Vincenzo Botta

Dante as Philosopher, Patriot and Poet

with an analysis of the Divina commedia, its plot and episodes

Vincenzo Botta

Dante as Philosopher, Patriot and Poet
with an analysis of the Divina commedia, its plot and episodes

ISBN/EAN: 9783337072933

Printed in Europe, USA, Canada, Australia, Japan

Cover: Foto ©Raphael Reischuk / pixelio.de

More available books at **www.hansebooks.com**

DANTE,

AS

PHILOSOPHER, PATRIOT, AND POET.

WITH AN ANALYSIS OF

THE DIVINA COMMEDIA,

ITS PLOT AND EPISODES.

BY VINCENZO BOTTA.

"Onorate l'altissimo poeta."—*Inferno*, iv.

NEW YORK:
CHARLES SCRIBNER & CO.,
124 GRAND STREET.
1865.

All' Italia,

che nella commemorazione

del sesto centenario dalla nascita

di Dante Allighieri

celebra il proprio rinascimento

alla vita di nazione,

L'Autore,

partecipando alla comune esultanza,

dedica quest' Opera

in umile tributo di devozione.

New York, *il Maggio del 1865.*

TABLE OF CONTENTS.

DANTE.

INTRODUCTION.

" THE poet," says Schiller, " is the son of his time, but pity for him if he is its pupil, or even its favorite. Let some beneficent deity snatch him, when a suckling, from the breast of his mother, and nurse him with the milk of a better time, that he may ripen to his full stature beneath a distant Grecian sky; and having grown to manhood, let him return, a foreign shape, into his century—not, however, to delight it by his presence, but, dreadful as the son of Agamemnon, to purify it." The ideal poet thus sketched by Schiller finds his highest historic illustration in the great national bard of Italy, the colossal central figure of the age in which he lived. Its master rather than its pupil, the object of its persecution rather than its favorite, early snatched away by the beneficent deity of sorrow, to be nurtured by the contemplation of a lofty ideal, which was revealed to him alone, he walked, a foreign shape, among his countrymen, whom he sought not to

2

delight, but to purify and elevate; and although six centuries have passed away, the stern voice of his muse still utters its terrible maledictions on evil-doers, and its menaces against the oppressors of his country; while it exalts the just, and speaks words of hope and comfort to the oppressed. But if he soared above his contemporaries, he was nevertheless the son of his time, the ideas and sentiments of which he reflected. We must, accordingly, glance at its character, in order fully to comprehend his relation to it.

The twelfth and thirteenth centuries mark that period of transition between ancient and modern times, in which Europe was emerging from the chaos that succeeded the fall of the Roman Empire; when new and foreign elements, combining with the remains of ancient civilization, had resulted in an organized society, although still convulsed by diverse and antagonistic elements; when the struggle between feudalism and democracy, the empire and the papacy, the monarchical system and the municipal régime, had combined to stimulate the human mind, and lead to those social transformations, of which the age of Dante, so great in its tendencies, its deeds, and even its contradictions, was the most remarkable result. It was an age of barbarism, superstition, anarchy, and tyranny; but it was also an age in which refinement and free thought began to appear, together with a longing for liberty, order, and social unity. Modern languages and nationalities were rapidly developing; England had established her birthright in the Magna Charta ; France had commenced the work of national organization ; the Spanish monarchy was advancing in resources and power ; Germany enjoying the conquests won in the reign of the glorious Hohenstauffens ; and the Christian world was gradually emancipating itself from the despotism of the Church, which had culminated in the great successor of Hildebrand, that terror of princes and heretics, Innocent III.

Meantime, the burgher class and the peasantry were rapidly becoming a power in the State ; the limits of the world were widened through the voyages of Marco Polo and other Italians ; ideas were enlarged, and commerce extended ; and while the human mind began to vindicate its independence, through the opposition of the Albigenses to the traditions of the papacy, as well as through the free songs of the Troubadours, the Universities of Paris and Bologna became centres of learning and genius ; science and theology were illustrated by the great names of Roger Bacon, St. Bonaventura, and Thomas Aquinas, and art found its highest expression in the cathedrals of Antwerp and Cologne.

In this work of social transformation, Italy had early taken the lead. Nourished more than any other nation by the Roman traditions, first awakened by the voice of Christianity, disorganized and reconstructed by the Northern invasions, morally and materially enriched by the Crusades, educated in the struggle between the papacy and the empire, Italy, even in the darkest periods of her history, enjoyed greater wealth, order, liberty, and refinement, than could be found in any other part of Western Europe. While England, Germany, and France, were yet shrouded in barbarism, and crushed by the iron heel of feudalism, the Italian States had attained a high degree of social progress. In their municipal organization, they enjoyed the freedom of self-government; Venice, Genoa, Pisa, held the sceptre of maritime commerce; their ships covered every sea, and their colonies dotted the shores of the Mediterranean; while they were rivalled by Florence and Milan, whose manufactories supplied Europe with commodities of every kind, and whose banks made loans alike to tradesmen and monarchs. Long before the birth of Dante, the Lombard League, in the North, had permanently asserted the independence of the cities on the battle-field of Legnano, and caused their rights to be recognized by the treaty of Constance. In the South, during the reign of Frederick II., a brilliant period had opened under the Arabian influence: education, science, art, and poetry were promoted; agriculture, commerce, and the administration of justice were improved; free institutions were established; the work of national unity was boldly undertaken, and to a great extent carried out; and the authority of the State was firmly vindicated against the encroachments of the Church. The great principles of Roman jurisprudence were revived in the schools of Padua and Bologna; while with the introduction of Arabian learning at the

College of Salerno, began a new era in the history of intellectual development. Under these vivifying agencies, the arts also began to flourish, leaving imperishable monuments in the magnificent palaces and churches which are still the admiration of the world, and in the illustrious names of Cimabue and Giotto, the greatest among the early regenerators of Italian art.

But this advanced civilization contained within itself two fatal elements of disintegration and decay: the first, that of State sovereignty, on which the municipal governments rested isolated and divided; the second, the papacy, whose influence, however beneficial it may have proved to the cause of general civilization in the early period of its history, could not but be antagonistic to that national unity which, if completed, would necessarily put an end to its supremacy. Hence, it has ever been the policy of the popes to foment local prejudices and ambitions, to promote discord among the republics, to discourage all progress, to ally themselves with the more ignorant and superstitious classes, and to invite foreign intervention as the only means through which they could consolidate and preserve their power. These two sources of discord, which have distracted Italy for so many centuries, and prevented her organization, find their parallel to-day in these United States, whose national existence is threatened by the same pernicious doctrine of State Rights, and by the Slave-Power, which, in its assertion of the dominion of man over man, and in the social

2*

results which it produces, is so akin to the papal institutions.

In opposition to these influences, a tendency toward nationality early manifested itself in the struggle between the empire and the papacy, which divided Italy into the two great parties of the Guelphs and the Ghibelins, who represented two opposing principles in Italian policy. With these two parties the life of Dante is so closely connected, that it would be impossible to comprehend his character, either as a statesman or a poet, without a glance at their history, and the issues involved in their contest.

The Italian people, in the tenth century, harassed by foreign invaders and the contentions of feudal lords, placed themselves under the protection of Otho the Great, of Germany; and from that time Italy, with the exception of a brief interval, remained united to the German Empire. The King of the Romans, being henceforth chosen by the Electors of Germany, became, after he had been crowned by the pope, the recognized head of the empire: the pope, in turn, was confirmed in power by the emperor, to whom, up to the thirteenth century, he acknowledged allegiance. Under Gregory VII., however, the papal Church not only asserted its independence of the empire, but claimed control over all emperors and kings. Hence arose that gigantic struggle which was still going on in the time of Dante.

In the reign of Henry IV., and in that of his successor, Henry V. (1056–1125), the ducal families of Welf and Wieblingen rose to power ; and their descendants, Conrad and Henry the Proud, became rival claimants for the imperial dignity—the one supporting the papal power, the other the imperial. The contest was transferred to Italy, where the war-cries of the contending parties, Welf and Wieblingen, were naturalized into *Guelfi* and *Ghibellini.*

From the time of Henry IV., Florence had taken sides with the Church, or the Guelph party ; but in 1248, the Ghibelins succeeded in overthrowing their rivals, only to be in turn driven out the following year. The Guelphs remained in power, and a general pacification took place, soon to be disturbed, however, by the discovery of a conspiracy of the Ghibelins, many of whom were beheaded, while others escaped or were banished. The refugees fled to Siena, where, aided by Manfred, King of Naples and Sicily, and son of the Emperor Frederick II., they organized a powerful army, met the Florentine Guelphs, and gained over them the memorable battle of Monteaperti, in 1260. Florence now again fell under the Ghibelins, who held the power until 1266, when the Guelphs regained it by the aid of Charles of Anjou, who, instigated by the pope, came at the head of a French army to seize the kingdom of Manfred. Having been crowned in Rome, Charles, on his way to take possession of the dominions thus conferred upon him, found at Benevento the gallant Manfred ready to dispute his claim. The battle which followed was at first fought with great bravery; but when victory was about to crown the arms of the Swabian prince, he found himself suddenly deserted by his most trusted officers. Overwhelmed by this treachery, the heroic Manfred, refusing to escape, with a little band of faithful followers, rushed into the thickest of the fight, and fell on the field. Thus Charles of Anjou took possession of the kingdom of Naples and Sicily as a fief from the pope. Meanwhile, Florence and the other northern cities arrayed themselves under the banner of the Guelphs, who had placed him on the throne. On the arrival of his vicar to take possession of the Florentine government, which had been surrendered to him for ten years, the Ghibelins departed from the city; and, although they long continued the struggle, they never regained their former ascendency. In vain did Conradin, the grandson of Frederick II., the last scion of the Swabian race, strive to reconquer the inheritance of his ancestors. Although, a few years later, the bells of the Sicilian Vespers tolled the knell of the French domination in Sicily, and gave the signal for the renewal of the contest to which that unfortunate young prince had bravely challenged his foes from the scaffold, the power of the Guelphs remained unimpaired in the Peninsula.

In that contest, the Guelphs and the Ghibelins not only represented the papal and imperial power, but that ever-existing antagonism between the plebeians and the patricians which lies at the foundation of all political parties. The Guelphs were, at first, the advocates of popular liberty, as expressed in the free municipalities; and being thus opposed to the imperial or aristocratic power, they became the natural allies of the popes, who succeeded, through their aid, in raising the papacy to a height which it had never before attained. On the other hand, the Ghibelins, believing in the necessity of a stronger government, in the prevailing anarchy, supported the claims of the emperors and their vassals; and thus, while they opposed the papacy, they aimed, at least indirectly, at the political consolidation of the Peninsula. With the fall of the Swabian family the Guelphs finally triumphed; the aristocracy was defeated; and the emperors found themselves confined, for the most part, to their German dominions. At the same time, a change of principles became apparent in both parties. While the Guelphs, secure in the possession of local freedom, ceased to oppose the nobility, which had now become almost identified with the people, resisted but faintly the empire, which was in its decline, they remained faithful to the cause of the popes, to whom they owed the final establishment of their power. The Ghibelins, on the other hand, opposed to the papacy, abandoning the claims of the aristocracy, remained devoted to national unity, which they sought to establish either by the revival of the empire, or by the elevation of a national chief. Thus, while the Guelphs represented the papal policy, the Ghibelins came to be the exponents of national rights—although many of them were mere adventurers, who sided with the emperors only to advance their own interests.

These struggles were not in vain; the public conscience was aroused from that lethargy into which it had fallen under the influence of the irresponsible authority of the Church; Christianity began to free itself from the outward forms with which it had been encumbered, and the aspiration for that individual and national liberty began to arise which is now recognized as constituting one of the essential principles of modern civilization. A century had not yet passed since Innocent III. had caused the kings of Europe to tremble on their thrones, and nations to fall at his feet, when the bull of Boniface VIII., claiming the right of interference in the administration of the State, was burned in Paris by the order of Philip the Fair, his former ally; and the pope himself, dressed in his pontifical robes, was dragged from the church, and driven, amidst the jeers of the populace, through the streets of Anagni—the caricature of a power which was fast declining.

It was in this age of transition that Dante was born and nurtured; it was by these influences that his genius was inspired. Early thrown into the turmoil of public life, he played a prominent part in the great drama of his century, as a soldier, a statesman, an ambassador, a supreme magistrate, in the most flourishing and advanced Republic of the middle ages. Although partisan writers have often profanely misrepresented his sentiments, and the intellectual despotism which since his time has presided over Italian literature has often concealed the philosophic and political ideas, which form the basis of his writings, beneath legends, idle interpretations, or questions of language and prosody, his transcendent genius has soared triumphant over all: and he stands forth as the philosopher whose intellect embraced all the knowledge of his time; the theologian who expressed in popular language the speculations of the divine science; the reformer who first boldly attacked the papal institutions as baneful to the welfare of Italy, as well as to the progress of the human mind; the statesman who expounded an entire system of government, corresponding to the highest exigencies of human society; the patriot who sacrificed his life to the good of his country; and, finally, the poet who sang the destiny of Italy and of humanity, made Christianity the subject of a sublime epic, and Christian virtue the object of all action. He experienced every reverse of fortune. He was a fugitive and a wanderer in his native land, and died an exile from the city of his birth and of his love. He wore the crown of thorns, which, from Socrates to Milton, has been the lot of all who have striven to elevate the race. But he left in his poem a work as enduring as literature itself, which, while it echoed the moans of a Past that was dying forever, saluted in sublime strains the morning of a new Civilization.

In the long period of her dismemberment, oppressed

by tyranny, and distracted by civil convulsions, Italy has
lived in the memory of her great poet, whose sublime
song has preserved her hopes and aspirations.   The
idea of national unity, which found in him its first
interpreter, descending through the ages, moved the
enthusiasm of Cola di Rienzo; awoke a patriotic
chord in the lyre of Petrarch; led the philosophic mind
of Machiavelli to impart a more practical direction to
the national sentiment; kindled the genius of modern
poets, from Alfieri to Monti, Niccolini, and Manzoni;
illumined the policy of princes, from the Visconti and
the Medici to Victor Emanuel; inspired the worship
of patriots, philosophers, and warriors, from Campanella
to Garibaldi, and the wisdom of statesmen, from Gero-
lamo Morone to Cavour.   And now, when the aspirations for which Dante lived and died are about to be
realized, and the hopes nourished by the tears and the
blood of generations begin to bear their fruit, regenerated Italy, as she enters the new epoch of her history,
on the return of the anniversary of his birth, rises, reverent and joyful, to do honor to him whose immortal
muse has for so many centuries never ceased to call
her from her grave.   Now Florence, at whose hands
he drank the bitter cup of his sorrow, on this day, when
political necessity intrusts to her keeping the national
Crown, offers to her Poet, as a solemn atonement for
the cruel ingratitude with which she persecuted her
noblest son, an Apotheosis worthy of his fame—a
triumph more grand than that which he proudly fore-

told, when, crushed by the calamities of his country, and stung by the bitter sense of personal wrong, he sang in prophetic strain :—

> If e'er the sacred poem that hath made
> Both heaven and earth copartners in its toil,
> And with lean abstinence, through many a year,
> Faded my brow, be destined to prevail
> Over the cruelty which bars me forth
> Of the fair sheepfold, where, a sleeping lamb,
> The wolves set on and fain had worried me;
> With other voice, and fleece of other grain,
> I shall forthwith return; and, standing up
> At my baptismal font, shall claim the wreath
> Due to the poet's temples.*

* Paradiso, xxv.

DANTE, a Christian name abbreviated from DU-RANTE, was born in Florence, May 14th, 1265, of the ancient and noble family of the ALLIGHIERI, believed to have been of Roman origin, but whose first ancestor recorded in history was Cacciaguida, a Florentine Knight, who died in the Crusade led by the Emperor Conrad III., in the middle of the twelfth century. A son of Cacciaguida, having inherited the maiden name of his mother, Aldighieria degli Aldighieri, a daughter of a lawyer of that name at Ferrara, became the founder of the Allighieri of Florence. Of this family, Bellincione, the grandfather of Dante, had seven children, the eldest of whom, Allighierio degli Allighieri, a jurisconsult and judge by profession, was the father of the poet. He was conspicuous among the leaders of the Guelph party, to which the Allighieri belonged ; and on its defeat at the battle of Monteaperti, he went into exile, thus preceding in the thorny path of proscription his most gifted son, the offspring of his second marriage, with Donna Bella.

It was in the ninth year of his age that Dante first met BEATRICE, who, according to the popular idea, inspired him with that transcendent love, the story of which he himself relates in the *Vita Nuova*, and which he has immortalized in the *Divina Commedia*. Concerning the nature of this love, there have been various opinions among commentators. While some have regarded it as the romantic devotion of an impassioned lover to an actual woman, by others Beatrice is considered as a purely symbolic character. Boccaccio, who wrote the life of Dante a few years after his death, and, as might be supposed, takes the romantic view of the question, relates that this first meeting took place at the house of Folco Portinari, the father of Beatrice, a man greatly esteemed by his countrymen, who had invited his friends, with their children, to visit him on the occasion of the Spring festival which the Florentines were accustomed to celebrate on the first of May. He describes Beatrice, then only eight years old, as a child of surpassing beauty, possessed of such dignity of manner, and such a charm of expression, that she was looked upon almost as an angel; and he adds that Dante, although so young, received her image into his heart with such affection, that from that day forward, never, as long as he lived, did it depart therefrom.

The *Vita Nuova*, composed from 1293 to 1300, contains thirty-one poems of different dates, accompanied by prose notes and interpretations, which connect them together, and explain their occasions and apparent meaning. It is essentially mystic in its character, and leaves the reader in doubt as to the nature of the love, whether real or symbolical, which it portrays. Dante here describes his first meeting with Beatrice, when love became the master of his soul; the devotion with which he followed her while a boy; and how, after nine years, this most gentle lady again appeared before him, clothed in pure white—and passing along the street, she turned her eyes towards the place where he stood very timidly, and by her ineffable courtesy saluted him with such grace, that, intoxicated with delight, he turned away from the crowd, and, betaking himself to his solitary chamber, he fell into a sweet slumber, in which a marvellous vision appeared to him. This vision he described in a sonnet, his first poetical composition, copies of which, as was often the custom in that age, were sent to the poets for their interpretation. The sonnet was well received, and poems in answer to it were returned—one particularly from Guido Cavalcanti, who, having thus made the acquaintance of Dante, conceived for him a friendship which terminated only with his death. Dante da Majano, however, another poet of some renown, showed very little sympathy with the mystic fancies of the lover, and, in a satirical response, advised the poet to seek the aid of the physician.

Thus Dante, according to the letter of the *Vita Nuova*, continued to dream and to love—to gaze at Beatrice from a distance, and to compose poems in her praise—abstaining, however, from naming her, fearful lest he should offend her purity or compromise her honor. He tells us that he attempted to conceal his affection, even by feigning love for another lady, to whom he dedicated the songs intended for Beatrice, and that this fiction went on for several years; and that at last Beatrice refused to salute him when they met. Then he relates that he returned home, locked himself in his chamber, where his lamentations could not be heard, and gave himself up to despair, until at length he fell asleep, with tears in his eyes, like a child who had been beaten. Again, at a wedding festival, he was so overpowered by her presence, that he was led away by his friends; and in answer to their inquiries as to what was the matter with him, he replied, " I have set my feet on that edge of life, beyond which no man can go with power to return."

On one occasion, having met with some ladies who knew the secret of his heart, Dante was questioned as to why he loved Beatrice, since he could not bear her presence; such a love, said they, must be indeed of a strange nature. " The object of my love," replied the poet, " was to obtain her salutation; and in that was all my blessedness, and the end of all my desires. But since she was pleased to refuse me this, my Lord Love has in his mercy placed all my beatitude in that which cannot fail me—that is, in praising my glorious lady." To which one of the ladies answered : " If thou speakest truly when thou sayest that thou lovest, thou must use the word love in another sense from that which it really means."

In a canzone, he describes a dream, or vision, in which he beholds the dead body of Beatrice, surrounded by women with unbound hair, who abandon themselves to mourning, as they cover the beautiful features with a snowy veil. Dark clouds obscure the sun; the stars

3*

are pale with grief. He beholds the slow and sorrowful funeral procession ; he sees a company of angels bearing away the soul of his beloved, enveloped in a white cloud. Tears gush from his closed eyes ; he cries, " O beautiful soul, how happy is he who can yet behold thee !" and he calls on Death to bear him away to Beatrice. The fair watchers at his bedside hasten to awaken him from his terrible dream, and ask the occasion of his grief. But in the sobs and groans with which he reveals it, they are unable to distinguish the name of Beatrice, and so the cause of his sorrow remained a poetical mystery to them.

This vision was the foreshadowing of approaching reality ; for the actual Beatrice soon after died, at the age of twenty-four, having been married for a few years to Simone de' Bardi, afterwards conspicuous in the political party of the Neri, by which Dante was so bitterly persecuted. Alluding to her death, which took place on the ninth day of the ninth month of the year, he traces some mysterious connection between Beatrice and the number nine, " three being the factor of nine, the Author of miracles Himself being three, Father, Son, and Holy Spirit, who are three in one ; this lady was accompanied by the number nine, that it might be understood that she was a miracle, whose only root is the marvellous Trinity." He calls her the glorious lady of his mind, the daughter of God, not of man ; he says that her aspect caused death to every other thought, and that her presence preserved man from all wrong, destroyed all enmity and all sensuous impulses, kindled the flame of charity, and put to flight pride and wrath.

That the Beatrice of the *Vita Nuova* is the same who reappears in the *Divina Commedia*, is evident from the conclusion, in which he says :—

"Soon after this a wonderful vision appeared to me, in which I saw things which made me purpose to speak no more of this blessed one until I could more worthily treat of her. And to attain to this, I study to the utmost of my power, as she truly knoweth. So that, if it shall please Him through whom all things live, that my life be prolonged for some years, I hope to speak of her as never was spoken of any woman. And then may it please Him who is the Lord of Grace that my soul may go to behold the glory of its lady, the blessed Beatrice, who in glory looks upon the face of Him, *qui est per omnia secula benedictus!*"

Admitting that the Beatrice of Dante was the daughter of Portinari, and not the mere personification of certain ideas so in accordance with the taste of the age, it is evident that the imagination of the poet transformed the actual woman into a pure ideal, and that little of her human nature remained. According to his own account, his relations with her were of the most formal kind. He first meets her at the age of nine years; nine years after, he passes her in the street, and in her salutation he experiences all the bliss a mortal can enjoy. At a wedding festival he is led away, overpowered by her presence. They meet again in public, and she refuses to recognize him. He expresses no sorrow or disappointment on the occasion of her marriage with another, and no desire for any more intimate relations with her himself. The *Vita Nuova* was composed during the most brilliant and active period of his life, while he was the recognized leader in political affairs, foreign ambassador, and chief magistrate of the Republic. Two years after the death of Beatrice, and while apparently lamenting her loss, he married Gemma Donati, who became the mother of his seven children ; and it seems highly improbable that, under these circumstances, he should write a book with the sole object of relating his attachment to another woman, in a form which, if not intended in a symbolic sense, would have been scarcely reconcilable with that discretion and sound judgment by which he was so eminently distinguished.

The *Vita Nuova*, therefore, must be regarded, not as the record of the early love of the poet, but rather of that new Life, of that intellectual development, in which he became conscious of the indwelling of the divine life ; when, his spiritual insight becoming more acute, finite objects revealed themselves to his mind as mere shadows of an infinite reality, to which he longed to unite himself.

But whatever semblance of personality may seem to attach to the Beatrice of the *Vita Nuova*, in the *Convito* and the *Divina Commedia* she becomes purely symbolic.

The *Convito*, the continuation of the *Vita Nuova*, and intended especially to assist it, as Dante himself says, furnishes the true key for the interpretation ; and here, after speculating on love and philosophy symbolized in Beatrice, " From this," he writes, " it may be seen who this lady is, and why she is called Philosophy ;" by which he means the highest aspiration of the human soul, the bride of the reason, which, becoming identified with it, elevates and sanctifies it ; in contradistinction to the philosophy of the schools, which he embodies in another lady, whom he represents as having at one time attracted him. It is therefore probable that he adopted the name of Beatrice from its literal signification—*Source of beatitude*—rather than from any reference to the wife of Bardi.

The symbolism of the Platonic writers derived its chief beauty from the degree of reality with which they invested their personifications, and this peculiarity was wonderfully intensified by the genius of Dante. Thus in the *Divina Commedia*, beholding Beatrice descend from heaven, Dante feels that love revive which thrilled him even in his childhood ; and when she lifts her veil, and reveals to him her second beauty, he regards her with that eagerness which a thirst of ten years had created. She reproaches him for his inconstancy, and says when she had changed her mortal for immortal he left her and gave himself to others, although nothing had been to him so pleasant as the contemplation of the beautiful limbs which enclosed her, and which are now scattered in dust.

These and other passages which are so vividly expressive of her womanhood, like the passionate words of Solomon to Shulamith, the symbol of Divine Wisdom, are always interpreted in a purely symbolic sense by the early commentators, with the exception of Boccaccio. Pietro and Jacopo, the sons of the poet, while they make no allusion to Beatrice as a woman, expressly say, that by the thirst of ten years, Dante referred to that period when, immersed in political life, he longed for the study of divine things, in which alone he could find rest ; and that by his love for the beautiful limbs, he meant the supernal pleasure he had enjoyed in the meditation of the Scriptures. But Beatrice is not alone in her symbolic character ; she is surrounded by other ladies personifying virtues or ideas—the Blessed Lady in heaven, Lucia, Leah, Rachel, Matilda, and the nymphs of the terrestrial paradise. He himself expresses the necessity of introducing sensible images for the understanding of transcendental ideas, and says :—

> For no other cause
> The Scripture, condescending graciously
> To your perception, hands and feet to God
> Attributes, nor so means : and Holy Church
> Doth represent with human countenance
> Gabriel, and Michäel, and him who made
> Tobias whole.

Thus Dante calls Beatrice the true praise of God, the glory of our kind, the fountain of all truth, and the splendor of eternal light. Her beauty none save her Maker can fully enjoy. She is Goddess—the prime delight of primal love. Her eyes are brighter than the stars; to look at them fulfils all desire. Her aspect is that of virtue; it reflects God himself. Possessing her, mankind possesses all things. On his being lost in the forest of barbarism, she descends from heaven to his succor; she absolves him of his sins; she reveals to him her beauty, which, for ten years of worldly life, has been concealed from him; she carries him with her from sphere to sphere; she unfolds to him the mysteries of the Divine Mind; till, reaching the heights of the Empyrean, he beholds her on a throne of glory, and thus addresses her—not as a mortal woman, but as the grand personification of the Divine Wisdom:—

> "O lady! thou in whom my hopes have rest;
> Who, for my safety, hast not scorned, in hell
> To leave the traces of thy footsteps marked;
> For all mine eyes have seen, I to thy power
> And goodness, virtue owe and grace. Of slave
> Thou hast to freedom brought me: and no means,
> For my deliverance apt, hast left untried.
> Thy liberal bounty still toward me keep:
> That, when my spirit, which thou madest whole,
> Is loosened from this body, it may find
> Favor with thee." So I my suit preferred:
> And she, so distant, as appeared, looked down,
> And smiled; then towards the eternal fountain turned.*

* Paradiso, xxxi.; Cf. also, Inferno, ii.; Purgatorio, vi., xv., xviii., xxiii., xxvii., xxx., xxxi., xxxii.; Paradiso, iii., iv., vii., xiv., xviii., xxiv., xxv., xxvii., xxx.

On the death of his father, Dante was, while yet a boy, intrusted to the care of Brunetto Latini, a philosopher, historian, poet, and statesman, who held the office of Secretary to the Florentine Republic. Being a Guelph, he was forced into exile soon after the battle of Monteaperti, and retired to France, where he wrote *Le Tresor*, an Encyclopædia of Mediæval Science. He was also the author of the *Tesoretto*, a poem on the conduct of life. After the triumph of Charles of Anjou and the fall of the Ghibelins, he returned to Florence, where he resumed his former office, and continued to exercise a considerable influence on the government until his death. Of him Filippo Villani says :—" He was worthy of being numbered with the most distinguished orators of antiquity. He was witty, learned, and shrewd ; ever ready to use his abilities in the service of others ; polished in manners ; a very useful person ; and, by the practice of all the virtues, would have been most happy if he had only been able to support with equanimity the evils of his turbulent country."

It was under the guidance of this eminent man that Dante received his early education and his first lessons in the art of government. He acquired the knowledge of several languages—Latin, French, and Provençal— and made himself acquainted with the various Italian dialects. He studied the Latin poets, and, above all, Virgil, whom he loved to address as the famous sage, his sweet and true father ; and to him, next to Beatrice, he gave the most prominent place in the *Commedia*.

Nor did he confine himself to poetry. Grammar, rhetoric, history, dialectics, geometry, music, and astronomy in turn occupied his attention, and he is represented as the most powerful orator of his time. Contemporary with Cimabue and Giotto, living in the dawn of modern art, a nature so broad and sympathetic as that of Dante could not fail to be greatly affected by its potent influence. Many of the most magnificent structures of Florence were erected in his time ; and the traveller of to-day may stand on the spot indicated by the inscription *Sasso di Dante*, inserted in the neighboring wall, where, according to tradition, it was his delight to sit and watch from day to day the growing beauty of the Duomo. Leonardo of Arezzo, his second biographer after Boccaccio, tells us that he was an excellent draughtsman, and he himself relates, in his *Vita Nuova*, that on a certain occasion he occupied himself in drawing figures of angels. By some of his biographers he is represented as the pupil of Cimabue. He was certainly the friend of the artists, the painters, and the musicians of his age : among them were Casella, who set to music several of his songs ; Oderigi da Gubbio, the celebrated miniature-painter ; and Giotto, who, according to Vasari, was assisted in his profession by the advice of Dante and by his designs. He took a leading part in the love-fêtes and brilliant festivities to which Florence, though in the midst of civil war, seems to have been much devoted. He delighted in the prac-

4

tice of all the elegant arts, and was the most accomplished man among his contemporaries.

Having passed his youth in these preparatory studies, he soon enlarged the sphere of his education, and sought alleviation from his sorrow for the mystical death of Beatrice in the study of philosophy. " I set myself," he says, " to read that book of Boëthius, but little known, with which he had consoled himself in prison and in exile ; and hearing that Tully had written a book treating of friendship, in which he had addressed some words of consolation to Lælius, a most excellent man, on the death of Scipio, his friend, I set myself to read that ; and although at first it was difficult to understand, I at length succeeded so far as my knowledge of the language and such little capacity as I had enabled me ; by means of which capacity I had already, like one dreaming, discovered many things, as may be seen in the *Vita Nuova*. And as it might happen that a man seeking silver should, beyond his expectation, find gold, which a hidden chance presents to him, not perhaps without divine direction, so I, who sought for consolation, found not only a remedy for my tears, but also acquaintance with authors, with knowledge, and with books."*

Through the study of philosophy his intellectual faculties were quickened, his spiritual insight was stimulated, and the moral bearing of all achievements became more defined. He was assiduous in his attendance at

* Convito.

the lectures and discussions of the Schools ; he turned his thoughts to the great problems of science with an intensity that no outward tumult could disturb, and devoted himself to study with such perseverance, that his sight at an early age became greatly impaired. Thirty months had scarcely passed from his reading of Cicero and Boëthius, when, as he says, philosophy became the mistress of his soul, which, as we have seen, he delighted to symbolize in Beatrice, and to whose worship he henceforth dedicated his life.

To complete his education, like the sages of old, he now travelled abroad—visited the Universities of Bologna, Padua, Cremona, Naples, and, at a later period, that of Paris. In these travels he became familiar with the prominent men of the time, and the prevailing systems of philosophy. Although he may have derived some ideas directly from the East, through the ambassadors of the Asiatic monarchies, who in the thirteenth century came to Rome, and from the missionaries returned from those countries, he chiefly owed his philosophic culture to the study of the Greek writers. These he probably did not read in the original, as his knowledge of the Greek language seems to have been limited. But, as far as regarded Plato, and through him Pythagoras and Socrates, Dante became acquainted with their doctrines in the Latin translations, particularly through the writings of Cicero, that great eclectic who preserved so much of the wisdom of the ancients ; and through those of the Fathers of the Church, St. Augustine, and other ecclesiastical writers of the Platonic school. Yet, while he was akin to Plato in the general tendency of his thoughts, and in the lofty symbolism by means of which he expressed them, he derived scientific ideas and forms from Aristotle, whose works he knew through Latin versions, the schoolmen, and the great *Commentary* of Averrhoes, whose speculations he often made his own. Ontologic and synthetic with Plato, he was psychologic and analytic with Aristotle, under whose guidance he anatomized nature, and examined the structure of the human mind and the organic construction of science, thus acquiring from the Peripatetic method discipline and strength, power of logic, of systematic classification and generalization. This mingling of the Idealism of Plato with the Realism of Aristotle is symbolized in the *Commedia*, where he points out in Limbo the illustrious shades of the two philosophers, sitting side by side above the ancient masters of science, dividing the royalty of the human intellect.

As in the study of ancient philosophy Dante derived his inspiration from the Academy and the Lyceum, so in theology, after the Scriptures and the Fathers, he revered as his teachers St. Bonaventura and St. Thomas Aquinas; the one the representative of the Realism, the other of the Idealism, of the middle ages. While from familiarity with the writings of the former his tendency to mysticism and symbolism was increased, from the study of the works of the latter his faculties of analysis, concentration, and encyclopædic combination were strengthened. His scientific system was the result of that eclectic power by which his mind was so distinguished, and through which, assimilating the elements of various doctrines, he produced a system which embraced the knowledge of the past and of his own age.

The *Convito*, or Banquet, a commentary on some of his poems, and the first philosophic treatise written in Italian prose, was composed during his exile. Although unfinished, and burdened by allegories and scholastic forms, it is characterized by depth of thought, purity of language, and beauty of style. It is particularly interesting for its allusions to the political parties and condition of Italy. In glancing at the general views of the poet on philosophy and its various departments, we shall follow the *Convito*, adding a few illustrations from the *Commedia*, to which that work may be considered as the philosophic introduction.

Philosophy, with Dante, consists in the loving practice of that wisdom which has its infinite source in the Deity, from whom it is reflected on other intelligences in degrees proportioned to their love. It rests on truth, and leads to virtue and to the possession of the supreme good. " How blind are those," he exclaims, " who never lift their eyes to the contemplation of that daughter of God ! She is the mother of all things, for in the creation of the world she stood before the Divine Mind. ' When the Lord prepared the heavens I was there,' she says ; ' when he set a compass upon the face of the

5*

depths ; when he established the clouds above ; when he straightened the fountains of the deep ; when he gave to the sea his decree, that the waters should not pass his commandment ; when he appointed the foundations of the earth ; then I was by him, as one brought up with him, and I was daily his delight, rejoicing always before him.' "

Having thus defined philosophy, Dante next considers how philosophic truth may be attained. On one side man is naturally impelled to acquire knowledge ; on the other, his intellectual power is limited.

> Since from things sensible alone we learn
> That which, digested rightly, after turns
> To intellectual,*

how then shall he rise to the possession of those truths which, surpassing all experimental knowledge, are the foundation of philosophy ? The poet solves this question, on which later philosophers have differed so widely, by asserting that some knowledge of things that do not come under the cognizance of the senses may be gained through " that inward light which manifests itself beneath the veil of external objects, and which, although not seen, is felt. The soul, imprisoned within the organs of the body, perceives that light, as a man in closing his eyes feels the action of the luminous air through that dim splendor which still penetrates his sight." Thus he admits the existence of a transcendental power constituting the very essence of the human intellect, although

* Paradiso, iv.

obscured by earthly conditions, and places the principle
of knowledge in God—

> In Him, who is truth's mirror: and Himself
> Parhelion unto all things, and naught else
> To Him.*

In the investigation of truth, Dante expressly incul-
cates the necessity of following the method of nature,
proceeding from the known to the unknown; from what
is evident to that which is obscure. In thus establishing induction as the basis of scientific method, he
anticipated Lord Bacon, whom he also preceded in
enumerating the causes of error and its remedies. The
first he ascribes to the senses, bad education, bad habits,
defective intellect, and the predominance of the passions. He laments the errors which spring from popular prejudice, and says that those who follow current
opinion without regard to its merits, are like the blind
led by the blind, or like sheep which follow each other
without discerning the cause of their movement. As
to the remedies which preserve the mind from error, he
holds that the senses should be distrusted in all things
which are beyond their capacity :—

> If mortals err
> In their opinion, when the key of sense
> Unlocks not, surely wonder's weapon keen
> Ought not to pierce thee; since thou find'st the wings
> Of reason to pursue the senses' flight
> Are short.†

---

* Paradiso, xxvi.   † Paradiso, ii.

Experience, "the fountain whence our arts derive their streams," must be carefully consulted, and too much caution cannot be exercised in forming opinions—

> And let this
> Henceforth be lead unto thy feet, to make
> Thee slow in motion, as a weary man,
> Both to the "yea" and to the "nay" thou seest not.
> For he among the fools is down full low,
> Whose affirmation, or denial, is
> Without distinction, in each case alike.
> Since it befalls, that in most instances
> Current opinion leans to false : and then
> Affection bends the judgment to her ply.*

He enforces a stern opposition to vulgar prejudice, and urges the control of the passions through devotion to wisdom. Then the clouds which obscure the intellect will gradually disappear, and, ascending above all doubt, it will attain the possession of truth, in which alone it can find rest.

> Well I discern, that by that truth alone,
> Enlightened, beyond which no truth may roam,
> Our mind can satisfy her thirst to know ;
> Therein she resteth, e'en as in his lair
> The wild beast, soon as she hath reached that bound
> And she hath power to reach it ; else desire
> Were given to no end. And thence doth doubt
> Spring, like a shoot, around the stock of truth ;
> And it is nature which, from height to height,
> On to the summit prompts us.†

* Paradiso, xiii.   † Paradiso, iv.

The cosmology of Dante is founded on the Christian doctrine of the Divine creation and the astronomical system of Ptolemy, embellished by ideas borrowed from the Greek and Arabian philosophers. The universe is the offspring of an infinite Power, which, subsisting in itself, consciously knows and loves itself, and in the same act manifests itself through new natures, which become the mirror of its splendor. The poet thus describes the origin of all ideas and existences—from one and unalterable substance :—

> That which dies not,
> And that which can die, are but each the beam
> Of that idea, which our Sovereign Sire
> Engendereth loving; for that lively light;
> Which passeth from his splendor, not disjoined
> From him, nor from his love triune with them,
> Doth, through his bounty, congregate itself,
> Mirrored, as 'twere, in new existences;
> Itself unalterable, and ever one.*

Creation he considers eternal, following in this respect the doctrines of Plato and Aristotle, which were also accepted by the early Fathers of the Greek Church, who believed that an infinite and immutable Being could not remain solitary for all eternity, but that he ever expressed himself in outward manifestations. The reason of the creation being eternal, the creation itself must of necessity have the same character. "As the Infinite is not made up of finites," says Barlow,

* Paradiso, xiii.

"neither is eternity composed of times, but is antecedent and subsequent to them. Duration, as comprehended by man, is *time;* but with God, is *eternity.* So, before all time—before that which had a beginning, or can have an end—the Infinite cause of all existences produced from Himself, in virtue of the perfection of his Divine nature, orders of intellectual beings approximate to his own. There never was, nor could be, an abstract eternal Being, dwelling apart from his creative energy. God, as correctly conceived by the human mind, is essentially the CREATOR. God, however, did not exercise his creative power of necessity, as understood by man; but out of the abundance of his love, and to manifest his glory. He created it out of the perfection of his own Divine Nature, which includes its essential activity and perfect liberty."*

Not that God from eternity created the world, as it appears, in time. Following the Aristotelian philosophy, Dante affirms that the eternal act' of the Creator brought forth into existence primeval matter—the Angels and the human soul, understanding for the former a universal principle, shapeless and confused, without quality or form, which, in its perpetual evolutions, receives all qualities and forms. "All things," says Daniello in his Commentary, "consist of matter and form. Matter is homogeneous, always the same, and ready to receive diverse forms; form is that which gives

* See "Critical, Historical, and Philosophical Contributions to the Study of the *Divina Commedia*," by H. C. Barlow.

existence to any thing." Perfection consists in pure act—that is, the full identification of form with matter. Hence, "the angelic substances occupy the upper portion of the intellectual world, because angelic creatures are always in pure act and perfect, but not *in potentia* or pure capacities, as are inferior things which occupy the lower portion; while man, who combines potentiality with form or act, holds the middle part, and unites together both the extremes." These ideas are thus expressed in the *Commedia*:—

> Not for increase to himself
> Of good, which may not be increased, but forth
> To manifest his glory by its beams;
> Inhabiting his own eternity,
> Beyond time's limit or what bound soe'er
> To circumscribe his being; as he willed,
> Into new natures, like unto himself,
> Eternal love unfolded: nor before,
> As if in dull inaction, torpid, lay,
> For, not in process of before or aft,
> Upon these waters moved the Spirit of God.
> Simple and mixed, both form and substance, forth
> To perfect being started, like three darts
> Shot from a bow three-corded. And as ray
> In crystal, glass, and amber, shines entire,
> E'en at the moment of its issuing; thus
> Did, from the eternal Sovereign, beam entire
> His threefold operation, at one act
> Produced coeval. Yet, in order, each
> Created his due station knew: those highest,
> Who pure intelligence were made; mere power,

> The lowest; in the midst, bound with strict league,
> Intelligence and power, unsevered bond.*

From primeval matter the heavenly bodies, the body of man, and the earth were developed, when the universe appeared girdled by the zone of infinite space, within which, in accordance with a universal law, the heavenly spheres revolve round the earth, which lies at the centre of the whole. God, a portion of the angelic natures and of the spirits of the blessed, dwell in the Empyrean, while others again inhabit the planets, which they influence, and over whose movements they preside. Here the poet mingles the astronomical ideas of his time with the doctrine of Averrhoes on the organism of the universe, which consisted, according to Renan, in a heaven eternal and incorruptible, composed of many orbs, which represented the members essential to its life. Heaven, the most noble of the animated beings, is moved by a soul, which, receiving its energy from the prime mover, is as the heart, whose vital influence is imparted to all the orbs of the cosmologic system. Each of these orbs has its special intelligence, which is its form, just as the rational soul is the form of man. These intelligences, hierarchically subordinate, constitute the chain of movers which propagate the movement of the first sphere down to the others. The moving power which they obey is desire, and, to attain the highest good, they move perpetually, thus manifest-

* Paradiso, xxix.

ing the desire which actuates them. Their intellect is always in act, uninfluenced by imagination and sensibility. They know themselves, and are conscious of whatever passes in the spheres beneath them, so that the first intelligence has the complete knowledge of all that occurs in the universe.*

Man is the noblest of all creatures under heaven, for he partakes more of the Divine Nature. "He comprehends within himself," says Dante, "all the faculties which belong to inferior beings, and is, besides, endowed with that direct ray of supreme intelligence which renders him a divine animal. His body, the instrument of a divine virtue in its exquisite organization, is superior to those of the other sentient beings. The human soul particularly delights to express itself in the mouth and in the eyes, the most spiritual portions of the human body—the windows through which shines forth the woman who dwells within the body. Inward emotions appear through the senses, as colors through glass. The mind, the deity of the soul, manifests itself through its intellectual faculties, which may be reduced to those of judging, reasoning, inventing, and of scientific construction. Through them man is essentially a distinct nature; and although animals may show signs of intelligence, these are not true expressions of that power, as the image in the mirror is not the person which it represents."

* See "Averroès et l'Averroisme," par Renan

The question of the origin of the human soul, which
has perplexed philosophers of all times, Dante solves by
referring it to a direct manifestation of God to the sentient principle, which, originating in generation, devel-
ops into an intellectual being when the primal mover
breathes into it the breath of intellectual life.

> Soon as in the embryo, to the brain
> Articulation is complete, then turns
> The primal Mover with a smile of joy
> On such great work of nature; and imbreathes
> New spirit replete with virtue, that what here
> Active it finds, to its own substance draws;
> And forms an individual soul, that lives,
> And feels, and bends reflective on itself.*

This manifestation of the Deity, although obscurely
revealed to the soul, renders it intelligent. It is in
virtue of reason, says Dante, that the human spirit
partakes of the Divine Nature, under the form of an
eternal intelligence. Yet the power of knowledge thus
conferred is felt only in its effects, in which alone it can
be observed. Man cannot know, *a priori*, from whence
his intellect derives its primal ideas, any more than he
can know the origin of his first affections. It is only
through induction that he discovers the source of his
intellectual and moral powers, in that breath of the
Divine Spirit to which he alludes in the verses
above quoted. An impersonal divine light is naturally

* Purgatorio, xxv.

resplendent to all spiritual creatures, the personality of whose intellect is created by the communication of that very element.   Dante here alludes to the theory of Averrhoes, who, disjoining the active from the passive intellect, destroyed the very nature of intellectual powers :—

> Spirit, substantial form, with matter joined,
> Not in confusion mixed, hath in itself
> Specific virtue of that union born,
> Which is not felt except it work, nor proved,
> But through effect, as vegetable life
> By the green leaf.   From whence his intellect
> Deduced its primal notices of things,
> Man therefore knows not, or his appetites
> Their first affections ; such in you, as zeal
> In bees to gather honey.*
> How babe of animal becomes, remains
> For thy considering.   At this point more wise
> Than thou has erred, making the soul disjoined
> From passive intellect.†

The subject of the immortality of the soul, the necessary result of that divine manifestation which renders it an intellectual being, is treated at some length in the *Convito*, and is thus alluded to in the *Commedia* :—

> Know ye not
> That we are worms, yet made at last to form
> The winged insect, imped with angel plumes,
> That to Heaven's justice unobstructed soars ?‡

---

* Purgatorio, xviii.   † Ibid., xxv.   ‡ Ibid., x.

> Call to mind from whence ye sprang.
> Ye were not formed to live the life of brutes,
> But virtue to pursue, and knowledge high.*

A lofty idea of the moral destiny of the race appears through all the writings of Dante. Moral perfection, in his view, is the great object for which man was created. His mystical love for Beatrice—divine ethics or wisdom—the prominent part he gives to that symbol—the symbolic virtues by which he surrounds it, and the manifest purpose of all his works, show that with him moral results had a pre-eminent importance. "He is not to be called a true lover of wisdom," he writes, "who loves it for the sake of gain, as do lawyers, physicians, and almost all persons who study, not in order to know, but to acquire riches or advancement, and who would not persevere in study should you give them what they desire to gain by it. As true friendship between men consists in each wholly loving the other, the true philosopher loves every part of wisdom, and wisdom every part of the philosopher, inasmuch as it draws all to itself, and allows no one of his thoughts to wander to other things."

Love, with him, is the perfection of moral life, the prime mover, the source of every virtue, the universal law which presides over all organic and rational development. The origin of the human soul, its natural impulse toward the Creator, and the influence of finite objects in leading it astray, he thus describes:—

* Inferno, xxvi.

Forth from his plastic hand, who charmed beholds
Her image ere she yet exist, the soul
Comes like a babe, that wantons sportively,
Weeping and laughing in its wayward moods;
As artless, and as ignorant of aught,
Save that her Maker being one who dwells
With gladness ever, willingly she turns
To whate'er yields her joy.   Of some slight good
The flavor soon she tastes; and, snared by that,
With fondness she pursues it; if no guide
Recall, no rein direct her wandering course.*

Free will, according to Dante, is the foundation of all merit:—

Ye have that virtue in you whose just voice
Uttereth counsel, and whose word should keep
The threshold of assent.   Here is the source
Whence cause of merit in you is derived.
E'en as the affections good or ill she takes,
Or severs, winnow'd, as the chaff.†

. . . . If this were so,
Free choice in you were none; nor justice would
There should be joy for virtue, woe for ill.
If, then, the present race of mankind err,
Seek in yourselves the cause, and find it there.‡

. . . . Those men
Who, reasoning, went to depth profoundest, marked
That innate freedom; and were thence induced
To leave their moral teaching to the world.§

* Purgatorio, xvi.   † Ibid.   ‡ Ibid.   § Ibid., xviii.

Man is destined to reach his highest development through the union of his soul with the Supreme Good, which he can only accomplish by rendering his will perfectly conformable to the divine will, as manifested in that harmony which makes "the universe resemble God."   In an age of scholastic dogmatism, Dante thus laid down those great principles derived from the Gospel, which have been too often disregarded; and asserted that true religion consisted not in forms, but in the constant exercise of duty, and in the perpetual effort to ascend to the heaven of ideal perfection, by assimilating to our spirit the Spirit of God which dwells within our hearts:—

> But lo! of those
> Who call "Christ, Christ!" there shall be many found,
> In judgment, farther off from him by far,
> Than such to whom his name was never known.
> Christians like these the Æthiop shall condemn,
> When that the two assemblages shall part;
> One rich eternally, the other poor.*

As a naturalist, Dante had an exquisite sentiment of the phenomena of terrestrial life; and from the acuteness of his mental insight, and his passionate study of nature, he had many glimpses of physical truths, which we find in curious hints as to causes and facts, which have only been established by the scientific researches of modern times.   Beneath the surface of his poetical

* Paradiso, xix.

fictions his Cosmos presents something of that unity and universality of plan which characterize the actual creation; and in the innumerable co-ordinate intelligences which he represents as presiding over the order of the universe, we see symbols of the permanent laws of nature, and of the correlative forces on which that order depends. (The principle of love—with him the law of all existences)—may be interpreted as a poetical allusion to the great law of attraction; and had Newton read the words of Virgil, when, having passed through the centre of the earth, he said that they had overpassed—

> That point to which from every part is dragged
> All heavy substance,*

they might have suggested to the mind of that great philosopher the law of gravitation more strikingly than the accidental fall of an apple. The distinct allusion to the existence of a Western World, in the episode—in which Ulysses narrates his wanderings through the sea, when, after passing the Straits of Gibraltar, and sailing westward for five months, he discovered a new land— may have had its influence with Columbus, to whom the *Commedia* was doubtless familiar, and thus Dante may have indirectly contributed to the discovery of the New World.†

In Canto XXV. of the *Purgatorio* the theory of generation is described, and the poet says :—

> With animation now endued,
> The active virtue (differing from a plant

---

* Inferno, xxxiv. † Ibid., xxvi.

No further, than that this is on the way,
And at its limit that) continues yet
To operate, that now it moves, and feels,
As sea-sponge clinging to the rock ; and there
Assumes the organic powers its seed conveyed.
This is the moment, son ! at which the virtue,
That from the generating heart proceeds,
Is pliant and expansive ; for each limb
Is in the heart. by forgeful nature planned.*

" To appreciate," says Barlow, " the physiological science shown by Dante in his masterly *resumé* of the formation of and development of a human being, from the first mysterious movings of embryonic life to the completion of the fœtal economy and the birth of an immortal soul, we must go back to that period when little or nothing more was known of the function of generation than what had been said by Aristotle, and repeated by his commentator Averrhoes. Had the poet been professor of physiology in the University of Bologna, and desired to preserve a memorial in his immortal work of the state of the science at that period, he could not have given a better account of it, or shown more judgment in the selection of his facts ; for not only does he avoid many of those errors into which his contemporaries and successors fell, but he seems to anticipate much of that true science which the latest investigations have brought to light, especially in reference to the development of embryonic life. With regard to this subject we have learned to search out

* Purgatorio, xxv.

their progressive changes, and to scrutinize the secret operations of nature'; but we cannot give a better or more philosophical account of the primary agent concerned than was given by Dante when, going to the fountain-head of life, he called the generating fluid ' perfect blood '—

> " Which by the thirsty veins is ne'er imbibed,
>   And rests as food superfluous to be taken
>   From the replenished table, in the heart
>   Derives effectual virtue that informs
>   The several human limbs."*

" The verses indicating the changes which the human embryo undergoes contain," continues Barlow, "a correct summary of the general law of the changes now known to take place in embryonic life, and which the French physiologists call *le principe des arrêts de développement ;* through which, as Milne Edwards describes it, each organic being, in its development, undergoes profound and various modifications, changing the character of its anatomic structure and its vital faculties as it passes from the embryonic state to the condition of a perfect animal." The same writer points out the manner in which Dante expresses the physiological fact noted by Elliotson, that " however a human embryo is always a human embryo, still man is at first a kind of zoophyte."

In Canto V. of the *Purgatorio*, Buonconte da Montefeltro, relating how his body was borne away by

* Purgatorio, xxv.

the overflowing of the stream near which he lay, the poet thus, through him, explains the phenomenon of the rain :—

> Thou know'st how in the atmosphere collects
> That vapor dank, returning into water
> Soon as it mounts where cold condenses it.
> That evil will, which in his intellect
> Still follows evil, came ; and raised the wind
> And smoky mist, by virtue of the power
> Given by his nature.   Thence the valley, soon
> As day was spent, he covered o'er with cloud,
> From Pratomagno to the mountain range ;
> And stretched the sky above ; so that the air
> Impregnate changed to water.   Fell the rain ;
> And to the fosses came all that the land
> Contained not ; and, as mightiest streams are wont,
> To the great river, with such headlong sweep,
> Rushed, that naught stayed its course.

" Had Dante," writes Barlow, alluding to this passage, " been thoroughly conversant with the modern theory of rain, he could not have expressed himself in more accurate language than this. His knowledge of physical science appears to have been much in advance of that of the age in which he lived, and of his more immediate successors. The mediæval meteorology of his commentators reads almost as nonsense in comparison with the few masterly words of the poet on the same subject. In the description of the storm of rain which caused the Archiano to overflow, and bear away the dead body of Buonconte to the Arno, where, whirled along its banks and rolled over its bed, the corpse became buried in the débris brought down by the river, Dante not only describes the circumstances with the pen of a poet, but, like a high-priest of nature, explains their causes also. In the words of Buonconte we have an accurate sketch of the formation of clouds and rain, by the mingling together of currents of air of different temperatures saturated with aqueous vapor. . . . . When rain falls from the upper region of the air we observe, at a considerable altitude, a thin, light veil, or a hazy turbidness ; as this increases, the lower clouds become diffused in it, and form a uniform sheet. Such is the *Stratus* cloud, described by Dante as covering the valley from Pratomagno to the ridge on the opposite side above Camaldoli. This cloud is a widely-extended, horizontal sheet of vapor, increasing from below and lying on or near the earth's surface. In the description given by Dante, the valley became covered in its entire breadth, so that to the cloud of vapor formed below was added the cloud of vapor precipitated from above ; the air impregnate changed to water, and a deluge of rain followed."

The same distinguished Dantophlist calls attention to the passage where the poet refers to the visive power of the mole :—

> Call to remembrance, reader, if thou e'er
> Hast on an Alpine height been taken by cloud,
> Through which thou saw'st no better than the mole
> Doth through opacous membrane.*

* Purgatorio, xvii.

" In the amount of vision here ascribed to the mole,"
says Barlow, " we have another instance how much
Dante's knowledge as a naturalist surpassed that of his
contemporaries and successors.   Until very lately, the
mole was considered to be blind.   It was reserved for
modern science to demonstrate the accuracy of Dante
and the truth of his description.   Not only has the
mole eyes, and nervous filaments passing to them from
the base of the brain, but it can see at least to distinguish light from darkness, which is all the power of
vision the natural habits of the animal require."

Barlow points out other passages which forcibly illus-
trate the insight of the poet into the mystery of final
causes.   " In the verses of the Paradiso, when speaking of love, he says :—

> This to the lunar sphere directs the fire,
> This moves the heart of mortal animals,
> This the brute earth together knits and binds :*

Three physical principles, combustion, vital action,
and attraction of cohesion, both of molecules and masses,
are expressed in a poetical manner, which almost seems
to anticipate in part the results of modern researches ;
for it matters little by what names things are called,
provided we understand what is meant ; and where
language is scarcely adequate to convey the whole idea
we desire to express, there must always be a surplus
sense, which the understanding will entertain according
to its capacity."   He refers also to the indications of

* Paradiso, i.

the meteoric phenomena of shooting or falling stars and of heat lightning, in that passage where Dante speaks of the fiery vapors which with such speed cut through the serene air at fall of night ;* and to the Southern Cross, which the poet describes in Canto I. of the *Purgatorio* :—

> To the right hand I turned, and fixed my mind
> On the other pole attentive, where I saw
> Four stars ne'er seen before save by the ken
> Of the first people.

" The principal stars of this constellation," says Barlow, " were known when Dante wrote, and in the description of them here given there is a reality attested by all who have seen them. They were once visible in our northern hemisphere. Without the aid of the telescope they appear as four stars, three of them of the first magnitude. In consequence of the precession of the equinoxes, writes Humboldt, the starry heavens are continually changing their aspect from every portion of the earth's surface. The early races of mankind beheld in the far north the glorious constellation of the southern hemisphere rise before them, which, after remaining long invisible, will again appear in those latitudes after a lapse of thousands of years. The Southern Cross began to become invisible in 52° 30′ north latitude, twenty-nine hundred years before our era, since, according to Galle, this constellation might previously have reached an altitude of

* Purgatorio, v.

more than 10°.   When it disappeared from the horizon of the countries of the Baltic, the great Pyramid
of Cheops had already been erected more than five
hundred years.   Dante, therefore, most truly says
that those stars were never seen before save by the
first people; meaning by these words not Adam and
Eve, as some writers would still have us believe, but
the early races which inhabited Europe and Asia."

The author to whom we are indebted for the above
quotations continues his scientific analysis of the *Commedia,* and, commenting on the following verses,—

> Mark the sun's heat ; how that to wine doth change,
> Mixed with the moisture filtered through the vine,—*

" It has been supposed," he remarks, " that Dante
drew his theory of wine from a passage of Cicero, in his
Cato Major de Senectute, repeated by Galileo three hundred years later.   But Cicero says no more than what
every vine-dresser from the days of Noah was perfectly aware of, that the sun ripened the grapes, and
that his warmth was necessary to the elaboration of
their juice.   Of the chemical action which then takes
place, as also of what occurs in vinous fermentations,
neither Cicero nor Dante nor Galileo was aware.
But Dante wisely conceived that ' the great minister
of nature' acted the chief part in the transmutation,
and the poet was right.   Without moisture and heat
there would be no life.   The sun is the great vivifying

* Purgatorio, xxv.

agent, and the absorption of his rays effects the change which the poet describes ; so that, as modern science has demonstrated, in quaffing the generous liquid thence derived we are actually drinking down sunbeams, and our souls are cheered and warmed by their inward effects as much as our bodily members are comforted by their outward radiance." He also alludes to the interesting fact in vegetable physiology, that flowers are only metamorphosed leaves, the discovery of which is commonly attributed to Goethe, but was first observed by Dante, and expressed in these words :—" Flowers and *other* leaves."*

Thus Dante was the representative not only of the art and poetry, but also of the science of his age ; and well might Raphael, in his admirable fresco of the Holy Sacrament, which every pilgrim of the beautiful has admired in the galleries of the Vatican, place prominent among the popes and the doctors of the Church, then the guardians of science and patrons of art, the noble figure of the poet, radiant with the severe light of philosophy, his glorious head girt with the laurel crown.

But genius, acquirements, and accomplishments were, with Dante, subordinate to the duties which bound him to his country. He felt, with Cicero, that devotion to the land of our birth excels and comprehends all other affections ; and this sentiment was early expressed in his life. At the age of twenty-four years we find him in the battle of Campaldino, in which the Florentine

* Purgatorio, xxxii.

army, commanded by Corso Donati, the leader of the Guelph party, defeated the Ghibelins of Arezzo. Dante fought valiantly in the foremost ranks of the cavalry led by Vieri dei Cerchi, who afterwards became the chief of the party of the Bianchi, with which the poet was for a few years associated. He himself alludes to this engagement in the *Commedia*; and in a letter since lost, but which is recorded by one of his early biographers, he described the battle, the emotions which he experienced, the danger he was in, his fears, his anxiety, and his intoxicating joy in the victory. Soon after, he took part in another engagement between the Florentines and the Pisans, in which the former conquered the castle of Caprona. From this time he devoted himself to the Republic, his influence becoming every day more powerful.

With the ascendency of the Guelphs, after the defeat of Manfred, in 1266, several reforms had been introduced,—among them the institution of the *Arti* or guilds into which the city was divided, the principal of which were the money-changers, the judges and notaries, the physicians and apothecaries, the wool-weavers or clothiers, the silk-weavers or mercers, the furriers, and the merchants. Each of the Arti had its consul and *gonfaloniere*, or standard-bearer. In 1282 the Priori were instituted, first to the number of three, then of six, and lastly of eight, who, elected by the guilds, had the management of public affairs. In 1292 a new constitution, under the direction of Giano della Bella, was adopted, by which the privileges of the Arti were confirmed, the nobles excluded from the administration, and a magistrate under the name of *Gonfaloniere di Giustizia* was instituted, with the duty of defending the rights of the people. To him a standard was given, and a body-guard of one thousand infantry.

In accordance with this constitution, Dante, renouncing his position as a nobleman, entered his name in the registers of the physicians and apothecaries, in common with others who, although not belonging to the profession, were engaged in the study of the natural sciences. He was soon intrusted with several foreign missions, and, in the capacity of ambassador, it is said that he visited Siena, Perugia, Venice, Ferrara, Rome, Naples, and Paris. His position in the government of Florence became so important, that, according to Boccaccio, no envoy from abroad was listened to, no answer to foreign powers returned, no reform introduced, no war declared, no peace made, without his counsel and consent. " In him," says the same writer, " popular confidence and hope were centred, and indeed all human and divine things were reflected."

The period in which Dante entered public life was also that in which his political views took a wider range, and his opinions became more settled and more defined. Up to this time his chief thought had been the advancement of the Guelphs and the welfare of his native city. Born of a Guelph family, educated in that political

6*

school, and surrounded by the associations and influences of that party, he had thus far been identified with it.　He might have regarded the establishment of local freedom as the first step towards national unity; he might have been dazzled by the splendor of Florence, then the great centre of European civilization.　It is certain, however, that in the first years of his career the nationality of Italy had not become a leading idea in his mind; and if it existed at all, it was undeveloped and confused.　But as he advanced in his philosophic and classical studies, and as his experience widened, his intellect more readily comprehended the relations of the national organism; he discovered, beneath the diversities that separated the different parts of the peninsula, the affinities that connected them together; and, rising above local partiality and ambition, he grasped the great idea of national unity, which from that time he never ceased to consider as the corner-stone of the future greatness of Italy.　As with the mystical death of Beatrice his soul had undergone a moral transformation, so now his political ideas were subjected to a radical change.　He ceased to be a Guelph and a Florentine, and became, as has been well said, the first Italian. But his aspirations were not confined to Italy alone; he conceived a plan of general organization, which, while it would place his country in an exalted position, would also establish the political union of the race, secure the permanent peace of the world, and result in the general progress of mankind.

To develop this fundamental idea, Dante composed his work *De Monarchia*, which may be considered the political introduction to the *Commedia*. Up to a recent date, it has been supposed that Dante composed this book at the period of his exile; but modern criticism, and particularly the researches of Karl Witte, have shown that that composition belongs to the first decade of his public career. Written in the rude Latin of the age, encumbered with scholastic subtilties and mediæval conceptions, this treatise is a candid, logical, and, at times, eloquent exposition of the political system of its author. It is divided into three parts; the first intended to show that mankind must be politically united in order to secure the object of its destiny; the second, to demonstrate that it belongs to Italy to effect that union; and the third, to assert the separation and the independence of the State from the Church.

The principles which Dante here advocates are so connected with the political ideas expressed in the *Divina Commedia*, that it is important to give a brief outline of the work. God is one, says Dante; nature is one; mankind is one,—one in its origin, its essence, and its destiny. Civilization should be one, composed of many nations free, yet united in one great confederation, headed by the ancient mistress of the world. Rome was the moral centre of Europe in the time of the empire; let Italy, the natural heir of Rome, take her place once more among nations. Was not Rome chosen to be the connecting link in the unity of the race ?   Was not the Roman empire destined to be the organ of universal aspiration, and the great leader of cosmopolitical action ?   The general causes which contributed to its first establishment, civil wars, wealth, and general decay, in the thirteenth century were still at work ; indeed, they were more potent than before. The restoration of the empire, therefore, was the necessary result of the conditions of the time, and the remedy which an overruling providence had given to the race.   And here he mingles legend with historic facts, and draws parallels from Roman history and the Bible.   He tells us how, in the same year in which David took the crown of Israel, Æneas landed on the coast of Italy ; and as from the family of David the Saviour was born, so the children of Æneas were destined to conquer the world, in order to establish that social unity which was necessary to the triumph of Christianity.   The Saviour Himself, the type of mankind, acknowledged the supremacy of the empire by being born under the reign of Augustus, and by submitting Himself to the sentence of the imperial courts. Let Rome, therefore, put on once more the mantle of empire, and, surrounding herself with the great intellects of the time, let her take the high place of cosmopolitan umpire in all questions arising between nations ; and let mankind, harmonious in the infinite variety of its functions, go forward under her guidance to the conquest of its perfection, which consists in the universal religion of human nature.

The arguments advanced by Dante for the establishment of Italian supremacy lost their force when Italy
ceased to hold the position at the head of contemporary
civilization which belonged to her in the thirteenth
century. But, apart from this, there is in his conception a breadth and comprehensiveness which entitle the
writer of the *Monarchia* to a place among the reformers
of all ages. His plan of social organization presents an
ideal in which the race appears as a great individuality,
endowed with immortal life in its collective character,
subject to that law of mutual responsibility among its
members which is destined at some future time to become the bond of all nations. It involves the principle
of indefinite progress developing through perpetually
extending associations. It embraces the unity of
mankind, not as the result of conquest, but of the harmonious distribution of national agencies for the highest
common object. It anticipates in some measure, as
has already been remarked, the plan adopted by Wash-
ington and his compeers in the Constitution of the
United States, differing, however, in this, that while
the American Republic extends to States geographically
and ethnographically integrant parts of the same country,
the Italian empire, as proposed by Dante, would have
embraced all the world, and have placed Italy, in relation
to other nations, as the sun to the planets, whose influence unites them in their harmonious movements, while
it gives them free scope in their appointed orbits.

In advocating the union of mankind under the lead-

ership of Italy, Dante did not intend to place other nations under her military despotism.   The revival of the
empire he contemplated was not that of the Asiatic
monarchies, neither was it that of Charlemagne or
Charles V.   His plan, grand in its conception, resting
on the basis of liberty, both national and individual,
was derived, on the one hand, from ancient Rome,
where the emperor was but a citizen charged with the
high office of tribune, and with the defence of popular
rights against the patricians ; on the other, from the
idea of modern governments founded on the political
union of municipalities belonging to the same nation.

Hence the idea of Dante did not necessarily involve
monarchical institutions, as is commonly believed, but
simply the concentration of social power into an individual or collective authority, which should exercise the
common sovereignty for the good of the people.   Admitting all forms of government, as circumstances
might require, the plan of Dante was adapted to all
nations, their different characters, traditions, and wants.
It was essentially liberal and democratic.   A nobleman
by birth, we have seen him enter the ranks of the
people, and give his cordial support to popular government.   If he occasionally recalls his family origin with
pride, he protests that there is no true nobility but that
of virtue and genius.   He compares aristocracy to a
mantle which the shears of time make shorter and
shorter ; he asserts that human worth rarely mounts
into the branches of genealogic trees ; he bitterly satir-

izes the aristocrats of his time who sprang from barterers and peddlers ; and he even says that those who
have not inherited the virtues of their fathers ought
neither to inherit their property. The high value he
placed on liberty, making even the empire subordinate
to it, we see from the noble tribute which he pays to
Cato, the great martyr of the Republic. He calls him
the most sacred of courageous men ; he represents him
as the guardian of the kingdom of purification, and,
kneeling before his august shade, he foretells the greatness to which he will be raised in the last day. And
while he condemns Brutus and Cassius, the murderers
of Cæsar, to the deepest abysses of hell, and exalts
Cæsar for having seized the standards of the eagle,
he carefully notes that he seized them *by the will
of Rome*, and mercilessly condemns Curio, his lieuten-
ant, to have his tongue forever cut off by the hand of
a demon, to be forever renewed, for having urged his
chief to cross the Rubicon without awaiting the call of
the people. He advocates the same principle when he
teaches that the government of nations belongs to
philosophy—that is, to wisdom united with the imperial
authority—and places the source of law not in the will
of rulers, but in that impersonal reason, of which the
people are the natural interpreters. Hence he causes
Virgil to praise him for his love of liberty, and to ex-
claim, while crossing the Stygian lake :—

There above
How many now hold themselves mighty kings

> Who here like swine shall wallow in the mire,
> Leaving behind them horrible dispraise.*

And descending deeper into the infernal regions, he points out the tyrants of all ages plunged into a river of blood, held down by demons in the form of centaurs, and guarded by the minotaur, the infamy of Crete, at once a beast and the son of a king, the living symbol of tyranny which feeds on human flesh.†

But his political views are not only democratic; they are deeply impressed with the stamp of nationality. This principle, which inspired the *Monarchia* and the *Commedia*, also finds expression in his *De Vulgari Eloquio*, an unfinished work written in Latin, in which the philologic element of the Italian nation is particularly examined. His knowledge of philology, a science of recent origin, was necessarily limited and imperfect; yet he forcibly expresses the idea of a national language, in opposition both to the local dialects and to the Latin then used by the Church and the upper classes. He clearly alludes to the division of the European languages into several families, as to the bases of distinct nationalities, and attributes a common origin to the Spanish, French, and Italian idioms. His remarks on the Italian dialects are particularly interesting, as affording the means of comparing the present condition of the language with the roots from which it has

---

* Inferno, viii.

† Inferno, xii., xxviii.; Purgatorio, i.; Paradiso, vi., xvi., and alibi, *passim.*

sprung. These dialects, according to Dante, were fourteen ; and he adds that each of them was so sub-divided, that all together they might reach the number of one thousand. He passes in review the chief of these varieties, and rejects them all, as not having the characteristics of a national language, which he insists does not belong to one or to another city, but is common to all.

The multitude of dialects which from time immemorial had prevailed throughout Italy, explains how, in the absence of a national centre, the Italian had not before appeared in literature. Although the primitive Italian songs are to be referred to the early part of the thirteenth century, it was only from 1220 to 1250 that the language began to be spoken at the court of Frederick II., in Palermo, when, under the auspices of that emperor, it was generally adopted by the Sicilian troubadours. From Sicily the new language soon made its way through the peninsula, and in Tuscany particularly it became the tongue of the poets of the thirteenth century,—first among them Guido Guinicelli, Guido Cavalcanti, and others of less note. It was this language, rough and poor in its vocabulary, unsettled and confused in its construction, which Dante made the vehicle of his thoughts, and which his genius moulded into a degree of perfection it has ever since maintained. While the early writers of English and French literature have no claim to be considered as models of style, the productions of Dante, after nearly six centuries,

7

remain the great standard of Italian composition. His language unites the softness of Petrarch with the richness of Boccaccio, and while it combines the harmony and the polish of the best writers, it surpasses all in chasteness and vigor. It is emphatically the national tongue, and Italy owes to him not only the first and the grandest expression of her living thought, but also the very organ of this expression, the great bond of her national life. Formed by the genius of the poet, he called forth all its harmonies, and caused it to echo in his poem from sphere to sphere, through the invisible universe, a grand pæan to the future of his country.

Dante not only acknowledged language as the basis of nationality, but he established that principle on the ethnographic character of the people. " When I say," he writes in the *Monarchia*, "that mankind may be governed by one ruler, I do not intend to propose that municipalities and municipal laws should originate from one source ; for nations, kingdoms, and cities have a character of their own, which makes it necessary that they should be ruled by different laws." And in the *Commedia*, seizing the true idea of national ethnography, he presents the colossal Eagle, symbol of the empire, as splendid in his individuality, as brilliant in the variety of his components, and causes him boldly to denounce the living usurpers who violate the sovereignty of nations, and the rulers who allow it to be violated. In the silvery whiteness of the temperate star of Jupiter, the spirits of the princes who rightly administered justice in the world appear to him clad in raiment of godly light. In their various and harmonious movements they describe certain signs through the heavens, which make the star seem silver streaked with gold, and which, as they are interpreted, express the divine command :—*Diligite justitiam qui judicatis terram.* And as at the shaking of a lighted brand innumerable sparks are scattered, a thousand twinkling lustres seem to descend, to ascend, and to form anew ; and he beholds the head and the neck of an Eagle in that streaming fire. Other beaming spirits move forth and take their places ; and soon the Eagle, with open wings, appears, and prominent among the living splendors which form it he recognizes David, who sang the Holy Spirit's song ; Trajan, who comforted the widow for her lost son ; Hezekiah, who retarded the coming of death by his prayers ; Constantine, who, to yield Rome to the shepherd, passed over to Constantinople, producing evil fruit from good intent ; and William, the good king, whom Sicily bewails. Now the stately bird rears his head and claps his wings, and there comes from his beak a voice, as one sound from many harp-strings, singing the praise of justice. Then the living symbol of the empire makes the heavens resound with his denunciations ; he upbraids Albert of Germany for his usurpation of Bohemia, and Philip the Fair for trampling on the rights of the Flemish and the Italian people ; he attacks Alphonso, whose luxury opened Spain to the Saracens ; and Wenceslaus of Bohemia,

whose effeminacy gave that land to the Germans.   He
loudly menaces

> The thirsting pride that maketh fool alike
> English and Scot, impatient of their bound.

He hurls his thunderbolts against the Kings of Portu-
gal and Norway, Charles, the halver of Naples and Jerusalem, Frederick of Aragon, James of Majorca and
James of Aragon—

> Who so renowned a nation and two crowns
> Have bastardized.

And, turning to Hungary, whose throne was in dispute
between two pretenders, and to Navarre, then under
foreign yoke, recognizing the right of revolution, he
exclaims :—

> O blest Hungary !
> If thou no longer patiently abidest
> Thy ill entreating : and O blest Navarre !
> If with thy mountainous girdle thou wouldst arm thee.

Then, from the small kingdom of Cyprus, his glance
pierces through the darkness of the future of Europe,
and, lamenting the oppression of the land, he foretells
the coming of revolutions and the fall of monarchies :—

> In earnest of that day, e'en now are heard
> Wailings and groans in Famagosta's streets
> And in Nicotia's, grudging at their beast,
> Who keepeth even footing with the rest.*

* Paradiso, xix., xx.

In the organization of Italy as a nation, as well as in all matters of government, Dante strongly opposed the interference of the papal Church. The papacy, which as an organized institution had gradually grown out of the necessities of the time, aided by the Carlovingians, whose usurpations it had sanctioned, reached the apex of its power in the reign of Gregory VII. " Charlemagne and Otho the Great," says Huillard Brèholles, in his *Historia Diplomatica Frederici Secundi*, " exercised a real supremacy over the papacy. But Gregory VII., mounting to the very sources of the spiritual and temporal power, indignant at this dependence, undertook to subject the empire to the Church, and the Church to the papacy. During the ten years of his pontificate (1073–1083) he could only accomplish one-half of his designs, and that which he took from the emperor he had the wisdom to transfer to the Church. The struggle which the successors of Gregory sustained against those of Henry IV., continued with alternate reverses and successes, in which the popes never lost sight of the double purpose of their predecessor. They sought more and more to discipline the Church; to introduce into it a powerful hierarchy ; to separate it from the ties of humanity by suppressing the marriage of priests ; to establish, in fact, in this great body an energetic centralization, which, proceeding from the brain, might communicate the impulsion through all the members. The submission of the Church to the papacy was, it may be said,

7*

an accomplished fact on the accession of Innocent III. (1198).   It then only remained to subject the temporal authority to the Holy See, and, uniting in one hand the two powers, to complete the intention of Gregory VII."

The same distinguished writer sums up the fundamental policy of the papacy during the first half of the thirteenth century in the following series of propositions :—

" The Church reserves to itself the patrimony of St. Peter, as a visible sign of the universal dominion which belongs to it.   The emperor is only its delegate, and consequently its inferior.   The empire, which is the highest expression of temporal power, is dependent on the Holy See.   The sovereign pontiff, who is superior to the head of the empire, is the monarch of monarchs."

This doctrine was reaffirmed at the time of Dante by Boniface VIII., in the famous bull *Unam Sanctam*, in which he proclaimed that " the Church possesses two swords, the spiritual and the temporal,—one for its own use, the other to be employed in its service by the kings and governors of the earth ; that the spiritual power as much surpasses in dignity and nobility every terrestrial power, as spiritual things excel temporal things ; that the spiritual power has the right to judge the temporal power, but that the spiritual, at least in its highest expression, which is the pope, can only be judged by God."

Familiar with Roman jurisprudence, and fully aware of the baneful effects of the papal government, Dante could not but detest such a monstrous theory; and it was chiefly to refute it that he wrote his *Monarchia*, particularly devoted to establish the supremacy of the State on the authority of God and on the principles of human reason, and to the overthrow of the arguments by which the claims of the Church were sustained. It required all the mental superiority and moral force of the writer thus openly to attack the papal power when the bloody code of Innocent III. was in full force; when the sovereignty of the popes was almost universally admitted as a corollary of the Christian doctrine; and when Boniface VIII. himself, on the occasion of the Jubilee held in 1300, appeared at the gates of St. Peter's with the imperial crown on his head, preceded by two swords, proclaiming himself to be emperor and pope. His treachery to Dante when ambassador at his court, the persecutions heaped on him when the triumph of the papal party was accomplished, and his secret flight from the Legations, while an exile, are evidences of the hatred with which he was regarded by the Church. Even twenty years after his death, Cardinal Beltrando del Pogetto, the legate of John XXII , not only prohibited the reading of the *Monarchia* under penalty of excommunication (a prohibition which, confirmed by the Church, is still in force), but he caused it to be burnt in the public square of Bologna; and strove, although in vain, to have the ashes of the author at Ravenna exhumed and scattered to the winds.

The expression of Dante's views on this subject is

not confined to the *Monarchia*; it pervades the whole
Commedia, in which, singing the apotheosis of a united
Italy, he borrows the lightning of heaven to smite the
papacy, her principal foe.   There, in the Inferno,
through the darkness of eternal night, he points out
the fiery abysses into which those popes are plunged
who have used spiritual power for the increase of their
temporal privileges.   The solitary valleys of the Purgatorio echo with laments that the sword is ingrafted on
the crook, and that two governments are mixed that ill
assort ; and the harmony of the Paradiso is disturbed
by the terrible denunciations which the Chief of the
Apostles hurls against his successors who had profaned
his seat. Emancipation from the papal yoke appears to
have been the great object of Dante in composing his
poem. He did not believe that the papacy, in its organic constitution, could be reconciled with the liberties
of Italy. Accordingly, foretelling the advent of a redeemer, he did not represent him as a messenger of
peace, but as a military chief, armed with an avenging
sword, through whose might the country was to be
regenerated.   The advent of such a messenger was with
him an article of religious faith ; and he believed that—

> The high Providence which did defend
> Through Scipio the world's empery for Rome,
> Would not delay its succor.*

* Paradiso, xxvii.   See also Inferno, xi., xix. ; Purgatorio, xvi., xix.,
xxiv. ; Paradiso, xxx., and alibi, *passim*.

The separation of Church and State being a predominant principle in the *Commedia*, the question arises, whether Dante acknowledged the spiritual sovereignty of the papacy, or whether he considered it as an accidental and transient feature of genuine Christianity. Looking at the poem in its literal signification, the early commentators, followed by many modern writers, have generally maintained, that while he opposed the temporal power of the popes, and condemned the abuses introduced into the Church, he never overstepped the bounds of strict orthodoxy, nor ceased to revere in their persons the legitimate successors of St. Peter, the guardians of Christianity, and the foundation of the visible unity of the Church ; while, on the contrary, others have striven to show that Dante, far from being the poet of papal Catholicism, was the precursor of Luther and of the Reformation, and have claimed for him the first rank among religious reformers.

Ugo Foscolo, the most accurate and independent among Italian critics at the beginning of the present century, took this view,* but it has only recently been systematically developed in the learned and ingenious writings of Rossetti.† According to this author, opposition to the papal power in the thirteenth century had so far gained ground as to induce a system of repression on the part of the Church, which culminated

* Ugo Foscolo. " Discorso sul testo del poema di Dante."

† G. Rossetti. " Sullo Spirito antipapale che produsse la Riforma e sua segreta influenza sulla letteratura d' Europa." See also his " Commento della *Divina Commedia*."

in the massacre of the Albigenses, ordered by Innocent III., and carried into execution by Simon de Montfort. The Inquisition, established by the same pope, affords further evidence that the public mind was freeing itself from the intellectual servitude of the preceding centuries. The Waldenses and other religious sects, which had either survived the destruction of those heretics or risen from their ashes, had continued the opposition : and in the time of Dante it was chiefly maintained by the order of the Templars, who, since their establishment in the East, had rapidly increased in numbers, wealth, and power, and formed a vast and formidable organization which extended throughout Europe. Their doctrines, expressed in symbols and rites chiefly derived from the East, centred in the great idea of liberty, symbolized by the sun. This Order at length became so obnoxious to the Church, that Clement V. determined on its destruction, which he accomplished with the aid of Philip the Fair. The grand master and other leading Templars were suddenly seized, put to torture, and burned at the stake ; while the Order itself was abolished by the pope throughout the world.

The principal poets of the time, according to Rossetti, either in communication with the Templars or bound together in secret associations, took a prominent part in this struggle. They adopted symbols and allegories, chiefly drawn from the language of love, in which they expressed their ideas of social and religious reform; by which they were able to communicate with each other, and to make themselves understood by the initiated. Thus the love of liberty, symbolized by the poets in the love of ideal women, was nourished and kept alive; and thus Dante, one of the principal leaders in that movement, wrote the *Commedia*, the esoteric Bible of the Templars, containing their principal doctrines and aspirations.

Without entering into any criticism of Rossetti's theory, it may be said that no positive evidence exists of the participation of Dante in any organized conspiracy against the papacy. Indeed, he so openly and boldly condemns that institution, as far at least as regards its temporal authority, that the possibility of an esoteric interpretation seems excluded by the text of the poem. His words on this subject are so clear and intelligible, that Ugo Foscolo suggests that the *Commedia* could not have been published before his death, as it would have exposed him to greater dangers than those which he actually incurred. At the same time, his expressions on the subject of the papacy as a spiritual power seem to indicate that while he recognized it as an accomplished fact, he strove to make it subservient to the high moral and political purposes which he had in view. Accordingly, he not only admits the fundamental distinction between the temporal and spiritual authority, but he insists that while the former belongs to the emperor, the latter belongs to the pope; the two being the suns which are destined to cast their

light from Rome over the kingdom of the world as
well as over that of God.* A glance at the religious
ideas of the poet, which are so closely connected with
his political system, seems necessary to a full understanding of the poem.

Dante was eminently a Christian, believing that only
through Christianity could the world be regenerated.
This idea pervades all his writings, and is the predom-
inating spirit of the *Commedia*, which, as he himself
says, was chiefly intended for the moral education of
the race. He accepted also, to some extent, the form
under which Christianity manifested itself in his time,
when the mission of the papal Church was far from
being closed. His moral sense was doubtless shocked
by the scandals which had penetrated into that institution; but he was by no means blind to the genuine
elements of religion which it contained, or to the salu-
tary influence which still it exerted. He could not fail
to be attracted by its metaphysical dogmas, its symbolism, the morality of most of its precepts, the æsthetic
beauty of its worship, and the heroic virtues and the
self-sacrifice which it had inspired. But while he revered what was worthy in Catholicism, he never
recognized the divine right it asserted over the human
conscience, which involves the destruction of all individual sovereignty, the birthright of every rational
being. Had he admitted such pretensions, it would
have been idle to insist on the separation of the State

---

* Purgatorio, xvi.

from the Church, which, as the popes at all times have rightly claimed, is the logical antithesis of that subjugation of the human reason to their authority, which they so strenuously assert ; and which implies the negation of the highest principles inherent to the moral nature of man, and which form the basis of all progress in individual and social life.

With Dante, therefore, the spiritual supremacy of the Church consists in the supremacy of that moral influence which the popes at an early period had obtained through their personal virtues, rather than from any prerogative bestowed on them from on high. The spiritual sovereignty he advocated was not that of Gregory VII., Innocent III., or Boniface VIII., but, as he expressly says, that of Linus, Cletus, Sextus, Callixtus, and Urban, all belonging to an age antecedent to the fifth century, when the power of the Holy See consisted in the virtue and sanctity of the pontiffs, whose lives were noble examples of humility and poverty, and who, far from claiming jurisdiction over the Empire and the Church, considered their mission restricted to the exercise of moral influence alone, and themselves subjects of the civil law. It was this supremacy that Dante wished to secure, when, on the death of Clement V., he wrote to the cardinals, urging them to elect an Italian pope, who, by returning the papal see from Avignon to Rome, should bring it under the influence of Italian civilization, and restore it to the purity of the Gospel.

8

The existing Church he personifies as the accursed she-wolf which prostitutes itself to many animals in wedlock vile, and corrupts Christianity, making it worse than idolatry. He satirizes the claim of the popes to infallibility even at the expense of historical truth ; he sneers at their assumed privilege of pardoning sins committed for the advancement of papal interests ; he places Cato, a pagan and a suicide, as guardian of the kingdom of expiation, and spares Manfred, although an excommunicated enemy of the Church ; he calls the papacy a cursed flower, which has turned the shepherd to a wolf, and has made both sheep and lambs to go astray ; he laments that the Gospel and the great teachers are cast aside, and that the popes and the cardinals never journey in their thought to Nazareth ; and, finally, he proclaims that the chair of St. Peter, although occupied by a legitimate pope, is vacant in the sight of God.*

Nor are the passages cited by commentators in proof of his orthodoxy by any means conclusive. He, indeed, professes reverence to the highest keys, but he never asserts that they are the only keys of heaven. He regards the first shepherd as a moral guide, but he subordinates him to the authority of the Old and the New Testament. He admits many, perhaps most, of the dogmas of the Catholic Church, but he never recognizes that which is the basis of the Catholic system, the infallibility of the Church, involving its exclusive possession

* Inferno, i., xi., xxvii. ; Purgatorio, i., iii. ; Paradiso, ix., xxvii.

of supernatural truth, and the consequent condemnation of all who die out of its pale. He believes in a Church, but his Church is as wide as humanity ; it embraces all creeds and doctrines, the good and the great of all ages, the illustrious pagans as well as the martyrs and apostles. This Church he symbolizes in the chariot which appears to him in the terrestrial paradise, drawn by the Gryphon, half eagle and half lion,—the God-man, surmounted by Beatrice, surrounded by the great teachers of religion, and the nymphs representing the Christian and moral virtues. It is this Church which he beholds transformed into the papal monster, an object of scandal and shame, and which he feels himself called to restore to its primitive purity, when he represents himself as charged with this mission by Beatrice before she reveals to him the mysteries of heaven ; or when, summoned before the council of the holy men of the Old and the New Testament, he is examined on his faith and consecrated as a religious reformer by St. Peter. In words borrowed from St. Paul, he speaks of this calling, of his hardships, and his weariness, and of the glories and revelations from which he derives comfort and hope.*

As men, governments, and forms of religion, in the mind of Dante, were subordinate to the great idea of nationality, so it was with political parties. It has been

---

* Inferno, xix. ; Purgatorio, xxx., xxxi., xxxii., xxxiii. ; Paradiso, v., xxiv., xxv.

seen that on the accession of Charles of Anjou to the
throne of Naples, the Guelphs became permanently established in power throughout the peninsula. Soon,
however, owing to jealousies and ambitions, and to new
issues arising from the conditions of the country, that
party became divided into two factions, reviving the old
antagonism between the plebeians and the patricians
which had before manifested itself in the Guelphs and
Ghibelins.   In Florence these factions were led by the
two rival families of the Cerchi and the Donati, whose
names were adopted by their followers. The Cerchi,
called also the *popolani minuti*, preserving the democratic
principle originally represented by the Guelphs, had
abandoned the support of the papacy, which a bitter
experience had shown could not be reconciled with
Italian liberty, and had thus joined the Ghibelins.
The Donati, or the *popolani grossi*, on the other hand,
remained faithful to the papal interest, but strove to
establish in the government a new aristocratic class
which had arisen from the increase of wealth and commerce.   It was to crush the growing influence of the
popolani grossi that the revolution of Giano della Bella had
taken place, which had resulted in the success of the popular party, and in the adoption of a more liberal constitution.

  Events soon occurred, however, which greatly com-
plicated the condition of parties.   The neighboring city
of Pistoja, like Florence, had become distracted by the
division of the Guelphs into two factions, which took
the names of *Bianchi* and *Neri*, from rival branches of

the ancient family of the Cancellieri, descended from the first and the second wife of one of its chiefs. From Bianca, the first wife, the Bianchi had taken their name ; while the other party, in a spirit of opposition, assumed the denomination of Neri. These two families, one represented by Guglielmo, the other by Bertacca Cancellieri, were the centre of the political agitation which prevailed in Pistoja. Lore, a young son of Guglielmo, playing one day with Petieri, a son of Bertacca, had slightly wounded his companion, and on his return home was sent by his father to apologize to the parents of the injured boy. Bertacca, an irascible and cruel man, refused to listen to any excuse, but caused Lore to be seized and one of his hands cut off. Thus bleeding and dismembered, the boy returned to his father, who at once called upon his friends and allies to aid him in avenging the inhuman deed. A sanguinary engagement followed, in which many on both sides were killed and wounded. Riot followed riot, and civil war became permanent, when Florence, the head of the Guelph League, to which Pistoja belonged, summoned the leaders of both parties, and confined them within the territory of the republic. But this new element only added fuel to the fire which already raged there. The rival chieftains of Pistoja allied themselves with the contending parties of Florence, which now assumed the names of Bianchi and Neri, and the war was renewed with added fury.

While Dante sought to reconcile the contending fac-

8*

tions, he naturally inclined toward the Bianchi, whose policy coincided, to some extent, with his own, and in whose ranks were some of his best friends. Among these, he was particularly attached to Vieri dei Cerchi, the chief of the party, a man of plebeian origin, of great wealth, accumulated by personal energy in commercial enterprise, valiant, ambitious, courteous, and attractive. The leader of the cavalry at the battle of Campaldino, Vieri had displayed great bravery, when, being required to select twelve horsemen for the assault, he had himself ridden forward, with his son and nephew by his side, and, turning to his troops, had said :—" We ourselves shall make the charge ; but any one of you may show his devotion to his country by joining us ;" words which brought Dante to his side among the number of those who volunteered for the charge, which was made with brilliant success.   Beside Vieri, the Bianchi recognized as one of their chiefs Guido Cavalcanti, the bosom friend of Dante, a nobleman, a warrior, a poet, and a philosopher.

The Neri, on the other hand, were led by Corso Donati, who, as has been said, commanded the Florentine army at Campaldino, and was brother to Forese and Piccarda, valued friends of the poet. " Corso," says Villani, " was a valorous knight, a good speaker, a most acute statesman, comely and of graceful carriage, but a worldly man and a conspirator, who, for the sake of attaining state and lordship, entered into many scandalous practices." Dino Compagni calls him the

Catiline of Florence, a shrewd, bold partisan, a friend of great lords, and an enemy of the people. Goaded by the overbearing violence of Corso, and the high-handed insults which he and his followers inflicted on the lower classes, the Florentines had, under the guidance of Giano della Bella, infused a stronger spirit of democracy into their constitution, and armed themselves anew against the aristocratic party. Apart from the hostility of Dante to the principles of Corso Donati, he had personal motives which estranged him from that leader. Haughty and proud himself, he could ill tolerate that imperious aristocrat, to whom, although inferior in social position, he was so superior in moral and intellectual attainments. Corso, too, was the mortal enemy of Guido Cavalcanti, whom he had attempted treacherously to put to death, and the poet and other friends had organized themselves into an armed company for his protection. He thus found himself an object of hatred to that demagogue, and he was soon destined to feel the power of his revenge.

Although the feud between the Bianchi and Neri had been for some time gathering strength, no important collision, up to the year 1300, seems to have taken place, and, to some extent, the civilities of common life continued to be exchanged between them. Villani relates that at a dinner-party given by Vieri dei Cerchi, in that year, Lady Filippo of the Bianchi was asked by the hostess to take her seat beside Lady Donati of the Neri. Messer Vieri jestingly remarked to his wife that she should have placed some one between them, as the ladies did not agree. This gave great offence to Lady Donati, who, with some resentful words, was in the act of leaving the room, when the host, distressed at having thus unintentionally offended the lady, rushed to her side, begged her pardon, and gently taking her arm, urged her to return. But Lady Donati, crimson with rage, by that act considered herself still further insulted. This conduct on her part provoked a severe retort from Messer Vieri. The husband demanded satisfaction; words were followed by blows. The first blood was shed; this called again for blood. A few days later, during the spring festival, a band of young men, belonging to the Bianchi, made their appearance on horseback in the streets, to witness the public games. They were attacked by another band of the Neri. An engagement followed, in which many on both sides were wounded. Another outbreak soon occurred between Guido Cavalcanti and Corso Donati and their followers, and Florence was distracted by riot and violence.

On the 15th of June, 1300, the same year in which he began the composition of his great poem, after a terrible conflict which had endangered the city, Dante, then thirty-five years of age, was elected one of the Priori, to whom the administration of public affairs was intrusted. Of his colleagues in office little record remains; but it is known that his uprightness, energy,

and genius soon placed him at the head of the government, and threw upon him the sole responsibility.
Although inclined towards the Bianchi, he held himself
above all parties, which he strove to pacify and to unite.
Finding, however, all attempts at conciliation fail, convinced that the safety of Florence could only be secured
by her deliverance from the turbulent leaders of both
factions, and indignant at an attempt of the Neri to
overthrow the legitimate authorities, he resolved, by a
decisive blow, to strike at the root of the evil. He
summoned the people to the square della Signoria, and
caused his colleagues to sign with him an ordinance
by which the principal leaders of the two parties were
banished from the city. This was proclaimed and carried into execution, and Florence was at last delivered
from the machinations and threats of these violent partisans. The boldness of the act was equalled by its
impartiality; for among the exiles there was not only
Corso Donati, his bitter enemy, but Guido Cavalcanti,
his best friend. It is true that the latter was soon pardoned and permitted to return, although he returned
only to die.

The republic now enjoyed comparative tranquillity,
and a period of peace and order seemed about to open.
But this calm was of short duration. The Neri who
remained in Florence, as well as those who had been
expelled, refused to be reconciled with the new condition, which consolidated the power in the hands of
their rivals, and they began to conspire both at home

and abroad.   Events occurred in the peninsula at this time which they hastened to turn to their advantage, and which greatly contributed to raise their hopes. Boniface VIII. had prevailed on Philip the Fair to undertake an expedition into Sicily, in order to overthrow the Ghibelin power represented by Frederick of Aragon, who had just then ascended the throne. Philip had placed his own brother, Charles de Valois, in command of the expedition, to whom the pope had promised the crown of the Eastern Empire. While Corso Donati was in Rome, urging the pontiff to induce the French prince to turn his arms against Florence, and to deliver her from the rule of the Bianchi, other prominent men of the Neri were in Bologna, where Charles held his court, striving to obtain the same object.

The Bianchi, becoming aware of this conspiracy, dispatched a delegation to Rome for the purpose of counteracting the schemes of their rivals ; and Dante was appointed chief of the embassy. Aware of the weakness of his colleagues, and of the necessity of his presence both in Florence and in Rome, he at first hesitated to accept the mission, saying :—" If I go, who is there to stay ? and if I stay, who is there to go ?"   He decided, however, to go. Boniface received the embassy with marked cordiality, urged the necessity of a reconciliation between the contending parties, and, dismissing the two other ambassadors, whom he had no cause to fear, he begged Dante to remain in Rome to complete the negotiations. Meantime he treacherously ordered Charles de Valois to enter Florence, ostensibly as a peace-maker, but in reality invested with authority to overthrow the existing government, and re-establish the Neri. This order was carried out on the 1st of November, 1301, when Charles entered the city at the head of his army. At first he proclaimed that he had come to bring the olive-branch of peace, and to reconcile the opposing parties. The historian Dino Compagni, a Bianco himself, was charged with the negotiations between the two factions, and the organization of a government in which they should each have an equal share. But the claims of the Neri were so exorbitant, that Dino, in his record of these events, declares that he soon abandoned in disgust all hope of pacification, and that his moral sentiment was so shocked by the plans of the leaders of that party, that, protesting that he would not play the *role* of Judas, he withdrew from the conference.

Meantime Corso Donati, still in exile, had learned that his return would not be unwelcome to Charles, and, under cover of night, he arrived at the gates of the city, where he was met by his partisans. Inflamed by his violent harangues, and led on by him, they entered, set free the prisoners, drove the Priori from the palace, set fire to the city, and, amidst the conflagration, gave themselves up to robbery, rapine, and murder. These orgies lasted for five days ; half the city was destroyed, and the people, whose leaders had been mur- .

dered or had escaped, remained impotent and terrified spectators of the awful scenes. In the midst of the burning ruins of Florence the Neri established a government of their own, at the head of which, under the auspices of Charles and Corso, they placed Cante dei Gabrielli, a violent and unscrupulous demagogue.

While these events were occurring Dante was still in Rome, detained there by the artifices of the pope. His house had been pillaged and burned, and his lands given up to devastation. A sentence of temporary banishment was soon passed against him, on the ground of his opposition to the advent of Charles de Valois, and also of his having illegally taken money in the discharge of his office; a charge, however, which he never condescended to notice, and of which his biographers have fully exonerated him. Failing to pay the fine which had been imposed upon him by the first sentence, a month after it was not only confirmed, but his property confiscated and his exile made perpetual, under penalty of being burnt alive if he were ever found within the territory of the republic. Thus betrayed by Boniface, and the victim of the conspiracy of Corso and his adherents, Dante, at the age of thirty-six, found himself deprived of the considerable property which he had inherited from his father, reduced almost to beggary, torn from his family, and an exile from the city of his birth, which he loved with an intense devotion, and where he had hoped to receive the poet's crown.

Leaving Rome, he came to Siena, where he first heard of the sentence passed against him. He then visited Arezzo, Bologna, and Forlì, everywhere arousing the companions of his misfortune, and calling them to the rescue of Florence. " Florence," he said, " we must recover ; Florence for Italy, and Italy for the world." The exiles held a council in the territory between Siena and Arezzo, where the Ghibelins, now almost entirely identified with the Bianchi, were still in possession of fortresses and castles. They established a provisional government, in which the poet held a prominent place; they organized an army, and appointed Scarpetta degli Ordelaffi, Podestà of Forlì, to command it. Meanwhile, Dante visited the different courts favorable to their cause, and succeeded in obtaining several thousand recruits, particularly from Bartolommeo della Scala, Lord of Verona, the chief of the Ghibelins, and his ardent friend.

In 1303 an attempt was made to take possession of Florence ; but the army of the exiles was defeated, and the prisoners mercilessly slaughtered by the Guelphs. Nor did the second attack, led by Alessandro della Romella, prove more successful. The vanguard of the united Bianchi and Ghibelins penetrated far into the city, but soon, repulsed by a stronger force, a panic ensued, which ended in a general flight. Dante was present at neither of these battles ; but he became greatly disheartened at the failures, which he, to a great extent, attributed to the cowardice of his allies, from whom he

9

grew more and more estranged, until finally he withdrew from all parties.

Indeed he had never been a partisan. Endowed with the sterling qualities of the statesman, and inspired by a noble patriotism, he regarded all organizations as means to an end ; and if he took part with them, it was not to become the slave of their traditions or of their prejudices, but only to make them subservient to higher aspirations. Hence his transition from one party to another; his partial adherence, first to the Guelphs, next to the Bianchi and the Ghibelins ; his endeavors to reconcile them into one great national party ; and, finally, his abandonment of all, far from indicating inconsistency, as has been asserted, were the result of his intense devotion to his country, and his untiring pursuit of whatever course he believed would best promote the highest interests of Italy. In his poem he often speaks of his independence of all parties. He causes his teacher, Brunetto Latini, to predict that he " shall be craved with keen hunger by all factions ;" and his ancestor, Caccaguida, to foretell, that of all the calamities which will befall him, that which shall gall him most will be the worthless and vile company amidst which he will be thrown.*

This lofty sentiment of personal independence led him, while passing judgment on his contemporaries, to distribute rewards and punishments according to their claims as patriots, not as partisans ; for patriotism he

* Inferno, xv. ; Paradiso, xvii.

esteemed as the highest virtue among those which elevate and endear life, and treason the most hideous crime which can deform human character, surpassing even parricide in its nature and dire effects: and so he condemns traitors to eternal misery, and, whether Guelphs or Ghibelins, shows them, side by side, imprisoned with Lucifer in the frozen lake of Antenora, in the lowest depths of hell.*

From the time of his banishment from Florence to that of his death, a period of about twenty years, we find Dante wandering from city to city, from monastery to monastery, from castle to castle, often finding hospitality from leaders of all parties, but always smarting under the sting of his own misfortunes and those of his country. In 1303 he found his first refuge and place of rest at the court of Bartolommeo della Scala, in Verona, who received him with such courtesy and kindness, that, as he says, " his granting always foreran his asking."† Not long after, he appears at Bologna, occupied in study ; next in Padua, where he received from his friend Giotto, then engaged in painting the chapel of the Madonna dell' Arena, the most generous and cordial hospitality. While in that city, he became the intimate friend of Madonna Pietra, of the noble family of the Scrovigni,—a relation which has been regarded by his biographers as having been of a more tender character. Here he summoned to him his eldest son,

* Inferno, xxxii. † Paradiso, xvii.

Pietro, then fourteen years of age, whose education he desired to direct. After two years' residence alternately at Bologna and Padua, we find him in Lunigiana, at the court of Franceschino Malaspina, who ruled that State in common with his two nephews, Conradin and Morello, distinguished for their warlike deeds and scholarly accomplishments, as well as for their sincere attachment to the poet.

While Dante was still in Lunigiana, a circumstance occurred which led to the continuance of the *Commedia*, which had been laid aside in the excitement of his public life, and his subsequent exile. During the disorders which followed the entrance of Charles de Valois into Florence, in 1301, when the house of the poet was pillaged and burned, Gemma, his wife, foreseeing the impending danger, caused some coffers, which contained, among other valued objects, the first cantos of the poem, to be removed and secreted in a safe place. Five years after that event, when the violence of passion had somewhat subsided, and more moderate men were at the head of the government, Gemma, finding it difficult to support and educate her numerous family by her own hands, sought to recover some of the confiscated property; and searching in the coffers for the deeds relating to it, found the manuscript of the first seven cantos of the Inferno. They were shown to several scholars, and their merit was at once recognized. They were sent to Morello Malaspina, with the request that he would use his influence with the poet to induce him to complete the work. Dante had regarded it as lost, and abandoned all thought of its completion; but he said, that since God had been pleased to preserve and restore it to him, he would endeavor to comply with the wishes of his friends. He accordingly devoted himself to the work, and re-wrote the cantos already composed.

Since the world is thus partly indebted to the wife of Dante for the preservation and the completion of his great poem, it may not be out of place here to refer to the charges brought against her by some of his biographers, who assert that she proved a second Xantippe to him, and that his matrimonial connection was most unfortunate. About 1293 Dante had married Gemma, of the family of the Donati, then politically connected with the Allighieri. He had lived with her but about seven years, when, in 1301, he was driven from Florence, and, it appears, never saw her again. Of the unhappiness of his marriage, however, there is no evidence, other than that the poet never alludes to his wife in his works, nor does it appear that he ever made any effort to induce her to join him in his exile. But neither did he speak of his children nor of his mother, whom he tenderly loved; his silence probably arising from the custom of the time, by which it was considered improper to bring before the public matters of a purely domestic character. On the other hand, his apparent neglect in having lived so long apart from her, finds abundant justification in his restricted circumstances, the unsettled condition of his life, which involved the necessity of constant

9*

changes, the numerous family of children dependent on her maternal protection, and, above all, in his unwavering hope of a speedy return to his home. Considering, then, the affectionate care she took of his family, providing for them even by the unaccustomed labor of her own hands, the devotion which prompted her to save his manuscripts and a part of his property from destruction, it would seem that the charges preferred against her are entirely groundless. It is true that his marriage, by placing him in relation with his political opponents, the Donati, may have caused him serious embarrassment, and the representations alluded to doubtless had their origin in this cause.

We trace Dante in his various wanderings up the valley of the Adige, as far as the Alps of the Tyrol; to the castle of the Ubaldini, in the mountains of the Casentino; to the monastery of Santa Croce di Fonte Avellana, on the Apennines of Umbria, where a chamber is still shown in which it is said he composed a part of his poem; to the castle of Colmollaro, near Gubbio, where he received the hospitality of Messer Bosone, a Ghibelin leader, his pupil and commentator; next to Udine, where he was entertained by Pagano della Torre, the Patriarch of Aquileja; and to the picturesque castle of Tolmino, in the Friuli, where a rock is still pointed out in the shadow of which he used to sit.

He visited also the monastery of Santa Croce del Corvo, situated on the shore of the Gulf of Spezzia, towards the borders of the dominions of the Malaspinas, where the most advanced point of Monte Caporione extends into the sea. His biographers relate that, in 1308, the hermits of St. Augustine, who lived there, one day saw a stranger of sad aspect, somewhat bent, as if oppressed by the burden of many sorrows, standing on that lovely spot, and gazing with kindling eyes at the charming picture which lay before him, encircled by a distant horizon, overhung by the blue sky reflected in the bluer sea. One of the monks approached and kindly addressed him; but the stranger, absorbed in the contemplation of the scene, made no reply. When again addressed and asked what he wished, sadly turning his eyes towards the speaker, he answered, *peace.* Frà Ilario, the Superior of the hermits, struck by his countenance, asked him aside; and learning who he was, manifested for him great sympathy and reverence. Dante then, taking from his breast a manuscript, presented it to the monk, saying :—" Here is a portion of my work. I leave it to you as a memorial of my respect, and I would ask that you would send a copy of it to Uguccione della Faggiuola, the Lord of Pisa, one of the three to whom I desire to dedicate the poem." On opening the book, Frà Ilario wondered how the poet could have written a work on such high subjects in the popular tongue; to which Dante answered, that he had begun the poem in Latin, but that he had finally decided to adopt the language which was more in conformity with the intelligence of the people. The monk, on sending the manuscript to Uguccione, wrote an account of this interview, and added, that of the other parts of the *Commedia*, the Purgatorio would be found with Morello Malaspina, and the Paradiso with Frederick of Aragon, King of Sicily.* It appears, however, that afterwards, disappointed by the policy pursued by that king, Dante withheld the contemplated dedication, and transferred it to Can Grande della Scala, Lord of Verona, the faithful champion of the national cause. The last thirteen cantos of the Paradiso, however, remained undiscovered for several months after the death of the poet, when his son, Jacopo, found them at Ravenna, in the house where he died; having had a dream, in which, according to Boccaccio, the luminous ghost of his father, clad in white garments, appeared to him, and pointed out the place where they had been hidden.

Soon after his visit to Monte Corvo, Dante was in Paris, a city which had long been frequented by Italian scholars and merchants. He devoted himself to the study of theology at the University, and attended, among others, the lectures of Sigier, a celebrated theologian of the time, and a disciple of Averrhoes, who appears to have taught very bold doctrines. The poet alludes to these lectures as being given in the *Vico degli strami*, so called from the straw on which the students sat, in the absence of benches, which were not yet introduced into the schools. He took different degrees

---

* Although some modern critics regard the letter of Frà Ilario as spurious, its authenticity has been established by others, particularly by Carlo Troya, in his *Veltro Allegorico*.

in theology, and on a certain public occasion, according to the prevailing custom, he discussed extemporaneously all questions on fourteen different subjects, and defended his positions against as many learned doctors. Admitted with honor to the highest degree, he was obliged to renounce it for the want of means necessary to pay the fee. Boccaccio asserts that from Paris Dante passed into England, then ruled by Edward II., and another biographer adds that he visited Oxford.

In 1308, on the death of Albert, Henry, Count of Luxemburg, was elected King of the Romans and Emperor of Germany, under the name of Henry VII. His election was confirmed by Clement V. ; and having received the imperial crown at Aix-la-Chapelle, at the hands of the Archbishop of Cologne, and settled the disputes among his German barons, he set out for Italy, where for nearly sixty years the imperial eagles had not been seen. Arrived at Lausanne, in the summer of 1310, at the head of a small army, he remained there to await re-enforcements, and to receive the delegations sent by the Italian cities to pay him homage. In the following October he crossed Mount Cenis, visited Turin and Asti, where he was greeted with demonstrations of loyalty, and reached Milan, where, on the day of the Epiphany, 1311, he received the iron crown. Here, and in the other cities through which he passed, he appointed vicars, recalled exiles, and strove to reconcile all parties. His eagerness in this respect was so great, and the favor he showed to the Guelphs so marked, that the Ghibelins complained that he was kinder to his enemies than to his friends.

We may judge of the high esteem in which the new emperor was held by the Italian people from the testimony of Dino Compagni and Villani, two contemporary chroniclers.   Dino describes him as descending from city to city, establishing peace and good-will, as though he had been an angel of God; and Villani, having given at some length the history of Henry, says:—"Let not the reader marvel that we have continued the history of his deeds without interruption. This we have done for two reasons; one, because all Christian people, and even the Greeks and Saracens, watched with great interest his progress and fortune, and there was little to observe elsewhere; the other, because in so short a time he experienced such great vicissitudes.   He was good, wise, just, and gracious; honest, brave, and fearless; a good Christian, and of modest lineage.   He had a magnanimous heart, and was much feared and held in awe.   He followed also this supreme virtue,—he was never disheartened by adversity, nor elated by success."

The advent of Henry in Italy could not but excite a lively interest in the hearts of all patriots, who saw in his triumph the dawn of a new era for their country. To Dante, particularly, that event was the glorious promise of the restoration of Italian unity, and all his hopes and enthusiasm revived.   He was in France when news reached him of the emperor's descent into Italy, and he hastened at once to join him. He addressed a letter " to Robert, King of Naples, to Frederick, King of Sicily, to the Senators of Rome, to the Dukes, Marquises, and Counts, and to all the people of Italy," which shows with what exaltation of mind he regarded the course of the emperor. " Behold now," says he, " the acceptable time in which the signs of consolation and of peace arise. Truly the new-born day begins to diffuse its light ; the aurora now appears in the East which dissipates the darkness of our misery, and the heavens, resplendent with tranquil clearness, strengthen the predictions of the nations. We who have long dwelt in the desert shall behold the expected joy, for the peaceful sun will arise, and slothful justice, which had retreated in darkness to its utmost limit, will return in all its splendor." Urging his countrymen to receive the emperor as the betrothed of Italy and the glory of the nation, he never forgets his own dignity nor the dignity of his country. " Rouse yourselves," exclaims he, " like freemen, and recollect that the emperor is only your first minister ; that he is made for you, and not you for him." *Non enim gens propter Regem, sed Rex propter gentem.*

But while most of the Italian cities, incited by Dante, arrayed themselves under the banner of Henry, the Florentines were busily plotting against him. They had, indeed, at first, shown some disposition to accept his rule, in common with the other cities of the Tuscan

League; but, owing to the intrigues of powerful Guelphs, of Robert of Anjou, King of Naples, and of Clement V., they now refused allegiance to him, declined to receive his delegates, and at last, to avoid the consequences of their vacillating policy, they took measures to resist his progress. They fortified Florence, formed an alliance with other discontented cities, and, in order to occupy the emperor elsewhere and prevent his approach, they incited revolts in the northern provinces.

At this policy, so fatal to the cause of Italy, the grief and indignation of Dante were extreme. After an interview with the emperor, in which he had enforced upon him the necessity of bold and energetic measures, he retired to the quiet solitude of Castle Porciano, in the Casentino, where he watched events with intense anxiety. Henry VII. meantime, from the influence of bad advisers, or from his own irresolute character, wasted his time and resources in overcoming the lesser obstacles in his way, and failed to strike the decisive blow. Dante now (April 16, 1311), from his retreat, addressed an eloquent letter to him, in which he implored him, in his own name and in that of his companions in exile, to put an end to his temporizing policy, and to march at once on the city which was the fruitful source of evil, "the viper which turned its fangs against the bosom of its mother, the contaminated sheep which spread disease among the flock, the incestuous Myrrha who delighted in unholy connections."

He insists that Florence is the key of the position, the possession of which will involve the submission of the other cities ; that his delays will bring certain ruin on him and on the cause, and ; assuming the language of an equal rather than that of a subject to his sovereign, he says :—" Why dost thou stop half way, as if the empire lay in Liguria ? Art thou he that shall come, or do we look for another ?"

Henry had just received this letter when the revolt of Brescia caused him to march on that city. Having previously recalled the exiled Guelphs and reconciled them with the Ghibelins, then in power, he had thought himself secure. But they were no sooner re-established than they drove out their rivals, made an alliance with Florence and Bologna, and openly rose against his authority. The emperor now laid siege to Brescia (May 14, 1311), but, as Dante had predicted, this proved a disastrous step. The imperial troops were decimated by disease ; and, while several months were lost in the siege, Florence gained time to prepare for resistance. Brescia at length surrendered (September 26, 1311), and the emperor forthwith departed for Genoa, where he was joined by the poet. His biographers relate that while in that city, Dante was the object of serious outrages on the part of the people, with whom he had dealt severely in his poem, particularly with Branca Doria, the most powerful among the nobility, whose soul he had described as in hell for having murdered

10

his father-in-law, while his body, still on earth, was animated by a demon.*

The emperor, meanwhile, having recruited his army, and furnished himself with additional means for carrying on the war, on the 12th of February, 1312, accompanied by Dante and other prominent exiles, sailed for Pisa with a fleet of thirty galleys. After spending a few months in that city, in order to complete his preparations, Henry, at the head of his army, left for Rome, where the troops of King Robert and of the Tuscan League had previously arrived, and were ready to oppose his coronation. On the 7th of May the imperial army reached Ponte Molle, which they found strongly guarded. They forced it and entered the city. Many engagements ensued, which were so far successful on the part of the emperor, that on the 1st of the following August he was crowned. He at once left Rome and pursued his way towards Florence.

On the 19th of September he arrived before the city, which, according to Villani, he could have taken by a bold movement; but, cautious, undecided, and still nourishing the vain hope that the Florentines would voluntarily submit, he lingered around the walls until the last opportunity was lost. A fever attacked his army, the emperor himself was taken ill, and, without striking a blow, he retired to Poggibonzi. Having thus failed to establish his authority in Tuscany, probably by

* Inferno, xxxiii.

the advice of Dante, he now decided to turn his arms against King Robert, who had so greatly contributed to his defeat. An alliance was concluded with Frederick, King of Sicily, money and troops were raised, and a fleet of one hundred and fifty galleys equipped. Fortune again seemed to smile on Henry, and the crown of Italy to be once more within his grasp. But only for a brief interval. He was taken ill on his way to Apuglia, in the town of Buonconvento, near Siena, where he died, August 24, 1313. His army dispersed, Italy was left more disturbed than ever, and a new source of grief was opened in the sorrowful heart of Dante. But he was not ungrateful to the emperor, although he had accomplished so little. Imagining the events described in his poem not as past, but as to come, he causes Beatrice to point out in the heights of the Empyrean the proud throne, surmounted by a crown, on which shall rest the soul of the great Harry.*

The course of Dante on the coming of Henry VII., has furnished narrow-minded critics occasion to charge him with having invoked foreign intervention in the affairs of the peninsula from motives of personal revenge. According to these writers, he abandoned the cause of the Guelphs only because he had been persecuted by that party, and urged the German emperor to take possession of Florence only that he might re-enter the city and chastise his enemies. But this charge is contradicted by the whole course of the poet himself. We have

* Paradiso, xxx.

seen that his relations with political parties were always subordinate to higher objects, and that the idea of the unity of Italy, far from having sprung up in his mind after his exile, was the result of his calm and philosophic speculation in the *Monarchia*, a work which, according to the best critics of the present day, was written in the most brilliant period of his public career. That the Guelph party was unable to carry out that idea, he had early become convinced ; hence we have seen him, at a period preceding his proscription, attach himself to the Bianchi, who had many points of similarity with the Ghibelins. If he looked to the German emperors for the carrying out of his political system, we must not lose sight of the fact that those princes, in the middle ages, were recognized as the highest representatives of civil authority, and that Italy was not a self-existing nation, but under the yoke of foreign potentates. Dante had sought in vain for an Italian chief who could expel those despots, and reduce the country to one government. Nothing now remained but to look to France or to Germany for that power ; and between the two he did not hesitate to choose. While France had at all times labored to secure in Italy the ascendency of the popes, the natural foes of Italian unity, Germany, for more than two centuries, had opposed them. She was, therefore, the natural ally of the Italian people in their struggle for national life. An alliance with France presented serious objections, formidable as she was in her position as a border state, in her strength and warlike character, and still more in the fact of her common origin. These dangers could not be feared in the case of Germany, a country heterogeneous, remote, divided, and harassed by intestine contentions. In any attempt at subjugation, the Italian people would be most likely to absorb the German; as in the seventh century, when the northern tribes, descending into Italy for conquest, became civilized and fused into the national stock. Add to this, that the German emperors derived their supremacy from Rome, as the successors of the Cæsars, and as such were Italians. Accordingly, Dante insisted on the necessity of Rome becoming the seat of the empire as well as the capital of the nation, and that any emperor of foreign birth should become a naturalized Italian, as his power was of Italian origin.

But it was no question with Dante as to who should be the redeemer of his country; it was, where he should be found. He would have accepted Can Grande della Scala, Uguccione della Faggiuola, the Malaspinas, Frederick of Sicily, or even Robert of Anjou, notwithstanding he says of him that he was more fit to be a preacher than a king. Although Frederick, after the death of Henry, withdrew his galleys and declined to serve the cause any longer, the poet did not despair. He still clung to his cherished idea, and, in the spirit of prophecy, foretold that since the South had failed in her duty, the power of the nation must pass to the North. Comparing Italy to a fleet, he thus predicted the events of to-day :—

> Yet before the date
> When through the hundredth in his reckoning dropped,
> Pale January must be shoved aside
> From winter's calendar, these heavenly spheres
> Shall roar so loud, that Fortune shall be fain
> To turn the poop where she has now the prow,
> So that the fleet run onward : and true fruit,
> Expected long, shall crown at last the bloom.*

After the death of Henry VII., Dante continued to roam through the country, and at the close of the year 1313 we find him in Pisa, at the court of the lord of that republic, Uguccione della Faggiuola. The most successful adventurer of his time, valiant and refined, a warrior and a poet, Uguccione had extended his dominions from Arezzo to Pisa and Lucca, and distinguished himself in the imperial army. Dante first met him at Arezzo, on his return from Rome, and was most favorably impressed by his manners, culture, and political aspirations. He now yielded to his entreaties and visited his court, hoping to find leisure to continue his poem, and also to be able to induce Uguccione to put himself at the head of the national movement. He found him, however, unwilling to risk his present position for an uncertain glory in the future. He had married his daughter to Corso Donati, and had allowed his ambition to be tempted by the pope, who had promised a cardinal's hat to one of his sons ; and he dreaded to

* Paradiso, xxvii.

endanger his relations with the court of Rome and the leader of the Guelph party. Becoming selfish, he became also despotic and cruel. A revolution ensued, led by Castruccio Castracane, a young patriot of Lucca, who had acquired great popularity for his boldness and gallantry. Uguccione was expelled from his dominions, and took refuge at the court of Verona, where he became general of the army ; and there he was again joined by the poet.

Verona was then under the rule of Can Grande della Scala, the brother of Bartolommeo, at whose court Dante had before resided. The poet had known Cane in his youth, and entertained for him a warm friendship. A chivalric and adventurous prince, an intrepid warrior, a skilful statesman, Can Grande had extended his dominions through northern Italy, and held the position of vicar-general of the empire. By his love of letters, and his fondness for poetry and the fine arts, he had attracted to Verona the most distinguished exiles, upon whom he lavished all his magnificent liberality. His splendid palace, adorned with pictures of battles, mythologic and pastoral scenes, its various departments decorated to suit the tastes and professions of his different guests, was at all times crowded with warriors, poets, and artists, who rendered his court brilliant and renowned. Had Dante sought only comfort and repose, it would seem that he might have been happy here. His fame as a poet gained him universal admiration ; he was surrounded by some of his best friends, and enjoyed the affectionate care of his son Pietro, who had settled in that city as a lawyer, and whose descendants still live in the noble family of the Sarego-Allighieri.* But, with all the esteem and friendship which were shown to him, he could not rest. The misfortunes of his country preyed on his sensitive spirit, and his soul was devoured by that slow-consuming fire which the exile only feels. Cacciaguida foreshadows the fate which awaited him when he says :—

> Thou shalt leave each thing
> Beloved most dearly ; this is the first shaft
> Shot from the bow of exile. Thou shalt prove
> How salt the savor is of other's bread ;
> How hard the passage to descend and climb
> By other's stairs.†

In his *Vulgare Eloquio* he says :—" I have pity for all unhappy ones ; but most for those, whosoever they are, that languish in exile, and visit their country only in dreams." He early addressed a pathetic letter to the people of Florence, beginning, " My people, what have I done to thee?" and entreating permission to return ; and in his *Convito*, striving again to move his country-

---

* The male line of Dante ceased in the youngest of his six sons. The noble family of the Saregos of Verona descend from Ginevra, only child of Pietro, who married Count Marco Antonio Sarego, whose family added the name of Allighieri to their own. At the request of the Corporation of Florence, the King of Italy has recently bestowed the honor of the Florentine patriciate upon the present Count Pietro Sarego-Allighieri and his descendants in the male line.

† Paradiso, xvii.

men to pity, he writes :—" Oh, why was not the Sovereign of the universe pleased to remove this sting from me! for then none would have sinned against me. I should have suffered no undeserved pain, nor would I have been thus subjected to exile and to misery. It has been the pleasure of Florence, the beautiful city, the famous daughter of Rome, to reject me from her sweet bosom, where I was born, where I grew to middle life, and where, if it may please her, I wish, from my heart, to end the time which yet remains to me, and then to rest there my worn-out spirit. Through almost all parts where our language is spoken, a wanderer, well-nigh a beggar, I have gone, showing, against my will, the wounds of fortune. Truly I have been a vessel without sail or rudder, driven to diverse ports and shores by that hot blast, the breath of grievous poverty."

But, much as he longed to return to Florence, he scorned all offers of pardon on terms derogatory to his dignity. In 1317, the Neri finding themselves secure in power, and no longer under the evil influence of Corso Donati, who had been murdered by the populace, the Florentine authorities proclaimed an ordinance of amnesty to exiles on condition of fine and penance; thus placing them on the level with pardoned convicts, who were, on the festival day of St. John, the patron of the city, required to present themselves at the church, holding a candle in their hands, when, with appropriate rites and offerings, they were restored to the rights of citizenship.   Several of the friends of Dante were.desirous that he should avail himself of this opportunity, and wrote to him urging his return.   In a reply to such a request made by a monk, one of his friends, he says :—" I have received your letter with all the reverence and affection which I feel for you, and I am very grateful for the interest which you take in my return. My obligation to you is the more deeply felt, as it is so seldom that the exile finds friends.   But as for the information which you give to me, I pray you to consider my position before you judge of my decision.   So I understand, through your letters and those of my nephew and of other friends, that I may avail myself of the ordinance just proclaimed for the restoration of the exiles ; that is, if I pay a certain sum, and submit myself to the ceremony of being offered, I may be absolved and return.   This proposal contains two things ridiculous and ill-advised.   I say ill-advised by those who mentioned them ; for you, wiser and more discreet, say nothing on this subject.   Is this then the glorious return of Dante Allighieri to his country, after nearly three lustres of suffering and exile ?   Did my innocence, patent to all, merit this ?   For this, the perpetual sweat and toil of study ?   Far from one, the housemate of philosophy, be so rash and earthen-hearted a humility as to allow himself to be offered up bound like a school-boy or a criminal !   Far from one, the preacher of justice, to pay those who have done him wrong, as for a favor. This is not the way for me to return to my country ;

but if another can be found that shall not derogate from the fame and honor of Dante, that I will enter on with no lagging steps; for if by none such may Florence be re-entered, by me then never! Can I not everywhere behold the mirror of the sun and the stars? speculate on sweetest truths under any sky, without giving myself up ingloriously, nay, ignominiously, to the populace and city of Florence? Nor shall I want for bread."

Having refused the amnesty, Dante continued to live at the court of Can Grande, chiefly occupied in the composition of the Paradiso, the first cantos of which he dedicated to his patron and friend. In his letter of dedication he alludes to the fame which his lordship everywhere enjoyed, and by which he himself had been attracted to his court. He says that his magnificence surpasses even its reputation, and, in token of his friendship, he begs him to accept the most sublime portion of his poem. He then dwells on the various interpretations of the work, its symbols and allegories; he explains the reason for the title of *Commedia;* speaks of its divisions; and, while he enters into an exposition of the first canto, he says that he must omit other details which would aid in the interpretation of the poem, as he is so oppressed by poverty. He hopes, however, that the generosity of his patron will find the means to place him out of need, that he may be allowed to write more on the subject.

This lament, which is often repeated in other works, seems to indicate that although Dante was kindly treated by Can Grande, his generosity was not of that exalted kind which he had experienced from his brother, Bartolommeo. Hence, while in the Paradiso he extols Cane for his liberality, and predicts his future glory, he plainly hints that he may say things not relished by his patron, and that, in consequence, he may even lose his place of refuge. It could not be supposed that the poet would long remain a favorite in a court in which, however hospitable, gayety and pleasure formed the chief occupation of life, and the power to minister to these tastes the surest means to favor and advancement. His frankness and his haughty bearing were little calculated to secure the partiality or good-will of the company among whom he found himself. Can Grande, although esteeming him far above all his other guests, often allowed himself to be amused at the embarrassment in which the insolence or the ridicule of the triflers of the court sometimes placed him. This, of course, added to his irritation and dissatisfaction. Petrarch relates, that Dante having a positive dislike for one of the courtiers who was the favorite of all for his buffoonery, Cane, one day, expressed some surprise that such a fool could make himself agreeable, while he who was so wise could not; to which the poet replied :—" You would not wonder, if you knew that friendship lies in similarity of tastes and of mind." It appears that coarse jests were allowed at the court of Can Grande, for which Dante had no taste, and which it was far below the dignity of the host to permit. It is related that, on one occasion, a boy was concealed under the table, who gathered the bones, which, according to the custom of the time, were thrown on the floor, and placed them all together at the feet of the poet. On rising from dinner the pile was discovered; the company seemed much amused, and Can Grande remarked that Dante must be a great eater of meat. To which he quickly retorted, alluding to his name of Cane:—"Sir, you would not see so many bones even if I were a dog (*un cane*)." From these and similar incidents handed down by tradition, it may be inferred that his life at that court was not a happy or congenial one. This unhappiness was still more aggravated by the office of judge, with which some of his early biographers say that he was intrusted, and which, it appears, was highly distasteful to him. Besides, while Cane recognized Frederick of Austria as the legitimate emperor, Dante, with Uguccione, supported Louis of Bavaria, to whom he dedicated his book, *De Monarchia*. Thus it is easy to understand how, even without any open rupture with his patron, he finally decided to abandon Verona.

In 1320, Dante passed to Ravenna, then ruled by the Polentas, whom he had long numbered among his friends. He had fought with Bernardino at the battle of Campaldino, and enjoyed the friendship of Guido Novello, the present ruler of the republic, a poet and a warrior, who felt himself honored by this visit, and received the poet with a hospitality worthy of the host and of the guest.   He called to his court his sons Pietro and Jacopo, whom he intrusted with honorable offices; he surrounded him with every comfort, and strove in many ways to make him forget his sorrows.   Thus enjoying the generous friendship of Guido, the love of his sons, and the tender care of several friends,—among whom were the sister of Uguccione della Faggiuola, her two daughters, and Giotto, who came to Ravenna to visit him,—he devoted himself to the completion of his work.   He continued to correspond with the scholars of his time, among them Giovanni del Virgilio, the most distinguished Latin poet of the age.   Two eclogues of this writer remain, addressed to Dante, whom he calls the harmonious swan, while he reserves for himself the name of vulgar crow.   In these verses Virgilio exhorts him to abandon the Italian language, and to sing in Latin the great events of the day, such as the death of Henry VII., the victories of Can Grande, and the wars of Liguria.   " But, above all," he says, " come to Bologna, to take the poetical crown which belongs to thee, although I fear that thy Guido will not allow thee to leave Ravenna, and the beautiful Pineta which adorns it on the coast of the Adriatic." Dante replied to these poems in two other Latin eclogues, in which he says that however happy he would be to receive the laurel crown in Bologna, he would be still happier to receive it in Florence.   " But," he concludes, " when new kingdoms shall be manifested through my cantos, and the inhabitants of the stars shall appear, then will be time to garland my gray hair with ivy and laurel."

In 1321, Dante was sent by Guido Novello on a diplomatic mission to the Republic of Venice, for the purpose, it appears, of forming an alliance to resist the growing power of the Guelphs, whom Guido, although himself of that party, had reason to fear. The Venetians, however, a few years before having been excommunicated by the pope, and their property and territory given to the first who should conquer them, had only succeeded in averting these penalties by making the most abject submission through their ambassador, who, it is said, was admitted into the pontifical presence only in the attitude of a dog walking on all fours, with a noose around his neck. The proud republic of Venice, therefore, far from consenting to enter into a new contest with the papal power, refused even to receive the ambassador of Guido, and Dante, disheartened, returned to Ravenna.

Broken down by a life of struggle and disappointment, his hair white from suffering rather than from age, the divine old man, as Giovanni del Virgilio calls him, fell ill on his return from Venice, and after lingering a few days, having received the last consolations of religion, died on the 14th of September, 1321, at the age of fifty-six years, mourned, says Boccaccio, by Guido and all the people of Ravenna.

Robed as a Franciscan friar, according to his own wish, at his feet a golden lyre with broken chords, his

hands resting on the open Scriptures, the remains of
Dante lay in state in the palace of the Polentas.   A
magnificent funeral followed; the bier was borne by
the most distinguished citizens of the city, and Guido
himself delivered the funeral oration.   He ordered a
worthy monument to be erected in the honor of the
departed poet, but whether he was able to carry out his
project, or whether, being himself soon after driven from
Ravenna, his pious wish remained unfulfilled, it is difficult to decide.   In 1483 a monument was erected by
Bernardo Bembo, Podestà of Ravenna, designed by
Lombardi, a celebrated architect and sculptor.   In
1692 it was restored by Cardinal Corsi, pontifical legate, and was again restored, in 1780, by Cardinal
Gonzaga.

A distinguished American writer thus describes the
monument :—" At an angle of one of the by-streets
of Ravenna is a small building, by no means striking
either as regards its architecture or decorations.   It is
fronted by a gate of open iron-work, surmounted by a
cardinal's hat—indicating that the structure was raised
or renovated by some church dignitary, a class who
appear invariably scrupulous to memorialize by inscriptions and emblems whatever public work they see fit to
promote.   A stranger might pass this little edifice un-
heeded, standing as it does at a lonely corner, and wear-
ing an aspect of neglect ; but as the eye glances through
the railing of the portal, it instinctively rests on a small
and time-stained bass-relief in the opposite wall, repre-

senting that sad, stern, and emaciated countenance, which, in the form of busts, engravings, frescoes, and portraits, haunts the traveller in every part of Italy. It is a face so strongly marked with the sorrow of a noble and ideal mind, that there is no need of the laurel wreath upon the head to assure us that we look upon the lineaments of a poet. And who could fail to stay his feet, and still the current of his wandering thoughts to a deeper flow, when he reads the entablature of the little temple, *Sepulchrum Dantis poetæ.*"* Of the several Latin inscriptions on the monument, none have particular claim to be noticed except the last two verses of the principal one, attributed to Dante himself, but which is more probably from the pen of Giovanni del Virgilio or some of his pupils.† Florence has again and again entreated Ravenna to restore to her keeping the sacred remains of the poet. In the sixteenth century Michael Angelo desired to erect a monument in his honor, if his ashes might be restored to Florence. But all negotiation failed: nor has the formal demand recently made by the corporation of Florence met with better success. Ravenna, proud of her sacred trust, declines to renounce it, on the ground that Dante, as the national poet, belongs

---

* Henry T. Tuckerman. "The Italian Sketch-Book."

† The inscription here alluded to is thus translated by an American poet :—

> The rights of monarchy, the heavens, the stream of fire, the pit
> In vision seen, I sang as far as to the fates seemed fit :
> But since my soul, an alien here, hath flown to nobler wars,
> And, happier now, hath gone to seek its Maker 'mid the stars,
> Here am I Dante shut, exiled from the ancestral shore
> Whom Florence, the of all least loving mother, bore.

11*

to no one city more than to another, and that his grave cannot be in a fitter place than that in which he found his last refuge. In 1829, a cenotaph in honor of the poet was erected by the Florentines in Santa Croce, where lie the remains of Michael Angelo, Machiavelli, Galileo, and Alfieri; but regenerated Italy will doubtless, ere long, give a nobler expression to the admiration and reverence with which she regards the great founder of her literature.

" Dante," says Boccaccio, " was of middle height; his face was long, his nose aquiline, his eyes large, his complexion dark, his hair and beard thick, crisp, and black; his countenance was sad and thoughtful, his gait grave, and his bearing wonderfully composed and polished. He was greatly inclined to solitude, familiar with few, and temperate in his habits; he seldom spoke save when spoken to, though a most eloquent person. He was assiduous in study, of tenacious memory, and marvellous capacity." According to a tradition preserved by Filippo Villani and others, confirmed by Vasari, a portrait of the poet in early life was painted by Giotto, with other frescoes, in the chapel of the palace of the Podestà, now used as a prison under the name of the Bargello. From two fires which occurred in the palace in the fourteenth century, the pictures became so defaced that the walls on which they were painted were whitewashed, and in the course of years the process was several times repeated. Although connoisseurs had long believed that the frescoes were not entirely destroyed, it was only in 1840, through the zeal of Seymour Kirkup, Richard H. Wilde, and Mr. Bezzi, that any investigation was made. The whitewash was removed, and the portrait of the poet, although considerably damaged, was brought to light and restored by Marini. It forms part of a group painted on the walls of the old chapel, where appear the figures of Corso Donati, of a cardinal, of a king, and by his side that of Dante. Two distinguished artists,* recently commissioned by the Italian government to inquire concerning the most authentic portrait of Dante, have reported this to be a copy from the original of Giotto, who, according to the chroniclers of the day, had painted the poet, not on the walls, but on a table attached to the altar of the chapel, and which may have been saved from the fires alluded to. Among existing portraits, the commissioners give the preference to one in miniature which is found in the Codice Riccardiano (1040), and next, to the one on the walls of the Duomo,† which they believe to be from the original of Taddeo Gaddi, a pupil of Giotto, which was once in the church of Santa Croce. They also call attention to a mask in colored plaster owned by the Marquises Torrigiani of Florence, which is said to be a copy of the original mask taken after death, from which the busts now most frequently seen have probably been copied.

---

* Signori Luigi Passerini and Gaetano Milanesi.
† Engraved by Raphael Morghen.

The conclusions of these connoisseurs are opposed by other artists of equal reputation, who defend the authenticity of the portrait in the palace of the Podestà, and give it a decided preference over all others.*   However this may be, it is certain that from the existing portraits in the Codici and the churches, as well as from those in the pictures of the Holy Sacrament and the Parnassus by Raphael, there is formed an ideal, which, varying in minor details, gives us the general type of the features of the poet, and of the changes which they underwent, through age and struggle, from the youthful picture of Giotto, marked by a touching sadness, feminine softness, and depth of expression, to those of a later period, when the bitter trials of his life had stamped themselves on his countenance, and given to it that expression which made the women of Verona say, as he passed, that he had come from the hell whence he could go and return at his pleasure, and bring news of those who were there.

* Among those who uphold the authenticity of the portrait of Giotto, Signori Cavalcaselle and Selvatico may be mentioned.

THE DIVINA COMMEDIA.

THE DIVINA COMMEDIA.

IN his dedication to Can Grande della Scala, Dante thus explains why he gave the title of *Commedia* to the poem to which posterity has added the epithet divine. "Comedy," he writes, "is a poetic narration, beginning with painful scenes and having a happy conclusion. It differs from tragedy, which is quiet and admirable in the beginning, and in the end horrible. Besides, the style of tragedy differs from that of comedy; the one is lofty and sublime, the other common and humble, according to the precept of Horace. The reason thus appears why this work is called *Commedia*. If we regard its subject, while at the beginning it is horrible and revolting, it is hell; at the conclusion it is happy, desirable, and attractive, it is paradise. And so the style is low and humble, because it is written in the language in which even little women converse."

The *Divina Commedia*, like other great national epics, is founded on the religious traditions of the age in which it was composed. Long before the time of Dante, the gods of Olympus had been dethroned, and a new religion had revealed to mankind a higher spiritual life on earth, and a heaven of justice, peace, and blessedness hereafter.   Founded on Monotheism, excluding alike Polytheism and Pantheism, embodying in its doctrines the loftiest principles of morality and right, and presenting, in the life of its divine founder, the most elevated type of virtue and self-sacrifice, Christianity appeared as an ideal religion, independent of all mythologies,—a living negation of the priesthood and of all ecclesiastical forms, relying exclusively on spirit and truth to produce the moral regeneration of mankind.   Owing, however, in part to the nature of the human mind, in part to the influence of the Greek and Roman mythological traditions, as well as those from the East and the North among which it developed, Christianity soon lost much of its spiritual character ; and the new religion not only grew into a vast hierarchical organization modelled on that of the empire, but it borrowed rites and ceremonies from the pagan worship, as well as new doctrines from the Platonic, Aristotelian, and Arabian philosophies. From these various elements there arose a mythology, half Christian half pagan, of which allegories, symbols, legends, and the personification of the virtues and vices formed the principal features, and which found expression in the romances of chivalry, in the songs of the Troubadours, in the fabliaux of the langue d'Oc, and in all the literature of the middle ages.

Prominent among the elements of this mythology were the fictions which related to the future life.   The Christian doctrine of the immortality of the soul, involving the punishment of the wicked and the reward of the just, passing through the popular imagination, assumed a material shape, and grew into an external form, through which it was believed that the palingenesy of man after death was to be effected. This belief had long before prevailed among the Egyptians and the Asiatic nations, whose traditions concerning the regions inhabited by departed souls, and their correspondence with the deeds done in the flesh, passing through the Greeks and the Romans, reappeared in the middle ages among the Mohammedans and Jews; and particularly among Christians, whose faith became intensified by the prevailing opinion that the reign of Antichrist was approaching, and that the end of the world was near at hand. Hence the visions, raptures, apparitions, and imaginary journeys through the infernal regions, purgatory, and paradise, which fill the ascetic and the theological works of that day, and of which the "Golden Legends," published in the thirteenth century, and the "Lives of the Saints," by the Bollandists, are inexhaustible mines. At the time of Dante, these imaginary creations had taken deep root in the public mind, and had become vital elements of religious thought as well as of art and literature; they were freely used by popes and priests in their letters and sermons, adopted by poets in their songs, sculptured on the doors and stalls of churches, and painted on cathedral walls and windows. But it was as subjects of dramatic representation that they most delighted the popular mind. Villani relates that, in the year 1304, a mystery representing the tortures of the infernal regions was performed in Florence, at the foot of the bridge alla Carraja, and that the number of persons assembled to witness the spectacle was so great, that the bridge gave way, and many of the audience were drowned. "Thus," says the chronicler, "that which was announced as a mere amusement became a sad reality, many people having indeed gone to see the other world."

It was these traditions and these popular ideas of mediæval Christianity that furnished Dante with the machinery of his great poem, and his descriptions of the invisible regions, while they embody all that the Christian religion reveals on the subject, are enriched with the beautiful creations of Grecian imagination, and the gloomy or fantastic myths of the North and the East, which together form the symbolic structure of the Inferno, Purgatorio, and Paradiso, into which the *Divina Commedia* is divided. Dante himself bears testimony to the allegoric character of his poem when, in his letter to Can Grande della Scala, he writes :—" To understand what here is said, it is necessary to know that this work has not only one sense but several: the literal, derived from the letter ; the allegoric, which arises from the things signified by the letter. Literally, the poem treats of the state of spirits after death ; but allegorically it signifies the present hell, in which man does either right or wrong in his pilgrimage on earth." His son Jacopo, who may be considered in some measure as the interpreter of the mind of his father, says the Inferno, Purgatorio, and Paradiso are figures representing man on the earth sunk in vice, striving to purify himself, or confirmed in virtue, through which the human soul attains happiness and rises to the contemplation of the Supreme Good. Accordingly, the poet himself often warns his readers to seek for the thought concealed in his mystic strains, and appeals to them to make their eyes keen to penetrate the veil of his subtle texture. Thus human depravity, purification, and moral perfection, are the great ideas embodied in the allegoric structure of the *Commedia*, which is symbolic in the conic form of the hell and purgatory, with the ancients an emblem of generative evolution; in the spheres of the paradise, involving the idea of the plurality of worlds; in the mysterious force by which the poet is borne from one to another, indicating the intellectual power of man in overcoming obstacles; in the general significance of the poem, which expresses throughout the doctrine of the immortality of the soul, the universal law of compensation, the mathematical connection between moral and physical order, and the gradual development of humanity from the lowest degree of barbarism through historic epochs to the highest civilization.

But the *Commedia* is not only symbolic in its outward form; it is equally so in the vision which it describes. It includes two distinct poems, the one philosophic and religious, the other historic and political; the two being throughout interwoven, each serving as an allegoric veil to the meaning of the other. The historic and political aspect has again two significations, intermingled yet distinct, corresponding to the political objects of the poet, the redemption of Italy and of the world. To this double interpretation Dante refers when he says that the hell of the present life is the allegoric subject of the poem ;—the hell of barbarism in which nations were ingulfed ; the brutal vices of princes and people ; the oppression of the good and the triumph of the wicked ; the hell of anarchy and of despotism which afflicted his country. And as we regard Italy or mankind in their progress towards union, peace, and civilization, or in the final attainment of their destiny, we find in the Purgatorio and in the Paradiso the complementary parts of the grand double epic, which contains at once the moral history of a nation and of humanity.

But, from whatever point of view the vision may be regarded, Dante stands forth not only as the painter of the immense picture which he unfolds before our eyes, but as the protagonist and the central symbol of the action which he portrays. Unlike the ancient poets, whose personality is lost in the events which they sing, he never disappears from his scenes. He carries us with him in his mystic journey, causes us to see what he sees, to hear what he hears, to feel what he feels. Whether passing through the fire and the ice of the infernal gulfs, ascending the solitary mountain of the penitents, or borne by the force of love from sphere to sphere, he is always the lover, the theologian, the philosopher, the Florentine, the Italian, bearing with him the memories of his youth and manhood, the sorrows and the hopes of his nation and of his race. Throughout ·the *Commedia*, the poet appears as the main subject of its action. His voice rings out clearly above the imaginative drapery and the supernatural machinery of the poem, and imparts a startling reality to the scenes it describes, and a truthfulness to the expression of ideas, passions, and emotions, which finds its parallel only in Shakspeare. We feel that beyond the grave the dead still live ; we listen to the story of their crimes and of their virtues; we share in the torments of the wicked and the joys of the blessed ; and in the realities of the invisible world we find the great epic of the present as well as of the future life. This personality, however, is never separated from the allegoric personification through which he represents man in his individual and social development ; and this double character, combining the living reality of the poet with the sublime idealism which he portrays, gives to his great work much of its philosophic and æsthetic originality.

It is this predominance of individuality, both in its real and symbolic character, which first appears in the *Commedia* as an element of poetic composition, that places Dante at the head of the modern school of progress, which is founded chiefly on this characteristic, and renders him the precursor and prophet of that great reformation that is still going on, in which man is striving

12*

to reconquer that spiritual sovereignty over himself of which he has been deprived by so many ages of despotism; and it is in this view that he is to be revered as the father of modern literature. He preceded the revival of learning by three centuries; he created a new language from the rude dialects of the people; he first introduced Christianity into poetry, which he caused to become the messenger of moral regeneration. He apotheosized woman in many symbols, particularly in those of Beatrice and the Virgin Mary, and exalted that divine element, first truly developed by Christianity, which has been characterized by Goethe as the eternal Feminine. He sanctified patriotism and liberty; and, blending mythology and science, legend and history, into one grand and harmonious work, he sang an ideal civilization which will be attained only when humanity shall have reached its highest limit of perfection. Thus, in the grandeur of its conception, and in its bearing on human destiny, the *Commedia* is superior to all other poems of ancient or modern literature. While Homer and Virgil sing the legends of Greece and Rome, Milton the fall of man, and Klopstock the advent of the Messiah, Dante sings the despair, the hope, and the triumph of the race.

As the *Commedia*, in its various interpretations, is symbolic, philosophic, historic, and political, it is epic in its unity and universality, lyric in its hymns, dramatic in its development, through dialogue and action, and didactic in its scientific discussions. As it is universal in its forms, it is universal in its subjects. It embraces the history and the aspirations of mankind, as expressed in the restoration of the empire, the exaltation of the Cæsars and of Henry VII., the condemnation of the papacy, and the judgments of men and governments in general. It is the exposition of a grand system of historic philosophy, as broad as humanity itself, which the poet, borrowing his illustration from the prophet Daniel, typifies in a huge old statue with a golden head, its members composed of different metals, symbols of the ages, placed on a mountain in mid-ocean, the back turned towards Egypt, the emblem of antiquity, and the face towards imperial Rome, emblem of the future. The statue is rent throughout, and from the fissure tears flow, the tears of mankind, which, gathered together, form the four rivers of hell, symbolic of the evils of a disunited race.*

It is chiefly from the various aspects of the human nature which it so vividly portrays, that the *Commedia* derives its claim to universality. The human type has always been, more or less, the object of æsthetic composition. We see it struggling through the gigantic and monstrous creations of ancient Egypt and India, and at length manifesting itself in the beautiful personifications of the gods and heroes of Greece. Before Dante, however, the artistic expression of human nature had always fallen short of its ideal. Even the perfection which it

* Inferno, xiv.

attained in the arts of Greece was limited to physical beauty, and never reached that moral grandeur to which it was elevated by Christianity. Subject to the necessity of an inexorable fate, the blind instrument of a mysterious power, in the poems of India and Greece man never appears as the personage to whom the deeds which they celebrate or represent could be attributed; not as the cause of his actions, but as a splendid mask behind which the hidden power moved or spoke. Thus the ideal man was deprived of that liberty, the essential characteristic of human personality, and the source of all moral action. With Dante, on the contrary, individual freedom is " the supreme gift bestowed on man, the most convincing proof of the goodness of the Creator." Accordingly, in his poem he regards it as the source of all merit and demerit, and the basis of all present and future rewards and punishments. He depicts all varieties of the human type under the action of this free and creative agency; considers them in their manifold aspects, tragic and comic, noble and ignoble, sublime and grotesque; and combines them all in one great composition, the true exponent of human life. All the extremes of human experience, the terrors of hell and the blessedness of paradise; all the elements and powers of man; his counterparts in good and evil, angels and demons; his crimes, his virtues, his despair, his hope, his hatred, and his love, indeed all the sentiments and passions that agitate the heart, are here represented. The poet of humanity, he places popes and emperors, kings and priests, masters and patricians, on the same footing with infidels and subjects, beggars and slaves, workmen and plebeians; all equal in hell or in paradise, distinguished by the only real cause of distinction, their moral character. His muse directs itself not to one class or to the other; not to the wise or to the ignorant, to the good or to evil-doers, but to mankind at large. It holds before all men a general type, through which they may learn to detest crime and love virtue, and to recognize themselves as children of the same Father, brothers of the same blood. Thus, with the *Divina Commedia* modern art was born, and after three centuries there appeared in its train Hamlet and Othello, followed by Don Carlos and Faust, the great representative productions of modern literature.

The appreciation of nature, in its grand and beautiful forms and wonderful design, constitutes another element of universality in the poem. "When the ancient world," says Humboldt, "had passed away, we find in the great and inspired founder of a new era, Dante Allighieri, occasional manifestations of the deepest sensibility to the charms of the terrestrial life of nature. He depicts with inimitable grace the morning fragrance, and the trembling light on the mirror of the gently moved and distant sea. He describes the bursting of the clouds and the swelling of the rivers when, after the battle of Campaldino, the body of Buonconte da Montefeltro was lost in the Arno. The entrance into the thick grove of the terrestrial paradise is drawn from

the poet's remembrance of the pine forest near Ravenna, where the matin song of the birds resounds
through the leafy boughs. The local fidelity of this
picture of nature contrasts in the celestial paradise with
the stream of light, flashing innumerable sparks, which
fall into the flowers on the shore, and then, as if inebri-
ated with their sweet fragrance, plunge back into the
stream, whilst others rise around them. It would
almost seem as if this fiction had its origin in the recol-
lection of that peculiar and rare phosphorescent condition of the ocean, when luminous points appear to
rise from the breaking waves, and, spreading themselves
over the surface of the waters, convert the liquid plain
into a moving sea of sparkling stars." To these examples may be added the many beautiful similes drawn from
the sea, boats, ships, sails, and the details of navigation
with which the *Commedia* abounds ; the descriptions of
lights and shadows, in the infinite variety of their com-
binations and degrees ; the rising and the setting of the
sun, as seen from different points of latitude ; the lightning and the shooting stars ; the whirlwind ; the phenomenon produced by the solar rays penetrating the dense
mists of the Alpine regions ; and other charming com-
parisons drawn from the fields and the vineyards, from
agricultural and pastoral life. It is these vivid illustrations drawn from external nature, mingled with similes
from science and history, which, added to the living
presence of the poet, give to the poem that wonderful
air of reality by which it is everywhere pervaded.

Besides man and nature, there are other types described in the *Commedia*, and first among them is that which comprehends all existing and possible types, God, the Infinite Power, Intelligence, and Love. With the ancient poets, the symbols of the Divine Nature were either material, or entirely disproportioned to the idea they intended to express. And so with those adopted by Christian art. Indeed, the more elevated was the conception of the Deity as revealed by Christianity, the more difficult became its artistic representation. Even the union of the Infinite with the finite, in the Incarnation, failed to bring it within the compass of art. Hence the Fathers of the Church earnestly opposed the Anthropomorphism which was early introduced into the new worship, as antagonistic to the spirituality of the Christian idea ; and although at a later period the figures of some of the saints, and particularly that of the Madonna, as depicted by Italian artists, received a typical character, no representation of Christ has ever been thus regarded by the Christian world. Although the best paintings of the Saviour may truthfully express some of the moral perfections of His humanity, yet they utterly fail to give even a remote idea of His Divinity.

This impossibility of rendering the Divine Ideal in æsthetic composition, which at a later epoch prompted Leonardo da Vinci to throw away his brush, after a vain effort to paint the head of Christ in his Last Supper, caused Dante to refrain from giving form or language to the Deity, although His living presence is constantly felt throughout the poem. His artistic merit, in this respect, is far superior to that of Homer, Milton, and Klopstock, who, by representing the Deity as an Emperor sitting on his throne, uttering his commands, and even discoursing on metaphysical questions, lower the conception of God, by divesting it of that spirituality so essential to any true idea of the Divine Nature. The God of Dante appears only in His mighty attributes; He is the first truth, the truth itself, the eternal light which dwells in itself, and of itself understands the past, the present, and the future. He is the Sun which illumines all intelligence, and warms all nature into love. He is the Supreme Good, the rays of whose splendor are diffused through the universe. He is Eternal Justice, recompensing every wrong. He is Wisdom, allotting a just meed unto all. He is the point whereto all times and places are present, and on which heaven and nature hang. And although the poet often makes use of expressions which might have been accepted by Giordano Bruno and Spinoza, yet he never subjects himself to the charge of Pantheism. He tempers the boldness of his philosophic speculations with his poetic fancies, makes the angels the intermediate link between God and nature, and nowhere confounds the infinitude of the Deity with His finite manifestations.*

Angels have been conceived under various forms, and endowed with different characteristics, varying according to the peculiarities of different nations. They ap-

* Paradiso, xxviii., xxix., and *alibi, passim*

pear in all ancient literatures, particularly in that of Persia, furnishing to philosophers a fertile subject of speculation, and to poets an inexhaustible source of æsthetic imagination. "The ancient Persians," says Hyde, "so firmly believed in the ministry of angels, and their superintendence over human affairs, that they gave their names to the months, and assigned to them distinct offices and provinces. The Jews followed their example in this respect, and held that every one had a tutelary or guardian angel from his birth. The Mohammedans are also great believers in angels, as were the Gentiles generally, especially in the East. It is not unusual, in Oriental phraseology, to call natural agents or phenomena angels; thus the winds or currents of air in motion, lightning, and fire, are so called. The rainbow being regarded as the messenger of the gods, its colors became those in which divine natures were supposed to be clothed."

This faith was accepted by Dante, as expressed in the angelogic system attributed to Dionysius the Areopagite, but probably the work of a Neo-platonic writer of the sixth century. They appear as the Divine agencies which distribute the bounties of God throughout nature, and preside over the harmonious movement of the universe. They are in heaven symbols of the innumerable existences which people the Cosmos, and on the earth of the forces of nature. Endowed with different degrees of perfection, and intrusted with different offices, the angels of the *Com-*

media are not individual personages, with distinct characters, as the Archangels Michael, Raphael, and others, described by Milton and Klopstock, who are rather heroes drawn after those of Homer. With Dante they are ministers of God in the government of the physical and moral world, the messengers and organs of Divine Providence. Clothed in a luminous, transparent integument, in accordance with the philosophic idea that no finite spirit can exist without some kind of body, they watch over the welfare of nations, families, and individuals; they fill the terrestrial and celestial atmosphere; they mingle with the blessed in paradise; they succor the penitent in purgatory; and they descend into hell, to punish the arrogance of the demons. But, whether fulfilling their duties in the other worlds or on the earth, or absorbed in the contemplation of Him whom to see is to be blessed, they appear in the *Commedia* as the highest creations in the universe, whose mission is to celebrate the glory of their Creator and to lead humanity on to its destiny.

Opposed to the Angels are the Demons, representing the evil spirit in its various manifestations, whose object is to impede the upward progress of man. We have here the elements of that eternal struggle between good and evil, which is the foundation of all mythologies and religions. As the angels are the types of moral beauty and holiness, the demons represent moral disorder and degradation; and the *Commedia* is the arena in which the conflict is carried on by man, aided on one side by the celestial powers, on the other tried and tempted by the angels who fell the victims of their own accursed pride. Strong in intellect and energetic in action, they concentrate their powers into an intense hatred of God, of man, and of that general order to which, against their will, they are made subordinate. Subjected by their fall to the shame of material transformation, they appear as monsters,—mean, treacherous, vulgar, and sometimes ridiculous. Aside from the part they play in the *Commedia*, the object of the poet was evidently to overthrow the evil spirits from the place they occupied in the popular imagination. Hence they always appear in the most repulsive aspect, unredeemed even by a single good quality ;—differing in this respect from those of the " Paradise Lost" and the " Messiah," in both of which poems Satan appears as presiding at the council of the infernal princes, defying the Deity, and planning bold schemes of warfare against His authority. In his indomitable pride he stands forth the highest of created intelligences, and, although so fallen, he still preserves much of his ancient grandeur. The Lucifer of Dante, on the contrary, colossal and monstrous. in his form, is imprisoned in the very depths of hell, firmly wedged in everlasting ice, symbolic of treason and death. Bound forever to the centre of the earth, choked by universal gravitation, oppressed by the burden of all creation, he is speechless for eternity, because he dared to excite rebellion. He is one and trine in his three monstrous faces, the parody of God, man, and nature, because he thought to wrench the sceptre of the universe from the hands of his Creator.   Without pride, without heroism, without power, he stands there, the symbol of degradation and of impotent hate.

Although the three Cantiche are integrant parts of the whole poem, and one cannot be fully understood if not regarded in its relation to the others, their style varies in accordance with their different subject, and the effect which they are intended to produce.   In the Inferno, which represents the material results of moral evil, it may be called statuesque, the forms and imagery being more material; the personages and scenes are described with a relief and boldness that gives them all the tangibility of sculpture.   In the Purgatorio, where the darkness diminishes and gradually disappears as the poet ascends its circles, the real becomes idealized, the characters spiritualized; the scenery is beautified by the mingling of light and shadow; delicious landscapes appear, and the descriptions are pictorial. Ascending to the heavenly spheres, the light becomes more intense, and the sound of music is everywhere heard,—the one affording the luminous body, the other vocal expression, to the spirits of the blessed.   The first Cantica may be also characterized as dramatic, the second as artistic and scientific, and the third as philosophic and contemplative; while as a whole, the poem, representing the contradictions of human life, is marked by great contrasts in its scenes and great variety in its style.   It combines sublimity with simplicity, strength with ardor, and intellectual speculation witn glowing imagination. Vigorous and concise, it may be said of Dante as has been said of Homer, that it is easier to wrench the club from the hand of Hercules than to take away a word from his verses without endangering their harmony and significance.

The poem is written in lines of eleven syllables, metrically arranged, with the accent falling regularly, in accordance with the laws of poetic harmony. Its versification is the *terza rima*, borrowed from the Provençal Troubadours, in which the stanzas are composed of three lines, one rhyming with two in the following stanzas, and so on, the last rhymes of each canto being, however, in couplets instead of triplets. In reference to the versification, a contemporary of the poet thus writes :—" I heard Dante say that a rhyme had never led him to say other than he would, but that many a time and often he had made words say for him what they were not wont to express for other poets."

The style of Dante is thus eloquently described by Thomas Carlyle :—" The three kingdoms, Inferno, Purgatorio, Paradiso, look out on one another like compartments of a great edifice ; a great supernatural world-cathedral, piled up there, stern, solemn, awful ; Dante's World of Souls ! It is, at bottom, the sincerest of all poems ; sincerity here, too, we find to be the measure of worth. It came deep out of the author's heart of hearts, and it goes deep and through long generations into ours. It has all been as if molten in the hottest furnace of his soul. It has made him lean for many years. Nor the general whole only; every compartment of it is worked out, with intense earnestness, into truth, into clear visuality. Each answers to the other; each finds its place, like a marble stone accurately hewn and polished. It is the soul of Dante, and in this the soul of the middle ages, rendered forever rhythmically visible there. Through all objects he pierces, as it were, down into the heart of Being. I know nothing so intense as Dante. Consider, for example, how he paints. He has a great power of vision; seizes the very type of a thing; presents that, and nothing more. There is a brevity, an abrupt precision in him. Tacitus is not briefer, more condensed; and then in Dante it seems a natural condensation, spontaneous to the man. One smiting word; and then there is silence, nothing more said. His silence is more eloquent than words. It is strange with what sharp, decisive grace he snatches the true likeness of a matter; cuts into the matter as with a pen of fire. The very movements in Dante have something brief; swift, decisive, almost military. The fiery, swift, Italian nature of the man, so silent, passionate, with its quick, abrupt movements, its silent, ' pale rages,' speaks itself in his verses. His painting is not graphic only : brief, true, and of a vividness as of fire in dark night ; taken on the wider scale, it is every way noble, and the outcome of a great soul. Francesca and her lover, what qualities in that ! A thing woven as out of rainbows on a ground of eternal black. A small flute-voice of infinite wail speaks there into our very heart of hearts. A touch of womanhood is it, too. She speaks of '*questa forma*' so innocent; and how, even in the pit of woe, it is a solace that he will never part from her. Saddest tragedy in these *alti guai!* And the raking winds in that *aer bruno*, whirl them away again, forever! I know not in the world an affection equal to that of Dante. It is a tenderness, a trembling, longing, pitying love; like the wail of Æolian harps, soft, soft, like a child's young heart; and then that stern, sore, saddened heart! I do not agree with much modern criticism, in greatly preferring the Inferno to the two other parts of the *Divina Commedia*. Such preference belongs, I imagine, to our general Byronism of taste, and is like to be a transient feeling. The Purgatorio and the Paradiso, especially the former, one would almost say, is even more excellent than it. It is a noble thing that Purgatorio, Mountain of Purification, an emblem of the noblest conception of that age. If sin is so fatal, and hell is and must be so rigorous, awful, yet in repentance, too, is man purified; repentance is the grand Christian act. It is beautiful how Dante works it out. The trembling of the ocean waves, under the first pure gleam of morning, dawning afar on the wandering Two, is as the type of an altered mood. Hope has now dawned; never-dying hope, if in company still with heavy sorrow. The obscure sojourn of demons and reprobates is under foot; a soft breathing of penitence mounts higher and higher to the throne of mercy itself. 'Pray for me,' the denizens of that Mount of Pain all say to him. 'Tell my Giovanna to pray for me, my daughter Giovanna; I think her mother loves me no more.' They toil painfully up by that winding steep, bent down like corbels of a building, some of them crushed together so for the sin of pride; yet, nevertheless, in years, in ages, and æons, they shall have reached the top, Heaven's gate, and by mercy been admitted in. The joy, too, of all, when one has prevailed; the whole mountain shakes with joy, and a psalm of praise rises, when one soul has perfected repentance, and got its sin and misery left behind. I call all this a noble embodiment of a true noble thought. But indeed the three compartments materially support one another, are indispensable to one another. The Paradiso, a kind of inarticulate music to me, is the redeeming side of the Inferno; the Inferno without it were untrue. All three make up the true Unseen World, as figured in the Christianity of the middle ages; a thing forever memorable, forever true, in the essence of it, to all men. It was, perhaps, delineated in no human soul with such depth of veracity as in this of Dante's; a man sent to sing it, to keep it long memorable. Very notable with what brief simplicity he passes out of the every-day reality into the invisible one; and in the second or third stanza we find ourselves in the World of Spirits, and dwell there as among things palpable, indubitable. To Dante they were so; the real world, as it is called, and its facts, were but the threshold to an infinitely higher fact of a world. At bottom, the one was as preternatural as the other. Has not each man a soul? He will not only be a Spirit, but is one. To the earnest Dante it is all one visible fact; he believes it, sees it; is the poet of it, in virtue of that."

To estimate aright the influence of Dante on Italian literature, it would be necessary to study its entire history. The creator of the national language, he is also the recognized founder of the national literature. While he lived, his poem, although only partially known, was sung by the people, and excited the dread of his enemies and the admiration of all Italy. The great number of Codici or ancient manuscripts, of printed editions, and of commentaries on the *Commedia*, are evidences of the popularity which it has at all times enjoyed, and of the interest which it has excited among learned men.* At the close of the fourteenth century

* The number of the *Codici* of the poem now extant in the libraries of Europe is estimated at four hundred and ninety-eight, of which Italy possesses about three hundred and ninety, and England sixty, the others being distributed among different countries. Five of these manuscripts belong to a period preceding 1350, some to the late part of the fourteenth century, and some others to the fifteenth and sixteenth centuries. Many are written on vellum, others on parchment, with numerous illuminations, and usually with an accompanying commentary, taken most frequently from the *Ottimo Commento*, and from the commentaries of Jacopo della Lana, of Pietro and Jacopo, sons of the poet, of Boccaccio, Benvenuto da Imola, and

it was recited both in France and Italy, as the rhapso-
dists of old recited the Iliad in Greece, one singer giving the narrative and the others the dialogue.   It is,
however, to Boccaccio that Italy is particularly indebted
for early promoting the study of Dante.   He wrote
the biography of the poet, and having transcribed the
entire poem with his own hand, presented it to Petrarch
as a precious gift of friendship.   This copy, with the
marginal notes of Petrarch, is still extant in the library
of the Vatican.

Although the strife between the Bianchi and Neri
was still raging, and the enemies of Dante and those
whom he had condemned to immortal infamy in the
Commedia were still living, the Florentine people at
length began to recognize the genius of the great
poet whom they had so cruelly persecuted.   In 1350,
the government, through the hands of Boccaccio, presented a certain sum to his daughter Beatrice, then a
-nun in the convent of Santo Stefano dell' Oliva, in

Buti, all of whom wrote during the fourteenth century. For the critical
history of the Codici of the *Divina Commedia*, their antiquity and value,
the *Prolegomeni Critici* to the edition of the poem by Karl Witte may be
referred to, as well as the work of Barlow, entitled, " Critical, Historical, and
Philosophical Contributions to the Study of the *Divina Commedia*." The
editions of the poem amount to about four hundred, of which more than
twenty were published in Italy from the invention of printing to the year
1500; the earliest having appeared in 1472. During the sixteenth century forty editions were published, three in the seventeenth, and thirty-
four in the eighteenth century. The commentaries of Landino, Vellutello,
Venturi, and Lombardi, as well as the more modern writings of Balbo,
Arrivabene, Pelli, Troya, Fraticelli, Costa, Brunone Bianchi, and others,
may be consulted with profit.

Ravenna; and in 1373 the republic established a free chair for the interpretation of the poem, to which Boccaccio was first called. On Sunday, the 3d of October of the same year, the father of Italian prose, leaving the solitude to which poverty and ill health had confined him, opened his lectures in the Church of Santo Stefano, near Ponte Vecchio, before an immense audience, who listened with religious devotion to the severe rebukes which the great poet hurled against their fathers and themselves. Boccaccio continued his lectures for two years, until his death, in 1375. He was succeeded by other eminent scholars, among whom were Filippo Villani, in 1391, Francesco Filelfo, in 1431, and Cristoforo Landino, in 1457. On the establishment of the Florentine Academy, by Cosimo de Medici, a new impulse was given to the study of Dante, through the labors of Marsilio Ficino, Benedetto Varchi, the historian Giambullari, Mazzoni, the teacher of Galileo, and Galileo himself, who lectured before the Academy on the Cosmography of the *Commedia*. Other cities rivalled Florence in her early recognition of the great poet. Public lectures on Dantean exegesis were everywhere established, and the study of the poem became the standard of the literary progress of the nation. Petrarch and Ariosto imitated passages from it; Tasso studied it with patient labor, and left numerous notes on the *Convito*; while Machiavelli adopted the entire political system of the poet, modifying it according to the requirements of the time. With the decline of

Dante's influence in the seventeenth century, the national sentiment declined, but in the eighteenth century he was restored to his ancient altar by those high-priests of literature, Alfieri, Gravina, Parini, Ugo Foscolo, and Monti.   Alfieri delighted in the study of Dante, and lost no opportunity to express his obligations to him as his teacher and guide.   Having set himself the task of extracting from the *Commedia* the most harmonious and expressive verses, he copied in his own minute handwriting two hundred pages, although his selection was confined to a portion of the poem ; and on the first page of the manuscript he wrote :—" Had I the courage to begin this work again, I would copy the entire poem, not omitting a word, convinced as · I am that there is more to learn from the errors of this poet than from the excellences of others."

It is only recently, however, since modern criticism has advanced to the dignity of a science, that the study of the *Commedia* has formed a distinct department, and one to which all nations have more or less contributed. In France, the translations of Ratisbonne and Lamenais have given popularity to the poem, and the critical works of Lenormant, Fauriel, Ozanam, and Quinet have added to it valuable illustrations.   England and America have not remained behind in offering noble tributes to the genius of the Italian poet, as is shown by the translations of Cary,* Wright, Pollock, Cayley,

---

* The translation of Francis H. Cary, which is natural, faithful, and elegant, is the one adopted for the selections here introduced.

Carlyle, Longfellow, Parsons, and Norton, and by the labors of the eminent critics Lord Vernon and Barlow. But it is in Germany, the classic land of philosophic criticism, that Dantophilism has made most rapid progress. In the universities of that country the *Divina Commedia* has become a special branch of study, on which public lectures have been given by the most distinguished critics.* The writings of Schlosser, Kopish, Ruth, Wegele, Paur, Blanc, Karl Witte, and Philalethes,† furnish a vast amount of valuable criticism and research in the various branches of history, theology, philosophy, and æsthetics, as connected with the interpretation of the great poem.

The influence of Dante on art is not less conspicuous than on literature. In his poem, Nature appears as matter stamped with the eternal idea of God, and Art is exalted as the means through which He elevates and advances the race. Art, says Dante, is closely akin to the Deity; she is the daughter of nature, whence she must draw all inspiration. No talent can

---

* The programme of lectures on the *Divina Commedia*, in the principal universities of Germany, during the first term of the scholastic year 1864-5, is as follows :—

GOTTINGEN (Hanover), Professor Fittman.—*On the life of Dante.*
WURBURG (Bavaria), Professor Wegele.—*On Dante and his Works.*
ERLANGEN (Bavaria), Professor Winterling.—*On the Divina Commedia.*
TUBINGEN (Wurtemberg), Professor Pièvre.—*On the Divina Commedia.*
VIENNA (Austria), Professor Mussafia.—*On Dante and his Works.*
GRATZ (Austria), Professor Lubin.—*On the Paradiso.*
BONN (Prussia), Professor Delius.—*On the Purgatorio.*
HEIDELBERG (Baden), Professor Ruth.—*On the Inferno.*
† *Nom de plume* of the present King of Saxony.

exist without art, for nature takes her inspiration from the celestial mind, and art derives its immutable rules from reason. If the artist disregards those rules, he produces, not artistic creations, but destructions. The poet often speaks of material means as inadequate to express ideas, the form according ill with the design of art, through the sluggishness of unreplying matter. He does not consider pleasure to be the ultimate object of art, which, in its highest expression, tends to elevate man's character and to increase his love for the Supreme Good. He says that the arts, these visible languages, cannot exist without high inspiration; and of himself he says, that he writes only under the dictation of love. To exert a moral influence through his work, the artist must be a moral man, and he cannot truly paint a figure, if he cannot be himself that figure. He often speaks also of the necessity of symbols to embody ideas and sentiments, and says that in their expression something divine must beam forth which shall transform them into artistic conceptions. He insists that the images be truthful, and clearly defined as figures impressed on wax.*

Thus the *Divina Commedia* is not only a great æsthetic work in itself, but contains a treasure of æsthetic hints and suggestions, and has ever been regarded by the greatest artists as an inexhaustible mine of inspiration. Giotto, as has been said, received from

* Inferno, xi.; Purgatorio, xii., xxvii., xxxiii., xxiv., xxx.; Paradiso, i., xiii., xxvii., and *alibi passim*.

Dante many suggestions and designs, and Orcagna re-produced the scenes of the Inferno in the frescoes of the Campo Santo at Pisa, and in those of Santa Maria Novella in Florence. The same inspiration may be discovered in the admirable paintings of the Last Judgment by Signorelli in Orvieto, and in those of the Cathedral of Bologna. The influence of Dante, however, is most conspicuous in Michael Angelo, so akin to him in his ideas, in his pure and lofty patriotism, as well as in his sublime imagination and bold execution. He took great delight in the study of the poem, and illustrated his own copy with designs on the margin, a work now unfortunately lost. In his Last Judgment, his Moses, and in the Creation of Man, this influence is particularly apparent. It manifests itself, although in a less degree, in Raphael, Leonardo da Vinci, and Titian. More recently, scenes from the *Commedia* have been reproduced, in various styles and with different degrees of merit, by Flaxman, Ary Scheffer, Gustav Dorè, and Blomberg, whose illustrations, dedicated to the King of Saxony, have just appeared. The same subjects have been painted by other distinguished artists, among whom are Lindenschmidt, whose " Dante and his Century" has attracted much attention, and Vogel von Vogelstein, whose picture, " The Triumph of Beatrice," has recently been presented to the Corporation of Florence. The same artist has also in his portfolio a series of designs representing the principal scenes in the poem and in the life of the poet.

The *Divina Commedia* may be considered as a grand dramatic composition, representing in its symbolic action both humanity in its struggle for the conquest of civilization, and Italy in its progress towards nationality. The Inferno, the Purgatorio, and the Paradiso are the three Acts, which represent the beginning, the development, and the conclusion of the drama ; and its principal personages are Dante, the protagonist ; Beatrice, the symbol of Divine Wisdom ; and Virgil, who here appears as the bard of the Roman empire, the precursor of Christianity, as he was regarded in the middle ages, and the symbol of human reason.　They are supported by innumerable other characters—departed souls, living persons, angels, demons, and the personifications of ideas and virtues.　The unity of the drama is maintained by the grouping of the scenes around the principal hero, who is ever present and ever prominent ; by the philosophic system which pervades it, and the moral and political object which it proposes.　The representation consists of one hundred scenes or cantos, of which each Act or Cantica contains thirty-three, with the exception of the Inferno, which is formed of thirty-four, the first two of which serve as the prologue to the whole.

THE PROLOGUE.

IN the introduction the poet makes us acquainted with the circumstances which led to the symbolic journey. He imagines himself lost in a gloomy forest. When seeking to ascend the mountain of civilization, he is opposed by a panther, a lion, and a she-wolf. The forest represents at once this life, in which man is lost in sin and barbarism, and Italy, distracted by political factions. The panther, the lion, and the she-wolf are symbols of lust, pride, and avarice, in a general sense, and also of the anarchy of the political parties in Italy; of France, or rather of Philip the Fair, Charles of Valois, and Robert of Anjou; and of the papacy and Rome under Boniface VIII. and his successors.

> In the midway of this our mortal life,
> I found me in a gloomy wood, astray
> Gone from the path direct: and e'en to tell,
> It were no easy task, how savage wild
> That forest, how robust and rough its growth,
> Which to remember only, my dismay
> Renews, in bitterness not far from death.
>
> *　　*　　*　　*　　*
>
> How first I entered it I scarce can say,
> Such sleepy dulness in that instant weighed
> My senses down, when the true path I left;
> But when a mountain's foot I reached, where closed
> The valley that had pierced my heart with dread,

I looked aloft, and saw his shoulders broad
Already vested with that planet's beam,
Who leads all wanderers safe through every way.
     Then was a little respite to the fear,
That in my heart's recesses deep had lain
All of that night, so pitifully passed :
And as a man, with difficult short breath,
Forespent with toiling, 'scaped from sea to shore,
Turns to the perilous wide waste, and stands
At gaze; e'en so my spirit, that yet failed,
Struggling with terror, turned to view the straits
That none hath passed and lived.   My weary frame
After short pause recomforted, again
I journeyed on over that lonely steep,
The hinder foot still firmer.   Scarce the ascent
Began, when lo ! a panther, nimble, light,
And covered with a speckled skin, appeared;
Nor, when it saw me, vanished; rather strove
To check my onward going; that oft-times,
With purpose to retrace my steps, I turned.
     The hour was morning's prime, and on his way
Aloft the sun ascended with those stars,
That with him rose when Love divine first moved
Those its fair works: so that with joyous hope
All things conspired to fill me, the gay skin
Of that swift animal, the matin dawn
And the sweet season.   Soon that joy was chased,
And by new dread succeeded, when in view
A lion came, 'gainst me as it appeared,
With his head held aloft and hunger-mad,
That e'en the air was fear-struck.   A she-wolf
Was at his heels, who in her leanness seemed
Full of all wants, and many a land hath made

Disconsolate ere now.   She with such fear
O'erwhelmed me, at the sight of her appalled,
That of the height all hope I lost.   As one,
Who, with his gain elated, sees the time
When all un'wares is gone, he inwardly
Mourns with heart-griping anguish; such was I
Haunted by that fell beast, never at peace,
Who coming o'er against me, by degrees
Impelled me where the sun in silence rests.

   While to the lower space with backward step
I fell, my ken discerned the form of one
Whose voice seemed faint through long disuse of speech.
When him in that great desert I espied,
" Have mercy on me," cried I out aloud,
" Spirit! or living man! whate'er thou be."

   He answered : " Now not man, man once I was,
And born of Lombard parents, Mantuans both
By country, when the power of Julius yet
Was scarcely firm.   At Rome my life was passed,
Beneath the mild Augustus, in the time
Of fabled deities and false.   A bard
Was I, and made Anchises' upright son
The subject of my song, who came from Troy,
When the flames preyed on Ilium's haughty towers.
But thou, say wherefore to such perils past
Return'st thou ? wherefore not this pleasant mount
Ascendest, cause and source of all delight ?"

   " And art thou then that Virgil, that well-spring
From which such copious floods of eloquence
Have issued ?" I with front abashed replied.
" Glory and light of all the tuneful train !
May it avail me, that I long with zeal
Have sought thy volume, and with love immense

Have conned it o'er.   My master thou, and guide!
Thou he from whom alone I have derived
That style, which for its beauty into fame
Exalts me.   See the beast, from whom I fled.
O save me from her, thou illustrious sage!
For every vein and pulse throughout my frame
She hath made tremble."   He, soon as he saw
That I was weeping, answered: "Thou must needs
Another way pursue, if thou wouldst 'scape
From out that savage wilderness.   This beast,
At whom thou criest, her way will suffer none
To pass, and no less hindrance makes than death.
So bad and so accursèd in her kind,
That never sated is her ravenous will,
Still after food more craving than before.
To many an animal in wedlock vile
She fastens, and shall yet to many more,
Until that greyhound come, who shall destroy
Her with sharp pain.   He will not life support
By earth nor its base metals, but by love,
Wisdom, and virtue; and his land shall be
The land 'twixt either Feltro.   In his might
Shall safety to Italia's plains arise,
For whose fair realm, Camilla, virgin pure,
Nisus, Euryalus, and Turnus fell.
He, with incessant chase, through every town
Shall worry, until he to hell at length
Restore her, thence by envy first let loose."

Commentators do not agree in the interpretation of
the above passage, where the poet predicts the advent of
a redeemer, under the symbol of a greyhound; but it is
commonly believed that it refers either to Can Grande

della Scala, to Uguccione della Faggiuola, or, in a general sense, to a chieftain who should arise at some future time.

Virgil now offers to conduct Dante through the realms of despair and expiation, promising that a worthier Spirit will lead him through the regions of the blessed. He accepts the offer; and while the air is imbrowned with shadows, and night is falling over the earth, the two poets depart.*

Dante expresses the fear that he has not sufficient virtue for this high enterprise. But Virgil exhorts him to take courage, and relates that in Limbo, the resting-place of his soul, he was called by a Lady, whose

> "eyes were brighter than the star
> Of day; and she, with gentle voice and soft,
> Angelically tuned, her speech addressed:
> 'O courteous shade of Mantua! thou whose fame
> Yet lives, and shall live long as nature lasts!
> A friend, not of my fortune but myself,
> On the wide desert in his road has met
> Hindrance so great, that he through fear has turned.
> Now much I dread lest he past help have strayed,
> And I be risen too late for his relief,
> From what in heaven of him I heard. Speed now,
> And by thy eloquent persuasive tongue,
> And by all means for his deliverance meet,
> Assist him. So to me will comfort spring.
> I, who now bid thee on this errand forth,
> Am Beatrice; from a place I come

* Inferno, i.

Revisited with joy.   Love brought me thence,
Who prompts my speech.   When in my Master's sight
I stand, thy praise to him I oft will tell.'
    "She then was silent, and I thus began:
'O Lady! by whose influence alone
Mankind excels whatever is contained
Within that heaven which hath the smallest orb,
So thy command delights me, that to obey,
If it were done already, would seem late.
No need hast thou further to speak thy will:
Yet tell the reason, why thou art not loath
To leave that ample space, where to return
Thou burnest, for this centre here beneath.' "

Here Beatrice narrates that a blessed Lady, residing
in high Heaven (*Divine Providence*), had come to Lucia
(*Divine Mercy*), and had recommended Dante to her;
that Lucia, the foe of all cruelty, had appeared to her.

    " 'She thus addressed me: " Thou true praise of God,
Beatrice! why is not thy succor lent
To him, who so much loved thee, as to leave
For thy sake all the multitude admires?
Dost thou not hear how pitiful his wail,
Nor mark the death, which in the torrent flood,
Swoln mightier than a sea, him struggling holds?"
Ne'er among men did any with such speed
Haste to their profit, flee from their annoy,
As when these words were spoken, I came here,
Down from my blessed seat, trusting the force
Of thy pure eloquence, which thee, and all
Who well have marked it, into honor brings.'
    "When she had ended, her bright beaming eyes

Tearful she turned aside; whereat I felt
Redoubled zeal to serve thee.   As she willed,
Thus am I come: I saved thee from the beast,
Who thy near way across the goodly mount
Prevented.   What is this comes o'er thee then?
Why, why dost thou hang back? why in thy breast
Harbor vile fear? why hast not courage there,
And noble daring; since three maids, so blest,
Thy safety plan, e'en in the court of heaven;
And so much certain good my words forebode?"
    As florets, by the frosty air of night
Bent down and closed, when day has blanched their leaves,
Rise all unfolded on their spiry stems;
So was my fainting vigor new restored,
And to my heart such kindly courage ran,
That I as one undaunted soon replied:
"O full of pity she, who undertook
My succor! and thou kind, who didst perform
So soon her true behest!   With such desire
Thou hast disposed me to renew my voyage,
That my first purpose fully is resumed.
Lead on: one only will is in us both.
Thou art my guide, my master thou, and lord."
    So spake I; and when he had onward moved,
I entered on the deep and woody way.*

* Inferno, ii.

INFERNO.

THE Inferno represents an immense cone, its apex extending to the centre of the earth, and its base opening at the surface; hollowed within are the infernal caverns, which descend spirally around the cone, divided into circular compartments, distant from each other, concentric, and narrowing as they descend. According to the calculation of Galileo, from the data given by the poet, the dimensions of the Inferno, expressed in numbers, would be four thousand miles in depth, and as many in breadth at its upper circumference. It is preceded by a vestibule, which opens beneath the forest at the " Fauces Averni" near Cuma, and consists of nine circles, with Dante a sacred number, arranged according to the sins punished within their limits, the punishments and the demons which preside over them having always a symbolic meaning. The order of the infernal regions is as follows :—1. The Vestibule; 2. The Limbo, where unbaptized infants, heathen sages, and poets dwell; 3. The Circle of Lust; 4. Gluttony; 5. Avarice and prodigality; 6. Anger, rage, and fury; 7. Atheism and infidelity; 8. Violence; 9. Fraud; 10. Treason. The poet imagines himself beginning his mystic journey at the age of thirty-five years, in Holy Week, in the year of the Jubilee, 1300. The time spent in the Inferno was computed to be about three days.

Descending to the dreary entrance, Dante marks, in color dim, over a lofty portal's arch, inscribed :—

> Through me you pass into the city of woe :
> Through me you pass into eternal pain :
> Through me among the people lost for aye.
> Justice the founder of my fabric moved :
> To rear me was the task of power divine,
> Supremest wisdom, and primeval love :
> Before me things create were none, save things
> Eternal, and eternal I endure.
> All hope abandon, ye who enter here.

He hesitates, but, reassured by his guide, they enter the vestibule.

> Here sighs, with lamentations and loud moans,
> Resounded through the air, pierced by no star,
> That e'en I wept at entering.   Various tongues,
> Horrible languages, outcries of woe,
> Accents of anger, voices deep and hoarse,
> With hands together smote that swelled the sounds,
> Made up a tumult, that forever whirls
> Round through that air with solid darkness stained,
> Like to the sand that in the whirlwind flies.
>   I then, with horror yet encompassed, cried :
> "O master ! what is this I hear ? what race
> Are these, who seem so overcome with woe ?"
>   He thus to me : " This miserable fate
> Suffer the wretched souls of those, who lived

Without or praise or blame, with that ill band
Of angels mixed, who nor rebellious proved,
Nor yet were true to God, but for themselves
Were only.   From his bounds Heaven drove them forth,
Not to impair his lustre; nor the depth
Of Hell receives them, lest the accursed tribe
Should glory thence with exultation vain."
    I then : "Master! what doth aggrieve them thus,
That they lament so loud?"   He straight replied :
"That will I tell thee briefly.   These of death
No hope may entertain : and their blind life
So meanly passes, that all other lots
They envy.   Fame of them the world hath none,
Nor suffers; mercy and justice scorn them both.
Speak not of them, but look, and pass them by."
    And I, who straightway looked, beheld a flag,
Which whirling ran around so rapidly,
That it no pause obtained : and following came
Such a long train of spirits, I should ne'er
Have thought that death so many had despoiled.
                    .... Forthwith
I understood, for certain, this the tribe
Of those ill spirits both to God displeasing
And to His foes.   These wretches, who ne'er lived,
Went on in nakedness, and sorely stung
By wasps and hornets, which bedewed their cheeks
With blood, that, mixed with tears, dropped to their feet,
And by disgustful worms was gathered there.

They reach the shore of Acheron, the river of sorrow,
which divides the vestibule into two parts, the one reserved for those who lived in a state of apathy both to
good and evil, the other Limbo, the first circle of hell.

On this bank they behold a throng of shades awaiting
the approach of Charon, eager to cross the river.

> .... And lo! toward us in a bark
> Comes on an old man, hoary white with eld,
> Crying: Woe to you, wicked spirits! hope not
> Ever to see the sky again.   I come
> To take you to the other shore across
> Into eternal darkness, there to dwell
> In fierce heat and in ice.   And thou, who there
> standest live spirit! get thee hence, and leave
> These who are dead.

But Virgil puts the grim boatman to silence by saying :—

> "Charon! thyself torment not: so 'tis willed
> Where will and power are one.   Ask thou no more."
> Straightway in silence fell the shaggy cheeks
> Of him the boatman o'er the livid lake,
> Around whose eyes glared wheeling flames.   Meanwhile
> Those spirits, faint and naked, color changed,
> And gnashed their teeth, soon as the cruel words
> They heard.   God and their parents they blasphemed,
> The human kind, the place, the time and seed
> That did engender them and give them birth.
>   Then all together sorely wailing drew
> To the cursed strand that every man must pass
> Who fears not God.   Charon, demoniac form,
> With eyes of burning coal, collects them all,
> Beckoning, and each, that lingers, with his oar
> Strikes.   As fall off the light autumnal leaves
>   ne still another following, till the bough
> Strews all its honors on the earth beneath;

E'en in like manner Adam's evil brood
Cast themselves, one by one, down from the shore
Each at a beck, as falcon at his call.
    Thus go they over through the umbered wave;
And ever they on the opposing bank
Be landed, on this side another throng
Still gathers. · " Son," thus spake the courteous guide,
" Those who die subject to the wrath of God
All here together come from every clime,
And to o'erpass the river are not loath :
For so Heaven's justice goads them on, that fear
Is turned into desire.   Hence ne'er hath passed
Good spirit.   If of thee Charon complain,
Now mayst thou know the import of his words."
    This said, the gloomy region trembling shook
So terribly, that yet with clammy dews
Fear chills my brow.   The sad earth gave a blast,
That, lightening, shot forth a vermilion flame,
Which all my senses conquered quite, and I
Down dropped, as one with sudden slumber seized.*

Awakened by a crash of thunder, the poet finds himself on the brink of the dread abyss, dark, deep, and overhung with thick clouds. Following Virgil, he descends to the edge of Limbo, in which the spirits of those who served not God aright, or from lack of baptism and of knowledge of the true God, are doomed to live forever in desire without hope.

    Here, as mine ear could note, no plaint was heard
Except of sighs, that made the eternal air
Tremble, not caused by tortures, but from grief

* Inferno, iii.

Felt by those multitudes, many and vast,
Of men, women, and infants.

To the inquiries of Dante, if any spirits ever came
forth thence, and were afterwards blessed, Virgil replies,
referring to the descent of Christ into hell :—

> " I was new to that estate,
> When I beheld a puissant One arrive
> Among us, with victorious trophy crowned.
> He forth the shade of our first parent drew,
> Abel his child, and Noah righteous man,
> Of Moses lawgiver for faith approved,
> Of patriarch Abraham, and David king,
> Israel with his sire and with his sons,
> Nor without Rachel whom so hard he won,
> And others many more, whom He to bliss
> Exalted.   Before these, be thou assured,
> No spirit of human kind was ever saved.'

A flame is now seen in the distance; the dark hemisphere is illumined, and the company of poets appear—
Horace, Ovid, and Lucan,—led by Homer, bearing
in his hand a sword, to indicate the mission of the
poet as legislator and founder of society.

> Meantime a voice I heard : " Honor the bard
> Sublime ! his shade returns, that left us late !"
> No sooner ceased the sound, than I beheld
> Four mighty spirits toward us bend their steps,
> Of semblance neither sorrowful nor glad.
>   So I beheld united the bright school
> Of him the monarch of sublimest song,
> That o'er the others like an eagle soars.

15*

> When they together short discourse had held,
> They turned to me, with salutation kind
> Beckoning me; at the which my master smiled:
> Nor was this all; but greater honor still
> They gave me, for they made me of their tribe;
> And I was sixth amid so learned a band.

They pass on together, and arrive at a magnificent castle, symbolizing Wisdom, girt seven times with lofty walls, and defended by a pleasant stream: the former, emblems of the moral and civil virtues in which wisdom consists; the latter, of eloquence, the means through which these virtues are communicated. They pass over the stream as over dry land; and enter, through seven gates,

> Into a mead with lively verdure fresh.
>   There dwelt a race, who slow their eyes around
> Majestically moved, and in their port
> Bore eminent authority: they spake
> Seldom, but all their words were tuneful sweet.
>   We to one side retired, into a place
> Open and bright and lofty, whence each one
> Stood manifest to view.   Incontinent,
> There on the green enamel of the plain
> Were shown me the great spirits, by whose sight
> I am exalted in my own esteem.

Here he sees the heroes and the heroines of antiquity: Electra, the mother of Dardanus, the founder of Troy; Hector, Æneas, and Cæsar; King Latinus, with his daughter Lavinia; Brutus, who expelled

Tarquin; Marcia, the wife of Cato; and, apart from all others, Saladin, the fierce rival of Richard Cœur de Lion. Looking upward, he beholds Aristotle, the master of the sapient throng, surrounded by the ancient philosophers, chief among whom are Socrates and Plato.*

Descending to the second circle, they behold Minos, the infernal judge, the symbol of conscience,

> Grinning with ghastly feature: he, of all
> Who enter, strict examining the crimes,
> Gives sentence, and dismisses them beneath,
> According as he foldeth him around:
> For when before him comes the ill-fated soul,
> It all confesses; and that judge severe
> Of sins, considering what place in hell
> Suits the transgression, with his tail so oft
> Himself encircles, as degrees beneath
> He dooms it to descend. Before him stand
> Alway a numerous throng; and in his turn
> Each one to judgment passing, speaks, and hears
> His fate, thence downward to his dwelling hurled.
> "O thou! who to this residence of woe
> Approachest!" when he saw me coming, cried
> Minos, relinquishing his dread employ,
> "Look how thou enter here; beware in whom
> Thou place thy trust; let not the entrance broad
> Deceive thee to thy harm." To him my guide:
> "Wherefore exclaimest? Hinder not his way
> By destiny appointed; so 'tis willed,
> Where will and power are one. Ask thou no more."

* Inferno, iv.

Now 'gin the rueful wailings to be heard.
Now am I come where many a plaining voice
Smites on mine ear.   Into a place I came
Where light was silent all.   Bellowing there groaned .
A noise, as of a sea in tempest torn
By warring winds.   The stormy blast of hell
With restless fury drives the spirits on,
Whirled round and dashed amain with sore annoy.
When they arrive before the ruinous sweep,
There shrieks are heard, there lamentations, moans,
And blasphemies 'gainst the good Power in heaven.
    I understood, that to this torment sad
The carnal sinners are condemned, in whom
Reason by lust is swayed.   As in large troops
And multitudinous, when winter reigns,
The starlings on their wings are borne abroad ;
So bears the tyrannous gust those evil souls.
On this side and on that, above, below,
It drives them : hope of rest to solace them
Is none, nor e'en of milder pang.   As cranes,
Chanting their dolorous notes, traverse the sky,
Stretched out in long array ; so I beheld
Spirits, who came loud wailing, hurried on
By their dire doom.

Here the shades of Semiramis, Dido, Cleopatra, Helen, Achilles, Parides, and Tristan appear, followed by thousands of others.   The poet desires to address two whom he sees approaching.   They are Francesca and Paolo, whose story, so full of pathos, tenderness, and grace, forms one of the most celebrated episodes of the *Commedia*.   Francesca was the daughter of Guido da Polenta, Lord of Ravenna, the sister of Bernardino, once companion in arms to Dante, and aunt of Guido Novello, his patron and friend. Young and beautiful, she had been married, against her will, to Lanciotto, a man of great courage, but deformed in person, while she was loved most tenderly by his more attractive brother Paolo, both sons of Malatesta, Lord of Rimini. Francesca and Paolo continued to love each other after her marriage, and, in 1289, being one day surprised by Lanciotto, they were slain on the spot. As the two shades, embracing each other, are borne by the wind near Dante, he thus speaks to his guide :—

      " Bard ! willingly
I would address those two together coming,
Which seem so light before the wind." He thus :
"Note thou, when nearer they to us approach.
Then by that love which carries them along,
Entreat; and they will come." Soon as the wind
Swayed them towards us, I thus framed my speech :
" O wearied spirits ! come and hold discourse
With us, if by none else restrained." As doves
By fond desire invited, on wide wings
And firm, to their sweet nest returning home,
Cleave the air, wafted by their will along ;
Thus issued, from that troop where Dido ranks,
They, through the ill air speeding : with such force
My cry prevailed, by strong affection urged.
 " O gracious creature and benign ! who go'st
Visiting, through this element obscure,
Us, whom the world, with bloody stain imbrued ;
If, for a friend, the King of all we owned,
Our prayer to Him should for thy peace arise,

Since thou hast pity on our evil plight.
Of whatsoe'er to hear or to discourse
It pleases thee, that will we hear, of that
Freely with thee discourse, while e'er the wind,
As now, is mute.   The land that gave me birth,
Is situate on the coast, where Po descends
To rest in ocean with his sequent streams.
    " Love, that in gentle heart is quickly learned,
Entangled him by that fair form, from me
Ta'en in such cruel sort, as grieves me still :
Love, that denial takes from none beloved,
Caught me with pleasing him so passing well,
That, as thou seest, he yet deserts me not.
Love brought us to one death : Caïna* waits
The soul, who spilt our life."   Such were their words;
At hearing which, downward I bent my looks,
And held them there so long, that the bard cried :
"What art thou pondering?"   I in answer thus :
" Alas ! by what sweet thoughts, what fond desire
Must they at length to that ill pass have reached!"
    Then turning, I to them my speech addressed,
And thus began : " Francesca ! your sad fate
Even to tears my grief and pity moves.
But tell me; in the time of your sweet sighs,
By what, and how Love granted, that ye knew
Your yet uncertain wishes ?"   She replied :
" No greater grief than to remember days
Of joy, when misery is at hand.   That kens
Thy learned instructor.   Yet so eagerly
If thou art bent to know the primal root,
From whence our love gat being, I will do

---

* The place in hell where the murderers of their own relatives are
punished.

As one, who weeps and tells his tale.   One day,
For our delight we read of Lancelot,
How him love thralled.   Alone we were, and no
Suspicion near us.   Oft-times by that reading
Our eyes were drawn together, and the hue
Fled from our altered cheek.   But at one point
Alone we fell.   When of that smile we read,
The wishèd smile, so rapturously kissed
By one so deep in love, then he, who ne'er
From me shall separate, at once my lips
All trembling kissed.   The book and writer both
Were love's purveyors.   In its leaves that day
We read no more."   While thus one spirit spake,
The other wailed so sorely, that heart-struck
I, through compassion fainting, seemed not far
From death, and like a corse fell to the ground.*

The poet now finds himself in the third circle, devoted to the punishment of the gluttonous.   As the vice of gluttony particularly dulls and deadens the intellectual powers of man, it is represented as punished in a region where darkness reigns supreme, presided over by the demon Cerberus, the devourer.

In the third circle I arrive, of showers
Ceaseless, accursed, heavy and cold, unchanged
Forever, both in kind and in degree.
Large hail, discolored water, sleety flaw
Through the dun midnight air streamed down amain ;
Stank all the land whereon that tempest fell.
  Cerberus, cruel monster, fierce and strange,
Through his wide threefold throat, barks as a dog

* Inferno, v.

Over the multitude immersed beneath.
His eyes glare crimson, black his unctuous beard,
His belly large, and clawed the hands with which
He tears the spirits, flays them, and their limbs
Piecemeal disparts.   Howling there spread, as curs,
Under the rainy deluge, with one side
The other screening, oft they rolled them round,
A wretched, godless crew.   When that great worm
Descried us, savage Cerberus, he oped
His jaws, and the fangs showed us; not a limb
Of him but trembled.   Then my guide, his palms
Expanding on the ground, thence filled with earth
Raised them, and cast it in his ravenous maw.
E'en as a dog, that yelling bays for food
His keeper, when the morsel comes, lets fall
His fury, bent alone with eager haste
To swallow it; so dropped the loathsome cheeks
Of demon Cerberus, who thundering stuns
The spirits, that they for deafness wish in vain.
    We, o'er the shades thrown prostrate by the brunt
Of the heavy tempest passing, set our feet
Upon their emptiness, that substance seemed.
    They all along the earth extended lay.

As the poet approaches, he is addressed by the shade
of a Florentine, called, from his gluttonous habits,
Ciacco, the pig.   He foretells the strife which will
distract Florence, and says that in all the city there are
but two just men, meaning, perhaps, Dante himself,
and Guido Cavalcanti, whom, however, the people
neglect; for avarice, envy, and pride have fired the
hearts of all.   Ciacco informs the poet of several other

Florentines recently condemned to this place, and as he falls among his blind companions, Dante and Virgil continue their way, and descend to the fourth circle, which is under the superintendence of Plutus, the infernal god of avarice, where the prodigal and the avaricious are doomed, with mutual upbraidings, to roll great weights against each other.*

On seeing Dante led by Virgil, or, as an old commentator says, Humanity led by Reason, Plutus opposes their entrance, but he is subdued by Virgil.

> Thus we, descending to the fourth steep ledge,
> Gained on the dismal shore, that all the woe
> Hems in of all the universe.   Ah me !
> Almighty Justice ! in what store thou heap'st
> New pains, new troubles, as I here beheld.
> Wherefore doth fault of ours bring us to this?
> E'en as a billow, on Charybdis rising,
> Against encountered billow dashing breaks ;
> Such is the dance this wretched race must lead,
> Whom more than elsewhere numerous here I found.
> From one side and the other, with loud voice,
> Both rolled on weights, by main force of their breasts,
> Then smote together, and each one forthwith
> Rolled them back voluble, turning again ;
> Exclaiming these, "Why holdest thou so fast ?"
> Those answering, " And why castest thou away ?"
> So, still repeating their despiteful song,
> They to the opposite point, on either hand,
> Traversed the horrid circle ; then arrived,

* Inferno, vi.

16

Both turned them round, and through the middle space
Conflicting met again.   At sight whereof
I, stung with grief, thus spake : "O say, my guide !
What race is this ?   Were these, whose heads are shorn,
On our left hand, all separate to the church ?"
    He straight replied : "In their first life, these all
In mind were so distorted, that they made,
According to due measure, of their wealth
No use.   This clearly from their words collect,
Which they howl forth, at each extremity
Arriving of the circle, where their crime
Contrary in kind disparts them.   To the church
Were separate those, that with no hairy cowls
Are crowned, both Popes and Cardinals, over whom
Avarice dominion absolute maintains."

The poet supposes that he may recognize some
among the number ; but Virgil replies :—

    "Vain thought conceivest thou.   That ignoble life
Which made them vile before, now makes them dark,
And to all knowledge indiscernible.
Forever they shall meet in this rude shock :
These from the tomb with clenchèd grasp shall rise,
Those with close-shavèd locks.   That ill they gave
And ill they kept, hath of the beauteous world
Deprived, and set them at this strife, which needs
No labored phrase of mine to set it off.
Now may'st thou see, my son ! how brief, how vain,
The goods committed into Fortune's hands,
For which the human race keep such a coil :
Not all the gold that is beneath the moon,
Or ever hath been, of these toil-worn souls
Might purchase rest for one."

A description of Fortune here follows, in which the poet mingles the ancient idea of Fate with the doctrine of the Arabians on the supreme created intelligence which presides over the world, and with those of his own age on Divine Providence. Fortune thus symbolizes the cosmical and social laws which affect the destinies of nations and races, independent of their control.

He whose transcendent wisdom passes all,
The heavens creating gave them ruling powers
To guide them; so that each part shines to each,
Their light in equal distribution poured.
By similar appointment he ordained
Over the world's bright images to rule,
Superintendence of a guiding hand
And general minister, which at due time
May change the empty vantages of life
From race to race, from one to other's blood,
Beyond prevention of man's wisest care:
Wherefore one nation rises into sway,
Another languishes, e'en as her will
Decrees, from us concealed, as in the grass
The serpent train.   Against her naught avails
Your utmost wisdom.   She with foresight plans,
Judges, and carries on her reign, as theirs
The other powers divine.   Her changes know
None intermission: by necessity
She is made swift, so frequent come who claim
Succession in her favors.   This is she,
So execrated e'en by those whose debt
To her is rather praise; they wrongfully
With blame requite her, and with evil word;

But she is blessed, and for that recks not:
Amidst the other primal beings glad,
Rolls on her sphere, and in her bliss exults.

The poets now cross the circle to the next steep, and reach a boiling well, whose murky waters expand into the Stygian lake of hatred and sadness, where the wrathful and the slothful are immersed.

               Intent I stood
To gaze, and in the marish sunk descried
A miry tribe, all naked, and with looks
Betokening rage.   They with their hands alone
Struck not, but with the head, the breast, the feet,
Cutting each other piecemeal with their fangs.
   The good instructor spake: "Now seest thou, son!
The souls of those, whom anger overcame.
· This too for certain know, that underneath
The water dwells a multitude, whose sighs
Into these bubbles make the surface heave,
As thine eye tells thee wheresoe'er it turn.
Fixed in the slime, they say: 'Sad once were we,
In the sweet air made gladsome by the sun,
Carrying a foul and lazy mist within:
Now in these murky settlings are we sad.'
Such dolorous strain they gurgle in their throats,
But word distinct can utter none."*

Arriving at the base of a lofty turret, a signal is raised and answered, and soon a small bark, ferried by Phlegyas, the demon of ire, is seen coming over the lake.

               * Inferno, vii.

Never was arrow from the cord dismissed,
That ran its way so nimbly through the air,
As a small bark, that through the waves I spied
Toward us coming, under the sole sway
Of one that ferried it, who cried aloud:
" Art thou arrived, fell spirit?"—" Phlegyas, Phlegyas,
This time thou criest in vain," my lord replied;
" No longer shalt thou have us, but while o'er
The slimy pool we pass."   As one who hears
Of some great wrong he hath sustained, whereat
Inly he pines; so Phlegyas inly pined
In his fierce ire.   My guide, descending, stepped
Into the skiff, and bade me enter next,
Close at his side; nor, till my entrance, seemed
The vessel freighted.   Soon as both embarked,
Cutting the waves, goes on the ancient prow,
More deeply than with others it is wont.

As they hold their course across the dead channel,
the shade of Filippo Argenti, a Florentine, noted for
his wealth and his proud and violent character, approaches, and thus addresses Dante :—

" Who art thou, that thus comest ere thine hour ?"
I answered : " Though I come, I tarry not;
But who art thou, that art become so foul ?"
" One, as thou seest, who mourn :" he straight replied.
To which I thus : " In mourning and in woe,
Cursed spirit ! tarry thou.   I know thee well,
E'en thus in filth disguised."   Then stretched he forth
Hands to the bark; whereof my teacher sage
Aware, thrusting him back : " Away ! down there
To the other dogs !" then, with his arms my neck

16*

Encircling, kissed my cheek, and spake: "O soul,
Justly disdainful! blest was she in whom
Thou wast conceived.   He in the world was one
For arrogance noted: to his memory
No virtue lends its lustre; even so
Here is his shadow furious.   There above
How many now hold themselves mighty kings
Who here like swine shall wallow in the mire,
Leaving behind them horrible dispraise."
I then: "Master! him fain would I behold
Whelmed in these dregs, before we quit the lake."
He thus: "Or ever to thy view the shore
Be offered, satisfied shall be that wish,
Which well deserves completion."   Scarce his words
Were ended, when I saw the miry tribes
Set on him with such violence, that yet
For that render I thanks to God, and praise.
"To Filippo Argenti!" cried they all:
And on himself the moody Florentine
Turned his avenging fangs.   Him here we left,
Nor speak I of him more.

The city of Dis, the beginning of the deeper hell,
standing on the other shore of the lake, appears in
sight, its towers and walls gleaming with the eternal
fire that inward burns.   The travellers are landed at
the gates, which are guarded by a thousand demons,
who, with ireful imprecations and gestures, forbid their
approach.   Virgil demands a secret parley, which is
granted, on condition that he comes alone :—

They spake: "Come thou alone; and let him go
Who hath so hardily entered this realm.

Alone return he by his witless way;
If well he know it, let him prove.   For thee
Here shalt thou tarry, who through clime so dark
Hast been his escort."   Now bethink thee, reader!
What cheer was mine at sound of those cursed words:
I did believe I never should return.

  "O my loved guide! who more than seven times
Security hast rendered me, and drawn
From peril deep, whereto I stood exposed,
Desert me not," I cried, "in this extreme.
And if our onward going be denied,
Together trace we back our steps with speed."
  My liege, who thither had conducted me,
Replied: "Fear not; for of our passage none
Hath power to disappoint us, by such high
Authority permitted.   But do thou
Expect me here; meanwhile, thy wearied spirit
Comfort, and feed with kindly hope, assured
I will not leave thee in this lower world."

After a short conference, the demons rush back, and close the gates.   Virgil returns with tardy steps, his eyes bent on the ground, and confidence banished from his brow.   He assures Dante, however, that he shall yet vanquish, and that a messenger from God will soon come to their succor.*

While they wait, the poet, lifting his eyes to the burning summit of a tower, sees standing there—

  At once three hellish furies stained with blood:
  In limb and motion feminine they seemed;

* Inferno, viii.

Around them greenest hydras twisting rolled
Their volumes; adders and cerastes crept
Instead of hair, and their fierce temples bound.

The furies are the symbols of remorse, while Medusa represents sensual pleasure, which dims the intellect and hardens the heart.

Their breast they each one clawing tore; themselves
Smote with their palms, and such shrill clamor raised,
That to the bard I clung, suspicion-bound.
"Hasten, Medusa: so to adamant
Him shall we change;" all looking down exclaimed:
"E'en when by Theseus' might assailed, we took
No ill revenge."—"Turn thyself round, and keep
Thy countenance hid: for if the Gorgon dire
Be shown, and thou shouldst view it, thy return
Upwards would be forever lost."   This said,
Himself, my gentle master, turned me round;
Nor trusted he my hands, but with his own
He also hid me.   Ye of intellect
Sound and entire, mark well the ore concealed
Under close texture of the mystic strain.
    And now there came o'er the perturbèd waves
Loud-crashing, terrible, a sound that made
Either shore tremble, as if of a wind
Impetuous, from conflicting vapors sprung,
That 'gainst some forest driving all his might,
Plucks off the branches, beats them down, and hurls
Afar; then, onward passing, proudly sweeps
His whirlwind rage, while beasts and shepherds fly.
    Mine eyes he loosed, and spake: "And now direct
Thy visual nerve along that ancient foam,
There, thickest where the smoke ascends."   As frogs

Before their foe the serpent, through the wave
Ply swiftly all, till at the ground each one
Lies on a heap; more than a thousand spirits
Destroyed, so saw I fleeing before one
Who passed with unwet feet the Stygian sound.
He, from his face removing the gross air,
Oft his left hand forth stretched, and seemed alone
By that annoyance wearied. I perceived
That he was sent from heaven; and to my guide
Turned me, who signal made, that I should stand
Quiet, and bend to him. Ah me! how full
Of noble anger seemed he! To the gate
He came, and with his wand touched it, whereat
Open without impediment it flew.
  " Outcasts of heaven! O abject race, and scorned!"
Began he, on the horrid grunsel standing,
" Whence doth this wild excess of insolence
Lodge in you? wherefore kick you 'gainst that will
Ne'er frustrate of its end, and which so oft
Hath laid on you enforcement of your pangs?
What profits, at the fates to butt the horn?
Your Cerberus, if ye remember, hence
Bears, still peeled of their hair, his throat and maw."

The angel turns back, and the poets enter the city,
which is overspread with burning sepulchres, their lids
suspended above them. Issuing from beneath, they
hear the lamentable moans of the tortured spirits of
arch-heretics, and of the followers of Epicurus, who
with the body make the spirit die.*
  They proceed by a secret pathway between the walls

* Inferno, ix.

and the sepulchres, conversing on the horror of the place.   Suddenly a voice is heard :—

> "O Tuscan! thou, who through the city of fire
> Alive art passing, so discreet of speech :
> Here, please thee, stay awhile.   Thy utterance
> Declares the place of thy nativity
> To be that noble land, with which perchance
> I too severely dealt."

The voice comes from Farinata degli Uberti, a noble Florentine, a leader of the Ghibelins, who had twice succeeded in defeating the Guelphs and expelling them from Florence.   After the battle of Monteaperti, the Ghibelins resolved to level Florence to the ground, a sentence which Farinata alone had efficiently opposed.   He is represented by Dante as the type of aristocratic haughtiness and indomitable passion, mingled with a noble devotion to his country.   The sound of his words causes Dante to approach closer to his guide, who says to him :—

> .... "What dost thou?   Turn:
> Lo! Farinata there, who hath himself
> Uplifted : from his girdle upwards, all
> Exposed, behold him."   On his face was mine
> Already fixed : his breast and forehead there
> Erecting, seemed as in high scorn he held
> E'en hell.   Between the sepulchres, to him
> My guide thrust me, with fearless hands and prompt ;
> This warning added : "See thy words be clear."
> He, soon as there I stood at the tomb's foot,

Eyed me a space; then in disdainful mood
Addressed me: "Say what ancestors were thine."
  I, willing to obey him, straight revealed
The whole, nor kept back aught: whence he, his brow
Somewhat uplifting, cried: "Fiercely were they
Adverse to me, my party, and the blood
From whence I sprang: twice, therefore, I abroad
Scattered them." "Though driven out, yet they each time
From all parts," answered I, "returned; an art
Which yours have shown they are not skilled to learn."

The poet is suddenly interrupted by the shade of
Cavalcante Cavalcanti, the father of Guido, his friend—

  Then, peering forth from the unclosed jaw,
Rose from his side a shade, high as the chin,
Leaning, methought, upon his knees upraised.
It looked around, as eager to explore
If there were other with me; but perceiving
That fond imagination quenched, with tears
Thus spake: "If thou through this blind prison go'st,
Led by thy lofty genius and profound,
Where is my son! and wherefore not with thee?"
  I straight replied: "Not of myself I come;
By him, who there expects me, through this clime
Conducted, whom perchance Guido thy son
Had in contempt." Already had his words
And mode of punishment read me his name,
Whence I so fully answered. He at once
Exclaimed, upstarting: "How! saidst thou, he *had?*
No longer lives he? Strikes not on his eye
The blessed daylight?" Then, of some delay
I made ere my reply, aware, down fell
Supine, nor after forth appeared he more.

This episode, while it records the poet's friendship
for Guido, gives relief to the proud character of Farinata, who still remains unmoved, as if absorbed by the
bitter remembrance of defeat which Dante had awakened in his breast.

> Meanwhile the other, great of soul, near whom
> I yet was stationed, changed not countenance stern,
> Nor moved the neck, nor bent his ribbed side.
> " And if," continuing the first discourse,
> " They in this art," he cried, " small skill have shown;
> That doth torment me more e'en than this bed.
> But not yet fifty times shall be relumed
> Her aspect, who reigns here queen of this realm,
> Ere thou shalt know the full weight of that art.
> So to the pleasant world mayst thou return,
> As thou shalt tell me why, in all their laws,
> Against my kin this people is so fell."
>   " The slaughter and great havoc," I replied,
> " That colored Arbia's flood with crimson stain—
> To these impute, that in our hallowed dome
> Such orisons ascend."   Sighing he shook
> The head, then thus resumed : "In that affray
> I stood not singly, nor, without just cause,
> Assuredly, should with the rest have stirred;
> But singly there I stood, when, by consent
> Of all, Florence had to the ground been razed,
> The one who openly forbade the deed."
>   *   *   *   *   *
>   Then conscious of my fault, and by remorse
> Smitten, I added thus : "Now shalt thou say
> To him there fallen, that his offspring still
> Is to the living joined; and bid him know

> That if from answer, silent, I abstained,
> 'Twas that my thought was occupied, intent
> Upon that error, which thy help hath solved."

After naming several personages lying in the sepulchres, among them the Emperor Frederick II. and Cardinal Ubaldini, Farinata withdraws from sight.*

The poets now reach a ledge of craggy rocks overhanging a profound abyss, which sends forth noxious exhalations. Here, as they wait to accustom themselves to the dire breath, Virgil unfolds the entire penal code of the *Commedia*, the fundamental principle of which is, that the penalty inflicted is proportioned, not to the crime itself, but to its effect on society ; a principle which distinguishes the Roman jurisprudence from that of the German nations. Accordingly, in the Inferno, violence, fraud, and treachery are punished more severely than anger, rage, and fury, and these again more severely than avarice and prodigality, lust and gluttony. Here also is explained the symbolic relation of the punishment to the crime.†

They now descend the rocky precipice to the seventh circle, where the violent are punished. But as violence may be committed against our neighbors, ourselves, or God, the circle is divided into three gulfs, corresponding to those three kinds of sin. It is guarded by the Minotaur, who feeds on human flesh ; and who, seeing the poets approach, gnaws itself, as if distracted with rage. He is commanded to give way, and—

* Inferno, x. † Ibid., xi.

17

> Like to a bull, that with impetuous spring
> Darts, at the moment when the fatal blow
> Hath struck him, but, unable to proceed,
> Plunges on either side; so saw I plunge
> The Minotaur; whereat the sage exclaimed:
> "Run to the passage! While he storms, 'tis well
> That thou descend." Thus down our road we took
> Through those dilapidated crags, that oft
> Moved underneath my feet, to weight like theirs
> Unused.

Virgil explains that the precipice was formed by the earthquake which preceded the descent of the Saviour into hell. They now reach the river of blood, in which those are punished who by violence have injured others. On the bank of the river they see thousands of centaurs, symbols of savage life uncontrolled by law, and directed only by brutal instinct and force. They are armed with keen arrows, and aim their shafts at whatsoever spirits emerge from out the blood farther than his guilt allows. On seeing Dante, Chiron, one of the centaurs, takes an arrow—

> And with the notch pushed back his shaggy beard
> To the cheek-bone, then, his great mouth to view
> Exposing, to his fellows thus exclaimed:
> "Are ye aware, that he who comes behind
> Moves what he touches? The feet of the dead
> Are not so wont."

Virgil informs the demon that Dante visits those regions by the will of a higher power, and asks for one of

his band on whose back they may ford the river.
Thus they pass

> The border of the crimson-seething flood,
> Whence from those steeped within, loud shrieks arose.

As they cross, their guide points out to them those
tyrants who were given to blood and rapine: Attila,
Alexander, Dionysius of Syracuse, Ezzolino, Obizzo,
and others.*

After passing the river, they enter a forest shadowed
by dusky foliage, whose gnarled branches bear thorns
filled with venom instead of fruit. Here the brute harpies make their nest :—

> Broad are their pennons, of the human form
> Their neck and countenance, armed with talons keen
> The feet, and the huge belly fledged with wings.
> These sit and wail on the drear mystic wood.

On all sides they hear sad plainings, but cannot see
from whom they come. Following the advice of Virgil, Dante breaks off a twig from one of those evil trees :

> And straight the trunk exclaimed, " Why pluck'st thou me ?"
> Then, as the dark blood trickled down its side,
> These words it added : " Wherefore tear'st me thus ?
> Is there no touch of mercy in thy breast ?
> Men once were we, that now are rooted here.
> Thy hand might well have spared us, had we been
> The souls of serpents." As a brand yet green,
> That, burning at one end, from the other sends
> A groaning sound, and hisses with the wind

* Inferno, xii.

That forces out its way, so burst at once
Forth from the broken splinter words and blood.
 I, letting fall the bough, remained as one
Assailed by terror; and the sage replied:
"If he, O injured spirit! could have believed
What he hath seen but in my verse described,
He never against thee had stretched his hand.
But I, because the thing surpassed belief,
Prompted him to this deed, which even now
Myself I rue. But tell me, who thou wast;
That, for this wrong, to do thee some amends
In the upper world (for thither to return
Is granted him) thy fame he may revive."
"That pleasant word of thine," the trunk replied,
"Hath so inveigled me, that I from speech
Cannot refrain, wherein if I indulge
A little longer, in the snare detained,
Count it not grievous."

Here the spirit relates that he is Pietro delle Vigne, former chancellor to the Emperor Frederick II., over whom he had gained unbounded influence. The courtiers, envious of the partiality with which he was treated, induced the emperor to believe that he had entered into a plot for poisoning him. In consequence of this supposed crime, he was condemned to lose his eyes, and to be imprisoned for life. Driven to despair by this cruel injustice, he dashed his head against a column to which he was chained, and died in the year 1245. Pietro thus relates his story :—

  "I it was, who held
Both keys to Frederick's heart, and turned the wards,

Opening and shutting, with a skill so sweet,
That besides me, into his inmost breast
Scarce any other could admittance find.
The faith I bore to my high charge was such,
It cost me the life-blood that warmed my veins;
The harlot who ne'er turned her gloating eyes
From Cæsar's household, common vice and pest
Of courts, 'gainst me inflamed the minds of all;
And to Augustus they so spread the flame,
That my glad honors changed to bitter woes.
My soul, disdainful and disgusted, sought
Refuge in death from scorn, and I became,
Just as I was, unjust toward myself.
By the new roots, which fix this stem, I swear,
That never faith I broke to my liege lord,
Who merited such honor; and of you,
If any to the world indeed return,
Clear he from wrong my memory, that lies
Yet prostrate under envy's cruel blow."

Pietro now explains how the soul is confined in those gnarled joints :—

                      "When departs
The fierce soul from the body, by itself
Thence torn asunder, to the seventh gulf
By Minos doomed, into the wood it falls,
No place assigned, but wheresoever chance
Hurls it; there sprouting, as a grain of spelt,
It rises to a sapling, growing thence
A savage plant.   The Harpies, on its leaves
Then feeding, cause both pain, and for the pain
A vent to grief.   We, as the rest, shall come
For our own spoils, yet not so that with them
We may again be clad; for what a man

17*

Takes from himself it is not just he have.
Here we perforce shall drag them ; and throughout
The dismal glade our bodies shall be hung,
Each on the wild thorn of his wretched shade."

The poet is still attentively listening to the voice, when he hears a noise as of the rushing of wild beasts hunted through a forest :—

　　　　　　　　　　　　　And lo! there came
Two naked, torn with briers, in headlong flight,
That they before them broke each fan o' th' wood.
" Haste now," the foremost cried, " now haste thee, death !"
The other, as seemed, impatient of delay,
Exclaiming, " Lano! not so bent for speed
Thy sinews, in the lists of Toppo's field."
And then, for that perchance no longer breath
Sufficed him, of himself and of a bush
One group he made. · Behind them was the wood
Full of black female mastiffs, gaunt and fleet,
As greyhounds that have newly slipped the leash.
On him, who squatted down, they stuck their fangs,
And having rent him piecemeal, bore away
The tortured limbs.

The poet learns from the shades that they are spirits who have, from various causes, committed suicide.*

From the forest they now pass to a plain of arid sand, where those who have been guilty of violence against God and against Nature are tormented :—

Vengeance of Heaven! Oh, how shouldst thou be feared
By all, who read what here mine eyes beheld !

* Inferno, xiii.

Of naked spirits many a flock I saw,
All weeping piteously, to different laws
Subjected; for on the earth some lay supine,
Some crouching close were seated, others paced
Incessantly around; the latter tribe
More numerous, those fewer who beneath
The torment lay, but louder in their grief.
  O'er all the sand fell slowly wafting down
Dilated flakes of fire, as flakes of snow
On Alpine summit, when the wind is hushed.
As, in the torrid Indian clime, the son
Of Ammon saw, upon his warrior band
Descending, solid flames, that to the ground
Came down; whence he bethought him with his troop
To trample on the soil; for easier thus
The vapor was extinguished, while alone:
So fell the eternal fiery flood, wherewith
The marl glowed underneath, as under stove
The viands, doubly to augment the pain.
Unceasing was the play of wretched hands,
Now this, now that way glancing, to shake off
The heat, still falling fresh.

The attention of the poet is attracted to a shade,
which scornfully defies the fiery tempest. It is Capaneus, one of the seven kings who besieged Thebes:

Straight he himself, who was aware I asked
My guide of him, exclaimed: "Such as I was
When living, dead such now I am. If Jove
Weary his workman out, from whom in ire
He snatched the lightnings, that at my last day
Transfixed me; if the rest he weary out,
At their black smithy laboring by turns,

In Mongibello, while he cries aloud,
' Help, help, good Mulciber !' as erst he cried
In the Phlegræan warfare ; and the bolts
Launch he, full aimed at me, with all his might ;
He never should enjoy a sweet revenge."
　　Then thus my guide, in accent higher raised
Than I before had heard him : " Capaneus !
Thou art more punished, in that this thy pride
Lives yet unquenched ; no torment, save thy rage,
Were to thy fiery pain proportioned full."

They pass on in silence until they reach a brook of
blood, which flows from the forest and runs through
the sandy plain.　As the poet walks along its stone-
built margin, Virgil thus explains to him how the rivers
of hell are formed from the tears of humanity :—

　" In midst of ocean," forthwith he began,
" A desolate country lies, which Crete is named :
Under whose monarch, in old times, the world
Lived pure and chaste.　A mountain rises there,
Called Ida, joyous once with leaves and streams,
Deserted now like a forbidden thing.
It was the spot which Rhea, Saturn's spouse,
Chose for the secret cradle of her son ;
And better to conceal him, drowned in shouts
His infant cries.　Within the mount, upright
An ancient form there stands, and huge, that turns
His shoulders towards Damiata ; and at Rome,
As in his mirror, looks.　Of finest gold
His head is shaped, pure silver are the breast
And arms, thence to the middle is of brass,
And downward all beneath well-tempered steel,
Save the right foot of potter's clay, on which

Than on the other more erect he stands.
Each part, except the gold, is rent throughout;
And from the fissure tears distil, which joined
Penetrate to that cave.   They in their course,
Thus far precipitated down the rock,
Form Acheron, and Styx, and Phlegethon;
Then by this straitened channel passing hence
Beneath, e'en to the lowest depth of all,
From there Cocytus, of whose lake (thyself
Shalt see it) I here give thee no account."*

Passing on, they meet a troop of spirits :—

They each one eyed us, as at eventide
One eyes another under a new moon;
And toward us sharpened their sight, as keen
As an old tailor at his needle's eye.
Thus narrowly explored by all the tribe,
I was agnized of one, who by the skirt
Caught me, and cried, " What wonder have we here ?"
And I, when he to me outstretched his arm,
Intently fixed my ken on his parched looks,
That, although smirched with fire, they hindered not
But I remembered him; and towards his face
My hand inclining, answered, " Ser Brunetto!
And are ye here ?"   He thus to me : " My son!
Oh, let it not displease thee, if Brunetto
Latini but a little space with thee
Turn back, and leave his fellows to proceed."
I thus to him replied : " Much as I can,
I thereto pray thee; and if thou be willing
That I here seat me with thee, I consent;
His leave, with whom I journey, first obtained."

* Inferno, xiv.

"O son!" said he, "whoever of this throng
One instant stops, lies then a hundred years,
No fan to ventilate him, when the fire
Smites sorest.   Pass thou therefore on.   I close
Will at thy garments walk, and then rejoin
My troop, who go mourning their endless doom."
     I dared not from the path descend to tread
On equal ground with him, but held my head
Bent down, as one who walks in reverent guise.

Having been informed of the circumstances which led
to the present journey—

     "If thou," he answered, "follow but thy star,
Thou canst not miss at last a glorious haven;
Unless in fairer days my judgment erred.
And if my fate so early had not chanced,
Seeing the heavens thus bounteous to thee, I
Had gladly given thee comfort in thy work.
But that ungrateful and malignant race,
Who in old times came down from Fesole,
Ay, and still smack of their rough mountain-flint,
Will for thy good deeds show thee enmity.
Nor wonder; for among ill-savored crabs
It suits not the sweet fig-tree lay her fruit.
Old fame reports them in the world for blind,
Covetous, envious, proud.   Look to it well:
Take heed thou cleanse thee of their ways.   For thee,
Thy fortune hath such honor in reserve,
That thou by either party shalt be craved
With hunger keen : but be the fresh herb far
From the goat's tooth.   The herd of Fesole
May of themselves make litter, not touch the plant,
. If any such yet spring on their rank bed,
In which the holy seed revives, transmitted

From those true Romans, who still there remained, ·
When it was made the nest of so much ill."
  "Were all my wish fulfilled," I straight replied,
"Thou from the confines of man's nature yet
Hadst not been driven forth; for in my mind
Is fixed, and now strikes full upon my heart,
The dear, benign, paternal image, such
As thine was, when so lately thou didst teach me
The way for man to win eternity:
And how I prized the lesson, it behooves,
That, long as life endures, my tongue should speak.
What of my fate thou tell'st, that write I down;
And, with another text to comment on,
For her I keep it, the celestial dame,
Who will know all, if I to her arrive.
This only would I have thee clearly note:
That, so my conscience have no plea against me,
Do Fortune as she list, I stand prepared.
Not new or strange such earnest to mine ear.
Speed Fortune then her wheel, as likes her best;
The clown his mattock; all things have their course."
Thereat my sapient guide upon his right
Turned himself back, then looked at me, and spake:
"He listens to good purpose who takes note."

Thus discoursing, they proceed on their way, till
Brunetto, seeing a company of spirits approach whom
he is forbidden to meet, commends to Dante his *Trésor*,
in which, he says, he still survives; turns back, and
runs at full speed to his place.*

Journeying on, they meet the shades of three Flor-

* Inferno, xv.

entines, who, recognizing Dante as one of their countrymen, inquire concerning the condition of their native city.   Whereupon :—

> " An upstart multitude and sudden gains,
> Pride and excess, O Florence ! have in thee
> Engendered, so that now in tears thou mourn'st !"
>   Thus cried I, with my face upraised, and they
> All three, who for an answer took my words,
> Looked at each other, as men look when truth
> Comes to their ear.   " If at so little cost,"
> They all at once rejoined, " thou satisfy
> Others who question thee, O happy thou !
> Gifted with words so apt to speak thy thought.
> Wherefore, if thou escape this darksome clime,
> Returning to behold the radiant stars,
> When thou with pleasure shalt retrace the past,
> See that of us thou speak among mankind."
>   This said, they broke the circle, and so swift
> Fled, that as pinions seemed their nimble feet.

The poets reach the termination of the seventh circle, which is separated from that below by an immense abyss.   Dante here unloosing the cord, the emblem of fortitude, with which his vest was girdled, gives it to Virgil, who casts it down into the chasm. Presently the hideous form of Geryon, the symbol of fraud, comes swimming up through the gross and murky air.*

> " Lo ! the fell monster with the deadly sting,
> Who passes mountains, breaks through fenced walls

* Inferno, xvi.

And firm embattled spears, and with his filth
Taints all the world." Thus me my guide addressed,
And beckoned him, that he should come to shore,
Near to the stony causeway's utmost edge.
  Forthwith that image vile of Fraud appeared,
His head and upper part exposed on land,
But laid not on the shore his bestial train.
His face the semblance of a just man's wore,
So kind and gracious was its outward cheer;
The rest was serpent all: two shaggy claws
Reached to the arm-pits; and the back and breast,
And either side, were painted o'er with nodes
And orbits. Colors variegated more,
Nor Turks nor Tartars e'er on cloth of state
With interchangeable embroidery wove,
Nor spread Arachne o'er her curious loom.
As oft-times a light skiff, moored to the shore,
Stands part in water, part upon the land;
Or, as where dwells the greedy German boor,
The beaver settles, watching for his prey;
So on the rim, that fenced the sand with rock,
Sat perched the fiend of evil. In the void
Glancing, his tail upturned its venomous fork,
With sting like scorpion's armed. Then thus my guide:
" Now need our way must turn few steps apart,
Far as to that ill beast, who couches there."

While Virgil parleys with the monster, Dante
approaches a tribe of the spirits of usurers, each
having suspended from his neck a purse bearing the
coat of arms of the family to which he belonged.
They are seated on the ground.

At the eyes forth gushed their pangs.
Against the vapors and the torrid soil
Alternately their shifting hands they plied.
Thus use the dogs in summer still to ply
Their jaws and feet by turns, when bitten sore
By gnats, or flies, or gadflies swarming round.

After a brief conversation, the poet returns to Virgil, whom he finds already seated on the back of the fierce Geryon, and who encourages him to mount before him.

As one, who hath an ague fit so near,
His nails already are turned blue, and he
Quivers all o'er, if he but eye the shade;
Such was my cheer at hearing of his words.
But shame soon interposed her threat, who makes
The servant bold in presence of his lord.
I settled me upon those shoulders huge,
And would have said, but that the words to aid
My purpose came not, "Look thou clasp me firm."
But he whose succor then not first I proved,
Soon as I mounted, in his arms aloft,
Embracing, held me up; and thus he spake:
"Geryon! now move thee: be thy wheeling gyres
Of ample circuit, easy thy descent.
Think on the unusual burden thou sustain'st."
As a small vessel, backening out from land,
Her station quits; so thence the monster loosed,
And, when he felt himself at large, turned round
There, where the breast had been, his forkèd tail.
Thus, like an eel, outstretched at length he steered,
Gathering the air up with retractile claws.

Not greater was the dread, when Phaëton
The reins let drop at random, whence high heaven,
Whereof signs yet appear, was wrapped in flames;
Nor when ill-fated Icarus perceived,
By liquefaction of the scalded wax,
The trusted pennons loosened from his loins,
His sire exclaiming loud, "Ill way thou keep'st,"
Than was my dread, when round me on each part
The air I viewed, and other object none
Save the fell beast.   He, slowly sailing, wheels
His downward motion, unobserved of me,
But that the wind, arising to my face,
Breathes on me from below.   Now on our right
I heard the cataract beneath us leap
With hideous crash; whence bending down to explore,
New terror I conceived at the steep plunge;
For flames I saw, and wailings smote mine ear:
So that, all trembling, close I crouched my limbs,
And then distinguished, unperceived before,
By the dread torments that on every side
Drew nearer, how our downward course we wound.
    As falcon that hath long been on the wing,
But lure nor birth has seen, while in despair
The falconer cries: "Ah me! thou swoop'st to earth,"
Wearied descends whence nimbly he arose
In many an airy wheel, and lighting sits
At distance from his lord in angry mood;
So Geryon lighting places us on foot
Low down at base of the deep-furrowed rock,
And, of his burden there discharged, forthwith
Sprang forward, like an arrow from the string.*

* Inferno, xvii.

They now reach the eighth circle, called *Malebolge,* or evil gulfs; formed by ten consecutive walls or bastions of dark ferruginous rock, each gulf becoming smaller and deeper as it approaches the central one, the deepest of all; at the bottom of which Lucifer is imprisoned, and to which each is connected by a bridge of rock, which unites them like the spokes of a wheel. The first chasm is peopled by the seducers of women, who are pursued and unmercifully scourged by horned demons.

> Ah! how they made them bound at the first stripe,
> None for the second waited, nor the third.

After recognizing some among the shades, the poets pass to the next arch, from where, in the foss below, they see the ghosts of flatterers immersed in horrid filth.

> Hence, in the second chasm we heard the ghosts,
> Who gibber in low melancholy sounds,
> With wide-stretched nostrils snort, and on themselves
> Smite with their palms.   Upon the banks a scurf,
> From the foul steam condensed, encrusting hung,
> That held sharp combat with the sight and smell.
> So hollow is the depth, that from no part,
> Save on the summit of the rocky span,
> Could I distinguish aught.   Thus far we came;
> And thence I saw, within the foss below,
> A crowd immersed in ordure, that appeared
> Draff of the human body.   There beneath,
> Searching with eye inquisitive, I marked

One with his head so grimed, 'twere hard to deem
If he were clerk or layman.   Loud he cried:
" Why greedily thus bendest more on me,
Than on these other filthy ones, thy ken ?"
   " Because, if true my memory," I replied,
" I heretofore have seen thee with dry locks;
And thou Alessio art, of Lucca sprung.
Therefore than all the rest I scan thee more."
   Then beating on his brain, these words he spake :
" Me thus low down my flatteries have sunk,
Wherewith I ne'er enough could glut my tongue."

Here Virgil points out Thais, the courtesan in the
Eunuch of Terence, the type of bad women, condemned to the place symbolic of their degradation.*

Canto XIX. opens with the following invective
against the Simoniacs, who suffer in the third gulf :—

   Woe to thee, Simon Magus! woe to you,
His wretched followers! who the things of God,
Which should be wedded unto goodness, them,
Rapacious as ye are, do prostitute
For gold and silver in adultery.
Now must the trumpet sound for you, since yours
Is the third chasm.

Observing the torments of these sinners, the poet
exclaims :—

   Wisdom supreme! how wonderful the art
Which thou dost manifest in heaven, in earth,

---

* Inferno, xviii.

18*

And in the evil world, how just a meed
Allotting by thy virtue unto all.
    I saw the livid stone, throughout the sides
And in its bottom full of apertures,
All equal in their width, and circular each.
*   *   *   *   *   *
    . . . . From out the mouth
Of every one emerged a sinner's feet,
And of the legs high upward as the calf.
The rest beneath was hid.   On either foot
The soles were burning; whence the flexile joints
Glanced with such violent motion, as had snapped
Asunder cords or twisted withs.   As flame,
Feeding on unctuous matter, glides along
The surface, scarcely touching where it moves;
So here, from heel to point, glided the flames.
    " Master ! say who is he than all the rest
Glancing in fiercer agony, on whom
A ruddier flame doth prey ?" I thus inquired.
    " If thou be willing," he replied, " that I
Carry thee down, where least the slope bank falls,
He of himself shall tell thee and his wrongs."
    I then: " As pleases thee, to me is best.
Thou art my lord ; and know'st that ne'er I quit
Thy will.   What silence hides that knowest thou."

Virgil then carries him down through a narrow
strait to the orifice where that spirit suffers.

    " Whoe'er thou art,
Sad spirit ! thus reversed, and as a stake
Driven in the soil," I in these words began ;
" If thou be able, utter forth thy voice."
    He shouted : " Ha ! already standest there ?
Already standest there, O Boniface !

By many a year the writing played me false.
So early dost thou surfeit with the wealth,
For which thou fearedst not in guile to take
The lovely lady, and then mangle her?"
    I felt as those who, piercing not the drift
Of answer made them, stand as if exposed
In mockery, nor know what to reply;
When Virgil thus admonished: "Tell him quick,
'I am not he, not he whom thou believest.'"
    And I, as was enjoined me, straight replied.
    That heard, the spirit all did wrench his feet,
And, sighing, next in woful accent spake:
"What then of me requirest? If to know
So much imports thee, who I am, that thou
Hast therefore down the bank descended, learn
That in the mighty mantle I was robed,
And of a she-bear was indeed the son,
So eager to advance my whelps, that there
My having in my purse above I stowed,
And here myself. Under my head are dragged
The rest, my predecessors in the guilt
Of simony. Stretched at their length, they lie
Along an opening in the rock. Midst them
I also low shall fall, soon as he comes,
For whom I took thee, when so hastily
I questioned. But already longer time
Hath passed, since my soles kindled, and I thus
Upturned have stood, than is his doom to stand
Planted with fiery feet, for after him,
One yet of deeds more ugly shall arrive,
From forth the west, a shepherd without law."

Dante, thus finding himself *tête-à-tête* with a pope,
takes occasion to address him in this satirical strain :—

          " Tell me now,
What treasures from St. Peter at the first
Our Lord demanded, when He put the keys
Into his charge ?   Surely He asked no more
But ' Follow me !'   Nor Peter, nor the rest,
Or gold or silver of Matthias took,
When lots were cast upon the forfeit place
Of the condemned soul.   Abide thou then;
Thy punishment of right is merited :
And look thou well to that ill-gotten coin,
Which against Charles thy hardihood inspired.
If reverence of the keys restrained me not,
Which thou in happier times didst hold, I yet
Severer speech might use.   Your avarice
O'ercasts the world with mourning, under foot
Treading the good, and raising bad men up.
Of shepherds like to you, the Evangelist
Was ware, when her, who sits upon the waves,
With kings in filthy whoredom he beheld;
She who with seven heads towered at her birth,
And from ten horns her proof of glory drew,
Long as her spouse in virtue took delight.
Of gold and silver ye have made you god,
Differing wherein from the idolater,
But he worships one, a hundred ye ?
Ah, Constantine ! to how much ill gave birth
Not thy conversion, but that plenteous dower,
Which the first wealthy Father gained from thee."
    Meanwhile, as thus I sung, he, whether wrath
Or conscience smote him, violent upsprang
Spinning on either sole.   I do believe
My teacher well was pleased, with so composed
A lip he listened ever to the sound

Of the true words I uttered.   In both arms
He caught, and, to his bosom lifting me,
Upward retraced the way of his descent.*

Virgil now bears his cherished burden to the steep
rock overhanging the fourth chasm, where those are
punished who, while living, presumed to predict future
events.

Earnest I looked
Into the depth that opened to my view,
Moistened with tears of anguish, and beheld
A tribe, that came along the hollow vale,
In silence weeping: such their step as walk
Choirs, chanting solemn litanies, on earth.
    As on them more direct mine eye descends,
Each wondrously seemed to be reversed
At the neck-bone, so that the countenance
Was from the reins averted; and because
None might before him look, they were compelled
To advance with backward gait.   Thus one perhaps
Hath been by force of palsy clean transposed,
But I ne'er saw it nor believe it so.
    Now, reader! think within thyself, so God
Fruit of thy reading give thee! how I long
Could keep my visage dry, when I beheld
Near me our form distorted in such guise,
That on the hinder parts fallen from the face
The tears down-streaming rolled.

His guide reproaches him for his weakness, and
points out to him the diviners, witches, and astrologers

* Inferno, xix.

of ancient times, among them Manto, the daughter of Tiresias of Thebes, by whom, according to tradition, Mantua was founded. In relating this legend, Dante describes the country surrounding the city of Mantua, and shows remarkable knowledge of physical geography. Among the astrologers and alchemists, the poet places Michael Scot, whose fame as a wizard is immortalized in Scott's " Lay of the Last Minstrel." *

From the next bridge the poets look into the fifth gulf, where public peculators are plunged in a lake of boiling pitch.

> In the Venetians' arsenal as boils
> Through wintry months tenacious pitch, to smear
> Their unsound vessels; for the inclement time
> Sea-faring men restrains, and in that while
> His bark one builds anew, another stops
> The ribs of his that hath made many a voyage.
> One hammers at the prow, one at the poop,
> This shapeth oars, that other cables twirls,
> The mizzen one repairs, and main-sail rent;
> So, not by force of fire but art divine,
> Boiled here a glutinous thick mass, that round
> Limed all the shore beneath. I that beheld,
> But therein naught distinguished, save the bubbles
> Raised by the boiling, and one mighty swell
> Heave, and by turns subsiding fall. While there
> I fixed my ken below, " Mark ! mark !" my guide
> Exclaiming, drew me towards him from the place
> Wherein I stood. . . . .

* Inferno, xx.

Behind me I discerned a devil black,
That running up advanced along the rock.
Ah! what fierce cruelty his look bespake.
In act how bitter did he seem, with wings
Buoyant outstretched, and feet of nimblest tread.
His shoulder, proudly eminent and sharp,
Was with a sinner charged; by either haunch
He held him, the foot's sinew griping fast.

The sinner proves to be an alderman of Lucca, and
the fiend dashes him down into the pitch, in haste to
return to that city for others, saying:—

That land hath store of such.   All men are there,
Except Bonturo, barterers: of "no"
For lucre there an "ay" is quickly made.
    Him dashing down o'er the rough rock, he turned,
Nor ever after thief a mastiff loosed
Sped with like eager haste.   That other sank,
And forthwith writhing to the surface rose.
But those dark demons, shrouded by the bridge,
Cried: "Here the hallowed visage saves not: here
Is other swimming than in Serchio's wave,
Wherefore, if thou desire we rend thee not,
Take heed thou mount not. o'er the pitch."   This said,
They grappled him with more than hundred hooks,
And shouted, "Covered thou must sport thee here:
So, if thou canst, in secret mayst thou filch."
E'en thus the cook bestirs him, with his grooms,
To thrust the flesh into the caldron down
With flesh-hooks, that it float not on the top.

Here Virgil bids Dante screen himself behind a

craggy rock, while he goes forward to speak to the
demons.

With storm and fury, as when dogs rush forth
Upon the poor man's back, who suddenly
From whence he standeth makes his suit; so rushed
Those from beneath the arch, and against him
Their weapons all they pointed.   He, aloud:
" Be none of you outrageous : ere your tine
Dare seize me, come forth from among you one,
Who having heard my words, decide he then
If he shall tear these limbs."   They shouted loud,
" Go, Malacoda !"   Whereat one advanced,
The others standing firm, and as he came,
" What may this turn avail him ?" he exclaimed.
.   " Believest thou, Malacoda ! I had come
Thus far from all your skirmishing secure,"
My teacher answered, " without will divine
And destiny propitious ?   Pass we then ;
For so Heaven's pleasure is, that I snould lead
Another through this savage wilderness."
Forthwith so fell his pride, that he let drop
The instrument of torture at his feet,
And to the rest exclaimed: " We have no power
To strike him."   Then to me my guide: " O thou
Who on the bridge among the crags dost sit
Low crouching, safely now to me return."
I rose, and towards him moved with speed ; the fiends
Meantime all forward drew: me terror seized,
Lest they should break the compact they had made.
*   *   *   *   *   *   *
I to my leader's side adhered, mine eyes
With fixed and motionless observance bent
On their unkindly visage.   They their hooks

Protruding, one the other thus bespake :
" Wilt thou I touch him on the hip ?"   To whom
Was answered : " Even so; nor miss thy aim."

Malacoda, their chief, however, forbids them to
molest him, and orders ten demons to guide the travellers.*

It hath been heretofore my chance to see
Horsemen with martial order shifting camp,
To onset sallying, or in muster ranged,
Or in retreat sometimes outstretched for flight :
Light-armèd squadrons and fleet foragers
Scouring thy plains, Arezzo ! have I seen,
And clashing tournaments, and tilting jousts,
Now with the sound of trumpets, now of bells,
Tabors, or signals made from castled heights,
And with inventions multiform, our own,
Or introduced from foreign land ; but ne'er
To such a strange recorder I beheld,
In evolution moving, horse nor foot,
Nor ship, that tacked by sign from land or star.
With the ten demons on our way we went ;
Ah, fearful company ! but in the church
With saints, with gluttons at the tavern's mess.
Still earnest on the pitch I gazed, to mark
All things whate'er the chasm contained, and those .
Who burned within.   As dolphins that, in sign
To mariners, heave high their archèd backs,
That thence forewarned they may advise to save
Their threatened vessel ; so, at intervals,
To ease the pain, his back some sinner showed,
Then hid more nimbly than the lightning-glance.
E'en as the frogs, that of a watery moat

* Inferno, xxi.

19

Stand at the brink, with the jaws only out,
Their feet and of the trunk all else concealed,
Thus on each part the sinners stood; but soon
As Barbariccia was at hand, so they
Drew back under the wave.   I saw, and yet
My heart doth stagger, one, that waited thus,
As it befalls that oft one frog remains,
While the next springs away : and Graffiacan,
Who of the fiends was nearest, grappling seized
His clotted locks, and dragged him sprawling up,
That he appeared to me an otter.

     *   *   *   *   *

                        " O Rubicant !
See that this hide thou with thy talons flay !"
Shouted together all the cursèd crew.

This peculator proves to be Ciampolo, of Navarre, formerly in the service of King Thibault, who died 1233.   His story, as he relates it to Virgil, is often interrupted by the demons, who, notwithstanding the order of their leader to leave him for a few moments, long to give vent to their cruelty.   Virgil asks him if there are other Italians in the pitch, to which the sinner replies :—

" If ye desire to see or hear," he thus
Quaking with dread resumed, " or Tuscan spirits
Or Lombard, I will cause them to appear.
Meantime let these ill talons bate their fury,
So that no vengeance they may fear from them,
And I, remaining in this self-same place,
Will, for myself but one, make seven appear,
:When my shrill whistle shall be heard: for so
Our custom is to call each other up."

After some parley, the demons agree to shield themselves behind the bank:—

Now, reader, of new sport expect to hear.
They each one turned his eyes to the other shore,
He first, who was the hardest to persuade.
The spirit of Navarre chose well his time,
Planted his feet on land, and at one leap
Escaping, disappointed their resolve.
Them quick resentment stung, but him the most,
Who was the cause of failure: in pursuit
He therefore sped, exclaiming, " Thou art caught !"
But little it availed ; terror outstripped
His following flight; the other plunged beneath,
And he with upward pinion raised his breast:
E'en thus the water-fowl, when she perceives
The falcon near, dives instant down, while
He enraged and spent retires.   That mockery
In Calcabrina fury stirred, who flew
After him, with desire of strife inflamed :
And, for the barterer had 'scaped, so turned
His talons on his comrade.   O'er the dike
In grapple close they joined ; but the other proved
A goshawk able to rend well his foe,
And in the boiling lake both fell.   The heat
Was umpire soon between them ; but in vain
To lift themselves they strove, so fast were glued
Their pennons.   Barbariccia, as the rest,
That chance lamenting, four in flight dispatched
From the other coast, with all their weapons armed.
They, to their post on each side speedily
Descending, stretched their hooks toward the fiends,
Who floundered, inly burning from their scars :

And we departing left them to that broil.*
In silence and in solitude we went,
One first, the other following his steps,
As minor friars journeying on their road.

Dante becomes alarmed lest the demons, finding themselves foiled, should pursue them. He manifests his fears to his guide, who suggests means of avoiding the danger :—

He had not spoke his purpose to the end,
When I from far beheld them with spread wings
Approach to take us.   Suddenly my guide
Caught me, even as a mother that from sleep
Is by the noise aroused, and near her sees
The climbing fires, who snatches up her babe
And flies ne'er pausing, careful more of him
Than of herself, that but a single vest
Clings round her limbs.   Down from the jutting beach
Supine he cast him to that pendent rock,
Which closes on one part the other chasm.
    Never ran water with such hurrying pace
Adown the tube to turn a land-mill's wheel,
When nearest it approaches to the spokes,
As then along that edge my master ran,
Carrying me in his bosom, as a child,
Not a companion.   Scarcely had his feet
Reached to the lowest of the bed beneath,
When over us the steep they reached : but fear
In him was none ; for that high Providence
Which placed them ministers of the fifth foss,
Power of departing thence took from them all.

Here they witness the punishments of the hypo-crites—

* Inferno, xxii.

Who paced with tardy steps around, and wept,
Faint in appearance and o'ercome with toil.
Caps had they on, with hoods, that fell low down
Before their eyes, in fashion like to those
Worn by the monks in Cologne.   Their outside
Was overlaid with gold, dazzling to view,
But leaden all within, and of such weight,
That Frederick's compared to these were straw.
Oh, everlasting wearisome attire !
   We yet once more with them together turned
To leftward, on their dismal moan intent.
But by the weight oppressed, so slowly came
The fainting people, that our company
Was changed at every movement of the step.*

From the bottom of this chasm to the opening of
the next the way is steep and craggy.   It is impossible
for Dante to ascend ; Virgil opens wide his arms and
takes him up :—

As one who, while he works,
Computes his labor's issue, that he seems
Still to foresee the effect : so lifting me
Up to the summit of one peak, he fixed
His eye upon another.   "Grapple that,"
Said he, " but first make proof, if it be such
As will sustain thee."   For one capped with lead
This were no journey.   Scarcely he, though light,
And I, though onward pushed from crag to crag,
Could mount.   And if the precinct of this coast
Were not less ample than the last, for him
I know not, but my strength had surely failed.

* Inferno, xxiii.

19*

But Malebolge all toward the mouth
Inclining of the nethermost abyss,
The site of every valley hence requires,
That one side upward slope, the other fall.
　　At length the point from whence the utmost stone
Juts down, we reached; soon as to that arrived,
So was the breath exhausted from my lungs,
I could no further, but did seat me there.

Virgil, however, does not allow him to rest.

　　" Now needs thy best of man."　So spake my guide;
" For not on downy plumes, nor under shade
Of canopy reposing, fame is won;
Without which whosoe'er consumes his days,
Leaveth such vestige of himself on earth,
As smoke in air, or foam upon the wave.
Thou therefore rise : vanquish thy weariness
By the mind's effort, in each struggle formed
To vanquish, if she suffer not the weight
Of her corporeal frame to crush her down.
A longer ladder yet remains to scale;
From these to have escaped sufficeth not.
If well thou note me, profit by my words."

Thus they mount up the steep and rugged path, and
with much difficulty reach the next bridge, where the
seventh chasm opens to their view, and they see numbers of loathsome and terrible serpents, hideous and
strange of shape, by which robbers are punished.

　　Amid this dread exuberance of woe
Ran naked spirits winged with horrid fear,

Nor hope had they of crevice where to hide,
Or heliotrope to charm them out of view.
With serpents were their hands behind them bound,
Which through their reins infixed the tail and head,
Twisted in folds before.   And lo! on one
Near to our side, darted an adder up,
And, where the neck is on the shoulders tied,
Transpierced him.   Far more quickly than e'er pen
Wrote O or I, he kindled, burned, and changed
To ashes all, poured out upon the earth.
When there dissolved he lay, the dust again
Uprolled spontaneous, and the self-same form
Instant resumed.   So mighty sages tell,
The Arabian Phœnix, when five hundred years
Have well-nigh circled, dies, and springs forthwith
Renascent : blade nor herb throughout his life
He tastes, but tears of frankincense alone
And odorous amomum : swaths of nard
And myrrh his funeral shroud.   As one that falls,
He knows not how, by force demoniac dragged
To earth, or through obstruction fettering up
In chains invisible the powers of man,
Who, risen from his trance, gazeth around,
Bewildered with the monstrous agony
He hath endured, and wildly staring sight,
So stood aghast the sinner when he rose.

Questioned as to who he was, the shade replies :—

    " Vanni Fucci am I called,
Not long since rained down from Tuscany
To this dire gullet.   Me the bestial life
And not the human pleased, mule that I was,
Who in Pistoia found my worthy den."

He relates that he is condemned to this place for having robbed a church, and falsely charged another man with the crime, for which the latter suffered death.*

> When he had spoke, the sinner raised his hands
> Pointed in mockery, and cried: "'Take them, God!
> I level them at thee." From that day forth
> The serpents were my friends; for round his neck
> One of them rolling twisted, as it said,
> "Be silent, tongue!" Another, to his arms
> Upgliding, tied them, riveting itself
> So close, it took from them the power to move.
> Pistoia! ah, Pistoia! why dost doubt
> To turn thee into ashes, cumbering earth
> No longer, since in evil act so far
> Thou hast outdone thy seed? I did not mark,
> Through all the gloomy circles of the abyss,
> Spirit, that swelled so proudly 'gainst his God;
> Not him, who headlong fell from Thebes. He fled,
> Nor uttered more; and after him there came
> A centaur full of fury, shouting, "Where,
> Where is the caitiff?" On Maremma's marsh
> Swarm not the serpent tribe as on his haunch
> They swarmed, to where the human face begins.
> Behind his head, upon the shoulders, lay
> With open wings a dragon, breathing fire
> On whomsoe'er he met.

The centaur Cacus speeds away in search of the blasphemous sinner. Presently the spirits of three Florentines appear and undergo a frightful transformation:—

* Inferno, xxiv.

If, O reader! now
Thou be not apt to credit what I tell,
No marvel; for myself do scarce allow
The witness of mine eyes.   But as I looked
Toward them, lo! a serpent with six feet
Springs forth on one, and fastens full upon him;
His midmost grasped the belly, a forefoot
Seized on each arm (while deep in either cheek
He fleshed his fangs); the hinder on the thighs
Were spread, 'twixt which the tail inserted curled
Upon the reins behind.   Ivy ne'er clasped
A doddered oak, as round the other's limbs
The hideous monster intertwined his own.
Then, as they both had been of burning wax,
Each melted into other, mingling hues,
That which was either now was seen no more.
Thus up the shrinking paper, ere it burns,
A brown tint glides, not turning yet to black,
And the clean white expires.   The other two
Looked on, exclaiming, "Ah! how dost thou change,
Agnello!   See!   Thou art nor double now,
Nor only one."   The two heads now became
One, and two figures blended in one form
Appeared, where both were lost.   Of the four lengths
Two arms were made: the belly and the chest,
The thighs and legs, into such members changed
As never eye hath seen.   Of former shape
All trace was vanished.   Two, yet neither, seemed
That image miscreate, and so passed on
With tardy steps.   As underneath the scourge
Of the fierce dog-star that lays bare the fields,
Shifting from brake to brake the lizard seems
A flash of lightning, if he thwart the road;

So toward the entrails of the other two
Approaching seemed an adder all on fire,
As the dark pepper-grain livid and swart.
In that part, whence our life is nourished first,
One he transpierced; then down before him fell
Stretched out. The pierced spirit looked on him,
But spake not; yea, stood motionless and yawned,
As if by sleep or feverous fit assailed.
He eyed the serpent, and the serpent him.
One from the wound, the other from the mouth,
Breathed a thick smoke, whose vapory columns joined.

    Lucan in mute attention now may hear,
Nor thy disastrous fate, Sabellus, tell,
Nor thine, Nasidius. Ovid now be mute
What if in warbling fiction he record
Cadmus and Arethusa, to a snake
Him changed, and her into a fountain clear,
I envy not; for never face to face
Two natures thus transmuted did he sing,
Wherein both shapes were ready to assume
The other's substance. They in mutual guise
So answered, that the serpent split his train
Divided to a fork, and the pierced spirit
Drew close his steps together, legs and thighs
Compacted, that no sign of juncture soon
Was visible: the tail, disparted, took
The figure which the spirit lost; its skin
Softening, his indurated to a rind.
The shoulders next I marked, that entering joined
The monster's arm-pits, whose two shorter feet
So lengthened, as the others dwindling shrunk.
The feet behind them twisting up became
That part that man conceals, which in the wretch

Was cleft in twain. While both the shadowy smoke
With a new color veils, and generates
The excrescent pile on one, peeling it off
From the other body, lo! upon his feet
One upright rose, and prone the other fell.
Not yet their glaring and malignant lamps
Were shifted, though each feature changed beneath.
Of him who stood erect, the mounting face
Retreated towards the temples, and what there
Superfluous matter came, shot out in ears
From the smooth cheeks; the rest, not backward dragged,
Of its excess did shape the nose; and swelled
Into due size protuberant the lips.
He, on the earth who lay, meanwhile extends
His sharpened visage, and draws down the ears
Into the head, as doth the slug his horns.
His tongue, continuous before and apt
For utterance, severs; and the other's fork
Closing unites. That done, the smoke was laid.
The soul, transformed into the brute, glides off,
Hissing along the vale, and after him
The other talking sputters; but soon turned
His new-grown shoulders on him, and in few
Thus to another spake: "Along this path
Crawling, as I have done, speed Buoso now."
So saw I fluctuate in successive change
The unsteady ballast of the seventh hold:
And here, if aught my pen have swerved, events
So strange may be its warrant. O'er mine eyes
Confusion hung, and on my thoughts amaze.*

* Inferno, xxv.

Florence, exult! for thou so mightily
Hast striven, that o'er land and sea thy wings
Thou beatest, and thy name spreads over hell.
Among the plunderers, such the three I found
Thy citizens; whence shame to me thy son,
And no proud honor to thyself redounds.
 But if our minds, when dreaming near the dawn,
Are of the truth presageful, thou ere long
Shalt feel what Prato (not to say the rest)
Would fain might come upon thee; and that chance
Were in good time, if it befell thee now.
Would so it were, since it must needs befall!
For as time wears me, I shall grieve the more.

The poets now retrace their steps up the projecting
rock until they reach the bridge that stretches over the
eighth gulf, and from thence they behold numberless
flames, wherein evil counsellors are consumed.

 As in that season, when the sun least veils
His face that lightens all, what time the fly
Gives way to the shrill gnat, the peasant then,
Upon some cliff reclined, beneath him sees
Fire-flies innumerous spangling o'er the vale,
Vineyard or tilth, where his day-labor lies;
With flames so numberless throughout its space
Shone the eighth chasm, apparent, when the depth
Was to my view exposed. As he, whose wrongs
The bears avenged, at its departure saw
Elijah's chariot, when the steeds erect
Raised their steep flight for heaven; his eyes, meanwhile,
Straining pursued them, till the flame alone,
Upsoaring like a misty speck, he kenned:

> E'en thus along the gulf moves every flame,
> A sinner so enfolded close in each,
> That none exhibits token of the theft.

Among other flames, they see one parted at the summit, where, swathed in confining fire, are the spirits of Ulysses and Diomede, guilty of the fraudulent invention of the horse of Troy, the carrying away of the Palladium, and the death of Deïdamia. Ulysses, narrating the history of his wanderings through the sea, intimates the existence of a western world, probably suggested by traditions handed down from the early discoveries of the Northmen.

> Of the old flame forthwith the greater horn
> Began to roll, murmuring, as a fire
> That labors with the wind, then to and fro
> Wagging the top, as a tongue uttering sounds,
> Threw out its voice, and spake: "When I escaped
> From Circe, who beyond a circling year
> Had held me near Caieta by her charms,
> Ere thus Æneas yet had named the shore;
> Nor fondness for my son, nor reverence
> Of my old father, nor return of love,
> That should have crowned Penelope with joy,
> Could overcome in me the zeal I had
> To explore the world, and search the ways of life,
> Man's evil and his virtue. Forth I sailed
> Into the deep illimitable main,
> With but one bark, and the small faithful band
> That yet cleaved to me. As Iberia far,
> Far as Marocco, either shore I saw,

20

And the Sardinian and each isle beside
Which round that ocean bathes.   Tardy with age
Were I and my companions, when we came
To the strait pass, where Hercules ordained
The boundaries not to be o'erstepped by man.
The walls of Seville to my right I left,
On the other hand already Ceuta passed.
'O brothers!' I began, 'who to the west
Through perils without number now have reached;
To this the short remaining watch, that yet
Our senses have to wake, refuse not proof
Of the unpeopled world, following the track
Of Phœbus.   Call to mind from whence ye sprang;
Ye were not formed to live the life of brutes,
But virtue to pursue and knowledge high.'
With these few words I sharpened for the voyage
The mind of my associates, that I then
Could scarcely have withheld them.   To the dawn
Our poop we turned, and for the witless flight
Made our oars wings, still gaining on the left.
Each star of the other pole night now beheld,
And ours so low, that from the ocean floor
It rose not.   Five times reillumed, as oft
Vanished the light from underneath the moon,
Since the deep way we entered, when from far
Appeared a mountain dim, loftiest methought
Of all I e'er beheld.   Joy seized us straight;
But soon to mourning changed.   From the new land
A whirlwind sprung, and at her foremost side
Did strike the vessel.   Thrice it whirled her round
With all the waves; the fourth time lifted up
The poop, and sank the prow—so Fate decreed—
And over us the booming billow closed."*

* Inferno, xxvi.

Another flame now appears, from whose top issues a confused sound, which shapes itself into words. It is the spirit of Count Guido da Montefeltro, who relates that he had been at first a warrior whose deeds bespake the nature of the fox rather than of the lion, famed for his knowledge in all the winding ways of subtlety, until at last, repenting, he became a Franciscan friar. Meanwhile, Boniface, the chief of the new Pharisees, waging war against the family of the Colonna, asked his advice as to the best mode of accomplishing their overthrow, at the same time offering him absolution for whatever sin he should commit in giving it.

> " Then, yielding to the forceful arguments,
> Of silence as more perilous I deemed,
> And answered : ' Father ! since thou washest me
> Clear of that guilt wherein I now must fall,
> Large promise with performance scant, be sure,
> Shall make thee triumph in thy lofty seat.' "

The pope, following this advice, promised to pardon the Colonna, and reinstate them in the possession of their property, provided they would pay him homage, and yield the coveted possession of the estate of Prenestino. They accepted the terms, but the pope retained all their possessions, and persecuted them even more bitterly than before. Thus seduced into sin by the holy father, Guido died; he here relates what followed :—

> " When I was numbered with the dead, then came
> Saint Francis for me ; but a cherub dark

He met, who cried : ' Wrong me not ; he is mine,
And must below to join the wretched crew,
For the deceitful counsel which he gave.
E'er since I watched him, hovering at his hair,
No power can the impenitent absolve ;
Nor to repent, and will, at once consist,
By contradiction absolute forbid.'
O misery ! how I shook myself, when he
Seized me, and cried, ' Thou haply thought'st me no
A disputant in logic so exact !'
To Minos down he bore me ; and the judge
Twined eight times round his callous back the tail,
Which biting with excess of rage, he spake :
' This is a guilty soul, that in the fire
' Must vanish.'   Hence, perdition-doomed, I rove
A prey to rankling sorrow, in this garb."
    When he had thus fulfilled his words, the flame
In dolor parted, beating to and fro,
And writhing its sharp horn.*

The poets pass on to the ninth gulf, where sowers
of scandal, schismatics, heretics, and fomenters of
discord are seen, with their limbs miserably maimed or
divided in various ways.

    Who, e'en in words unfettered, might at full
Tell of the wounds and blood that now I saw,
Though he repeated oft the tale ?   No tongue
So vast a theme could equal, speech and thought
Both impotent alike.   If in one band
Collected, stood the people all, who e'er
Poured on Apulia's happy soil their blood,

* Inferno, xxvii.

Slain by the Trojans, and in that long war,
When of the rings the measured booty made
A pile so high, as Rome's historian writes
Who errs not; with the multitude, that felt
The grinding force of Guiscard's Norman steel,
And those the rest, whose bones are gathered yet
At Ceperano, there where treachery
Branded the Apulian name, or where beyond
Thy walls, O Tagliacozzo, without arms
The old Alardo conquered; and his limbs
One were to show transpierced, another his
Clean lopped away: a spectacle like this
Were but a thing of naught to the hideous sight
Of the ninth chasm.   A rundlet, that hath lost
Its middle or side stave, gapes not so wide
As one I marked, torn from the chin throughout
Down to the hinder passage: 'twixt the legs
Dangling his entrails hung, the midriff lay
Open to view, and wretched ventricle,
That turns the englutted aliment to dross.
    While eagerly I fix on him my gaze,
He eyed me, with his hands laid his breast bare,
And cried, "Now mark how I do rip me: lo!
How is Mahomet mangled: before me
Walks Ali weeping, from the chin his face
Cleft to the forelock; and the others all,
Whom here thou seest, while they lived, did sow
Scandal and schism, and therefore thus are rent.
A fiend is here behind, who with his sword
Hacks us thus cruelly, slivering again
Each of this ream, when we have compassed round
The dismal way; for first our gashes close
Ere we repass before him.   But, say who

20*

Art thou, that standest musing on the rock,
Haply so lingering to delay the pain
Sentenced upon thy crimes ?"—" Him death not yet,"
My guide rejoined, " hath overta'en, nor sin
Conducts to torment; but, that he may make
Full trial of your state, I who am dead
Must through the depths of hell, from orb to orb,
Conduct him.   Trust my words; for they are true."
    More than a hundred spirits, when that they heard,
Stood in the foss to mark me, through amaze
Forgetful of their pangs.

Among others, the poet sees the shade of Mosca of
the family of the Uberti, who murdered Buondelmonte
dei Buondelmonti to avenge the Amidei, whom he had
offended by promising to marry a lady of that family,
and then breaking his engagement and marrying another.
This event, which happened in 1215, was the first
cause of those divisions in Florence which afterwards
occasioned the rise of the Guelph and Ghibelin parties.
He sees also the ghost of Bertrand de Born, Vicomte
de Hautefort, the Provençal troubadour, who instigated
Prince Henry to raise the standard of rebellion against
his father, Henry II. of England.

                              I there
Still lingered to behold the troop, and saw
Thing, such as I may fear without more proof
To tell of, but that conscience makes me firm,
The boon companion, who her strong breast-plate
Buckles on him, that feels no guilt within,
And bids him on and fear not.   Without doubt

I saw, and yet it seems to pass before me,
A headless trunk, that even as the rest
Of the sad flock paced onward.   By the hair
It bore the severed member, lantern-wise,
Pendent in hand, which looked at us, and said,
" Woe's me!"   The spirit lighted thus himself;
And two there were in one, and one in two.
How that may be, He knows who ordereth so.
     When at the bridge's foot direct he stood,
His arm aloft he reared, thrusting the head
Full in our view, that nearer we might hear
The words, which thus it uttered : " Now behold
This grievous torment, thou, who breathing go'st
To spy the dead : behold, if any else
Be terrible as this.   And, that on earth
Thou mayst bear tidings of me, know that I
Am Bertrand, he of Born, who gave King John*
The counsel mischievous.   Father and son
I set at mutual war.   For Absalom
And David more did not Ahitophel,
Spurring them on maliciously to strife.
For parting those so closely knit, my brain
Parted, alas! I carry from its source,
That in this trunk inhabits.   Thus the law
Of retribution fiercely works in me."†

Dante here relates to Virgil how, in the cave which

---

* The passage relating to this event, as it stands in the best Codici,
reads *re giovane*, not *re Giovanni*, as it is written in many Codici and
editions from which Cary translated.   It was not John who was instigated
by Bertrand to raise the standard of rebellion against Henry II., but prince
Henry, commonly called the young.

† Inferno, xxviii.

they had just passed, he had seen Geri del Bello, one of
his own relatives, who had been murdered, and who
pointed at him with menacing look, for his death
remained still unavenged.   Meanwhile, they reach the
bridge that crosses the tenth bolgia, where forgers,
afflicted by diverse plagues and diseases, are confined.

More rueful was it not methinks to see
The nation in Ægina droop, what time
Each living thing, e'en to the little worm,
All fell, so full of malice was the air,
(And afterward, as bards of yore have told,
The ancient people were restored anew
From seed of emmets) than was here to see
The spirits, that languished through the murky vale,
Up-piled on many a stack.   Confused they lay,
One o'er the belly, o'er the shoulders one
Rolled of another; sideling crawled a third
Along the dismal pathway.   Step by step
We journeyed on, in silence looking round,
And listening those diseased, who strove in vain
To lift their forms.   Then two I marked, that sat
Propped 'gainst each other, as two brazen pans
Set to retain the heat.   From head to foot,
A tetter barked them round.   Nor saw I e'er
Groom currying so fast, for whom his lord
Impatient waited, or himself perchance
Tired with long watching, as of these each one
Plied quickly his keen nails, through furiousness
Of ne'er abated pruriency.   The crust
Came drawn from underneath in flakes, like scales
Scraped from the bream, or fish of broader mail.

Of the two shades, one is Grifolino of Arezzo, who promised Albero, son of the bishop of Siena, that he would teach him the art of flying, and, because he did not keep his promise, Albero prevailed on his father to have him burnt as a necromancer.

> Then to the bard I spake: "Was ever race
> Light as Siena's? Sure not France herself
> Can show a tribe so frivolous and vain."

The other is the ghost of Capochio, who forged metals by the power of alchemy. Having been a fellow-student of Dante in natural philosophy, he says to him :—

> "If I scan thee right,
> Thou needs must well remember how I aped
> Creative nature by my subtle art."*

Two pale and furious shades now appear. They bury their fangs deep in the necks of Capochio and Grifolino, drag them down the pavement, and flesh their jaws in them.

> When vanished the two furious shades, on whom
> Mine eye was held, I turned it back to view
> The other cursèd spirits.   One I saw
> In fashion like a lute, had but the groin
> Been severed where it meets the forked part.
> Swoln dropsy, disproportioning the limbs
> With ill-converted moisture, that the paunch
> Suits not the visage, opened wide his lips,

* Inferno, xxix.

Gasping as in the hectic man for drought,
One towards the chin, the other upward curled.

He is Adamo of Brescia, who, at the instigation of
Guido, Alessandro, and their brother, the lords of Romena, counterfeited the coin of Florence, for which
he was burned alive.   He thus relates his sufferings :—

"O ye! who in this world of misery,
Wherefore I know not, are exempt from pain,"
Thus he began, "attentively regard
Adamo's woe.   When living, full supply
Ne'er lacked me of what most I coveted;
One drop of water now, alas! I crave.
The rills, that glitter down the grassy slopes
Of Casentino, making fresh and soft
The banks whereby they glide to Arno's stream,
Stand ever in my view; and not in vain;
For more the pictured semblance dries me up,
Much more than the disease, which makes the flesh
Desert these shrivelled cheeks.   So from the place,
Where I transgressed, stern Justice urging me,
Takes means to quicken more my laboring sighs.
There is Romena, where I falsified
The metal with the Baptist's form impressed,
For which on earth I left my body burnt.
But if I here might see the sorrowing soul
Of Guido, Alessandro, or their brother,
For Branda's limpid spring I would not change
The welcome sight.   One is e'en now within,
If truly the mad spirits tell, that round
Are wandering.   But wherein besteads me that?
My limbs are fettered.   Were I but so light,

That I each hundred years might move one inch,
I had set forth already on this path,
Seeking him out amidst the shapeless crew,
Although eleven miles it wind, not less
Than half of one across.   They brought me down
Among this tribe; induced by them, I stamped
The florins with three carats of alloy."

" Who are the abject pair," I next inquired,
" That, closely bounding thee upon thy right,
Lie smoking, like a hand in winter steeped,
In the chill stream?"   " When to this gulf I dropped,
He answered, "here I found them: since that hour
They have not turned, nor ever shall, I ween,
Till Time hath run his course.   One is that dame,
The false accuser of the Hebrew youth;
Sinon the other, that false Greek from Troy.
Sharp fever drains the reeky moistness out,
In such a cloud upsteamed."   When that he heard,
One, galled perchance to be so darkly named,
With clinched hand smote him on the bracèd paunch,
That like a drum resounded: but forthwith
Adamo smote him on the face, the blow
Returning with his arm, that seemed as hard.

" Though my o'erweighty limbs have ta'en from me
The power to move," said he, " I have an arm
At liberty for such employ."   To whom
Was answered: " When thou wentest to the fire,
Thou hadst it not so ready at command,
Then readier when it coined the impostor gold."

And thus the dropsied: " Ay, now speak'st thou true;
But there thou gavest not such true testimony,
When thou wast questioned of the truth, at Troy."

" If I spake false, thou falsely stamp'dst the coin,"

Said Sinon; "I am here for but one fault,
And thou for more than any imp beside."

"Remember," he replied, "O perjured one!
The horse remember, that did teem with death;
And all the world be witness to thy guilt."

"To thine," returned the Greek, "witness the thirst
Whence thy tongue cracks, witness the fluid mound
Reared by thy belly up before thine eyes,
A mass corrupt." To whom the coiner thus:

"Thy mouth gapes wide as ever to let pass
Its evil saying. Me if thirst assails,
Yet I am stuffed with moisture. Thou art parched:
Pains rack thy head: no urging wouldst thou need
To make thee lap Narcissus' mirror up."

I was all fixed to listen, when my guide
Admonished: "Now beware! A little more,
And I do quarrel with thee." I perceived
How angrily he spake, and towards him turned
With shame so poignant, as remembered yet
Confounds me. As a man that dreams of harm
Befallen him, dreaming wishes it a dream,
And that which is, desires as if it were not;
Such then was I, who, wanting power to speak,
Wished to excuse myself, and all the while
Excused me, though unweeting that I did.

"More grievous fault than thine has been, less shame,"
My master cried, "might expiate. Therefore cast
All sorrow from thy soul; and if again
Chance bring thee, where like conference is held,
Think I am ever at thy side. To hear
Such wrangling is a joy for vulgar minds."*

* Inferno, xxx.

The poets now advance to the ninth circle, which is encompassed with giants, and is divided into four chasms, one within the other, each devoted to the punishment of traitors. In the first, *Caïna*, so called from Cain, are the betrayers of their relatives; in the second, *Antenora*, from Antenor of Troy, are the traitors to their country; in the third, *Ptolomea*, from Ptolemy the betrayer of Pompey, are those who deceive under the semblance of kindness; and in the fourth, *Giudecca*, from Judas, in the midst of which is Lucifer, imprisoned in ice, are those who betray their benefactors.

Turning our back upon the vale of woe,
We crossed the encircled mound in silence.   There
Was less than day and less than night, that far
Mine eye advanced not: but I heard a horn
Sounded so loud, the peal it rang had made
The thunder feeble.   Following its course
The adverse way, my strainèd eyes were bent
On that one spot.   So terrible a blast
Orlando blew not, when that dismal rout
O'erthrew the host of Charlemain, and quenched
His saintly warfare.   Thitherward not long
My head was raised, when many a lofty tower
Methought I spied.   "Master," said I, "what land
Is this?"   He answered straight: "Too long a space
Of intervening darkness has thine eye
To traverse: thou hast therefore widely erred
In thy imagining.   Thither arrived
Thou well shalt see, how distance can delude
The sense.   A little therefore urge thee on."
Then tenderly he caught me by the hand:

21

"Yet know," said he, "ere farther we advance,
That it less strange may seem, these are not towers,
But giants.   In the pit they stand immersed,
Each from his navel downward, round the bank."

As they approach, the forms of the giants appear more distinct.   As the walls of the castle of Montereggion, near Siena, are crowned with round turrets, so the shore which encompasses the abyss

Was turreted with giants, half their length
Uprearing, horrible, whom Jove from heaven
Yet threatens, when his muttering thunder rolls. . . .

They here encounter, among others, Antæus, as he issues forth from the cave, five ells in height, without the head; and Virgil thus speaks to him :—

"O thou, who in the fortunate vale, that made
Great Scipio heir of glory, when his sword
Drove back the troop of Hannibal in flight,
Who thence of old didst carry for thy spoil
An hundred lions; and if thou hadst fought
In the high conflict on thy brethren's side,
Seems as men yet believed, that through thine arm
The sons of earth had conquered; now vouchsafe
To place us down beneath, where numbing cold
Locks up Cocytus.   Force not that we crave
Or 'Tityus' help or Typhon's.   Here is one
Can give what in this realm ye covet.   Stoop
Therefore, nor scornfully distort thy lip.
He in the upper world can yet bestow
Renown on thee; for he doth live, and looks
For life yet longer, if before the time

Grace call him not unto herself." Thus spake
The teacher.   He in haste forth stretched his hands,
And caught my guide.   Alcides whilom felt
That grapple, straitened sore.   Soon as my guide
Had felt it, he bespake me thus: "This way,
That I may clasp thee;" then so caught me up,
That we were both one burden.   As appears
The tower of Carisenda, from beneath
Where it doth lean, if chance a passing cloud
So sail across, that opposite it hangs;
Such then Antæus seemed, as at mine ease
I marked him stooping.   I were fain at times
To have passed another way.   Yet in the abyss,
That Lucifer with Judas low ingulfs,
Lightly he placed us; nor, there leaning, stayed;
But rose, as in a bark the stately mast.*

Thus landed in the deepest circle of the Inferno, where traitors are imprisoned in ice, symbolic of the coldness of heart which leads to the crime, the poet thus exclaims :—

Could I command rough rhymes and hoarse to suit
That hole of sorrow, o'er which every rock
His first abutment rears, then might the vein
Of fancy rise full springing; but not mine
Such measures, and with faltering awe I touch
The mighty theme; for to describe the depth
Of all the universe, is no emprize
To jest with, and demands a tongue not used
To infant babbling.   But let them assist
My song, the tuneful maidens, by whose aid

* Inferno, xxxi.

Amphion walled in Thebes; so with the truth
My speech shall best accord.   Oh! ill-starred folk,
Beyond all others wretched! who abide
In such a mansion, as scarce thought finds words
To speak of, better had ye here on earth
Been flocks or mountain-goats.   At dawn we stood
In the dark pit beneath the giants' feet,
But lower far than they, and I did gaze
Still on the lofty battlement, a voice
Bespake me thus: "Look how thou walkest.   Take
Good heed, thy soles do tread not on the heads
Of thy poor brethren."   Thereupon I turned,
And saw before and underneath my feet
A lake, whose frozen surface liker seemed
To glass than water.   Not so thick a veil
In winter e'er hath Austrian Danube spread
O'er his still course, nor Tanais far remote
Under the chilling sky.   Rolled o'er that mass
Had Tabernich or Pietrapana fallen,
Not e'en its rim had creaked.   As peeps the frog
Croaking above the wave, what time in dreams
The village gleaner oft pursues her toil,
So, to where modest shame appears, thus low
Blue pinched and shrined in ice the spirits stood,
Moving their teeth in shrill note like the stork.
His face each downward held; their mouth the cold,
Their eyes expressed the dolor of their heart.

Here the poet beholds at his feet two shades closely
joined together.   Hearing the voice of Dante, they
bend their necks—

And when their looks were lifted up to me,
Straightway their eyes, before all moist within,

Distilled upon their lips, and the frost bound
The tears betwixt those orbs, and held them there.
Plank unto plank hath never cramp closed up
So stoutly.   Whence, like two enragèd goats,
They clashed together: them such fury seized.

He learns that one of these spirits is Camiccione dei
Pazzi, who had treacherously murdered his kinsman,
Ubertino, and who here waits for his relative, Carlino,
a traitor to his country, whose deeper guilt will wash
out his.   They now reach Antenora, and, passing along
in that eternal cold over the heads of the ghosts imprisoned below, the poet strikes, with his foot, a violent
blow against the face of one, who thus speaks:

"Now who art thou, that smiting others' cheeks,
Through Antenora roamest, with such force
As were past sufferance, wert thou living still?"
"And I am living, to thy joy perchance,"
Was my reply, "if fame be dear to thee,
That with the rest I may thy name enroll."
"The contrary of what I covet most,"
Said he, "thou tenderest: hence! nor vex me more,
Ill knowest thou to flatter in this vale."
Then seizing on his hinder scalp I cried:
"Name thee, or not a hair shall tarry here."
"Rend all away," he answered, "yet for that
I will not tell, nor show thee, who I am,
Though at my head thou pluck a thousand times."
Now I had grasped his tresses, and stripped off
More than one tuft, he barking, with his eyes
Drawn in and downward, when another cried,
"What ails thee, Bocca?   Sound not loud enough

21*

> Thy chattering teeth, but thou must.bark outright?
> What devil wrings thee?"—" Now," said I, " be dumb,
> Accursed traitor!   To thy shame, of thee
> True tidings will I bear."—" Off!" he replied;
> " Tell what thou list: but, as thou 'scape from hence,
> To speak of him whose tongue hath been so glib,
> Forget not."

Bocca degli Abati, the shade here alluded to, had caused the defeat of the Guelphs at Monteaperti. During the engagement, he cut off the hand of the bearer of the Florentine standard, causing it to fall, and thus spread terror through the army. He relates that the spirit who revealed his name was Buoso of Cremona, of the family of Duera, who was bribed by Guy de Montfort to leave a pass open to the army of Charles of Anjou, between Piedmont and Parma, the defence of which had been intrusted to him by the Ghibelins. He names other traitors who are there; and passing on, the poet—

> Beheld two spirits by the ice
> Pent in one hollow, that the head of one
> Was cowl unto the other; and, as bread
> Is ravened up through hunger, the uppermost
> Did so apply his fangs to the other's brain,
> Where the spine joins it.   Not more furiously
> On Menalippus' temples Tydeus gnawed,
> Than on that skull and on its garbage he.
>   " O thou! who show'st so beastly sign of hate
> 'Gainst him thou prey'st on, let me hear," said I,
> " The cause, on such condition, that if right

Warrant thy grievance, knowing who ye are,
And what the color of his sinning was,
I may repay thee in the world above,
If that, wherewith I speak, be moist so long."*

Ugolino de Gherardeschi, a nobleman of Pisa belonging to the Guelph party, with the aid of the Archbishop Ruggieri, had expelled from the city Nino of Gallura, his nephew, the ruler of the republic, and taken possession of the government (1288). But Ruggieri soon after betrayed him, and, with the aid of the populace, whom he excited to fury, seized him, his two sons, and three grandchildren, and caused them all to be imprisoned in a tower on the piazza of the Anziani. The key of the tower was then thrown in the Arno, and the unhappy prisoners were left to die of starvation. At the words of Dante—

His jaws uplifting from their fell repast,
That sinner wiped them on the hairs o' the head,
Which he behind had mangled, then began :
" Thy will obeying, I call up afresh
Sorrow past cure ; which, but to think of, wrings
My heart, or ere I tell on 't. But if words,
That I may utter, shall prove seed to bear
Fruit of eternal infamy to him,
The traitor whom I gnaw at, thou at once
Shalt see me speak and weep. Who thou mayst be
I know not, nor how here below art come :
But Florentine thou seemest of a truth,
When I do hear thee. Know, I was on earth

* Inferno, xxxii.

Count Ugolino, and the Archbishop he,
Ruggieri.   Why I neighbor him so close,
Now list.   That through effect of his ill thoughts
In him my trust reposing, I was ta'en
And after murdered, need is not I tell.
What therefore thou canst not have heard, that is,
How cruel was the murder, shalt thou hear,
And know if he have wronged me.   A small grate
Within that mew, which for my sake the name
Of famine bears, where others yet must pine,
Already through its opening several moons
Had shown me, when I slept the evil sleep
That from the future tore the curtain off.
This one, methought, as master of the sport,
Rode forth to chase the gaunt wolf, and his whelps,
Unto the mountain which forbids the sight
Of Lucca to the Pisan.   With lean brachs
Inquisitive and keen, before him ranged
Lanfranchi with Sismondi and Gualandi.
After short course the father and the sons
Seemed tired and lagging, and methought I saw
The sharp tusks gore their sides.   When I awoke,
Before the dawn, amid their sleep I heard
My sons (for they were with me) weep and ask
For bread.   Right cruel art thou, if no pang
Thou feel at thinking what my heart foretold;
And if not now, why use thy tears to flow?
Now had they wakened; and the hour drew near
When they were wont to bring us food; the mind
Of each misgave him through his dream, and I
Heard, at its outlet underneath, locked up
The horrible tower: whence, uttering not a word,
I looked upon the visage of my sons.

I wept not: so all stone I felt within.
They wept: and one, my little Anselm, cried,
' Thou lookest so!   Father, what ails thee ?'   Yet
I shed no tear, nor answered all that day
Nor the next night, until another sun
Came out upon the world.   When a faint beam
Had to our doleful prison made its way,
And in four countenances I descried
The image of my own, on either hand
Through agony I bit; and they, who thought
I did it through desire of feeding, rose
O' the sudden, and cried, ' Father, we should grieve
Far less, if thou wouldst eat of us: thou gavest
These weeds of miserable flesh we wear;
And do thou strip them off from us again.'
Then, not to make them sadder, I kept down
My spirit in stillness.   That day and the next
We all were silent.   Ah, obdurate earth !
Why open'dst not upon us ?   When we came
To the fourth day, then Gaddo at my feet
Outstretched did fling him, crying, ' Hast no help
For me, my father ?'   There he died; and e'en
Plainly as thou seest me, saw I the three
Fall one by one 'twixt the fifth day and sixth :
Whence I betook me, now grown blind, to grope
Over them all, and for three days aloud
Called on them who were dead.   Then, fasting got
The mastery of grief."   Thus having spoke,
Once more upon the wretched skull his teeth
He fastened, like a mastiff's 'gainst the bone,
Firm and unyielding.

The poet, glowing with indignation at this horrible

recital, thus raises his voice against Pisa, who had allowed such crime within her walls :—

Oh, thou Pisa ! shame
Of all the people who their dwelling make
In that fair region, where the Italian voice
Is heard; since that thy neighbors are so slack
To punish, from their deep foundations rise
Capraia and Gorgona, and dam up
The mouth of Arno ; that each soul in thee
May perish in the waters.   What if fame
Reported that thy castles were betrayed
By Ugolino, yet no right hadst thou
To stretch his children on the rack.   For them,
Brigata, Uguccione, and the pair
Of gentle ones, of whom my song hath told,
Their tender years, thou modern Thebes, did make
Uncapable of guilt.

The poets continue to descend to the region below, where suffer those who have betrayed under the semblance of kindness.   The ghosts are—

.... Skarfed in rugged folds of ice,
Not on their feet were turned, but each reversed.
   There, very weeping suffers not to weep ;
For, at their eyes, grief, seeking passage, finds
Impediment, and rolling inward turns
For increase of sharp anguish : the first tears
Hang clustered, and like crystal visors show,
Under the socket brimming all the cup.

Dante here meets, among others, the shade of Alberigo dei Manfredi, one of the Frati Gaudenti, or joyous friars, who, having quarrelled with some of his brotherhood, invited them to a banquet under pretence of reconciliation, and, at a given signal, assassins rushed in and murdered those whom he had marked for destruction. The poet asking who he was—

"The friar Alberigo," answered he,
"Am I, who from the evil garden plucked
Its fruitage, and am here repaid, the date
More luscious for my fig."—"Ha!" I exclaimed,
"Art thou too dead?"—"How in the world aloft
It fareth with my body," answered he,
"I am right ignorant. Such privilege
Hath Ptolomea, that oft-times the soul
Drops hither, ere by Atropos divorced.
And that thou mayst wipe out more willingly
The glazed tear-drops that o'erlay mine eyes,
Know that the soul, that moment she betrays,
As I did, yields her body to a fiend
Who after moves and governs it at will,
Till all its time be rounded: headlong she
Falls to this cistern. And perchance above
Doth yet appear the body of a ghost,
Who here behind me winters. Him thou know'st
If thou but newly art arrived below.
The years are many that have passed away,
Since to this fastness Branca Doria came.'
"Now," answered I, "methinks thou mockest me;
For Branca Doria never yet hath died,
But doth all natural functions of a man,
Eats, drinks, and sleeps, and putteth raiment on."
He thus: "Not yet unto that upper foss
By th' evil talons guarded, where the pitch

Tenacious boils, had Michel Zanche reached,
When this one left a demon in his stead
In his own body, and of one his kin,
Who with him treachery wrought.   But now put forth
Thy hands and ope mine eyes."   I oped them not.
Ill manners were best courtesy to him.
Ah, Genoese !   Men perverse in every way,
With every foulness stained, why from the earth
Are ye not cancelled ?   Such as one of yours
I with Romagna's darkest spirit found,
As,· for his doings, even now in soul
Is in Cocytus plunged, and yet doth seem
In body still alive upon the earth.*

In the fourth and last gulf of the ninth circle are imprisoned the spirits of those traitors who have betrayed their benefactors.   They are buried in thick and transparent ice ; some lie prone, some stand upright, others upon their heads, and others again on their faces and feet, arched like a bow.   Chief among them, in the centre of the gulf, is the grim monarch of hell, whose wings, like the sails of a gigantic windmill, fan the air with their ceaseless motion, and freeze all around in an eternal chillness.

The poet imagines that Lucifer, being expelled from heaven, fell headlong on the southern hemisphere with such violence, that he sank down to the centre of the earth ; and that the terrified earth projected its solid mass on the northern hemisphere, so that the sea which

* Inferno, xxxiii.

then covered it rushed on the southern hemisphere—
while the internal space through which Lucifer passed
threw itself up and formed the mountain of Purgatory.
Colossal and monstrous in his form as the highest
mountain, the arch-enemy is here imprisoned at the
centre of the earth, firmly wedged in everlasting ice,
with half of his form looking upward to his awful kingdom, while his legs protrude towards the southern
hemisphere.   He has three faces, symbolic of the three
vices, and of the three powers which prevent Italy and
man from attaining their destiny.   In each of his three
mouths he champs a sinner: in the middle one, Judas,
the betrayer of Christ; in the two others, Brutus and
Cassius, the murderers of Cæsar, the enemies of civilization and of the empire.

When to the point we came,

Whereat my guide was pleased that I should see
The creature eminent in beauty once,
He from before me stepped and made me pause.
　　" Lo!" he exclaimed, " lo Dis; and lo the place,
Where thou hast need to arm thy heart with strength."
　　How frozen and how faint I then became,
Ask me not, reader! for I write it not;
Since words would fail to tell thee of my state.
I was not dead nor living.   Think thyself,
If quick conception work in thee at all,
How I did feel.   That emperor, who sways
The realm of sorrow, at mid-breast from the ice
Stood forth; and I in stature am more like
A giant, than the giants are his arms.

22

Mark now how great that whole must be, which suits
With such a part.   If he were beautiful
As he is hideous now, and yet did dare
To scowl upon his Maker, well from him
May all our misery flow.   Oh, what a sight!
How passing strange it seemed, when I did spy
Upon his head three faces: one in front
Of hue vermilion, the other two with this
Midway each shoulder joined and at the crest;
The right 'twixt wan and yellow seemed; the left
To look on, such as come from whence old Nile
Stoops to the lowlands.   Under each shot forth
Two mighty wings, enormous as became
A bird so vast.   Sails never such I saw
Outstretched on the wide sea.   No plumes had they,
But were in texture like a bat; and these
He flapped i' th' air, that from him issued still
Three winds, wherewith Cocytus to its depth
Was frozen.   At six eyes he wept: the tears
Adown three chins distilled with bloody foam.
At every mouth his teeth a sinner champed,
Bruised as with ponderous engine; so that three
Were in this guise tormented.   But far more
Than from that gnawing, was the foremost panged
By the fierce rending, whence oft-times the back
Was stripped of all its skin.   "That upper spirit,
Who hath worst punishment," so spake my guide,
"Is Judas, he that hath his head within,
And plies the feet without.   Of th' other two,
Whose heads are under, from the murky jaw
Who hangs, is Brutus: lo! how he doth writhe,
And speaks not.   The other, Cassius, that appears
So large of limb.   But night now reascends;
And it is time for parting.   All is seen."

Dante now clings round the neck of Virgil, who, watching for the moment when the wings of Lucifer are opened, catches the shaggy sides of the demon, and steps down from pile to pile along his thick hairy sides and the jagged ice of Cocytus, in which he lies immovable. They descend through his fell as through a tree or a perpendicular wall, which affords some points of support, till, reaching the place where the thigh of the demon turned upon the swelling of his haunches, the very centre of the earth, Virgil turns himself with great dexterity, and places his head where his feet had been, as the descent now ceases, and the ascent to the opposite hemisphere begins. Dante notes that this action of turning was performed with pain and struggling, the centripetal force being so great that bodies were here subject to immense resistance. The poets at length issue forth at a rocky opening in the hemisphere opposite to that from which they entered ; and, following the sound of a brooklet which descends along the hollow of the rock, they return

> To the fair world : and heedless of repose
> We climbed, he first, I following his steps,
> Till on our view the beautiful lights of heaven
> Dawned through a circular opening in the cave :
> Thence issuing, we again beheld the stars.*

* Inferno, xxxiv.

THE kingdom of darkness is conquered, and victory crowns the struggling soul. Man, in the development of his higher nature, has conquered the beasts which opposed his advance; he has put to silence and forced into his service the demons who threatened him with destruction. Guided by wisdom, he has traversed the abysses of iniquity, descended the precipices and depths of misery, and surveyed all the gloomy region of evil. "The abhorred worm that boreth through the world" he has made the means of his exit from the realm of despair, and now hell is forever closed behind him. The second Act in the drama of humanity opens, and the poet begins the ascent of the mountain of expiation, which leads to the heaven of justice and happiness.

> O'er better waves to speed her rapid course
> The light bark of my genius lifts the sail,
> Well pleased to leave so cruel sea behind;
> And of that second region will I sing,
> In which the human spirit from sinful blot
> Is purged, and for ascent to Heaven prepares.

The Purgatorio, as imagined by Dante, rises from the ocean in the southern hemisphere, an immense conic mountain, the antipode of Mount Zion, which, at the time of the poet, was considered as the centre of the circumference of the earth. The mountain is divided into several cornices, which, beginning at the base, ascend in a wide spiral form around the cone, and represent the different degrees of human progress. In its construction, therefore, it is the reverse of the Inferno, the circles of which, symbolic of ever-increasing iniquity, narrow as they descend. As he mounts upward, the poet feels his task lighter. His strength increases, his nature becomes more and more elevated and spiritualized, till, reaching the top of the mountain, where lies the terrestrial paradise, he is at length blessed by the vision of the triumphant Beatrice. The ascent of the Purgatorio is accomplished in about four days. Its principal divisions are: 1. The shore of humility; 2. The region inhabited by the spirits of the negligent, which, extending from the base of the mountain upward, forms the vestibule of the purgatory, in which four kinds of negligents undergo purification; 3. The circle of pride; 4. Of envy; 5. Of irascibility; 6. Of sloth and indifference; 7. Of parsimony and profusion; 8. Of free living; 9. Of concupiscence; 10. The terrestrial paradise.

On issuing from the interior of the earth, the poet thus describes the change of scene :—

> Sweet hue of eastern sapphire, that was spread
> O'er the serene aspect of the pure air,
> High up as the first circle, to mine eyes

> Unwonted joy renewed, soon as I 'scaped
> Forth from the atmosphere of deadly gloom,
> That had mine eyes and bosom filled with grief.
> The radiant planet, that to love invites,
> Made all the orient laugh, and veiled beneath
> The Pisces' light, that in his escort came.

Having saluted the four stars of the Southern Cross, which made heaven joyous with their light, Dante beholds Cato of Utica, the guardian of the kingdom of progress.

> I saw an old man standing by my side
> Alone, so worthy of reverence in his look,
> That ne'er from son to father more was owed.
> Low down his beard, and mixed with hoary white,
> Descended, like his locks, which, parting, fell
> Upon his breast in double fold.   The beams
> Of those four luminaries on his face
> So brightly shone, and with such radiance clear
> Decked it, that I beheld him as the sun.

Cato inquires who they are and whence they came.

> My guide, then laying hold on me, by words
> And intimations, given with hand and head,
> Made my bent knees and eye submissive pay
> Due reverence; then thus to him replied:
> " Not of myself I come; a Dame from heaven
> Descending, him besought me in my charge
> To bring.   But since thy will implies, that more
> Our true condition I unfold at large,
> Mine is not to deny thee thy request.
> This mortal ne'er hath seen the furthest gloom;

But erring by his folly had approached
So near, that little space was left to turn.
Then, as before I told; I was dispatched
To work his rescue; and no way remained
Save this which I have ta'en.   I have displayed
Before him all the regions of the bad;
And purpose now those spirits to display,
That under thy command are purged from sin.
How I have brought him would be long to say.
From high descends the virtue, by whose aid
I to thy sight and hearing him have led.
Now may our coming please thee.   In the search
Of liberty he journeys': that how dear,
They know who for her sake have life refused.
Thou knowest, to whom death for her was sweet
In Utica, where thou didst leave those weeds,
That in the last great day will shine so bright.
For us the eternal edicts are unmoved:
He breathes, and I of Minos am not bound,
Abiding in that circle, where the eyes
Of thy chaste Marcia beam, who still in look
Prays thee, O hallowed spirit! to own her thine.
Then by her love we implore thee, let us pass
Through thy seven regions: for which, best thanks
I for thy favor will to her return,
If mention there below thou not disdain."

The answer of Cato is characteristic :—

" Marcia so pleasing in my sight was found,"
He then to him rejoined, " while I was there,
That all she asked me I was fain to grant.
Now that beyond the accursèd stream she dwells,
She may no longer move me, by that law,

Which was ordained me, when I issued thence.
Not so, if Dame from heaven, as thou sayst,
Moves and directs thee; then no flattery needs.
Enough for me that in her name thou ask."

He bids them go, and directs Virgil to gird his companion with a slender reed, symbolic of simplicity and patience; to lave his face till all sordid stain is wiped from it; and, pointing out the shore where they may obtain the reed, he disappears.

The dawn had chased the matin hour of prime,
Which fled before it, so that from afar
I spied the trembling of the ocean stream.
　We traversed the deserted plain, as one
Who, wandered from his track, thinks every step
Trodden in vain till he regain the path.
　When we had come, where yet the tender dew
Strove with the sun, and in a place where fresh
The wind breathed o'er it, while it slowly dried;
Both hands extended on the watery grass
My master placed, in graceful act and kind.
Whence I, of his intent before apprised,
Stretched out to him my cheeks suffused with tears.
There to my visage he anew restored
That hue which the dun shades of hell concealed.
　Then on the solitary shore arrived,
That never sailing on its waters saw
Man that could after measure back his course,
He girt me in such manner as had pleased
Him who instructed; and, O strange to tell!
As he selected every humble plant,

Wherever one was plucked, another there
Resembling, straightway in its place arose.*

As the sun rises, the poets, lingering by the shore,
behold a light coming swiftly over the sea, growing
larger and brighter as it approaches; then two wings
appear, and Virgil exclaims :—

        " Down, down; bend low
Thy knees; behold God's angel : fold thy hands.
Now shalt thou see true ministers indeed.
Lo! how all human means he sets at naught;
So that nor oar he needs, nor other sail
Except his wings, between such distant shores.
Lo! how straight up to heaven he holds them reared,
Winnowing the air with those eternal plumes,
That not like mortal hairs fall off or change."
  As more and more toward us came, more bright
Appeared the bird of God, nor could the eye
Endure his splendor near : I mine bent down.
He drove ashore in a small bark so swift
And light, that in its course no wave it drank.
The heavenly steersman at the prow was seen,
Visibly written " Blessèd" in his looks.
Within, a hundred spirits and more there sat.
  " In Exitu Israel de Egypto,"
All with one voice together sang, with what
In the remainder of that hymn is writ.
Then, soon as with the sign of holy cross
He blessed them, they at once leaped out on land.
He, swiftly as he came, returned.   The crew,

              * Purgatorio, i.

There left, appeared astounded with the place,
Gazing around, as one who sees new sights.
From every side the sun darted its beams,
And with his arrowy radiance from mid-heaven
Had chased the Capricorn, when that strange tribe,
Lifting their eyes toward us: "If ye know,
Declare what path will lead us to the mount."
Them Virgil answered: "Ye suppose, perchance,
Us well acquainted with this place: but here,
We, as yourselves, are strangers. Not long erst
We came, before you but a little space,
By other road so rough and hard, that now
The ascent will seem to us as play." The spirits,
Who from my breathing had perceived I lived,
Grew pale with wonder. As the multitude
Flock round a herald sent with olive-branch,
To hear what news he brings, and in their haste
Tread one another down; e'en so at sight
Of me those happy spirits were fixed, each one
Forgetful of its errand to depart
Where, cleansed from sin, it might be made all fair.
Then one I saw darting before the rest
With such fond ardor to embrace me, I
To do the like was moved. O shadows vain!
Except in outward semblance: thrice my hands
I clasped behind it, they as oft returned
Empty into my breast again. Surprise
I need must think was painted in my looks,
For that the shadow smiled and backward drew.
To follow it I hastened, but with voice
Of sweetness it enjoined me to desist.
Then who it was I knew, and prayed of it,
To talk with me it would a little pause.

It answered : " Thee as in my mortal frame
I loved, so loosed from it I love thee still,
And therefore pause : but why walkest thou here ?"

Dante here recognizes the shade of Casella, " the musician in whose company," says Landino, " he often recreated his spirits, wearied by severer studies." Explaining to him the occasion of his visit to the invisible world, the poet thus asks of him a song :—

" If new law taketh not from thee
Memory or custom of love-tuned song,
That whilom all my cares had power to suage ;
Please thee therewith a little to console
My spirit, that encumbered with its frame,
Travelling so far, of pain is overcome."
" Love, that discourses in my thoughts,"* he then
Began in such soft accents, that within
The sweetness thrills me yet.   My gentle guide,
And all who came with him, so well were pleased,
That seemed naught else might in their thoughts have room.
Fast fixed in mute attention to his notes
We stood, when lo ! that old man venerable
Exclaiming, " How is this, ye tardy spirits ?
What negligence detains you loitering here ?
Run to the mountain to cast off those scales,
That from your eyes the sight of God conceal."
As a wild flock of pigeons, to their food
Collected, blade or tares, without their pride
Accustomed, and in still and quiet sort,
If aught alarm them, suddenly desert

* *Amor che nella mente mi ragiona ;* the first verse of a canzone in the *Convito* of Dante.

> Their meal, assailed by more important care;
> So I that new-come troop beheld, the song
> Deserting, hasten to the mountain side,
> As one who goes, yet, where he tends, knows not.
> Nor with less hurried step did we depart.*

Reproached by Cato for thus loitering on their way, the poets hasten towards the mountain; and, meeting a troop of spirits, they beg them to show them the entrance :—

> As sheep, that step from forth their fold, by one,
> Or pairs, or three at once; meanwhile the rest
> Stand fearfully, bending the eye and nose
> To ground, and what the foremost does, that do
> The others, gathering round her if she stops,
> Simple and quiet, nor the cause discern;
> So saw I moving to advance the first,
> Who of that fortunate crew were at the head,
> Of modest mien, and graceful in their gait.
> When they before me had beheld the light
> From my right side fall broken on the ground,
> So that the shadow reached the cave; they stopped,
> And somewhat back retired : the same did all
> Who followed, though unweeting of the cause.

Virgil explains to them the reason why the form of Dante casts a shadow, and assures them that he is here from a virtue derived from heaven.   They then point out to them the entrance to the mountain; and one of the number, comely, fair, and gentle of aspect, bearing the

* Purgatorio, ii.

mark of a wound on his forehead and another on his breast, manifests himself to the poet as Manfred, the King of Naples and Sicily, and prays him on his return to the earth to go and relate to his good daughter Costanza, the wife of Peter III., King of Aragon, and mother to Frederick, King of Sicily, tidings of him, and of what had happened after he had fallen on the battle-field.

> " When by two mortal blows
> My frame was shattered, I betook myself
> Weeping to Him, who of free will forgives.
> My sins were horrible : but so wide arms
> Hath goodness infinite, that it receives
> All who turn to it.   Had this text divine
> Been of Cosenza's shepherd better scanned,
> Who then by Clement on my hunt was set,
> Yet at the bridge's head my bones had lain,
> Near Benevento, by the heavy mole
> Protected ; but the rain now drenches them,
> And the wind drives, out of the kingdom's bounds,
> Far as the stream of Verde, where, with lights
> Extinguished, he removed them from their bed.
> Yet by their curse we are not so destroyed,
> But that the eternal love may turn, while hope
> Retains her verdant blossom."

Manfred asks Dante to commend him to his daughter, whose prayers may profit him.*

The poet, aided by his guide, now ascends slowly and wearily the almost perpendicular slope till they reach a level ledge, where they rest. Dante here

* Purgatorio, iii.

demands of his guide how far they must journey, for,
he says, the hill mounts higher than the sight of man.

He thus to me: " Such is this steep ascent,
That it is ever difficult at first,
But more a man proceeds, less evil grows.
When pleasant it shall seem to thee, so much
That upward going shall be easy to thee
As in a vessel to go down the tide,
Then of this path thou wilt have reached the end.
There hope to rest thee from thy toil.   No more
I answer, and thus far for certain know."
As he his words had spoken, near to us
A voice there sounded: " Yet ye first perchance
May to repose you by constraint be led."
At sound thereof each turned ; and on the left
A huge stone we beheld, of which nor
Nor he before was ware.   Thither we drew ;
And there were some, who in the shady place
Behind the rock were standing, as a man
Through idleness might stand.   Among them one,
Who seemed to be much wearied, sat him down,
And with his arms did fold his knees about,
Holding his face between them downward bent.
   " Sweet Sir !" I cried, " behold that man who shows
Himself more idle than if laziness
Were sister to him."   Straight he turned to us,
And, o'er the thigh lifting his face, observed,
Then in these accents spake : " Up then, proceed,
Thou valiant one."   Straight who it was I knew ;
Nor could the pain I felt (for want of breath
Still somewhat urged me) hinder my approach.
And when I came to him, he scarce his head

Uplifted, saying, " Well hast thou discerned,
How from the left the sun his chariot leads."

Dante recognizes, in this ideal of laziness, Belacqua, an excellent master of the harp and lute, who had been very negligent in his temporal affairs. The poet is moved to laughter by his lazy and broken words, and asks him why he does not strive to mount the hill.

Then he : " My brother ! of what use to mount,
When, to my suffering, would not let me pass
The bird of God, who at the portal sits ?
Behoves so long that heaven first bear me round
Without its limits, as in life it bore ;
Because I, to the end, repentant sighs
Delayed ; if prayer do not aid me first,
That riseth up from heart which lives in grace,
What other kind avails, not heard in heaven ?"*

Proceeding upward, they meet a troop of spirits, who express surprise that the figure of Dante casts a shadow, and inquire concerning his condition ; when they learn that he is yet in the flesh, they flock around him in crowds, saying :—

" O spirit ! who go'st on to blessedness,
With the same limbs that clad thee at thy birth,"
Shouting they came : "a little rest thy step.
Look if thou any one among our tribe
Hast e'er beheld, that tidings of him there
Thou mayst report. Ah, wherefore go'st thou on ?

* Purgatorio, iv.

Ah, wherefore tarriest thou not?   We all
By violence died, and to our latest hour
Were sinners, but then warned by light from heaven;
So that, repenting and forgiving, we
Did issue out of life at peace with God,
Who, with desire to see Him, fills our heart."
    Then I: "The visages of all I scan,
Yet none of ye remember.   But if aught
That I can do may please you, gentle spirits!
Speak, and I will perform it; by that peace,
Which, on the steps of guide so excellent
Following, from world to world, intent I seek."

Here the shade of Giacopo del Cassero, a citizen of
Fano, relates his story.   He had spoken ill of Azzo da
Este, Marquis of Ferrara, who for this sent his assassins to put him to death.   He was overtaken at Oriaco,
a place near the Brenta, where his "life-blood" was
shed.   The next who speaks is Buonconte di Montefeltro, who had fallen in the battle of Campaldino.
As his body had never been found, Dante asks what
became of it.

    "Oh!" answered he, "at Casentino's foot
A stream there courseth, named Archiano, sprung
In Apennine above the hermit's seat.
E'en where its name is cancelled, there came I,
Pierced in the throat, fleeing away on foot,
And bloodying the plain.   Here sight and speech
Failed me; and, finishing with Mary's name,
I fell, and tenantless my flesh remained.
I will report the truth; which thou again

Tell to the living.   Me God's angel took,
While he of hell exclaimed : ' O thou from heaven !
Say wherefore hast thou robbed me ?   Thou of him
The eternal portion bear'st with thee away,
For one poor tear that he deprives me of.
But of the other, other rule I make.' "

He relates that the evil spirit raised a storm, that the Archiano overflowed, and his body was hurled along into the Arno, and there buried.

Buonconte has scarcely concluded when another shade thus speaks :—

" Ah ! when thou to the world shalt be returned,
And rested after thy long road," so spake
Next the third spirit, " then remember me.
I once was Pia.   Siena gave me life ;
Maremma took it from me.   That he knows,
Who me with jewelled ring had first espoused."

The unfortunate lady whose ghost is here introduced, belonged to the family of the Tolomei of Siena.   She married Count Nello della Pietra, who murdered her in 1295, in Maremma.   The reason which prompted the deed, and the kind of death to which she was subjected, as well as its cause, remained a mystery.   According to some chroniclers, the Count made way with her for the purpose of marrying another ; according to others, for revenge.   In the six lines alluding to her death, as a secret known only to her husband, whom she abstains from accusing ; to the matrimonial ring first given to her, then to another ; and in her prayer to be remem-

23*

bered among the living, we have a picture, a history,
and a tragedy.*

Entreating the poet to obtain for them the prayers of
their friends on earth, the shades crowd around him, as

> •   When from their game of dice men separate,
> He who hath lost remains in sadness fixed,
> Revolving in his mind what luckless throws
> He cast : but, meanwhile, all the company
> Go with the other ; one before him runs,
> And one behind his mantle twitches, one
> Fast by his side bids him remember him.
> He stops not ; and each one, to whom his hand
> Is stretched, well knows he bids him stand aside ;
> And thus he from the press defends himself.
> E'en such was I in that close-crowding throng ;
> And turning so my face around to all,
> And promising, I 'scaped from it with pains.

The poets continue their ascent, when the solitary
shade of Sordello, the Lombard Troubadour, appears,
looking towards them.

> We soon approached it.   O thou Lombard spirit
> How didst thou stand, in high abstracted mood,
> Scarce moving with slow dignity thine eyes.
> It spoke not aught, but let us onward pass,
> Eying us as a lion on his watch.
> But Virgil, with entreaty mild, advanced,
> Requesting it to show the best ascent.
> It answer to his question none returned ;
> But of our country and our kind of life

* Purgatorio, v.

Demanded.   When my courteous guide began,
" Mantua," the shadow, in itself absorbed,
Rose towards us from the place in which it stood,
And cried, " Mantuan! I am thy countryman,
Sordello."   Each the other then embraced.

Witnessing the sweet scene, the poet thus exclaims :

Ah, slavish Italy! thou inn of grief!
Vessel without a pilot in loud storm !
Lady no longer of fair provinces !
But brothel-house impure ! this gentle spirit,
Even from the pleasant sound of his dear land,
Was prompt to greet a fellow-citizen
With such glad cheer : while now thy living ones
In thee abide not without war ; and one
Malicious gnaws another ; ay, of those
Whom the same wall and the same moat contains.
Seek, wretched one ! around thy sea-coasts wide ;
Then homeward to thy bosom turn ; and mark,
If any part of thee sweet peace enjoy.
What boots it, that thy reins Justinian's hand
Refitted, if thy saddle be unpressed ?
Naught doth he now but aggravate thy shame.
Ah, people ! thou obedient still shouldst live,
And in the saddle let thy Cæsar sit,
If well thou markedst that which God commands.
Look how that beast to fellness hath relapsed,
From having lost correction of the spur,
Since to the bridle thou hast set thine hand,
O German Albert ! who abandon'st her
That is grown savage and unmanageable,
When thou shouldst clasp her flanks with forked heels.
Just judgment from the stars fall on thy blood ;

And be it strange and manifest to all;
Such as may strike thy successor with dread;
For that thy sire and thou have suffered thus,
Through greediness of yonder realms detained,
The garden of the empire to run waste.
Come, see the Capulets and Montagues,
The Filippeschi and Monaldi, man
Who carest for naught! those sunk in grief, and these
With dire suspicion racked.　Come, cruel one!
Come, and behold the oppression of the nobles,
And mark their injuries; and thou mayst see
What safety Santafiore can supply.
Come and behold thy Rome, who calls on thee,
Desolate widow, day and night with moans,
" My Cæsar, why dost thou desert my side?"
Come, and behold what love among thy people:
And if no pity touches thee for us,
Come, and blush for thine own report.　For me,
If it be lawful, O Almighty Power!
Who wast in earth for our sakes crucified,
Are thy just eyes turned elsewhere? or is this
A preparation, in the wondrous depth
Of thy sage counsel made, for some good end,
Entirely from our reach of thought cut off?
So are the Italian cities all o'erthronged
With tyrants, and a great Marcellus made
Of every petty factious villager.
　　My Florence! thou mayst well remain unmoved,
At this digression, which affects not thee:
Thanks to thy people, who so wisely speed.
Many have justice in their heart, that long
Waiteth for counsel to direct the bow,
Or ere it dart unto its aim: but thine

Have it on their lip's edge.   Many refuse
To bear the common burdens : readier thine
Answer uncalled, and cry, " Behold I stoop !"
    Make thyself glad, for thou hast reason now,
Thou wealthy ! thou at peace ! thou wisdom-fraught !
Facts best will witness if I speak the truth.
Athens and Lacedæmon, who of old
Enacted laws, for civil arts renowned,
Made little progress in improving life
Towards thee, who usest such nice subtlety,
That to the middle of November scarce
Reaches the thread thou in October weavest.
How many times within thy memory,
Customs, and laws, and coins, and offices
Have been by thee renewed, and people changed.
    If thou remember'st well and canst see clear,
Thou wilt perceive thyself like a sick wretch,
Who finds no rest upon her down, but oft
Shifting her side, short respite seeks from pain.*

When Sordello understands that the shade with
whom he has been speaking is Virgil,—

    As one, who aught before him suddenly
Beholding, whence his wonder riseth, cries,
" It is, yet is not," wavering in belief;
Such he appeared; then downward bent his eyes,
And, drawing near with reverential step,
Caught him, where one of mean estate might clasp
His lord.   " Glory of Latium !" he exclaimed,
" In whom our tongue its utmost power displayed;
Boast of my honored birth-place ! what desert

* Purgatorio, vi.

Of mine, what favor, rather, undeserved,
Shows thee to me?   If I to hear that voice
Am worthy, say if from below thou comest,
And from what cloister's pale."—" Through every orb
Of that sad region," he replied, " thus far
Am I arriv'ed, by heavenly influence led;
And with such aid I come.   Not for my doing,
But for not doing, have I lost the light
Of that high Sun, whom thou desirest, and who
By me too late was known.   There is a place
There underneath, not made by torments sad,
But by dun shades alone; where mourning's voice
Sounds not of anguish sharp, but breathes in sighs.
There I with little innocents abide,
Who by death's fangs were bitten, ere exempt
From human taint."

The day declines, and Sordello invites the poets to come with him to a beautiful valley, where they may rest for the night, and from whence they may behold the shades of the monarchs who have been guilty of negligence.   From an eminence they see the valley.

Refulgent gold, and silver thrice refined,
And scarlet grain and ceruse, Indian wood
Of lucid dye serene, fresh emeralds
But newly broken, by the herbs and flowers
Placed in that fair recess, in color all
Had been surpassed, as great surpasses less.
Nor Nature only there lavished her hues,
But of the sweetness of a thousand smells
A rare and undistinguished fragrance made.

Sordello points out the shades of the Emperor Rodolph, Ottocar, King of Bohemia, Philip III. of France, Henry of Navarre, Peter III. of Aragon, Charles I. of Naples, Henry III. of England, and in a few words characterizes each.*

> Now was the hour that wakens fond desire
> In men at sea, and melts their thoughtful heart
> Who in the morn have bid sweet friends farewell,
> And pilgrim newly on his road with love
> Thrills, if he hear the vesper-bell from far,
> That seems to mourn for the expiring day :
> When I, no longer taking heed to hear,
> Began, with wonder, from those spirits to mark
> One risen from its seat, which with its hand
> Audience implored.   Both palms it joined and raised,
> Fixing its steadfast gaze toward the east,
> As telling God, "I care for naught beside."
> "Te Lucis Ante," so devoutly then
> Came from its lip, and in so soft a strain,
> That all my sense in ravishment was lost.
> And the rest after, softly and devout,
> Followed through all the hymn, with upward gaze
> Directed to the bright supernal wheels.

The spirits now meekly look up, as if in expectation. Two angels are seen descending, armed with flame-illumined swords,—

> * Broken and mutilated of their points.
> Green as the tender leaves but newly born,
> Their vesture was, the which, by wings as green
> Beaten, they drew behind them, fanned in air.

* Purgatorio, vii.

A little over us one took his stand,
The other lighted on the opposing hill,
So that the troop were in the midst contained.

Sordello informs the poets that the angels have come to guard the valley against the serpent, who will soon appear. The three now descend into the valley to hold converse with the shades, among which Dante recognizes that of his friend Nino de Visconti, of Pisa, nephew to Count Ugolino, a chief of the Guelphs, and a judge in Gallura, of Sardinia, who had fought with him in the battle of Campaldino.

Mutually towards each other we advanced.
"Nino, thou courteous judge! what joy I felt
When I perceived thou wert not with the bad."

While they are speaking, Sordello

Cried: "Lo there our enemy!"
And with his hand pointed that way to look.
Along the side, where barrier none arose
Around the little vale, a serpent lay,
Such haply as gave Eve the bitter food.
Between the grass and flowers, the evil snake
Came on, reverting oft his lifted head;
And, as a beast that smooths its polished coat,
Licking his back. I saw not, nor can tell,
How those celestial falcons from their seat
Moved, but in motion each one well descried.
Hearing the air cut by their verdant plumes,
The serpent fled; and, to their stations, back
The angels up returned with equal flight.

The poet, here addressing Conrad Malaspina, eulogizes his family; when Conrad foretells that he will soon have still better cause for the good opinion he expresses, in the kind reception he will receive by his descendant, Morello.*

The day dawns, and Dante, overcome by sleep, sinks down upon the grass where they had been seated.

> In that hour,
> When near the dawn the swallow her sad lay,
> Remembering haply ancient grief, renews;
> And when our minds, more wanderers from the flesh,
> And less by thought restrained, are, as 'twere, full
> Of holy divination in their dreams;
> Then, in a vision, did I seem to view
> A golden-feathered eagle in the sky,
> With open wings, and hovering for descent;
> And I was in that place, methought, from whence
> Young Ganymede, from his associates reft,
> Was snatched aloft to the high consistory.
> "Perhaps," thought I within me, "here alone
> He strikes his quarry, and elsewhere disdains
> To pounce upon the prey." Therewith, it seemed,
> A little wheeling in his aëry tour,
> Terrible as the lightning, rushed he down,
> And snatched me upward even to the fire.
> There both, I thought, the eagle and myself,
> Did burn; and so intense the imagined flames,
> That needs my sleep was broken off.

The eagle by which the poet imagines himself

* Purgatorio, viii.

24

snatched from the earth and carried to the sphere of fire, is the symbol of genius, which descends on the poet, and, lifting him up to the highest heavens, inflames him with the love of humanity, to whose progress he feels himself consecrated. Awakening terror-stricken from his dream, Dante finds Virgil at his side, who tells him that while he was sleeping, Lucia had come and borne him upwards in her arms to the place where they then were, and that, pointing out the entrance to the Purgatorio, she had disappeared.

Entering a breach as of a wall, they see a portal with three steps,—the lowest of white marble, smooth and polished ; the next broken and of a dark hue ; and a third of porphyry, symbolizing purity of conscience, contrition, and love. An angel guards the entrance ; he wears an ash-colored robe, and bears a naked sword in his hand. Hearing from Virgil that they had come by the order of a heavenly lady, he admits them to the realm of expiation. Before him Dante thrice prostrates himself, and the angel inscribes the letter *P* (*Peccata*) seven times on the forehead of the poet with the blunted point of his drawn sword, denoting the seven capital sins. Then drawing from beneath his vestment two keys, one of gold and the other of silver, symbolic of science and virtue, he opens the gate, saying :—

> "Enter, but this warning hear,
> He forth again departs who looks behind."

As they advance, the penitents sing the hymn, "We praise thee, O God!"

In accents blended with sweet melody.
The strains came o'er mine ear, e'en as the sound
Of choral voices, that in solemn chant
With organ mingle, and, now high and clear
Come swelling, now float indistinct away.*

The extensive region lying at the base of the Purga-torio, which the poets have passed, is the abode of the negligent, who outnumber all other sinners. After passing the gate, they ascend a winding path up the rock till they reach an open space or cornice extending around the mountain, the ascending side of which is of white marble, wonderfully wrought with sculptured stories of humility, designed for the contemplation of the proud, who here expiate their sin. The dignity of art as an educational power has never been so nobly asserted as in the following passages :—

The angel (who came down to earth
With tidings of the peace so many years
Wept for in vain, that oped the heavenly gates
From their long interdict) before us seemed,
In a sweet act, so sculptured to the life,
He looked no silent image. One had sworn
He had said "Hail!" for she was imaged there,
By whom the key did open to God's love;
And in her act as sensibly impressed
That word, "Behold the handmaid of the Lord,"
As figure sealed on wax.

* Purgatorio, ix.

Next engraven on the rock he sees,

The cart and kine, drawing the sacred ark,
That from unbidden office awes mankind.
Before it came much people; and the whole
Parted in seven quires.   One sense cried "Nay,"
Another, "Yes, they sing."   Like doubt arose
Betwixt the eye and smell, from the curled fume
Of incense breathing up the well-wrought toil.
Preceding the blest vessel, onward came
With light dance leaping, girt in humble guise,
Israel's sweet harper: in that hap he seemed
Less, and yet more, than kingly.   Opposite,
At a great palace, from the lattice forth
Looked Michol, like a lady full of scorn
And sorrow.   To behold the tablet next,
Which, at the back of Michol whitely shone,
I moved me.   There, was storied on the rock
The exalted glory of the Roman prince,
Whose mighty worth moved Gregory to earn
His mighty conquest, Trajan the Emperor.
A widow at his bridle stood, attired
In tears and mourning.   Round about them trooped
Full throng of knights; and overhead in gold
The eagles floated, struggling with the wind.
The wretch appeared amid all these to say:
"Grant vengeance, Sire! for, woe beshrew this heart,
My son is murdered."   He replying seemed:
"Wait now till I return."   And she, as one
Made hasty by her grief: "O Sire! if thou
Dost not return?"—"Where I am, who then is,
May right thee."—"What to thee is other's good,
If thou neglect thy own?"—"Now comfort thee,"
At length he answers.   "It beseemeth well

My duty be performed, ere I move hence:
So justice wills; and pity bids me stay."
  He, whose ken nothing new surveys, produced
That visible speaking, new to us and strange,
The like not found on earth.   Fondly I gazed
Upon those patterns of meek humbleness,
Shapes yet more precious for their artist's sake;
When "Lo!" the poet whispered, "where this way
(But slack their pace) a multitude advance.
These to the lofty steps shall guide us on."
  Mine eyes, though bent on view of novel sights,
Their loved allurement, were not slow to turn.
  Reader! I would not that amazed thou miss
Of thy good purpose, hearing how just God
Decrees our debts be cancelled.   Ponder not
The form of suffering.   Think on what succeeds:
Think that, at worst, beyond the mighty doom
It cannot pass.   "Instructor!" I began,
"What I see hither tending, bears no trace
Of human semblance, nor of aught beside
That my foiled sight can guess."   He answering thus:
"So courbed to earth, beneath their heavy terms
Of torment stoop they, that mine eye at first
Struggled as thine.   But look intently thither;
And disentangle with thy laboring view,
What, underneath those stones, approacheth: now,
E'en now, mayst thou discern the pangs of each."
  Christians and proud! O poor and wretched ones!
That, feeble in the mind's eye, lean your trust
Upon unstaid perverseness: know ye not
That we are worms, yet made at last to form
The wingèd insect, imped with angel plumes,
That to Heaven's justice unobstructed soars?
  24*

Why buoy ye up aloft your unfledged souls?
Abortive then and shapeless ye remain,
Like the untimely embryon of a worm.
  As, to support incumbent floor or roof,
For corbel, is a figure sometimes seen,
That crumples up its knees unto its breast;
With the feigned posture, stirring ruth unfeigned
In the beholder's fancy; so I saw
These fashioned, when I noted well their guise.
  Each, as his back was laden, came indeed
Or more or less contracted; and it seemed
As he, who showed most patience in his look,
Wailing exclaimed: "I can endure no more."*

The spirits, as they pass round the first circle, recite
the Lord's Prayer:—

  "O Thou Almighty Father! who dost make
The heavens thy dwelling, not in bounds confined,
But that, with love intenser, there Thou view'st
Thy primal effluence; hallowed be Thy name:
Join, each created being, to extol
Thy might; for worthy humblest thanks and praise
Is Thy blest Spirit.   May Thy kingdom's peace
Come unto us; for we, unless it come,
With all our striving, thither tend in vain.
As, of their will, the angels unto Thee
Tender meet sacrifice, circling Thy throne
With loud hosannas; so of theirs be done
By saintly men on earth.   Grant us, this day,
Our daily manna, without which he roams
Through this rough desert retrograde, who most

* Purgatorio, x.

Toils to advance his steps.   As we to each
Pardon the evil done us, pardon Thou,
Benign, and of our merit take no count.
'Gainst the old adversary, prove Thou not
Our virtue, easily subdued; but free
From his incitements, and defeat his wiles.
This last petition, dearest Lord! is made
Not for ourselves; since that were needless now;
But for their sakes who after us remain."

Here one of the shades reveals himself as Umberto, son of the Count Santafiore, of Siena, who, in his arrogance, forgot nature, " the common mother," and became so scornful of his fellow-men, that he was at last murdered.   While the poet stoops to listen to his story, another spirit, bowed beneath his burden, recognizes and calls him by name.   It is his friend Oderigi da Gubbio, the friend of Giotto, the glory of the art of illuminating, then held in high esteem.   Oderigi confesses that his fame is now obscured by that of Franco da Bologna, formerly his pupil, the founder of the Bolognese school of painting, to whom, while living, he had been unkind, fearing he would surpass him, and for this sin he now suffers the penalty.   But the law of progress in art is irresistible.

O powers of man! how vain your glory, nipped
E'en in its height of verdure, if an age
Less bright succeed not.   Cimabue thought
To lord it over painting's field; and now
The cry is Giotto's, and his name eclipsed.

Thus hath one Guido from the other snatched
The lettered prize : and he, perhaps, is born
Who shall drive either from their nest.

The two here referred to are Guido Cavalcanti and
Guido Guinicelli, from whom he snatched the prize of
letters.   In saying that he perhaps is born who shall
drive either from their nest, Dante doubtless referred to
himself.   Now Oderigi, fully convinced of the vanity
of worldly reputation, thus exclaims :—

      .... " The noise
Of worldly fame is but a blast of wind,
That blows from diverse points, and shifts its name,
Shifting the point it blows from.   Shalt thou more
Live in the mouths of mankind, if thy flesh
Part shrivelled from thee, than if thou hadst died
Before the coral and the pap were left ;
Or e'er some thousand years have passed ? and that
Is, to eternity compared, a space
Briefer than is the twinkling of an eye
To the heaven's slowest orb.   He there, who treads
So leisurely before me, far and wide
Through Tuscany resounded once ; and now
Is in Siena scarce with whispers named :
There was he sovereign, when destruction caught
The maddening rage of Florence, in that day
Proud as she now is loathsome.   Your renown
Is as the herb, whose hue doth come and go ;
And his might withers it, by whom it sprang
Crude from the lap of earth."

The shade pointed out by Oderigi is the spirit of
Provenzano Salvani, who, while living, presumed to

seize the supreme power in Siena. He is here never resting, curved under an enormous weight.*

Virgil desiring Dante to look where they are treading, he observes that the stone is wrought with sculptures exhibiting various instances, in history and fable, of the punishment of pride.

> As, in memorial of the buried, drawn
> Upon earth-levelled tombs, the sculptured form
> Of what was once, appears (at sight whereof
> Tears often stream forth, by remembrance waked,
> Whose sacred stings the piteous often feel),
> So saw I there, but with more curious skill
> Of portraiture o'erwrought, whate'er of space
> From forth the mountain stretches.   On one part
> Him I beheld, above all creatures erst
> Created noblest, lightening fall from heaven:
> On the other side, with bolt celestial pierced,
> Briareus; cumbering earth he lay, through dint
> Of mortal ice-stroke.   The Thymbræan god,
> With Mars, I saw, and Pallas, round their sire,
> Armed still, and gazing on the giant's limbs
> Strewn o'er the ethereal field.   Nimrod I saw:
> At foot of the stupendous work he stood,
> As if bewildered, looking on the crowd
> Leagued in his proud attempt on Sennaar's plain.
>   O Niobe! in what a trance of woe
> Thee I beheld, upon that highway drawn,
> Seven sons on either side thee slain.   O Saul!
> How ghastly didst thou look, on thine own sword
> Expiring, in Gilboa, from that hour
> Ne'er visited with rain from heaven, or dew.

Purgatorio, xi.

O fond Arachne! thee I also saw,
Half spider now, in anguish, crawling up
The unfinished web thou weavedst to thy bane.

*   *   *   *   *   *

What master of the pencil or the style
Had traced the shades and lines, that might have made
The subtlest workman wonder? Dead, the dead;
The living seemed alive: with clearer view,
His eye beheld not, who beheld the truth,
Than mine what I did tread on, while I went
Low bending. Now swell out, and with stiff necks
Pass on, ye sons of Eve! veil not your looks,
Lest they descry the evil of your path.

An angel now appears.

The goodly shape approached us, snowy white
In vesture, and with visage casting streams
Of tremulous lustre like the matin star.
His arms he opened, then his wings; and spake:
" Onward! the steps, behold, are near; and now
The ascent is without difficulty gained."
A scanty few are they, who, when they hear
Such tidings, hasten. O, ye race of men!
Though born to soar, why suffer ye a wind
So slight to baffle ye? He led us on
Where the rock parted; here, against my front,
Did beat his wings; then promised I should fare
In safety on my way.

Dante finding himself lightened in his ascent, Virgil
explains to him that it is owing to the touch of the
angel's wing, which, purifying him from pride, has removed from his forehead the first of the letters there

inscribed; and that when all shall be erased, he will feel no sense of labor in his upward way.

> Then like to one, upon whose head is placed
> Somewhat he deems not of, but from the becks
> Of others, as they pass him by; his hand
> Lends therefore help to assure him, searches, finds,
> And well performs such office as the eye
> Wants power to execute: so stretching forth
> The fingers of my right hand, did I find
> Six only of the letters, which his sword,
> Who bare the keys, had traced upon my brow.
> The leader, as he marked mine action, smiled.*

The poets now reach the second cornice, where the shades of those whose lives had been stained with envy undergo purification. As they go on, they hear invisible spirits singing songs which record examples of love and affection, the poet thus introducing music as an instrument of moral progress. Multitudes of shades appear, imploring the prayers of the saints.

> I do not think there walks on earth this day
> Man so remorseless, that he had not yearned
> With pity at the sight that next I saw.
> Mine eyes a load of sorrow teemed, when now
> I stood so near them, that their semblances
> Came clearly to my view. Of sackcloth vile
> Their covering seemed; and, on his shoulder, one
> Did stay another, leaning; and all leaned
> Against the cliff. E'en thus the blind and poor,
> Near the confessionals, to crave an alms,

* Purgatorio, xii.

Stand, each his head upon his fellow's sunk;
So most to stir compassion, not by sound
Of words alone, but that which moves not less,
The sight of misery.   And as never beam
Of noonday visiteth the eyeless man,
E'en so was heaven a niggard unto these
Of his fair light: for; through the orbs of all,
A thread of wire, impiercing, knits them up,
As for the taming of a haggard hawk.

It were a wrong, methought, to pass and look
On others, yet myself the while unseen.
To my sage counsel therefore did I turn.
He knew the meaning of the mute appeal,
Nor waited for my questioning, but said:
"Speak; and be brief, be subtile in thy words."

On that part of the cornice, whence no rim
Engarlands its steep fall, did Virgil come;
On the other side me were the spirits, their cheeks
Bathing devout with penitential tears,
That through the dread impalement forced a way.

I turned me to them, and "O shades!" said I,
"Assured that to your eyes unveiled shall shine
The lofty light, sole object of your wish,
So may Heaven's grace clear whatsoe'er of foam
Floats turbid on the conscience, that thenceforth
The stream of mind roll limpid from its source;
As ye declare (for so shall ye impart
A boon I dearly prize) if any soul
Of Látium dwell among ye: and perchance
That soul may profit, if I learn so much."

"My brother! we are, each one, citizens
Of one true city.   Any, thou wouldst say,
Who lived a stranger in Italia's land."

So heard I answering, as appeared, a voice
That onward came some space from whence I stood.
    A spirit I noted, in whose look was marked
Expectance.   Ask ye how ?   The chin was raised
As in one reft of sight.   "Spirit," said I,
"Who for thy rise art tutoring (if thou be
That which didst answer to me), or by place,
Or name, disclose thyself, that I may know thee."
    "I was," it answered, "of Siena : here
I cleanse away with these the evil life,
Soliciting with tears that He, who is,
Vouchsafe Him to us.   Though Sapia named,
In sapience I excelled not ; gladder far
Of other's hurt, than of the good befell me.
That thou mayst own I now deceive thee not,
Hear, if my folly were not as I speak it.
When now my years sloped waning down the arch,
It so bechanced, my fellow-citizens
Near Colle met their enemies in the field ;
And I prayed God to grant what He had willed.
There were they vanquished, and betook themselves
Unto the bitter passages of flight.
I marked the hunt ; and waxing out of bounds
In gladness, lifted up my shameless brow,
And, like the merlin cheated by a gleam,
Cried, ' It is over.   Heaven ! I fear thee not.'
Upon my verge of life I wished for peace
With God ; nor yet repentance had supplied
What I did lack of duty, were it not
The hermit Piero, touched with charity,
In his devout oraisons thought on me.
But who art thou that question'st of our state,
Who go'st, as I believe, with lids unclosed,

25

And breathest in thy talk?"—"Mine eyes," said I,
"May yet be here ta'en from me; but not long;
For they have not offended grievously
With envious glances.   But the woe beneath
Urges my soul with more exceeding dread.
That nether load already weighs me down."
　　She thus: "Who then, among us here aloft,
Hath brought thee, if thou weenest to return?"
　　"He," answered I, "who standeth mute beside me.
I live: of me ask therefore, chosen spirit!
If thou desire I yonder yet should move
For thee my mortal feet."—"Oh!" she replied,
"This is so strange a thing, it is great sign
That God doth love thee.   Therefore with thy prayer
Sometime assist me: and, by that I crave,
Which most thou covetest, that if thy feet
E'er tread on Tuscan soil, thou save my fame
Amongst my kindred.   Them shalt thou behold
With that vain multitude, who set their hope
On Telamone's haven; there to fail
Confounded, more than when the fancied stream
They sought, of Dian called: but they, who lead
Their navies, more than ruined hopes shall mourn."*

Here other shades implore the poet to comfort them
and to tell them who he is.   He replies that he comes
from the banks of Arno: whereupon one of the spirits,
that of Guido del Duca, inveighs against the vices of the
cities watered by that river.   He says of himself:—

"Envy so parched my blood, that had I seen
A fellow-man made joyous, thou hadst marked
A livid paleness overspread my cheek.

* Purgatorio, xiii.

Such harvest reap I of the seed I sowed.
O man ! why place thy heart where there doth need
Exclusion of participants in good ?"*

The poets journeying on their upward way, Dante is
dazzled by an unusual splendor, against which he strives
in vain to shield his sight. It is the radiance of the
angel of God, who comes to purify him of another sin,
and to admit him to the region beyond. As they go
on, the poet inquires of Virgil :—

" How can it chance, that good distributed,
The many, that possess it, makes more rich,
Than if 'twere shared by few ?"   He answering thus :
" Thy mind, reverting still to things of earth,
Strikes darkness from true light.   The highest good,
Unlimited, ineffable, doth so speed
To love, as beam to lucid body darts,
Giving as much of ardor as it finds.
The sempiternal effluence streams abroad,
Spreading, wherever charity extends.
So that the more aspirants to that bliss
Are multiplied, more good is there to love,
And more is loved ; as mirrors, that reflect,
Each unto other, propagated light."

While Dante narrates an ecstatic vision, in which he
had beheld many illustrious examples of patience, a fog.
slowly gathering, envelops them in darkness.†

Hell's dunnest gloom, or night unlustrous, dark,
Of every planet 'reft, and palled in clouds,

* Purgatorio, xiv.   † Ibid., xv.

Did never spread before the sight a veil
In thickness like that fog, nor to the sense
So palpable and gross.　Entering its shade,
Mine eye endured not with unclosèd lids;
Which marking, near me drew the faithful guide,
Offering me his shoulder for a stay.
　　As the blind man behind his leader walks,
Lest he should err, or stumble unawares
On what might harm him or perhaps destroy;
I journeyed through that bitter air and foul,
Still listening to my escort's warning voice,
"Look that from me thou part not."　Straight I heard
Voices, and each one seemed to pray for peace,
And for compassion, to the Lamb of God
That taketh sins away.　Their prelude still
Was "Agnus Dei;" and through all the choir,
One voice, one measure ran, that perfect seemed
The concord of their song.　"Are these I hear
Spirits, O master?" I exclaimed; and he,
"Thou aim'st aright: these loose the bonds of wrath."

The shade of Marco Lombardo now addresses Dante
through the dense mist, and enters upon a discussion
concerning the existence of evil.　He shows that although the action of the human soul is always determined by motives, it has also the power of creating those
motives; and thus it enjoys the prerogative of free-will,
which is the source of moral evil.　As for social evil,
Marco attributes it to the union of civil authority with
spiritual power.

　　　　　　　"Laws indeed there are:
But who is he observes them?　None; not he,
Who goes before, the shepherd of the flock,

Who chews the cud but doth not cleave the hoof.
Therefore the multitude, who see their guide
Strike at the very good they covet most,
Feed there and look no further.   Thus the cause
Is not corrupted nature in yourselves,
But ill-conducting, that hath turned the world
To evil.   Rome, that turned it unto good,
Was wont to boast two suns, whose several beams
Cast light on either way, the world's and God's.
One since hath quenched the other; and the sword
Is grafted on the crook; and, so conjoined,
Each must perforce decline to worse, unawed
By fear of other.   If thou doubt me, mark
The blade: each herb is judged of by its seed.
That land, through which Adice and the Po
Their waters roll, was once the residence
Of courtesy and valor, ere the day
That frowned on Frederick; now secure may pass
Those limits, whosoe'er hath left, for shame,
To talk with good men, or come near their haunts.
Three aged ones are still found there, in whom
The old time chides the new: these deem it long
Ere God restore them to a better world:
The good Gherardo; of Palazzo he,
Conrad; and Guido of Castello, named
In Gallic phrase more fitly the plain Lombard.
On this at last conclude.   The Church of Rome,
Mixing two governments that ill assort,
Hath missed her footing, fallen into the mire,
And there herself and burden much defiled."*

They now issue forth from the dense vapor, and
salute the setting sun.   The poet has a vision of many

* Purgatorio, xvi.

25*

noted examples of anger ; when a light, outshining far
our earthly beam, strikes on his closed lids, and he
hears the voice of an angel, who comes to marshal
them on their upward way. He feels the waving of
his wing, and hears whispered in his ear the words:
" Blessed they, the peacemakers !" Thus they ascend
to the fourth cornice or circle, where the sin of indifference is punished.   Virgil here presents the moral system
of the Purgatorio, explains the nature and the genesis
of human passions, and shows them to be the offspring
of that love which is the universal law of nature.*

As Dante listens to his guide, suddenly a multitude
of shades, impelled by the eagerness of love, are heard
chanting stories of holy zeal and of noble deeds, mingled with others relating to the sins of indifference and
idleness.†

As these shades pass out of sight, Dante falls into
a dream, in which worldly happiness appears to him as
a Syren, and her true character is exposed by a lady, the
symbol of philosophy.

> . . . . Before me, in my dream, a woman's shape
> There came, with lips that stammered, eyes aslant,
> Distorted feet, hands maimed, and color pale.
>   I looked upon her : and, as sunshine cheers
> Limbs numbed by nightly cold, e'en thus my look
> Unloosed her tongue ; next, in brief space, her form
> Decrepit raised erect, and faded face
> With love's own hue illumed.   Recovering speech,

* Purgatorio, xvii.   † Ibid., xviii.

She forthwith, warbling, such a strain began,
That I, how loath soe'er, could scarce have held
Attention from the song.   " I," thus she sang,
" I am the Syren, she, whom mariners
On the wide sea are wildered when they hear:
Such fulness of delight the listener feels.
I, from his course, Ulysses by my lay
Enchanted drew.   Whoe'er frequents me once,
Parts seldom: so I charm him, and his heart,
Contented, knows no void."   Or ere her mouth
Was closed, to shame her, at my side appeared
A dame of semblance holy.   With stern voice
She uttered: " Say, O Virgil! who is this?"
Which hearing, he approached, with eyes still bent
Toward that goodly presence: the other seized her,
And, her robes tearing, opened her before,
And showed the belly to me, whence a smell,
Exhaling loathsome, waked me.   Round I turned
Mine eyes: and thus the teacher: " At the least
Three times my voice hath called thee.   Rise, begone.
Let us the opening find where thou mayst pass."

While Dante follows his guide, he hears a voice
saying:—

    " Come, enter here," in tone so soft and mild,
As never met the ear on mortal strand.
    With swan-like wings dispread and pointing up,
Who thus had spoken marshalled us along,
Where, each side of the solid masonry,
The sloping walls retired; then moved his plumes,
And fanning us, affirmed that those, who mourn,
Are blessèd, for that comfort shall be theirs.

They reach the fifth cornice, where the sin of avarice is cleansed, and here

A race appeared before me, on the ground
All downward lying prone and weeping sore.
"My soul hath cleaved to the dust," I heard
With sighs so deep, they well-nigh choked the words.

In answer to Virgil's inquiries, the spirit of Pope Adrian points out to them the ascending path; he relates the events of his life, and explains that he and his companions are kept prostrate on the ground for the sin of covetousness.

     . . . . "E'en as our eyes
Fastened below, nor e'er to loftier clime
Were lifted; thus hath justice levelled us,
Here on the earth.   As avarice quenched our love
Of good, without which is no working; thus
Here justice holds us prisoned, hand and foot
Chained down and bound, while heaven's just Lord shall
       please,
So long to tarry, motionless, outstretched."
   My knees I stooped, and would have spoke; but he,
Ere my beginning, by his ear perceived
I did him reverence; and "What cause," said he,
"Hath bowed thee thus?"—"Compunction," I rejoined,
"And inward awe of your high dignity."
   "Up," he exclaimed, "brother! upon thy feet
Arise; err not: thy fellow-servant I,
(Thine and all others') of one Sovereign Power.*

         * Purgatorio, xix.

Meantime the poet hears songs recording illustrious examples of poverty, and learns that he who sings is the spirit of Hugh Capet. He narrates the history of his reign, denounces his successors, particularly Philip the Fair, Charles of Anjou, and Charles de Valois, and foretells the fall of his dynasty.

As the poets continue on their way, the mountain suddenly trembles, as if nodding to its fall, and voices from every side shout forth, " Glory be to God in the highest !" It is the sign that a soul has closed the period of its purification and is about to enter Paradise.*

The travellers are overtaken by a shade, which proves to be that of the poet Statius, who is here introduced as the symbol of the moral power inherent to poetical genius. He explains to them the laws which preside over the realms of expiation, to which he had been condemned for his prodigality, and that it is for his release that the mountain, but now exulting, shook through every pendent cliff and rocky bound. In revealing himself as Statius, the spirit, unaware of the presence of Virgil, says that he owes to him all his fame ; his was the breast at which he hung ; he the muse from whom he drank his inspiration, and whose authority had ever been sacred with him ; and that to have lived coëval with the Mantuan he would stay another period in his banishment from heaven.

* Purgatorio, xx.

The Mantuan, when he heard him, turned to me;
And holding silence, by his countenance
Enjoined me silence: but the power which wills
Bears not supreme control: laughter and tears
Follow so closely on the passion prompts them,
They wait not for the motions of the will
In natures most sincere.   I did but smile,
As one who winks; and thereupon the shade
Broke off, and peered into mine eyes, where best
Our looks interpret.   "So to good event
Mayst thou conduct such great emprize," he cried.
"Say, why across thy visage beamed, but now,
The lightning of a smile?"   On either part
Now am I straitened; one conjures me speak,
The other to silence binds me: whence a sigh
I utter, and the sigh is heard.   "Speak on,"
The teacher cried: "and do not fear to speak;
But tell him what so earnestly he asks."
Whereon I thus: "Perchance, O ancient spirit!
Thou marvell'st at my smiling.   There is room
For yet more wonder.   He who guides my ken
On high, he is that Mantuan, led by whom
Thou didst presume of men and gods to sing.
If other cause thou deem'dst for which I smiled,
Leave it as not the true one; and believe
Those words, thou spakest of him, indeed the cause."
	Now down he bent to embrace my teacher's feet;
But he forbade him: "Brother! do it not:
Thou art a shadow, and behold'st a shade."*

The angel here erases with his wing another emblem
of sin from the forehead of the poet, and, following

* Purgatorio, xxi.

Virgil and Statius, he enters the next circle, where the vice of gluttony is atoned for. Virgil asks Statius how he had been saved, not having been a Christian, to which

> He answering thus: " By thee conducted first,
> I entered the Parnassian grots, and quaffed
> Of the clear spring; illumined first by thee,
> Opened mine eyes to God. Thou didst, as one,
> Who, journeying through the darkness, bears a light
> Behind, that profits not himself, but makes
> His followers wise, when thou exclaimedst, 'Lo!
> A renovated world, Justice returned,
> Times of primeval innocence restored,
> And a new race descended from above.'
> Poet and Christian both to thee I owed."

As they discourse on other poets who dwell in Limbo, engarlanded with laurels, they reach a tree hung with goodly fruits, breathing sweet fragrance, and watered by a crystal stream.*

They hear sounds of weeping and the chanting of hymns. A crowd of spirits, silent and devout, appear, gazing at the fruits of the tree, which they are forbidden to gather. Their eyes are dark and hollow; their visages are pale, and so lean that the bones stare through the skin. One amidst them turns his deep-sunken eyes on Dante, and the poet recognizes him as Forese, a brother of Corso Donati, a relative of his wife, and one of his dearest friends. Forese explains

* Purgatorio, xxii.

that gluttony is the cause of his suffering, and that this
sin is here purified by hunger and thirst for the fruit
and the water, the sight of which inflames the desire
for food and drink. He then inveighs against the
immodest dress of the Florentine ladies :—

> " A time to come
> Stands full within my view, to which this hour
> Shall not be counted of an ancient date,
> When from the pulpit shall be loudly warned
> The unblushing dames of Florence, lest they bear
> Unkerchiefed bosoms to the common gaze.
> What savage women hath the world e'er seen,
> What Saracens, for whom there needed scourge
> Of spiritual or other discipline,
> To force them walk with covering on their limbs?
> But did they see, the shameless ones, what Heaven
> Wafts on swift wing toward them while I speak,
> Their mouths were oped for howling; they shall taste
> Of sorrow (unless foresight cheat me here)
> Or ere the cheek of him be clothed with down,
> Who is now rocked with lullaby asleep."*

Walking by the side of Dante, Forese points out to
him the principal shades in the circle, among them that
of Buonagiunta di Lucca, a celebrated troubadour of the
age, who, on seeing Dante, whispered the name of
Gentucca, a lady of Lucca, whom the poet had loved.
Approaching, Buonagiunta thus speaks :—

* Purgatorio, xxiii.

> "Woman is born,
> Whose brow no wimple shades yet, that shall make
> My city please thee, blame it as they may.
> Go then with this forewarning. If aught else
> My whisper too implied, the event shall tell.
> But say, if of a truth I see the man
> Of that new lay the inventor, which begins
> With 'Ladies, ye that con the lore of love.' "
>   To whom I thus: "Count of me but as one,
> Who am the scribe of love; that, when he breathes,
> Take up my pen, and, as he dictates, write."

Here Buonagiunta praises Dante for the new style, inspired by nature, which he had introduced into poetry, and which placed him above all his contemporaries, and particularly above Buonagiunta himself, whose poems had all the artificiality of the age.

As they are about to part, Forese asks Dante when he shall see him again. The poet replies that however soon he may return, his wishes will have arrived before him, the condition of Florence becoming every day worse. Forese, knowing that his brother Corso is the principal cause of these calamities, foretells the violent death which he will soon meet.

> "Go now," he cried: "lo! he, whose guilt is most,
> Passes before my vision, dragged at heels
> Of an infuriate beast. Toward the vale,
> Where guilt hath no redemption, on it speeds,
> Each step increasing swiftness on the last;
> Until a blow it strikes, that leaveth him
> A corse most vilely shattered. No long space

26

Those wheels have yet to roll" (therewith his eyes
Looked up to heaven), "ere thou shalt plainly see
That which my words may not more plainly tell.
I quit thee: time is precious here: I lose
Too much, thus measuring my pace with thine."
    As from a troop of well-ranked chivalry,
One knight, more enterprising than the rest,
Pricks forth at gallop, eager to display
His prowess in the first encounter proved;
So parted he from us, with lengthened strides;
And left me on the way with those twain spirits,
Who were such mighty marshals of the world.

On their way they come to another tree, beneath
whose boughs, thick with blooming fruit, a multitude
of spirits raise their hands, striving in vain to gather it.
From its branches are heard warnings not to come near
it, but to pass on, and leave this plant, taken from the
tree whereof Eve tasted. Voices are heard, recounting
ancient examples of gluttony. The angel of God
now appears in dazzling light, erases another sign from
the forehead of the poet, and points out the way which
leads to the next circle, where carnal sinners are purified.

    As when, to harbinger the dawn, springs up
On freshened wing the air of May, and breathes
Of fragrance, all impregned with herb and flowers;
E'en such a wind I felt upon my front
Blow gently, and the moving of a wing
Perceived, that, moving, shed ambrosial smell;
And then a voice: "Blessed are they, whom grace
Doth so illume, that appetite in them

> Exhaleth no inordinate desire,
> Still hungering as the rule of temperance wills."*

Proceeding on their way, Statius explains to Dante how shades, which have no need of food, may suffer from want of it. He treats of the problem of generation, and other subjects relating to animal life, and its progress towards the intellectual life. He gives his views on the state of the soul after death, the aërial body which it takes on its arrival in the other world, and its capability of manifesting its feelings and emotions. While Dante listens to this discussion, the rocky precipice on which they walk sends forth a blazing fire, leaving only a narrow path between the rock and the edge of the cornice. Walking one by one, the poet fearing the fire on one hand and the precipice on the other, they hear voices from the flames, commending examples of chastity.†

As the poet walks on between the setting sun and the fire in which the shades are purified, his passing shadow makes the umbered flame burn ruddier. The spirits marvel at the light, and ask the cause of it. Dante tells them that he is a living man, who, through the intercession of a celestial lady, has come to visit the kingdoms of death. He in turn questions them as to who they are, and who are those who have just passed. The shades appear astounded at seeing him, but, soon recovering, the spirit of Guido Guinicelli

---

* Purgatorio, xxiv.　　　　† Ibid., xxv.

speaks, and explains the nature of the sins of which they had been guilty. Guido was a poet, who flourished in the last part of the thirteenth century. He belonged to one of the noble families of Bologna, and in the history of the time he figures as a warrior and a Ghibelin. His poems, according to Dante, marked a decided progress in poetical composition.

       With such pious joy,
As the two sons upon their mother gazed
From sad Lycurgus rescued; such my joy
(Save that I more repressed it) when I heard
From his own lips the name of him pronounced,
Who was a father to me, and to those
My betters, who have ever used the sweet
And pleasant rhymes of love. So naught I heard,
Nor spake; but long time thoughtfully I went,
Gazing on him; and, only for the fire,
Approached not nearer. When my eyes were fed
By looking on him; with such solemn pledge,
As forces credence, I devoted me
Unto his service wholly. In reply
He thus bespake me: " What from thee I hear
Is graved so deeply on my mind, the waves
Of Lethe shall not wash it off, nor make
A whit less lively. But as now thy oath
Has sealed the truth, declare what cause impels
That love, which both thy looks and speech bewray."
 " Those dulcet lays," I answered; " which, as long
As of our tongue the beauty does not fade,
Shall make us love the very ink that traced them."

Guido celebrates the praise of Arnault Daniel, the

Provençal troubadour, whose spirit stands before him,
and commending his soul to the prayers of the poet—

> Haply to make way
> For one that followed next, when that was said,
> He vanished through the fire, as through the wave
> A fish, that glances diving to the deep.*

The angel of God now again appears standing before
the flame, and singing, " Blessed are the pure in heart."
As the poets approach, he orders them to pass through
the fire, and to listen to the song they will hear issuing
from thence.

> I, when I heard his saying, was as one
> Laid in the grave.   My hands together clasped,
> And upward stretching, on the fire I looked,
> And busy fancy conjured up the forms
> Erewhile beheld alive consumed in flames.
> The escorting spirits turned with gentle looks
> Toward me; and the Mantuan spake: " My son,
> Here torment thou mayst feel, but canst not death.
> Remember thee, remember thee, if I
> Safe e'en on Geryon brought thee; now I come
> More near to God, wilt thou not trust me now?
> Of this be sure; though in its womb that flame
> A thousand years contained thee, from thy head
> No hair should perish.   If thou doubt my truth,
> Approach; and with thy hands thy vesture's hem
> Stretch forth, and for thyself confirm belief.
> Lay now all fear, oh! lay all fear aside.
> Turn hither, and come onward undismayed."

* Purgatorio, xxvi.

26*

The poet still hesitates, when Virgil reminds him that this wall of fire divides him from Beatrice:

> As at Thisbe's name the eye
> Of Pyramus was opened (when life ebbed
> Fast from his veins) and took one parting glance,
> While vermeil dyed the mulberry; thus I turned
> To my sage guide, relenting, when I heard
> The name that springs forever in my breast.
> He shook his forehead; and, "How long," he said,
> "Linger we now?" then smiled, as one would smile
> Upon a child that eyes the fruit and yields.
> Into the fire before me then he walked;
> And Statius, who erewhile no little space
> Had parted us, he prayed to come behind.
> I would have cast me into molten glass
> To cool me, when I entered; so intense
> Raged the conflagrant mass. The sire beloved,
> To comfort me, as he proceeded, still
> Of Beatrice talked. "Her eyes," saith he,
> "E'en now I seem to view." From the other side
> A voice, that sang, did guide us; and the voice
> Following, with heedful ear, we issued forth,
> There where the path led upward. "Come," we heard,
> "Come, blessed of my Father." Such the sounds
> That hailed us from within a light, which shone
> So radiant, I could not endure the view.
> "The sun," it added, "hastes: and evening comes.
> Delay not: ere the western sky is hung
> With blackness, strive ye for the pass."

Issuing from this fire of purification, Dante and the

two other poets continue their upward ascent until
nightfall, when they stop to rest—

As the goats,
That late have skipped and wantoned rapidly
Upon the craggy cliffs, ere they had ta'en
Their supper on the herb, now silent lie
And ruminate beneath the umbrage brown,
While noonday rages; and the goatherd leans
Upon his staff, and leaning watches them:
And as the swain, that lodges out all night
In quiet by his flock, lest beast of prey
Disperse them: even so all three abode,
I as a goat, and as the shepherds they,
Close pent on either side by shelving rock.

Thus lying and gazing on the stars, which shine
above them with unusual glory, Dante falls asleep. In
his dream, Leah, the symbol of active life, appears.

About the hour,
As I believe, when Venus from the east
First lightened on the mountain, she whose orb
Seems alway glowing with the fire of love,
A lady young and beautiful, I dreamed,
Was passing o'er a lea; and, as she came,
Methought I saw her ever and anon
Bending to cull the flowers; and thus she sang:
"Know ye, whoever of my name would ask,
That I am Leah! for my brow to weave
A garland, these fair hands unwearied ply.
To please me at the crystal mirror, here
I deck me. But my sister Rachel, she

Before her glass abides the livelong day,
Her radiant eyes beholding, charmed no less,
Than I with this delightful task.   Her joy
In contemplation, as in labor mine."

As the dawn approaches, Dante awakes and finds his guide already risen.   Virgil tells him that on this day he will find the delicious fruit which man so eagerly roams in quest of, and, thus encouraged, the poet soon reaches the summit of the mountain where lies the terrestrial paradise.   Here Virgil thus speaks to him:

                              " Both fires, my son,
The temporal and eternal, thou hast seen;
And art arrived, where of itself my ken
No farther reaches.   I, with skill and art,
Thus far have drawn thee.   Now thy pleasure take
For guide.   Thou hast o'ercome the steeper way,
O'ercome the straiter.   Lo! the sun, that darts
His beam upon thy forehead: lo! the herb,
The arborets and flowers, which of itself
This land pours forth profuse.   Till those bright eyes
With gladness come, which, weeping, made me haste
To succor thee, thou mayst or seat thee down,
Or wander where thou wilt.   Expect no more
Sanction of warning voice or sign from me,
Free of thy own arbitrament to choose,
Discreet, judicious.   To distrust thy sense
Were henceforth error.   I invest thee then
With crown and mitre, sovereign o'er thyself."*

* Purgatorio, xxvii.

Through that celestial forest, whose thick shade
With lively greenness the new-springing day
Attempered, eager now to roam, and search
Its limits round, forthwith I left the bank;
Along the champaign leisurely my way
Pursuing o'er the ground, that on all sides
Delicious odor breathed.   A pleasant air,
That intermitted never, never veered,
Smote on my temples, gently, as a wind
Of softest influence: at which the sprays,
Obedient all, leaned, trembling, to that part
Where first the holy mountain casts his shade;
Yet were not so disordered, but that still
Upon their top the feathered quiristers
Applied their wonted art, and with full joy
Welcomed those hours of prime, and warbled shrill
Amid the leaves, that to their jocund lays
Kept tenor; even as from branch to branch,
Along the piny forests on the shore
Of Chiassi, rolls the gathering melody,
When Eolus hath from his cavern loosed
The dripping south.

Approaching a brooklet, whose crystal waters wind
through the May-bloom and the grass, in the perpetual
shadow of the forest, he beholds Matilda, the symbol
of the Christian doctrine—

A lady all alone, who, singing, went,
And culling flower from flower, wherewith her way
Was all o'er painted.   "Lady beautiful!
Thou, who (if looks, that use to speak the heart,
Are worthy of our trust) with love's own beam
Dost warm thee," thus to her my speech I framed;

"Ah! please thee hither towards the streamlet bend
Thy steps so near, that I may list thy song.
Beholding thee and this fair place, methinks,
I call to mind where wandered and how looked
Proserpine, in that season, when her child
The mother lost, and she the bloomy spring."
　　As when a lady, turning in the dance,
Doth foot it featly, and advances scarce
One step before the other to the ground;
Over the yellow and vermilion flowers
Thus turn'd she at my suit, most maiden-like,
Veiling her sober eyes; and came so near,
That I distinctly caught the dulcet sound.
Arriving where the limpid waters now
Laved the green sward, her eyes she deigned to raise,
That shot such splendor on me, as I ween
Ne'er glanced from Cytherea's, when her son
Had sped his keenest weapons to her heart.
Upon the opposite bank she stood and smiled;
As through her graceful fingers shifted still
The intermingling dyes, which without seed
That lofty land unbosoms.

Matilda informs him that she has come hither to
answer all his doubts. She explains to him that this
mountain, once the dwelling of guiltless man, rises so
high towards heaven, that the contending elements
never disturb it; the circumambient air still circles
there with its first impulse; the plants impregnate with
their efficacy the voyaging breeze, whose subtile plume
wafts it abroad to other climes, producing many a tree
of various virtue; the stream springs not from vapor

that the cold converts, but issues from a fountain solid, undecaying, and sure, by the Omnific Will feeding all with full supply. On one side, called Lethe, it has the power to take away all remembrance of offences; on the other, called Eunoe, in flavor exceeding that of all things else, it brings back remembrance of good deeds done; and both must be tasted before its power is felt.*

Matilda now, turning towards the poet, cries :—

> "My brother! look and hearken!"
> And lo! a sudden lustre ran across
> Through the great forest on all parts, so bright,
> I doubted whether lightning were abroad;
> But that, expiring ever in the spleen
> That doth unfold it, and this during still,
> And waxing still in splendor, made me question
> What it might be: and a sweet melody
> Ran through the luminous air.   Then did I chide,
> With warrantable zeal, the hardihood
> Of our first parent; for that there, where earth
> Stood in obedience to the heavens, she only,
> Woman, the creature of an hour, endured not
> Restraint of any veil, which had she borne
> Devoutly, joys, ineffable as these,
> Had from the first, and long time since, been mine.
>   While, through that wilderness of primy sweets
> That never fade, suspense I walked, and yet
> Expectant of beatitude more high;
> Before us, like a blazing fire, the air

* Purgatorio, xxviii.

Under the green boughs glowed; and, for a song,
Distinct the sound of melody was heard......
    Onward a space, what seemed seven trees of gold
The intervening distance to mine eye
Falsely presented; but, when I was come
So near them, that no lineament was lost
Of those, with which a doubtful object, seen
Remotely, plays on the misdeeming sense;
Then did the faculty, that ministers
Discourse to reason, these for tapers of gold
Distinguish; and i' the singing trace the sound
" Hosanna."   Above, their beauteous garniture
Flamed with more ample lustre, than the moon
Through cloudless sky at midnight, in her noon.
    I turned me, full of wonder, to my guide;
And he did answer with a countenance
Charged with no less amazement: whence my view
Reverted to those lofty things, which came
So slowly moving towards us, that the bride
Would have outstripped them on her bridal day.

The vision described in this and in the following
cantos contains the fundamental ideas of the poem, and
fully unfolds its plot and scope.   The tapers of gold
typify the seven gifts of the Holy Spirit: wisdom, intellect, science, prudence, courage, piety, and the fear of
God.   They are represented as moving slowly towards
the poet, showing that these gifts can only be acquired
through the slow process of moral education.   The
luminous streamers which the golden tapers leave behind are emblematic of the intellectual illumination
bestowed on man in the accomplishment of his destiny.

The elders represent the twenty-four prophets, whose office was to transmit the divine light to humanity; and the four animals the four Evangelists, who communicated to it the doctrine of Christian truth and hope. The chariot represents the Church of God, its two wheels signifying the Old and the New Testament; the Gryphon, half eagle and half lion, is the symbol of Christ in His twofold nature; and the nymphs personify the Christian and moral virtues. The two old men who attend the car are St. Luke and St. Paul, followed by the great doctors, St. Augustine, St. Gregory, St. Jerome, St. Ambrose, and St. Bernard. The poet thus describes the sublime pageant of the Church, preceded by the golden tapers :—

> I straightway marked a tribe behind them walk,
> As if attendant on their leaders, clothed
> With raiment of such whiteness, as on earth
> Was never. On my left, the watery gleam
> Borrowed, and gave me back, when there I looked,
> As in a mirror, my left side portrayed.
> When I had chosen on the river's edge
> Such station, that the distance of the stream
> Alone did separate me; there I stayed
> My steps for clearer prospect, and beheld
> The flames go onward, leaving, as they went,
> The air behind them painted as with trail
> Of liveliest pencils; so distinct were marked
> All those seven listed colors, whence the sun
> Maketh his bow, and Cynthia her zone.
> These streaming gonfalons did flow beyond

27

My vision; and ten paces, as I guess,
Parted the outermost.   Beneath a sky
So beautiful, came four-and-twenty elders
By two and two, with flower-de-luces crowned.
All sang one song: " Blessed be thou among
The daughters of Adam ! and thy loveliness
Blessed forever."   After that the flowers
And the fresh herblets on the opposite brink
Were free from that elected race ; as light
In heaven doth second light, came after them
Four animals, each crowned with verdurous leaf.
With six wings each was plumed ; the plumage full
Of eyes ; and the eyes of Argus would be such
Were they endued with life.   Reader ! more rhymes
I will not waste in shadowing forth their form ;
For other need so straitens, that in this
I may not give my bounty room.   But read
Ezekiel ; for he paints them, from the north
How he beheld them come by Chebar's flood,
In whirlwind, cloud, and fire ; and even such
As thou shalt find them charactered by him,
Here were they ; save as to the pennons ; there,
From him departing, John accords with me.
    The space, surrounded by the four, enclosed
A car triumphal : on two wheels it came,
Drawn at a Gryphon's neck ; and he above
Stretched either wing uplifted, 'tween the midst
And the three listed hues, on each side, three ;
So that the wings did cleave or injure none ;
And out of sight they rose.   The members, far
As he was bird, were golden ; white the rest,
With vermeil interveined.   So beautiful
A car, in Rome, ne'er graced Augustus' pomp,

Or Africanus': e'en the sun's itself
Were poor to this; that chariot of the sun,
Erroneous, which in blazing ruin fell
At Tellus' prayer devout, by the just doom
Mysterious of all-seeing Jove.   Three nymphs
At the right wheel came circling in smooth dance:
The one so ruddy, that her form had scarce
Been known within a furnace of clear flame;
The next did look, as if the flesh and bones
Were emerald; snow new-fallen seemed the third.
Now seemed the white to lead, the ruddy now;
And from her song who led, the others took
Their measure, swift or slow.   At the other wheel,
A band quaternion, each in purple clad,
Advanced with festal step, as, of them, one
The rest conducted; one, upon whose front
Three eyes were seen.   In rear of all this group,
Two old men I beheld, dissimilar
In raiment, but in port and gesture like,
Solid and mainly grave; of whom, the one
Did show himself some favored counsellor
Of the great Coan; him, whom Nature made
To serve the costliest creature of her tribe:
His fellow marked an opposite intent;
Bearing a sword, whose glitterance and keen edge,
E'en as I viewed it with the flood between,
Appalled me.   Next, four others I beheld,
Of humble seeming: and, behind them all,
One single old man, sleeping as he came,
With a shrewd visage.   And these seven, each
Like the first troop were habited; but wore
No braid of lilies on their temples wreathed.
Rather, with roses and each vermeil flower,

A sight, but little distant, might have sworn,
That they were all on fire above their brow.
   When as the car was o'er against me, straight
Was heard a thundering, at whose voice it seemed
The chosen multitude were stayed ; for there,
With the first ensigns, made they solemn halt.*

The seven candlesticks of gold, shedding the polar light of heaven, now stand firmly fixed. Forthwith the saintly tribe between them and the Gryphon turn to the car as to their rest ; and one of them thrice chants a hymn to Beatrice, while the others take up the song.

                 At the last audit, so
The blest shall rise, from forth his cavern each
Uplifting lightly his new-vested flesh ;
As, on the sacred litter, at the voice
Authoritative of that elder, sprang
A hundred ministers and messengers
Of life eternal. " Blessed thou, who comest !"
And, " Oh !" they cried, " from full hands scatter ye
Unwithering lilies :" and, so saying, cast
Flowers overhead and round them on all sides.
   I have beheld, ere now, at break of day,
The eastern clime all roseate ; and the sky
Opposed, one deep and beautiful serene ;
And the sun's face so shaded, and with mists
Attempered, at his rising, that the eye
Long while endured the sight : thus, in a cloud
Of flowers, that from those hands angelic rose,
And down within and outside of the car
Fell showering, in white veil, with olive wreathed,

             * Purgatorio, xxix.

A virgin in my view appeared, beneath
Green mantle, robed in hue of living flame:
And o'er my spirit, that so long a time
Had from her presence felt no shuddering dread,
Albeit mine eyes discerned her not, there moved
A hidden virtue from her, at whose touch
The power of ancient love was strong within me.
   No sooner on my vision streaming, smote
The heavenly influence, which years past and e'en
In childhood thrilled me, than towards Virgil I
Turned me leftward; panting like a babe
That flees for refuge to his mother's breast,
If aught have terrified or worked him woe;
And would have cried: "There is no dram of blood
That doth not quiver in me.   The old flame
Throws out clear tokens of reviving fire."
But Virgil had bereaved us of himself;
Virgil, my best-loved father, Virgil, he
To whom I gave me up for safety; nor
All our prime mother lost, availed to save
My undewed cheeks from blur of soiling tears.
   "Dante! weep not, that Virgil leaves thee; nay,
Weep thou not yet: behooves thee feel the edge
Of other sword; and thou shalt weep for that."
   As to the prow or stern, some admiral
Paces the deck, inspiriting his crew,
When mid the sail-yards all hands ply aloof;
Thus, on the left side of the car, I saw
(Turning me at the sound of mine own name,
Which here I am compelled to register)
The virgin stationed, who before appeared
Veiled in that festive shower angelical.
Towards me, across the stream, she bent her eyes,
   27*

Though from her brow the veil descending, bound
With foliage of Minerva, suffered not
That I beheld her clearly : then with act
Full royal, still insulting o'er her thrall,
Added, as one who, speaking, keepeth back
The bitterest saying, to conclude the speech :
" Observe me well.   I am, in sooth, I am
Beatrice.   What ! and hast thou deigned at last
Approach the mountain ?   Knewest not, O man !
Thy happiness is here ?"   Down fell mine eyes
On the clear fount ; but there, myself espying,
Recoiled, and sought the greensward ; such a weight
Of shame was on my forehead.   With a mien
Of that stern majesty, which doth surround
A mother's presence to her awe-struck child,
She looked ; a flavor of such bitterness
Was mingled in her pity.   There her words
Brake off ; and suddenly the angels sang,
" In thee, O gracious Lord ! my hope hath been :"
But went no further than, " Thou, Lord ! hast set
My feet in ample room."   As snow that lies,
Amidst the living rafters on the back
Of Italy, congealed, when drifted high
And closely piled by rough Sclavonian blasts ;
Breathe but the land whereon no shadow falls,
And straightway melting it distils away,
Like a fire-wasted taper : thus was I,
Without a sigh or tear, or ever these
Did sing, that, with the chiming of heaven's sphere,
Still in their warbling chime : but when the strain
Of dulcet symphony expressed for me
Their soft compassion, more than could the words,
" Virgin ! why so consumest him ?" then, the ice,

Congealed about my bosom, turned itself
To spirit and water; and with anguish forth
Gushed, through the lips and eyelids, from the heart.
   Upon the chariot's same edge still she stood,
Immovable; and thus addressed her words
To those bright semblances with pity touched:
" Ye in the eternal day your vigils keep;
So that nor night nor slumber, with close stealth,
Conveys from you a single step, in all
The goings on of time; thence, with more heed
I shape mine answer, for his ear intended,
Who there stands weeping; that the sorrow now
May equal the transgression.   Not alone
Through operation of the mighty orbs,
That mark each seed to some predestined aim,
As with aspect or fortunate or ill,
The constellations meet; but through benign
Largess of heavenly graces, which rain down
From such a height as mocks our vision, this man
Was, in the freshness of his being, such,
So gifted virtually, that in him
All better habits wondrously had thrived.
The more of kindly strength is in the soil,
So much doth evil seed and lack of culture
Mar it the more, and make it run to wildness.
These looks sometime upheld him; for I showed
My youthful eyes, and led him by their light
In upright walking.   Soon as I had reached
The threshold of my second age, and changed
My mortal for immortal; then he left me,
And gave himself to others.   When from flesh
To spirit I had risen, and increase
Of beauty and of virtue circled me,

I was less dear to him, and valued less.
His steps were turned into deceitful ways,
Following false images of good, that make
No promise perfect.   Nor availed me aught
To sue for inspirations, with the which,
I, both in dreams of night, and otherwise,
Did call him back; of them, so little recked him.
Such depth he fell, that all device was short
Of his preserving, save that he should view
The children of perdition.   To this end
I visited the purlieus of the dead:
And one, who hath conducted him thus high,
Received my supplications, urged with weeping.
It were a breaking of God's high decree,
If Lethe should be passed and such food tasted
Without the cost of some repenting tear.*

" O thou!" her words she thus without delay
Resuming, turned their point on me, to whom
They, with but lateral edge, seemed harsh before:
" Say thou, who stand'st beyond the holy stream,
If this be true.   A charge, so grievous, needs
Thine own avowal."   On my faculty
Such strange amazement hung, the voice expired
Imperfect, ere its organs gave it birth.

A little space refraining, then she spake:
" What dost thou muse on ?   Answer me.   The wave
On thy remembrances of evil yet
Hath done no injury."   A mingled sense
Of fear and of confusion, from my lips
Did such a " Yea" produce, as needed help
Of vision to interpret.   As when breaks,
In act to be discharged, a cross-bow bent

* Purgatorio, xxx.

Beyond its pitch, both nerve and bow o'erstretched ;
The flagging weapon feebly hits the mark :
Thus, tears and sighs forth gushing, did I burst
Beneath the heavy load : and thus my voice
Was slackened on its way.   She straight began :
" When my desire invited thee to love
The good, which sets a bound to our aspirings ;
What bar of thwarting foss or linkèd chain
Did meet thee, that thou so shouldst quit the hope
Of further progress ? or what bait of ease,
Or promise of allurement, led thee on
Elsewhere, that thou elsewhere shouldst rather wait ?"
   A bitter sigh I drew, then scarce found voice
To answer ; hardly to these sounds my lips
Gave utterance, wailing : " Thy fair looks withdrawn,
Things present, with deceitful pleasures, turned
My steps aside."   She answering spake : " Hadst thou
Been silent, or denied what thou avow'st,
Thou hadst not hid thy sin the more ; such eye
Observes it.   But whene'er the sinner's cheek
Breaks forth into the precious-streaming tears
Of self-accusing, in our court the wheel
Of justice doth run counter to the edge.
Howe'er, that thou mayst profit by thy shame
For errors past, and that henceforth more strength
May arm thee, when thou hear'st the Siren-voice ;
Lay thou aside the motive to this grief,
And lend attentive ear, while I unfold
How opposite a way my buried flesh
Should have impelled thee.   Never didst thou spy,
In art or nature, aught so passing sweet,
As were the limbs that in their beauteous frame
Enclosed me, and are scattered now in dust.

If sweetest thing thus failed thee with my death,
What afterward, of mortal, should thy wish
Have tempted?   When thou first hadst felt the dart
Of perishable things, in my departing
For better realms, thy wing thou shouldst have pruned
To follow me; and never stooped again,
To 'bide a second blow, for a slight girl,
Or other gaud as transient and as vain.
The new and inexperienced bird awaits
Twice, it may be, or thrice, the fowler's aim;
But in the sight of one whose plumes are full,
In vain the net is spread, the arrow winged."
    I stood, as children silent and ashamed
Stand, listening, with their eyes upon the earth,
Acknowledging their fault, and self-condemned;
And she resumed: "If but to hear thus pains thee,
Raise thou thy beard, and lo! what sight shall do."
    With less reluctance yields a sturdy holm,
Rent from its fibres by a blast, that blows
From off the pole, or from Iarbas' land,
Than I at her behest my visage raised:
And thus the face denoting by the beard,
I marked the secret sting her words conveyed.
    No sooner lifted I mine aspect up,
Than I perceived those primal creatures cease
Their flowery sprinkling; and mine eyes beheld
(Yet unassured and wavering in their view)
Beatrice; she who towards the mystic shape,
That joins two natures in one form, had turned:
And even under shadow of her veil,
And parted by the verdant rill that flowe'
Between, in loveliness she seemed as much
Her former self surpassing, as on earth

All others she surpassed.   Remorseful goads
Shot sudden through me.   Each thing else, the more
Its love had late beguiled me, now the more
Was loathsome.   On my heart so keenly smote
The bitter consciousness, that on the ground
O'erpowered I fell: and what my state was then,
She knows, who was the cause.   When now my strength
Flowed back, returning outward from the heart,
The lady, whom alone I first had seen,
I found above me.   "Loose me not," she cried:
"Loose not thy hold:" and lo! had dragged me high
As to my neck into the stream; while she,
Still as she drew me after, swept along,
Swift as a shuttle, bounding o'er the wave.
      The blessèd shore approaching, then was heard
So sweetly, "Tu asperges me," that I,
May not remember, much less tell the sound.
      The beauteous dame, her arms expanding, clasped
My temples, and immerged me where 'twas fit
The wave should drench me: and, thence raising up,
Within the fourfold dance of lovely nymphs
Presented me so laved; and with their arm
They each did cover me.   "Here are we nymphs,
And in the heaven are stars.   Or ever earth
Was visited of Beatrice, we,
Appointed for her handmaids, tended on her.
We to her eyes will lead thee: but the light
Of gladness, that is in them, well to scan,
Those yonder three, of deeper ken than ours,
Thy sight shall quicken."   Thus began their song:
And then they led me to the Gryphon's breast,
Where, turned toward us, Beatrice stood.
"Spare not thy vision.   We have stationed thee

Before the emeralds, whence love, erewhile,
Hath drawn his weapons on thee." As they spake,
A thousand fervent wishes riveted
Mine eyes upon her beaming eyes, that stood,
Still fixed toward the Gryphon, motionless.
As the sun strikes a mirror, even thus
Within those orbs the twifold being shone ;
Forever varying, in one figure now
Reflected, now in other. Reader! muse
How wondrous in my sight it seemed, to mark
A thing, albeit steadfast in itself,
Yet in its imaged semblance mutable.

Full of amaze, and joyous, while my soul
Fed on the viand, whereof still desire
Grows with satiety ; the other three,
With gesture that declared a loftier line,
Advanced : to their own carol, on they came
Dancing, in festive ring angelical.

"Turn, Beatrice!" was their song : "Oh! turn
Thy saintly sight on this thy faithful one,
Who, to behold thee, many a wearisome pace
Hath measured. Gracious at our prayer, vouchsafe
Unveil to him thy cheeks ; that he may mark
Thy second beauty, now concealed." O splendor!
O sacred light eternal! who is he,
So pale with musing in Pierian shades,
Or with that fount so lavishly imbued,
Whose spirit should not fail him in the essay
To represent thee such as thou didst seem,
When under cope of the still-chiming heaven
Thou gavest to open air thy charms revealed ?*

* Purgatorio, xxxi.

Dante remains absorbed in the contemplation of Beatrice, but the sacred virgins warn him not to gaze on her too fixedly. Now the glorious pageant moves on to the sound of angelic music, and a new vision appears to the poet.

> As when, their bucklers for protection raised,
> A well-ranged troop, with portly banners curled,
> Wheel circling, ere the whole can change their ground;
> E'en thus the goodly regiment of heaven,
> Proceeding, all did pass us, ere the car
> Had sloped his beam.   Attendant at the wheels
> The damsels turned; and on the Gryphon moved
> The sacred burden, with a pace so smooth,
> No feather on him trembled.   The fair dame,
> Who through the wave had drawn me, 'companied
> By Statius and myself, pursued the wheel,
> Whose orbit, rolling, marked a lesser arch.

The lofty tree which is here alluded to is symbolic of humanity, despoiled of leaves and flowers by the sin of our first parents.

> Through the high wood, now void (the more her blame
> Who by the serpent was beguiled), I passed,
> With step in cadence to the harmony
> Angelic.   Onward had we moved, as far,
> Perchance, as arrow at three several flights
> Full winged had sped, when from her station down
> Descended Beatrice.   With one voice
> All murmured " Adam;" circling next a plant
> Despoiled of flowers and leaf, on every bough.
> Its tresses, spreading more as more they rose,
> Were such, as midst their forest wilds, for height,

28

The Indians might have gazed at.   " Blessed thou,
Gryphon ! whose beak hath never plucked that tree
Pleasant to taste : for hence the appetite
Was warped to evil."   Round the stately trunk
Thus shouted forth the rest, to whom returned
The animal twice-gendered : " Yea ! for so
The generation of the just are saved."
And turning to the chariot-pole, to foot
He drew it of the widowed branch, and bound
There, left unto the stock whereon it grew.

    As when large floods of radiance from above
Stream, with that radiance mingled, which ascends
Next after setting of the scaly sign,
Our plants then burgein, and each wears anew
His wonted colors, ere the sun have yoked
Beneath another star his flamy steeds;
Thus putting forth a hue more faint than rose,
And deeper than the violet, was renewed
The plant, erewhile in all its branches bare.
Unearthly was the hymn which then arose.
I understood it not, nor to the end
Endured the harmony.   Had I the skill
To pencil forth how closed the unpitying eyes,
Slumbering, when Syrinx warbled (eyes that paid
So dearly for their watching), then like painter
That with a model paints, I might design
The manner of my falling into sleep.
But feign who will the slumber cunningly,
I pass it by to when I waked ; and tell,
How suddenly a flash of splendor rent
The curtain of my sleep, and one cries out,
" Arise : what dost thou ?"   As the chosen three,
On Tabor's mount, admitted to behold
The blossoming of that fair tree, whose fruit

Is coveted of angels, and doth make
Perpetual feast in heaven; to themselves
Returning, at the word whence deeper sleeps
Were broken, they their tribe diminished saw;
Both Moses and Elias gone, and changed
The stole their master wore; thus to myself
Returning, over me beheld I stand
The piteous one, who, cross the stream, had brought
My steps. "And where," all doubting, I exclaimed,
"Is Beatrice?"—"See her," she replied,
"Beneath the fresh leaf, seated on its root.
Behold the associate choir, that circles her.
The others, with a melody more sweet
And more profound, journeying to higher realms,
Upon the Gryphon tend." If there her words
Were closed, I know not; but mine eyes had now
Ta'en view of her, by whom all other thoughts
Were barred admittance. On the very ground
Alone she sat, as she had there been left
A guard upon the wain, which I beheld
Bound to the twiform beast. The seven nymphs
Did make themselves a cloister round about her;
And in their hands upheld those lights secure
From blast Septentrion and the gusty south.

The history of the Church is now foreshadowed. The first descent of the eagle symbolizes the Roman emperors by whom it was preserved; the second, the coming of Constantine and other monarchs, who, by endowing it with wealth and power, transformed it into a monster. The fox introduced is emblematic of the frauds through which the Papal Church extended its dominions; the dragon is Satan, who inspired the popes with ambition and covetousness; the harlot, the papacy itself; and the giant, the monarchs of France, the allies of the papacy, who, to pervert the holy see more thoroughly, removed it to Avignon, beyond the influence of Italian civilization.

> " A little while thou shalt be forester here;
> And citizen shalt be, forever with me,
> Of that true Rome, wherein Christ dwells a Roman.
> To profit the misguided world, keep now
> Thine eyes upon the car; and what thou seest,
> Take heed thou write, returning to that place."
> Thus Beatrice: at whose feet inclined,
> Devout, at her behest, my thought and eyes,
> I, as she bade, directed. Never fire,
> With so swift motion, forth a stormy cloud
> Leaped downward from the welkin's farthest bound,
> As I beheld the bird of Jove descend
> Down through the tree; and, as he rushed, the rind
> Disparting crush beneath him; buds much more,
> And leaflets. On the car, with all his might
> He struck; whence, staggering, like a ship it reeled,
> At random driven, to starboard now, o'ercome,
> And now to larboard, by the vaulting waves.
> Next, springing up into the chariot's womb,
> A fox I saw, with hunger seeming pined
> Of all good food. But, for his ugly sins
> The saintly maid rebuking him, away
> Scampering he turned, fast as his hide-bound corpse
> Would bear him. Next, from whence before he came
> I saw the eagle dart into the hull
> O' the car, and leave it with his feathers lined:
> And then a voice, like that which issues forth

From heart with sorrow rived, did issue forth
From heaven, and, " O poor bark of mine !" it cried,
" How badly art thou freighted."   Then it seemed
That the earth opened, between either wheel;
And I beheld a dragon issue thence,
That through the chariot fixed his forked train;
And, like a wasp, that draggeth back the sting,
So drawing forth his baleful train, he dragged
Part of the bottom forth; and went his way
Exulting.   What remained, as lively turf
With green herb, so did clothe itself with plumes,
Which haply had, with purpose chaste and kind,
Been offered; and therewith were clothed the wheels,
Both one and other, and the beam, so quickly,
A sigh were not breathed sooner.   Thus transformed,
The holy structure, through its several parts,
Did put forth heads; three on the beam, and one
On every side: the first like oxen horned;
But with a single horn upon their front,
The four.   Like monster, sight hath never seen.
O'er it methought there sat, secure as rock
On mountain's lofty top, a shameless whore,
Whose ken roved loosely round her.   At her side,
As 'twere that none might bear her off, I saw
A giant stand; and ever and anon
They mingled kisses.   But, her lustful eyes
Chancing on me to wander, that fell minion
Scourged her from head to foot all o'er; then full
Of jealousy, and fierce with rage, unloosed
The monster, and dragged on, so far across
The forest, that from me its shades alone
Shielded the harlot and the new-formed brute.*

* Purgatorio, xxxii.

28*

"The heathen, Lord! are come:" responsive thus,
The trinal now, and now the virgin band
Quaternion, their sweet psalmody began,
Weeping; and Beatrice listened, sad
And sighing, to the song, in such a mood,
That Mary, as she stood beside the cross,
Was scarce more changed.   But when they gave her place
To speak, then, risen upright on her feet,
She, with a color glowing bright as fire,
Did answer: "Yet a little while, and ye
Shall see me not; and, my beloved sisters!
Again a little while, and ye shall see me."

Before her then she marshalled all the seven;
And, beckoning only, motioned me, the dame,
And that remaining sage, to follow her.

So on she passed; and had not set, I ween,
Her tenth step to the ground, when, with mine eyes,
Her eyes encountered; and, with visage mild,
"So mend thy pace," she cried, "that if my words
Address thee, thou mayst still be aptly placed
To hear them."   Soon as duly to her side
I now had hastened: "Brother!" she began,
"Why makest thou no attempt at questioning,
As thus we walk together?"   Like to those
Who, speaking with too reverent an awe
Before their betters, draw not forth the voice
Alive unto their lips, befell me then
That I in sounds imperfect thus began:
"Lady! what I have need of, that thou know'st;
And what will suit my need."   She answering thus:
"Of fearfulness and shame, I will that thou
Henceforth do rid thee; that thou speak no more,
As one who dreams."

Here Beatrice foretells the advent of a messenger from God, symbolized in the number five hundred, five, and ten, which, written in Roman characters, gives the word DVX, that is, a military leader, who will slay the foul one, and the giant her accomplice. She charges the poet to repeat to the world her prophecy, and to proclaim that whoever shall rob or pluck the tree of humanity will make himself guilty before God, who for his own use, and not for that of the Church, or of any other institution, created and hallowed it.

       " Thus far be taught of me :
The vessel which thou saw'st the serpent break,
Was, and is not: let him, who hath the blame,
Hope not to scare God's vengeance with a sop.
Without an heir forever shall not be
That eagle, he, who left the chariot plumed,
Which monster made it first and next a prey.
Plainly I view, and therefore speak, the stars
E'en now approaching, whose conjunction, free
From all impediment and bar, brings on
A season, in the which, one sent from God
(Five hundred, five, and ten, do mark him out),
That foul one, and the accomplice of her guilt,
The giant, both shall slay. And if perchance
My saying, dark as Themis or as Sphinx,
Fail to persuade thee (since like them it foils
The intellect with blindness), yet ere long
Events shall be the Naïads, that will solve
This knotty riddle, and no damage light
On flock or field. Take heed; and as these words
By me are uttered, teach them even so

To those who live that life, which is a race
To death : and when thou writest them, keep in mind
Not to conceal how thou hast seen the plant,
That twice hath now been spoiled.   This whoso robs,
This whoso plucks, with blasphemy of deed
Sins against God, who for His use alone
Creating hallowed it.   For taste of this,
In pain and in desire, five thousand years
And upward, the first soul did yearn for him
Who punished in himself the fatal gust.

   " Thy reason slumbers, if it deem this height,
And summit thus inverted, of the plant,
Without due cause : and were not vainer thoughts,
As Elsa's numbing waters, to thy soul,
And their fond pleasures had not dyed it dark
As Pyramus the mulberry ; thou hadst seen,
In such momentous circumstance alone,
God's equal justice morally implied
In the forbidden tree.   But since I mark thee,
In understanding, hardened into stone,
And, to that hardness, spotted too and stained,
So that thine eye is dazzled at my word ;
I will, that, if not written, yet at least
Painted thou take it in thee, for the cause,
That one brings home his staff inwreathed with palm."

   I thus : " As wax by seal, that changeth not
Its impress, now is stamped my brain by thee.
But wherefore soars thy wished-for speech so high
Beyond my sight, that loses it the more,
The more it strains to reach it ?"—" To the end
That thou mayst know," she answered straight, " the school
That thou hast followed ; and how far behind,
When following my discourse, its learning halts :

And mayst behold your art, from the divine
As distant, as the disagreement is
'Twixt earth and heaven's most high and rapturous orb."
  " I not remember," I replied, " that e'er
I was estranged from thee; nor for such fault
Doth conscience chide me." Smiling she returned:
" If thou canst not remember, call to mind
How lately thou hast drunk of Lethe's wave;
And, sure as smoke doth indicate a flame,
In that forgetfulness itself conclude
Blame from thy alienated will incurred.
From henceforth, verily, my words shall be
As naked, as will suit them to appear
In thy unpractised view." More sparkling now,
And with retarded course, the sun possessed
The circle of mid-day, that varies still
As the aspect varies of each several clime:
When, as one sent in vaward of a troop
For escort, pauses, if perchance he spy
Vestige of somewhat strange and rare; so paused
The sevenfold band, arriving at the verge
Of a dun umbrage hoar, such as is seen,
Beneath green leaves and gloomy branches, oft
To overbrow a bleak and alpine cliff.
And, where they stood, before them, as it seemed,
I, Tigris and Euphrates both, beheld
Forth from one fountain issue; and, like friends,
Linger at parting. " O enlightening beam !
O glory of our kind ! beseech thee say
What water this, which, from one source derived,
Itself removes to distance from itself ?"
  To such entreaty answer thus was made:
" Entreat Matilda, that she teach thee this."

And here, as one who clears himself of blame
Imputed, the fair dame returned: "Of me
He this and more hath learned; and I am safe
That Lethe's water hath not hid it from him."
    And Beatrice: "Some more pressing care,
That oft the memory 'reaves, perchance hath made
His mind's eye dark.   But lo, where Eunoe flows!
Lead thither; and, as thou art wont, revive
His fainting virtue."   As a courteous spirit,
That proffers no excuses, but as soon
As he hath token of another's will,
Makes it his own; when she had ta'en me, thus
The lovely maiden moved her on, and called
To Statius, with an air most lady-like:
"Come thou with him."   Were further space allowed,
Then, Reader! might I sing, though but in part,
That beverage, with whose sweetness I had ne'er
Been sated.   But, since all the leaves are full,
Appointed for this second strain, mine art
With warning bridle checks me.   I returned
From the most holy wave, regenerate,
E'en as new plants renewed with foliage new,
Pure and made apt for mounting to the stars.*

* Purgatorio, xxxiii.

PARADISO.

MAN, according to DANTE, attains his perfection when, his intellectual and moral faculties having received their full development, he becomes possessed of the supreme Good, to which his nature aspires. This possession, however, both in the present and the future life, is proportioned to the capacity of each individual soul to realize in itself the infinite Ideal. Thus led by BEATRICE, the poet ascends to the heavenly spheres,—the abodes of those spirits who have reached different degrees of perfection, approaching nearer and nearer to the highest point, where human nature reaches its full beatitude, and becomes identified with absolute truth, justice, and happiness, or the infinite Good. The Paradiso, the third Act of the *Divina Commedia*, represents the apotheosis of man, consummated in this union, in which the object of his individual and social relations is accomplished, the wisdom of creation becomes manifest, and the perfection of nature, art, and society is attained.

This final triumph is gained chiefly through knowledge, the foundation of all progress and civilization, the true golden ladder by which humanity ascends to the Empyrean, where its image appears, shining within the "three circles of equal measure and of different hue, the symbol of the Divine nature, one and trine." In accordance with this view, Dante tells us, in the *Convito*, that by the heavens he means the sciences, which he fancifully compares with the celestial spheres. He draws a parallel between the one and the other; finds analogies between the order of ideas and the order of the heavens; and strives to show that grammar corresponds to the Moon, dialectics to Mercury, rhetoric to Venus, arithmetic to the Sun, music to Mars, geometry to Jupiter, astrology to Saturn, physics and metaphysics to the fixed stars, ethics to the Primum Mobile, and theology to the Empyrean. Deriving his symbols from the Arabians, he causes the spheres (*the sciences*) to be moved by intelligences which he distributes hierarchically, according to certain qualities of the planets : the angels presiding over the movements of the Moon, the archangels over Mercury, the Thrones over Venus; while the Sun, Mars, and Jupiter, are moved by the Dominions, Virtues, and Principalities ; and the Powers, Cherubim, and Seraphim, impel the Heaven of the Fixed Stars, the Primum Mobile, and the Empyrean. Thus, as the Inferno and the Purgatorio properly consist each of nine circles, the Paradiso is divided into nine spheres, encircled by the Empyrean, the heaven of the visible presence of God. The Earth lies immobile at the centre of the Universe ; around it the celestial spheres move in circular and concentric orbits, which widen and move more swiftly as they are nearer the Primum Mobile, the heaven which communicates its movement to the other globes through subordinate intelligences.

The heavenly spheres, the abodes of the blessed spirits, are distributed in the following order : 1. The Moon, the nearest to the Earth, where dwell those who have broken their religious vows. 2. Mercury, the sphere of patriotic and active rulers. 3. Venus, the planet of lovers. 4. The Sun, the abode of philosophers and theologians. 5. Mars, the world of Christian warriors. 6. Jupiter, containing the spirits of righteous rulers. 7. Saturn, the heaven of contemplative minds. 8. Fixed Stars, where live in eternal blessedness the hosts who celebrate the triumph of Christ. 9. Primum Mobile, the heaven of the Divine Glory. 10. The Empyrean, the abode of the Visible Presence of God. To these spheres Dante ascends with Beatrice, borne by the same force which causes them to revolve, and illumined by the light which, as they ascend, shines brighter and brighter from the eyes of his divine guide.

The Paradiso thus opens :—

His glory, by whose might all things are moved,
Pierces the universe, and in one part
Sheds more resplendence, elsewhere less. In heaven,
That largeliest of his light partakes, was I,
Witness of things, which, to relate again,
Surpasseth power of him who comes from thence ;
For that, so near approaching its desire,

> Our intellect is to such depth absorbed,
> That memory cannot follow.   Nathless all,
> That in my thoughts I of that sacred realm
> Could store, shall now be matter of my song.

The aid of the Muses has hitherto sustained the poet ; but henceforth he requires the inspiration of Apollo himself, whom he thus invokes :—

>   O power divine !
> If thou to me of thine impart so much,
> That of that happy realm the shadowed form
> Traced in my thoughts I may set forth to view ;
> Thou shalt behold me of thy favored tree
> Come to the foot, and crown myself with leaves :
> For to that honor thou, and my high theme
> Will fit me.   If but seldom, mighty Sire !
> To grace his triumph, gathers thence a wreath
> Cæsar, or bard (more shame for human wills
> Depraved), joy to the Delphic god must spring
> From the Peneian foliage, when one breast
> Is with such thirst inspired.   From a small spark
> Great flame hath risen : after me, perchance,
> Others with better voice may pray, and gain,
> From the Cyrrhæan city, answer kind.

Beatrice and Dante stand on the summit of the mountain of the Purgatorio :—

> I saw Beatrice turned, and on the sun
> Gazing, as never eagle fixed his ken.
> As from the first a second beam is wont
> To issue, and reflected upwards rise,
> Even as a pilgrim bent on his return ;   .

So of her act, that through the eyesight passed
Into my fancy, mine was formed; and straight,
Beyond our mortal wont, I fixed mine eyes
Upon the sun.   Much is allowed us there,
That here exceeds our power; thanks to the place
Made for the dwelling of the human kind.
   I suffered it not long; and yet so long,
That I beheld it bickering sparks around,
As iron that comes boiling from the fire.
And suddenly upon the day appeared
A day new-risen; as he, who hath the power,
Had with another sun bedecked the sky.
   Her eyes fast fixed on the eternal wheels,
Beatrice stood unmoved; and I with ken
Fixed upon her, from upward gaze removed,
At her aspect, such inwardly became
As Glaucus, when he tasted of the herb
That made him peer among the ocean gods:
Words may not tell of that trans-human change;
And therefore let the example serve, though weak,
For those whom grace hath better proof in store.
   If I were only what thou didst create,
Then newly, Love! by whom the heaven is ruled;
Thou know'st, who by thy light didst bear me up.
When as the wheel which thou dost ever guide,
Desired Spirit! with its harmony,
Tempered of thee and measured, charmed mine ear,
Then seemed to me so much of heaven to blaze
With the sun's flame, that rain or flood ne'er made
A lake so broad.   The newness of the sound,
And that great light, inflamed me with desire,
Keener than e'er was felt, to know their cause.

In answer to his doubts, Beatrice—

After utterance of a piteous sigh,
She towards me bent her eyes, with such a look,
As on her frenzied child a mother casts:
Then thus began: " Among themselves all things
Have order; and from hence the form, which makes
The universe resemble God.   In this
The higher creatures see the printed steps
Of that eternal worth, which is the end
Whither the line is drawn.   All natures lean,
In this their order, diversely: some more,
Some less approaching to their primal source.
Thus they to different havens are moved on
Through the vast sea of being, and each one
With instinct given, that bears it in its course:
This to the lunar sphere directs the fire;
This moves the hearts of mortal animals;
This the brute earth together knits, and binds.
Nor only creatures, void of intellect,
Are aimed at by this bow; but even those,
That have intelligence and love, are pierced.
That Providence, who so well orders all,
With her own light makes ever calm the heaven,
In which the substance, that hath greatest speed,
Is turned: and thither now, as to our seat
Predestined, we are carried by the force
Of that strong cord, that never loses dart
But at fair aim and glad.   Yet is it true,
That as, oft-times, but ill accords the form
To the design of art, through sluggishness
Of unreplying matter; so this course
Is sometimes quitted by the creature, who
Hath power, directed thus, to bend elsewhere:
As from a cloud the fire is seen to fall,

From its original impulse warped, to earth,
By vicious fondness.   Thou no more admire
Thy soaring (if I rightly deem), than lapse
Of torrent downwards from a mountain's height.
There would in thee for wonder be more cause,
If, free of hindrance, thou hadst stayed below,
As living fire unmoved upon the earth."
So said, she turned toward the heaven her face.*

The poet thus distinguishes those who will not be able to follow him in his adventurous track, and those few who will :—

All ye, who in small bark have following sailed,
Eager to listen, on the adventurous track
Of my proud keel, that singing cuts her way,
Backward return with speed, and your own shores
Revisit; nor put out to open sea,
Where, losing me, perchance ye may remain
Bewildered in deep maze.   The way I pass,
Ne'er yet was run; Minerva breathes the gale:
Apollo guides me; and another Nine,
To my rapt sight, the arctic beams reveal.
Ye other few who have outstretched the neck
Timely for food of angels, on which here
They live, yet never know satiety;
Through the deep brine ye fearless may put out
Your vessel; marking well the furrow broad
Before you in the wave, that on both sides
Equal returns—

  * * * * *

The increate perpetual thirst, that draws
Toward the realm of God's own form, bore us

     * Paradiso, i.

29*

> Swift almost as the heaven ye behold.
> Beatrice upward gazed, and I on her;
> And in such space as on the notch a dart
> Is placed, then loosened flies, I saw myself
> Arrived, where wondrous thing engaged my sight;
> Whence she, to whom no care of mine was hid,
> Turning to me, with aspect glad as fair,
> Bespake me: " Gratefully direct thy mind
> To God, through whom to this first star we come."

They now enter the moon.

> Meseemed as if a cloud had covered us,
> Translucent, solid, firm, and polished bright,
> Like adamant, which the sun's beam had smit.
> Within itself the ever-during pearl
> Received us; as the wave a ray of light
> Receives, and rests unbroken.

Dante asks of Beatrice the cause of the dark spots on the moon, which he refers to different degrees of density and rarity in that satellite, and to the light of the sun, thus differently distributed among its parts. This theory, however, which comes nearer to the conclusion of modern science, is refuted at length by Beatrice, who introduces the erroneous notions of astronomy then prevailing, to explain that phenomenon.*

The moon, the lowest sphere of the Paradise, is inhabited by the spirits of those who have violated their religious vows.

* Paradiso, ii.

As through translucent and smooth glass, or **wave**
Clear and unmoved, and flowing not so deep
As that its bed is dark, the shape returns
So faint of our impictured lineaments,
That, on white forehead set, a pearl as strong
Comes to the eye; such saw I many a face,
All stretched to speak; from whence I straight conceived,
Delusion opposite to that, which raised,
Between the man and fountain, amorous flame.
  Sudden, as I perceived them, deeming these
Reflected semblances, to see of whom
They were, I turned mine eyes, and nothing saw;
Then turned them back, directed on the light
Of my sweet guide, who, smiling, shot forth beams
From her celestial eyes. "Wonder not thou,"
She cried, "at this my smiling, when I see
Thy childish judgment; since not yet on truth
It rests the foot, but, as it still is wont,
Makes thee fall back in unsound vacancy.
True substances are these, which thou behold'st,
Hither through failure of their vow exiled.
But speak thou with them; listen, and believe,
That the true light, which fills them with desire,
Permits not from its beams their feet to stray."

Among the spirits who seem most eager to converse,
the poet recognizes his friend Piccarda, the sister of
Forese and Corso Donati, a relative of his wife. Piccarda had taken refuge in the convent of St. Clare, and
become a nun, to avoid a marriage contracted for her
against her will by her family. Her brother Corso,
enraged at her escape, aided by a band of hired ruffians,
stormed the convent, carried off his sister by force, and

obliged her to marry the man to whom he had promised
her hand.   She died soon after.   The meeting and the
recognition of Piccarda are thus described :—

Straight to the shadow, which for converse seemed
Most earnest, I addressed me; and began,
As one by over-eagerness perplexed :
" O spirit, born for joy ! who in the rays
Of life eternal, of that sweetness know'st
The flavor, which, not tasted, passes far
All apprehension ; me it well would please,
If thou wouldst tell me of thy name, and this
Your station here."   Whence she with kindness prompt,
And eyes glistering with smiles: " Our charity,
To any wish by justice introduced,
Bars not the door ; no more than she above,
Who would have all her court be like herself.
I was a virgin sister in the earth :
And if thy mind observe me well, this form,
With such addition graced of loveliness,
Will not conceal me long; but thou wilt know
Piccarda, in the tardiest sphere thus placed,
Here mid these other blessèd also blest,
Our hearts, whose high affections burn alone
With pleasure from the Holy Spirit conceived,
Admitted to his order, dwell in joy.
And this condition, which appears so low,
Is for this cause assigned us, that our vows
Were, in some part, neglected and made void."
Whence I to her replied : " Something divine
Beams in your countenances wondrous fair ;
From former knowledge quite transmuting you.
Therefore to recollect was I so slow.

But what thou sayst hath to my memory
Given now such aid, that to retrace your forms
Is easier.   Yet inform me, ye, who here
Are happy; long ye for a higher place,
More to behold, and more in love to dwell ?"
    She with those other spirits gently smiled;
Then answered with such gladness, that she seemed
With love's first flame to glow: " Brother ! our will
Is, in composure, settled by the power
Of charity, who makes us will alone
What we possess, and naught beyond desire :
If we should wish to be exalted more,
Then must our wishes jar with the high will
Of Him, who sets us here; which in these orbs
Thou wilt confess not possible, if here
To be in charity must needs befall,
And if her nature well thou contemplate.
Rather it is inherent in this state
Of blessedness, to keep ourselves within
The divine will, by which our wills with His
Are one.   So that as we, from step to step,
Are placed throughout this kingdom, pleases all,
Even as our King, who in us plants His will;
And in His will is our tranquillity :
It is the mighty ocean, whither tends
Whatever it creates and nature makes."
    Then saw I clearly how each spot in heaven
Is Paradise, though with like gracious dew
The supreme virtue shower not over all.

She then thus relates to him how she had entered the
convent, and how she was taken away.   She also points
out Constance, daughter of Ruggieri, King of Sicily,

who was also taken by force from a monastery, married
to the Emperor Henry VI., and afterwards became the
mother of Frederick II.

> " Exalted worth and perfectness of life
> The Lady higher up inshrine in heaven,
> By whose pure laws upon your nether earth
> The robe and veil they wear; to that intent,
> That e'en till death they may keep watch, or sleep,
> With their great bridegroom, who accepts each vow,
> Which to his gracious pleasure love conforms.
> I from the world, to follow her, when young
> Escaped; and, in her vesture mantling me,
> Made promise of the way her sect enjoins.
> Thereafter men, for ill than good more apt,
> Forth snatched me from the pleasant cloister's pale
> God knows how, after that, my life was framed.
> This other splendid shape, which thou behold'st
> At my right side, burning with all the light
> Of this our orb, what of myself I tell
> May to herself apply.　From her, like me
> A sister, with like violence were torn
> The saintly folds, that shaded her fair brows.
> E'en when she to the world again was brought
> In spite of her own will and better wont,
> Yet not for that the bosom's inward veil
> Did she renounce.　This is the luminary
> Of mighty Constance, who from that loud blast,
> Which blew the second over Suabia's realm,
> That power produced, which was the third and last."
>   She ceased from further talk, and then began
> " Ave Maria" singing; and with that song
> Vanished, as heavy substance through deep wave.

> Mine eye, that, far as it was capable,
> Pursued her, when in dimness she was lost,
> Turned to the mark where greater want impelled,
> And bent on Beatrice all its gaze.
> But she, as lightning, beamed upon my looks ;
> So that the sight sustained it not at first.
> Whence I to question her became less prompt.*

Beatrice solves several doubts on metaphysical subjects by which the mind of the poet is perturbed : she interprets the doctrine of Plato regarding the return of the soul to the stars, and explains how Piccarda and Constance, having yielded to violence, had lost some portion of the merit which they would have acquired by their good intentions. The poet here asks of Beatrice if man may supply the failure of his vows by other works.† On proceeding to solve this question, his guide thus sings the praise of liberty :—

> " Supreme of gifts which God creating gave
> Of His free bounty, sign most evident
> Of goodness, and in His account most prized,
> Was liberty of will ; the boon, wherewith
> All intellectual creatures, and them sole,
> He hath endowed."

In the discussion which follows, Dante accepts the doctrine taught by mediæval theology, which, measuring the sacrifice by the value of the gift sacrificed, considered religious vows as the highest expression of religious worship. This theory, which is the basis of the monastic orders and the ecclesiastical hierarchy in the

* Paradiso, iii.   † Ibid., iv.

Papal Church, assumes that the apex of moral perfection consists in the sacrifice of what is noblest in human nature. The theologians of that age had not yet seen that the suicide of the soul is no less criminal than that of the body, and that it can only be justified by the good intentions which may have prompted it in a state of society morally disorganized. No man can bind his faculties, essentially free, to a life in opposition to the laws of nature and the exigencies of social organization; nor can he disregard the sacred inviolability of his own conscience, morally bound to follow the light which illuminates the soul in the progress of its intellectual development. Religious vows, therefore, involving the sacrifice of one's own personality, whether encouraged by the Papal Church or by the religion of the Brahmins, are essentially immoral, and ought not to be recognized in any system of civil government. Dante himself seems to have felt the error of the theory which he borrowed from the notions of his time; for he not only placed in Paradise the spirits of those who violated their vows, but he says that no vow is legitimate which is not accepted by God; who, being the author of human personality, cannot but regard its sacrifice as a criminal attempt to destroy His own noblest work.

> " Take then no vow at random : ta'en with faith,
> Preserve it; yet not bent, as Jephthah once,
> Blindly to execute a rash resolve,
> Whom better it had suited to exclaim,

'I have done ill,' than to redeem his pledge
By doing worse: or, not unlike to him
In folly, that great leader of the Greeks;
Whence, on the altar, Iphigenia mourned
Her virgin beauty, and hath since made mourn
Both wise and simple, even all, who hear
Of so fell sacrifice.   Be ye more staid,
O Christians! not, like feather, by each wind
Removable; nor think to cleanse yourselves
In every water.   Either Testament,
The Old and New, is yours: and for your guide,
The shepherd of the Church.   Let this suffice
To save you.   When by evil lust enticed,
Remember ye be men, not senseless beasts;
Nor let the Jew, who dwelleth in your streets,
Hold you in mockery.   Be not as the lamb,
That, fickle wanton, leaves its mother's milk,
To dally with itself in idle play."
*   *   *   *   *
Though mainly prompt new question to propose,
Her silence and changed look did keep me dumb,
And as the arrow, ere the cord is still,
Leapeth unto its mark; so on we sped
Into the second realm.   There I beheld
The dame, so joyous, enter, that the orb
Grew brighter at her smiles; and, if the star
Were moved to gladness, what then was my cheer,
Whom nature hath made apt for every change!
    As in a quiet and clear lake the fish,
If aught approach them from without, do draw
Towards it, deeming it their food; so drew
Full more than thousand splendors towards us;
And in each one was heard: "Lo! one arrived
To multiply our loves!" and as each came,
30

The shadow, streaming forth effulgence new,
Witnessed augmented joy.   Here, Reader! think,
If thou didst miss the sequel of my tale,
To know the rest how sorely thou wouldst crave;
And thou shalt see what vehement desire
Possessed me, soon as these had met my view,
To know their state.   " O born in happy hour!
Thou, to whom grace vouchsafes, or ere thy close
Of fleshly warfare, to behold the thrones
Of that eternal triumph; know, to us
The light communicated, which through heaven
Expatiates without bound.   Therefore, if aught
Thou of our beams wouldst borrow for thine aid,
Spare not; and, of our radiance, take thy fill."
     Thus of those piteous spirits one bespake me;
And Beatrice next: " Say on; and trust
As unto gods."—" How in the light supreme
Thou harbor'st, and from thence the virtue bring'st,
That, sparkling in thine eyes, denotes thy joy,
I mark: but, who thou art, am still to seek;
Or wherefore, worthy spirit! for thy lot
This sphere assigned, that oft from mortal ken
Is veiled by other's beams."   I said; and turned
Toward the lustre, that with greeting kind
Erewhile had hailed me.   Forthwith, brighter far
Than erst, it waxed: and, as himself the sun
Hides through excess of light, when his warm gaze
Hath on the mantle of thick vapors preyed;
Within its proper ray the saintly shape
Was, through increase of gladness, thus concealed;
And, shrouded so in splendor, answered me,
E'en as the tenor of my song declares.*

* Paradiso, v.

The spirit proves to be the Emperor Justinian, who speaks of his own actions, and particularly of the formation of the code which bears his name. He then relates the history of Rome, from the foundation of the city to his own reign. He celebrates the deeds of Julius Cæsar and of Augustus, and believes that the safety of the world will be secured by the revival of the empire. Hence he denounces those who oppose the imperial eagles,—the Guelphs, the monarchs of France and of Naples, their allies, as well as the Ghibelins themselves, who fight for the empire for selfish purposes.

    .... " Judge then for thyself
Of those, whom I erewhile accused to thee,
What they are, and how grievous their offending,
Who are the cause of all your ills.   The one
Against the universal ensign rears
The yellow lilies ; and with partial aim,
That, to himself, the other arrogates :
So that 'tis hard to see who most offends.
Be yours, ye Ghibelins, to veil your hearts
Beneath another standard : ill is this
Followed of him, who severs it and justice :
And let not with his Guelphs the new-crowned Charles
Assail it ; but those talons hold in dread,
Which from a lion of more lofty port
Have rent the casing.   Many a time ere now
The sons have for the sire's transgression wailed :
Nor let him trust the fond belief, that Heaven
Will truck its armor for his lilied shield.

    " This little star is furnished with good spirits,

Whose mortal lives were busied to that end,
That honor and renown might wait on them:
And, when desires thus err in their intention,
True love must needs ascend with slacker beam.
But it is part of our delight, to measure
Our wages with the merit; and admire
The close proportion.   Hence doth heavenly justice
Temper so evenly affection in us,
It ne'er can warp to any wrongfulness.
Of diverse voices is sweet music made:
So in our life the different degrees
Render sweet harmony among these wheels.
   " Within the pearl, that now encloseth us,
Shines Romeo's light, whose goodly deed and fair
Met ill acceptance.   But the Provençals,
That were his foes, have little cause for mirth.
Ill shapes that man his course, who makes his wrong
Of other's worth.   Four daughters were there born
To Raymond Berenger; and every one
Became a queen: and this for him did Romeo,
Though of mean state and from a foreign land.
Yet envious tongues incited him to ask
A reckoning of that just one, who returned
Twelve-fold to him for ten.   Aged and poor
He parted thence: and if the world did know
The heart he had, begging his life by morsels,
'Twould deem the praise it yields him scanty dealt."

Romeo, to whom the poet here alludes, had long and
faithfully served Raymond Berenger, Count of Prov-
ence; and when an account was required of him, of
the revenues he had carefully husbanded and his master
as lavishly disbursed, " he demanded the little mule,"

says Villani, "the staff, and the scrip, with which he had first entered into the Count's service—a stranger pilgrim from the shrine of St. James in Galicia—and departed as he came; nor was it ever known whence he was, or whither he went."*

The spirit of Justinian now returns to his orbit, and joins the other bright beings who dwell there :—

> Thus chanting saw I turn that substance bright,
> With four-fold lustre to its orb again,
> Revolving; and the rest, unto their dance,
> With it, moved also; and, like swiftest sparks,
> In sudden distance from my sight were veiled.
>   Me doubt possessed; and "Speak," it whispered me,
> "Speak, speak unto thy lady; that she quench
> Thy thirst with drops of sweetness."   Yet blank awe,
> Which lords it o'er me, even at the sound
> Of Beatrice's name, did bow me down
> As one in slumber held.   Not long that mood
> Beatrice suffered : she, with such a smile,
> As might have made one blest amid the flames,
> Beaming upon me, thus her words began :
> " Thou in thy thought art pondering (as I deem,
> And what I deem is truth) how just revenge
> Could be with justice punished : from which doubt
> I soon will free thee; so thou mark my words;
> For they of weighty matter shall possess thee."

Here Beatrice instructs the poet on the problem of salvation, reconciling Divine justice with the crucifixion of Jesus Christ, and the necessity of His sufferings, with the punishment of the people who put Him to death.

* Paradiso, vi.

30*

Then referring to the immortality of the soul and the
final resurrection, she concludes :—

> " The angels, O my brother ! and this clime
> Wherein thou art, impassible and pure,
> I call created, even as they are
> In their whole being.   But the elements
> Which thou hast named, and what of them is made,
> Are by created virtue informed : create,
> Their substance; and create, the informing virtue
> In these bright stars, that round them circling move.
> The soul of every brute and of each plant,
> The ray and motion of the sacred lights,
> Draw from complexion with meet power endued.
> But this our life the eternal good inspires
> Immediate, and enamors of itself;
> So that our wishes rest forever here.
>
> " And hence thou mayst by inference conclude
> Our resurrection certain, if thy mind
> Consider how the human flesh was framed,
> When both our parents at the first were made."*

Dante finds himself in the planet Venus :—

> I was not ware that I was wafted up
> Into its orb; but the new loveliness,
> That graced my lady, gave me ample proof
> That we had entered there.   And as in flame
> A sparkle is distinct, or voice in voice
> Discerned, when one its even tenor keeps,
> The other comes and goes; so in that light
> I other luminaries saw, that coursed

* Paradiso, vii.

In circling motion, rapid more or less,
As their eternal vision each impels.
    Never was blast from vapor charged with cold,
Whether invisible to eye or no,
Descended with such speed; it had not seemed
To linger in dull tardiness, compared
To those celestial lights, that towards us came,
Leaving the circuit of their joyous ring,
Conducted by the lofty seraphim.
And after them, who in the van appeared,
Such an Hosanna sounded as hath left
Desire, ne'er since extinct in me, to hear
Renewed the strain.   Then, parting from the rest,
One near us drew, and sole began: " We all
Are ready at thy pleasure, well disposed
To do thee gentle service.   We are they,
To whom thou in the world erewhile didst sing;
' O ye! whose intellectual ministry
Moves the third heaven:' and in one orb we roll,
One motion, one impulse, with those who rule
Princedoms in heaven; yet are of love so full,
That to please thee 'twill be as sweet to rest."
    After mine eyes had with meek reverence
Sought the celestial guide, and were by her
Assured, they turned again unto the light,
Who had so largely promised : and with voice
That bore the lively pressure of my zeal,
" Tell who ye are," I cried.   Forthwith it grew
In size and splendor, through augmented joy;
And thus it answered: "A short date, below,
The world possessed me.   Had the time been more,
Much evil, that will come, had never chanced.
My gladness hides thee from me, which doth shine

> Around, and shroud me, as an animal
> In its own silk enswathed. 'Thou lovedst me well,
> And hadst good cause ; for had my sojourning
> Been longer on the earth, the love I bare thee
> Had put forth more than blossoms."

The shade reveals himself as Charles Martel, the son of Charles II., King of Naples, who had inherited from his mother Maria, sister of Ladislaus IV., King of Hungary, the right to that crown. Charles was crowned at Naples ; but before he could obtain possession of his kingdom he died, in 1295, at the age of twenty-three years. Four years before his death he had married Clemenza, daughter of Rudolph of Hapsburg, Emperor of Germany, by whom he had a son, Carlo Roberto, or Carobert, who, in 1308, was elected King of Hungary. Dante had met Charles Martel in Naples, in his official visits to that city, and entertained for him a warm friendship. He had seen him again in 1295, when Charles came to Florence to meet his father and brothers, released from their condition as hostages in the hands of the Aragons. Accompanied by two hundred young cavaliers, dressed like the King in Hungarian costume, the young prince was received by the Florentines with great demonstrations of affection, and in these festivities Dante had taken a prominent part. Charles here describes the lands over which he had the right to rule, and says that, had it not been for the ill policy followed by his ancestor, Charles of Anjou, which resulted in the massacre of the Sicilian Vespers, his dynasty would not have been expelled from Sicily. If his brother Robert would remember that event, he would not allow the courtiers whom he had brought with him from Catalonia to devour the people over whom he rules. His bark is already overladen, and needs not more freight. He, the son of Charles II., so liberal and splendid, is too penurious himself, and too greedy, to have ministers who add to the burdens which he imposes on the people. Here the spirit answers the question proposed by Dante, how a covetous son can spring from a liberal father. A philosophical dissertation follows, on the causes why children differ in disposition from their parents. Nature has made all things right, and directed to certain ends; she has accordingly endowed men with different qualities, so as to render possible the various offices required by civil society. It is only by following his calling that man can succeed.

> .... "Nature ever,
> Finding discordant fortune, like all seed
> Out of its proper climate, thrives but ill.
> And were the world below content to mark
> And work on the foundation nature lays,
> It would not lack supply of excellence.
> But ye perversely to religion strain
> Him, who was born to gird on him the sword,
> And of the fluent phraseman make your king:
> Therefore your steps have wandered from the path."*

The next canto opens with an apostrophe to the beautiful Clemenza, the daughter of Charles Martel

* Paradiso, viii.

and wife of Louis X., King of France, who was still living when these verses were written.

> And now the visage of that saintly light
> Was to the sun, that fills it, turned again,
> As to the good, whose plenitude of bliss
> Sufficeth all.   O ye misguided souls!
> Infatuate, who from such a good estrange
> Your hearts, and bend your gaze on vanity,
> Alas for you!—And lo! toward me, next,
> Another of those splendent forms approached,
> That, by its outward brightening, testified
> The will it had to pleasure me.   The eyes
> Of Beatrice, resting, as before,
> Firmly upon me, manifested forth
> Approval of my wish.   "And O," I cried,
> "Blest spirit! quickly be my will performed;
> And prove thou to me, that my inmost thoughts
> I can reflect on thee."   Thereat the light,
> That yet was new to me, from the recess,
> Where it before was singing, thus began,
> As one who joys in kindness.

The spirit reveals itself to be that of Cunizza, sister of Ezzelino III., the tyrant who, descending from his castle of Romano, situated on a hill between the Marca Trevigiana, Padua, and Venice, had carried slaughter and conflagration through the surrounding country. Cunizza had been beloved by Sordello, and thus finds herself in the planet Venus; but she does not regret the love which prevents her from rising higher in heaven. She points out the lustrous splendor of Folco of Genoa, a celebrated Provençal poet, commonly called Folques of Marseilles. She says, that before the memory of Folco shall perish on the earth, many ages will have passed; and she exclaims :—

> " Consider thou
> If to excel be worthy man's endeavor,
> When such life may attend the first."

She takes occasion to inveigh against the people of the Marca Trevigiana and of Padua, for their vices, and foretells many calamities which afterwards befell them. The spirit of Folco—

> . . . . . that other joyance, meanwhile waxed
> A thing to marvel at, in splendor glowing,
> Like choicest ruby stricken by the sun.
> For, in that upper clime, effulgence comes
> Of gladness, as here laughter: and below,
> As the mind saddens, murkier grows the shade.

Folco now relates the story of his love for a lady believed to have been Adalagia, wife of Baral of Marseilles, at whose court he lived. On her death he became a monk, and was soon after elected bishop of that city, then archbishop of Toulouse. He explains the reason why his passion did not prevent him from entering heaven :—

> And yet there bides
> No sorrowful repentance here, but mirth,
> Not for the fault (that doth not come to mind),
> But for the virtue, whose o'erruling sway

And providence have wrought thus quaintly.   Here
The skill is looked into, that fashioneth
With such effectual working, and the good
Discerned, accruing to the lower world
From this above.

He then points out the spirit of Rahab, the harlot of
Jericho, sparkling as the sunbeam on clear water.   She
is blessed—

.."For that she favored first the high exploit
Of Joshua on the holy land, whereof
The Pope recks little now.   Thy city, plant
Of him, that on his Maker turned the back,
And of whose envying so much woe hath sprung,
Engenders and expands the cursèd flower,
That hath made wander both the sheep and lambs,
Turning the shepherd to a wolf.   For this,
The Gospel and great teachers laid aside,
The decretals, as their stuffed margins show,
Are the sole study.   Pope and Cardinals,
Intent on these, ne'er journey but in thought
To Nazareth, where Gabriel oped his wings.
Yet it may chance, ere long, the Vatican,
And other most selected parts of Rome,
That were the grave of Peter's soldiery,
Shall be delivered from the adulterous bond."*

The poet invites the reader to rise with him to the
point in those lofty spheres where the equator inter-
sects the zodiac, to the sun, which is the fourth heaven,
where, led by Beatrice, he finds himself borne with the
velocity of thought.

* Paradiso, ix.

For Beatrice, she who passeth on
So suddenly from good to better, time
Counts not the act, oh then how great must needs
Have been her brightness! What there was i' th' sun
(Where I had entered), not through change of hue,
But light transparent—did I summon up
Genius, art, practice—I might not so speak,
It should be e'er imagined: yet believed
It may be, and the sight be justly craved.
And if our fantasy fail of such height,
What marvel, since no eye above the sun
Hath ever travelled? Such are they dwell here,
Fourth family of the Omnipotent Sire,
Who of His Spirit and of His offspring shows;
And holds them still enraptured with the view.
And thus to me Beatrice: " Thank, oh thank
The Sun of angels, Him, who by His grace
To this perceptible hath lifted thee."

   Never was heart in such devotion bound,
And with complacency so absolute
Disposed to render up itself to God,
As mine was at those words: and so entire
The love for Him, that held me, it eclipsed
Beatrice in oblivion. Naught displeased
Was she, but smiled thereat so joyously,
That of her laughing eyes the radiance brake,
And scattered my collected mind abroad.
   Then saw I a bright band, in liveliness
Surpassing, who themselves did make the crown,
And us their centre: yet more sweet in voice,
Than, in their visage, beaming. Cinctured thus,
Sometime Latona's daughter we behold,
When the impregnate air retains the thread

3¹

That weaves her zone.   In the celestial court,
Whence I return, are many jewels found,
So dear and beautiful, they cannot brook
Transporting from that realm : and of these lights
Such was the song.   Who doth not prune his wing
To soar up thither, let him look from thence
For tidings from the dumb.   When, singing thus,
Those burning suns had circled round us thrice,
As nearest stars around the fixed pole ;
Then seemed they like to ladies, from the dance
Not ceasing, but suspense, in silent pause,
Listening, till they have caught the strain anew :
Suspended so they stood : and, from within,
Thus heard I one, who spake : " Since with its beam
The grace, whence true love lighteth first his flame,
That after doth increase by loving, shines
So multiplied in thee, it leads thee up
Along this ladder, down whose hallowed steps
None e'er descend, and mount them not again ;
Who from his vial should refuse thee wine
To slake thy thirst, no less constrained were,
Than water flowing not unto the sea.
Thou fain wouldst hear what plants are these, that bloom
In the bright garland, which, admiring, girds
This fair dame round, who strengthens thee for heaven."

The voice is that of Thomas Aquinas, the pupil of
Albertus Magnus, the angel of the schools.   He points
out to the poet the great luminaries of the Church :
Gratian, the Benedictine monk, author of an abridg-
ment of the canon law ; Peter Lombard, professor at
the University of Paris, then bishop of the same city ;
Solomon, endowed with sapience so profound, that no

second has ever risen with a mind of such wide amplitude; St. Dionysius the Areopagite, to whom was shown the nature and the ministry of the angels; then St. Ambrose, the teacher of St. Augustine; Boëthius, the saintly soul that shows the world's deceitfulness to all who hear him; Isidore, archbishop of Seville; the venerable Bede; Richard of St. Victor; and Sigier, the teacher of the poet while in Paris. Forthwith—

> As clock, that calleth up the spouse of God
> To win her bridegroom's love at matin's hour,
> Each part of other fitly drawn and urged,
> Sends out a tinkling sound, of note so sweet,
> Affection springs in well-disposèd breast;
> Thus saw I move the glorious wheel; thus heard
> Voice answering voice, so musical and soft,
> It can be known but where day endless shines.*
>   O fond anxiety of mortal men!
> How vain and inconclusive arguments
> Are those, which make thee beat thy wings below!
> For statutes one, and one for aphorisms
> Was hunting; this the priesthood followed; that,
> By force or sophistry, aspired to rule;
> To rob, another; and another sought,
> By civil business, wealth; one, moiling, lay
> Tangled in net of sensual delight;
> And one to wistless indolence resigned;
> What time from all these empty things escaped,
> With Beatrice, I thus gloriously
> Was raised aloft, and made the guest of heaven.

* Paradiso, x.

Dante here beholds the light in which the spirit of Aquinas dwells, smiling with gladness. A member of the Dominican Order, St. Thomas is introduced to exalt the life of St. Francis of Assisi; as, in the following canto, St. Bonaventura, of the Franciscan Order, celebrates the praise of St. Dominic, with the manifest intention of condemning all sectarian spirit between the various denominations of Christianity, and of rebuking the monks of the two orders for their jeal-ousies and quarrels. Corresponding to certain tempo-rary wants of society, these religious institutions had been powerful instruments of civilization, which, on its first rising from barbarism, could not but receive an impulse through the saintly devotion, the ardent zeal, and the Christian virtues, of which their founders were noble examples. The poet felt particular veneration for the saint of Assisi, a bold reformer of the Church, who had united a tender sympathy with the charms and beauties of nature, to a character ennobled by the sen-timent of his entire dependence on God, and had em-bodied in his life of poverty and self-denial the ideal of the religion of Christ. He was born in Assisi, 1182; in early life, called by the voice of God, he renounced all worldly goods, and, against the will of his father, com-menced a new life as a begging friar, living in humility and poverty. Followed by many religious enthusiasts, in 1210 he founded the Order of Franciscans, and con-secrated the noble ladies of Assisi, St. Clare and St. Agnes, who felt themselves called to imitate him. His

Order was approved by Innocent III., under the influence of a dream, in which he saw the saint propping up the Church with his shoulders; the institution was confirmed by Honorius III. St. Francis visited Egypt, in order to preach the Gospel, but soon returned to Italy. According to the legend, in 1226, while on Mount Vernia, he received the *stigmata*, or marks resembling the wounds of Christ, on his body; and two years after, when he died, he was seen by Father Elias, the friend of Frederick II., ascending to heaven, in the form of a brilliant star, on a white cloud—the birds, whom the saint loved (his brothers, as he delighted to call them), singing his requiem as he ascended. St. Thomas thus alludes to the principal events in the life of St. Francis, and particularly to his marriage with poverty, a figure which was adopted by Cimabue and Giotto, in the history of the saint painted by them in the church of the Franciscans of Assisi :—

> " Between Tupino, and the wave that falls
> From blest Ubaldo's chosen hill, there hangs ·
> Rich slope of mountain high, whence heat and cold
> Are wafted through Perugia's eastern gate;
> And Nocera with Gualdo, in its rear,
> Mourn for their heavy yoke. Upon that side,
> Where it doth break its steepness most, arose ·
> A sun upon the world, as duly this
> From Ganges doth: therefore let none, who speak
> Of that place, say Ascesi; for its name
> Were lamely so delivered; but the East,
> To call things rightly, be it henceforth styled.

31*

He was not yet much distant from his rising,
When his good influence 'gan to bless the earth.
A dame, to whom none openeth pleasure's gate
More than to death, was, 'gainst his father's will,
His stripling choice: and he did make her his,
Before the spiritual court, by nuptial bonds,
And in his father's sight: from day to day,
Then loved her more devoutly. She, bereaved
Of her first husband, slighted and obscure,
Thousand and hundred years and more, remained
Without a single suitor, till he came.
Nor aught availed, that, with Amyclas, she
Was found unmoved at rumor of his voice,
Who shook the world: nor aught her constant boldness
Whereby with Christ she mounted on the cross,
When Mary stayed beneath. But not to deal
Thus closely with thee longer, take at large
The lovers' titles—Poverty and Francis.
Their concord and glad looks, wonder and love,
And sweet regard gave birth to holy thoughts,
So much, that venerable Bernard first
Did bare his feet, and, in pursuit of peace
So heavenly, ran, yet deemed his footing slow.
O hidden riches! O prolific good!
Egidius bares him next, and next Sylvester,
And follow, both, the bridegroom: so the bride
Can please them. Thenceforth goes he on his way,
The father and the master, with his spouse,
And with that family, whom now the cord
Girt humbly: nor did abjectness of heart
Weigh down his eyelids, for that he was son
Of Pietro Bernardone, and by men
In wondrous sort despised. But royally

His hard intention he to Innocent
Set forth; and, from him, first received the seal
On his religion.   Then, when numerous flocked
The tribe of lowly ones, that traced *his* steps,
Whose marvellous life deservedly were sung
In heights empyreal; through Honorius' hand
A second crown, to deck their Guardian's virtues,
Was by the eternal Spirit inwreathed : and when
He had, through thirst of martyrdom, stood up
In the proud Soldan's presence, and there preached
Christ and His followers, but found the race
Unripened for conversion; back once more
He hasted (not to intermit his toil),
And reaped Ausonian lands.   On the hard rock,
'Twixt Arno and the Tiber, he from Christ
Took the last signet, which his limbs two years
Did carry.   Then, the season come that he,
Who to such good had destined him, was pleased
To advance him to the meed, which he had earned
By his self-humbling; to his brotherhood,
As their just heritage, he gave in charge
His dearest lady : and enjoined their love
And faith to her; and, from her bosom, willed
His goodly spirit should move forth, returning
To its appointed kingdom; nor would have
His body laid upon another bier."

Here St. Thomas pays a tribute of veneration to St.
Dominic, the founder of the Order to which he belonged, and rebukes the Dominicans of his own time,
who had abandoned the spirit of their patriarch, and
given themselves up to a worldly life.*

* Paradiso, xi.

Soon as its final word the blessed flame
Had raised for utterance, straight the holy mill
Began to wheel; nor yet had once revolved,
Or e'er another, circling, compassed it,
Motion to motion, song to song, conjoining;
Song, that as much our muses doth excel,
Our Syrens with their tuneful pipes, as ray
Of primal splendor doth its faint reflex.
As when, if Juno bid her handmaid forth,
Two arches parallel, and tricked alike,
Span the thin cloud, the outer taking birth
From that within (in manner of that voice
Whom love did melt away, as sun the mist),
And they who gaze, presageful call to mind
The compact made with Noah, of the world
No more to be o'erflowed; about us thus,
Of sempiternal roses, bending, wreathed
Those garlands twain; and to the innermost
E'en thus the external answered. When the footing,
And other great festivity, of song,
And radiance, light with light accordant, each
Jocund and blithe, had at their pleasure stilled
(E'en as the eyes, by quick volition moved,
Are shut and raised together), from the heart
Of one among the new lights moved a voice,
That made me seem like needle to the star,
In turning to its whereabout.

This light proves to be the spirit of St. Bonaventura,
who sings the praise of St. Dominic, the Castilian
monk :—

  " The loving minion of the Christian faith,
  The hallowed wrestler, gentle to his own,

And to his enemies terrible.   So replete
His soul with lively virtue, that when first
Created, even in the mother's womb,
It prophesied.   When, at the sacred font,
The spousals were complete 'twixt faith and him,
Where pledge of mutual safety was exchanged,
The dame, who was his surety, in her sleep
Beheld the wondrous fruit, that was from him
And from his heirs to issue.   And that such
He might be construed, as indeed he was,
She was inspired to name him of his owner,
Whose he was wholly; and so called him Dominic.
And I speak of him, as the laborer,
Whom Christ in His own garden chose to be
His helpmate.   Messenger he seemed, and friend
Fast knit to Christ; and the first love he showed,
Was after the first counsel that Christ gave.
Many a time his nurse, at entering, found
That he had risen in silence, and was prostrate,
As who should say, 'My errand was for this.'
O happy father! Felix rightly named.
O favored mother! rightly named Joanna;
If that do mean, as men interpret it.
Not for the world's sake, for which now they toil
Upon Ostiense and Taddeo's lore,
But for the real manna, soon he grew
Mighty in learning; and did set himself
To go about the vineyard, that soon turns
To wan and withered, if not tended well:
And from the see (whose bounty to the just
And needy is gone by, not through its fault,
But his who fills it basely), he besought,
No dispensation for commuted wrong,

Nor the first vacant fortune, nor the tenths
That to God's paupers rightly appertain,
But, 'gainst an erring and degenerate world,
License to fight, in favor of that seed
From which the twice twelve scions gird thee round.
Then, with sage doctrine and good-will to help,
Forth on his great apostleship he fared,
Like torrent bursting from a lofty vein;
And, dashing 'gainst the stocks of heresy,
Smote fiercest, where resistance was most stout.
Thence many rivulets have since been turned,
Over the garden catholic to lead
Their living waters, and have fed its plants."

St. Bonaventura deplores the decline of the true
faith which had given birth to religious orders, and
points out other spirits who are dancing in the circle.*

Let him, who would conceive what now I say,
Imagine (and retain the image firm
As mountain rock, the whilst he hears me speak),
Of stars, fifteen, from midst the ethereal host
Selected, that, with lively ray serene,
O'ercome the massiest air: thereto imagine
The wain, that, in the bosom of our sky,
Spins ever on its axle night and day,
With the bright summit of that horn, which swells
Due from the pole, round which the first wheel rolls,
To have ranged themselves in fashion of two signs
In heaven, such as Ariadne made,
When death's chill seized her; and that one of them
Did compass in the other's beam; and both

* Paradiso, xii.

In such sort whirled around, that each should tend
With opposite motion : and, conceiving thus,
Of that true constellation, and the dance
Twofold, that circled me, he shall attain
As 'twere the shadow ; for things there as much
Surpass our usage, as the swiftest heaven
Is swifter than the Chiana.   There was sung
No Bacchus, and no Io Pæan, but
Three Persons in the Godhead, and in one
Person that nature and the human joined.

St. Thomas now instructs the poet in the mystery of creation, explaining the metaphysical relation of created things to the Deity, and exalts Adam and Jesus as the ideals of humanity.   He warns Dante against assenting to any proposition without having duly examined it.

" Let not the people be too swift to judge ;
As one who reckons on the blades in field,
Or e'er the crop be ripe.   For I have seen
The thorn frown rudely all the winter long,
And after bear the rose upon its top ;
And bark, that all her way across the sea
Ran straight and speedy, perish at the last
E'en in the haven's mouth.   Seeing one steal,
Another bring his offering to the priest,
Let not Dame Birtha and Sir Martin thence
Into heaven's counsels deem that they can pry :
For one of these may rise, the other fall."*

When the great spirit of Aquinum ceases, Beatrice, conscious of the unexpressed desire of Dante, says :—

* Paradiso, xiii.

　　　　　　　　　　　　" Need there is (though yet
He tells it to you not in words, nor e'en
In thought) that he should fathom to its depth
Another mystery.　Tell him, if the light,
Wherewith your substance blooms, shall stay with you
Eternally, as now; and, if it doth,
How, when ye shall regain your visible forms,
The sight may without harm endure the change,
That also tell."　As those, who in a ring
Tread the light measure, in their fitful mirth
Raise loud the voice, and spring with gladder bound;
Thus, at the hearing of that pious suit, .
The saintly circles, in their tourneying
And wondrous note, attested new delight.
　　Whoso laments, that we must doff this garb
Of frail mortality, thenceforth to live
Immortally above; he hath not seen
The sweet refreshing of that heavenly shower.
　　Him, who lives ever, and forever reigns
In mystic union of the Three in One,
Unbounded, bounding all, each spirit thrice
Sang, with such melody, as, but to hear,
For highest merit were an ample meed.

Solomon, the goodliest light, now, with voice as
gentle as that with which the angel once saluted Mary,
thus replies :—

　　" Long as the joy of Paradise shall last,
Our love shall shine around that raiment, bright
As fervent; fervent as, in vision, blest;
And that as far, in blessedness, exceeding,
As it hath grace, beyond its virtue, great.
Our shape, regarmented with glorious weeds

Of saintly flesh, must, being thus entire,
Show yet more gracious.   Therefore shall increase
Whate'er, of light, gratuitous imparts
The Supreme Good; light, ministering aid,
The better to disclose His glory; whence,
The vision needs increasing, must increase
The fervor which it kindles; and that too
The ray that comes from it.   But as the gleed
Which gives out flame, yet in its whiteness shines
More livelily than that, and so preserves
Its proper semblance; thus this circling sphere
Of splendor shall to view less radiant seem,
Than shall our fleshly robe, which yonder earth
Now covers.   Nor will such excess of light
O'erpower us, in corporeal organs made
Firm, and susceptible of all delight."
    So ready and so cordial an "Amen"
Followed from either choir, as plainly spoke
Desire of their dead bodies; yet perchance
Not for themselves, but for their kindred dear,
Mothers and sires, and those whom best they loved,
Ere they were made imperishable flame.
    And lo! forthwith there rose up round about
A lustre, over that already there;
Of equal clearness, like the brightening up
Of the horizon.   As at evening hour
Of twilight, new appearances through heaven
Peer with faint glimmer, doubtfully descried;
So, there, new substances, methought, began
To rise in view beyond the other twain,
And wheeling, sweep their ampler circuit wide.
    O genuine glitter of eternal Beam!
With what a sudden whiteness did it flow,

32

O'erpowering vision in me.　But so fair,
So passing lovely, Beatrice showed,
Mind cannot follow it, nor words express
Her infinite sweetness.　Thence mine eyes regained
Power to look up; and I beheld myself,
Sole with my lady, to more lofty bliss
Translated: for the star, with warmer smile
Impurpled, well denoted our ascent.

The poet now finds himself with Beatrice in the planet Mars, which contains the spirits of those who died in defence of the Christian faith.　They appear to him as lights, forming two luminous lists in the form of a cross, extending over the surface of the planet, along which they move.

　　　　　　　With such mighty sheen
And mantling crimson, in two listed rays
The splendors shot before me, that I cried,
" God of Sabaoth! that dost prank them thus!"
　As leads the galaxy from pole to pole,
Distinguished into greater lights and less,
Its pathway, which the wisest fail to spell;
So thickly studded, in the depth of Mars,
Those rays described the venerable sign,
That quadrants in the round conjoining frame.
　Here memory mocks the toil of genius.　Christ
Beam'd on that cross; and pattern fails me now;
But whoso takes his cross, and follows Christ,
Will pardon me for that I leave untold,
When in the fleckered dawning he shall spy
The glitterance of Christ.　From horn to horn,
And 'tween the summit and the base, did move

Lights scintillating, as they met and passed.
Thus oft are seen with ever-changeful glance,
Straight or athwart, now rapid and now slow,
The atomies of bodies, long or short,
To move along the sunbeam, whose slant line
Checkers the shadow interposed by art
Against the noontide heat.   And as the chime
Of minstrel music, dulcimer, and harp
With many strings, a pleasant dinning makes
To him, who heareth not distinct the note;
So from the lights, which there appeared to me,
Gathered along the cross a melody,
That, indistinctly heard, with ravishment
Possessed me.   Yet I marked it was a hymn
Of lofty praises; for there came to me
" Arise," and " Conquer," as to one who hears
And comprehends not.   Me such ecstasy
O'ercame, that never, till that hour, was thing
That held me in so sweet imprisonment.*

   True love, that ever shows itself as clear
In kindness, as loose appetite in wrong,
Silenced that lyre harmonious, and stilled
The sacred chords, that are by Heaven's right hand
Unwound and tightened.   How to righteous prayers
Should they not hearken, who, to give me will
For praying, in accordance thus were mute ?
He hath in sooth good cause for endless grief,
Who, for the love of thing that lasteth not,
Despoils himself forever of that love.

   As oft along the still and pure serene,
At nightfall, glides a sudden trail of fire,
Attracting with involuntary heed

* Paradiso, xiv.

The eye to follow it, erewhile at rest;
And seems some star that shifted place in heaven,
Only that, whence it kindles, none is lost,
And it is soon extinct; thus from the horn,
That on the dexter of the cross extends,
Down to its foot, one luminary ran
From mid the cluster shone there; yet no gem
Dropp'd from its foil: and through the beamy list,
Like flame in alabaster, glowed its course.
   So forward stretched him (if of credence aught
Our greater muse may claim) the pious ghost
Of old Anchises, in the Elysian bower,
When he perceived his son. "O thou, my blood!
O most exceeding grace divine! to whom,
As now to thee, hath twice the heavenly gate
Been e'er unclosed?" So spake the light: whence I
Turned me toward him; then unto my dame
My sight directed: and on either side
Amazement waited me; for in her eyes
Was lighted such a smile, I thought that mine
Had dived unto the bottom of my grace
And of my bliss in Paradise. Forthwith,
To hearing and to sight grateful alike,
The spirit to his proem added things
I understood not, so profound he spake:
Yet not of choice, but through necessity,
Mysterious; for his high conception soared
Beyond the mark of mortals. When the flight
Of holy transport had so spent its rage,
That nearer to the level of our thought
The speech descended; the first sounds I heard
Were: "Blest be thou, Triunal Deity!
That such favor in my seed vouchsafed."

Then followed: "No unpleasant thirst, though long,
Which took me reading in the sacred book,
Whose leaves or white or dusky never change,
Thou hast allayed, my son! within this light,
From whence my voice thou hear'st: more thanks to her,
Who, for such lofty mounting, has with plumes
Begirt thee.   Thou dost deem thy thoughts to me
From Him transmitted, who is first of all,
E'en as all numbers ray from unity;
And therefore dost not ask me who I am,
Or why to thee more joyous I appear,
Than any other in this gladsome throng.
The truth is as thou deem'st; for in this life
Both less and greater in that mirror look,
In which thy thoughts, or ere thou think'st, are shown.
But, that the love, which keeps me wakeful ever,
Urging with sacred thirst of sweet desire,
May be contented fully; let thy voice,
Fearless, and frank, and jocund, utter forth
Thy will distinctly, utter forth the wish,
Whereto my ready answer stands decreed."
    I turned me to Beatrice; and she heard
Ere I had spoken, smiling an assent,
That to my will gave wings; and I began:
"To each among your tribe, what time ye kenned
The nature, in whom naught unequal dwells,
Wisdom and love were in one measure dealt;
For that they are so equal in the sun,
From whence ye drew your radiance and your heat,
As makes all likeness scant.   But will and means,
In mortals, for the cause ye well discern,
With unlike wings are fledge.   A mortal, I
Experience inequality like this;

32*

And therefore give no thanks, but in the heart,
For thy paternal greeting. This howe'er
I pray thee, living topaz! that ingemm'st
This precious jewel; let me hear thy name."
    "I am thy root, O leaf! whom to expect
Even, hath pleased me." Thus the prompt reply
Prefacing, next it added: "He, of whom
Thy kindred appellation comes, and who,
These hundred years and more, on its first ledge
Hath circuited the mountain, was my son,
And thy great grandsire. Well befits, his long
Endurance should be shortened by thy deeds.
    "Florence, within her ancient limit-mark,
Which calls her still to matin prayers and noon,
Was chaste and sober, and abode in peace.
She had no armlets and no head-tires then;
No purfled dames; no zone, that caught the eye
More than the person did. Time was not yet,
When at his daughter's birth the sire grew pale,
For fear the age and dowry should exceed,
On each side, just proportion. House was none
Void of its family: nor yet had come
Sardanapalus, to exhibit feats
Of chamber prowess. Montemalo yet
O'er our suburban turret rose; as much
To be surpassed in fall, as in its rising.
I saw Bellincion Berti walk abroad
In leathern girdle, and a clasp of bone;
And, with no artful coloring on her cheeks,
His lady leave the glass. The sons I saw
Of Nerli, and of Vecchio, well content
With unrobed jerkin; and their good dames handling
The spindle and the flax: O happy they!

Each sure of burial in her native land,
And none left desolate a-bed for France.
One waked to tend the cradle, hushing it
With sounds that lulled the parent's infancy:
Another, with her maidens, drawing off
The tresses from the distaff, lectured them
Old tales of Troy, and Fesole, and Rome.
A Salterello and Cianghella we
Had held as strange a marvel, as ye would
A Cincinnatus or Cornelia now.
  " In such composed and seemly fellowship,
Such faithful and such fair equality,
In so sweet household, Mary at my birth
Bestowed me, called on·with loud cries; and there,
In your old baptistery, I was made
Christian at once and Cacciaguida; as were,
My brethren Eliseo and Moronto.
  " From Valdipado came to me my spouse;
And hence thy surname grew. I followed then
The Emperor Conrad; and his knighthood he
Did gird on me; in such good part he took
My valiant service. After him I went
To testify against that evil law,
Whose people, by the shepherd's fault, possess
Your right usurped. There I by that foul crew
Was disentangled from the treacherous world,
Whose base affection many a spirit soils;
And from the martyrdom came to this peace."*

The poet feels disposed to boast of his ancestry,
whereupon he is reminded of his vanity by a smile from
Beatrice. Meantime, Cacciaguida continues his de-

* Paradiso, xv.

scription of Florence as it was in his time. He enu-
merates the principal families of the city, and laments
the introduction of strangers, who, by traffic, growing
in wealth, but not in refinement, were the cause of the
corruption of the city, and of its decline.*

Dante now thus addresses his ancestor :—

> " O plant, from whence I spring! revered and loved!
> Who soar'st so high a pitch, that thou as clear,
> As earthly thought determines two obtuse
> In one triangle not contained, so clear
> Dost see contingencies, ere in themselves
> Existent, looking at the point whereto
> All times are present; I, the while I scaled
> With Virgil the soul-purifying mount,
> And visited the nether world of woe,
> Touching my future destiny have heard
> Words grievous, though I feel me on all sides
> Well squared to Fortune's blows.   Therefore my will
> Were satisfied to know the lot awaits me.
> The arrow, seen beforehand, slacks his flight."
> So said I to the brightness, which erewhile
> To me had spoken; and my will declared,
> As Beatrice willed, explicitly.
> Nor with oracular response obscure,
> Such as, or e'er the Lamb of God was slain,
> Beguiled the credulous nations : but, in terms
> Precise, and unambiguous lore, replied
> The spirit of paternal love, enshrined,
> Yet in his smile apparent; and thus spake :
> " Contingency, whose verge extendeth not
> Beyond the tablet of your mortal mould,

* Paradiso, xvi.

Is all depictured in the eternal light:
But hence deriveth not necessity,
More than the tall ship, hurried down the flood,
Is driven by the eye that looks on it.
From thence as to the ear sweet harmony
From organ comes, so comes before mine eye
The time prepared for thee.   Such as driven out
From Athens, by his cruel stepdame's wiles,
Hippolytus departed; such must thou
Depart from Florence.   This they wish, and this
Contrive, and will ere long effectuate, there,
Where gainful merchandise is made of Christ
Throughout the livelong day.   The common cry
Will, as 'tis ever wont, affix the blame
Unto the party injured: but the truth
Shall, in the vengeance it dispenseth, find
A faithful witness.   Thou shalt leave each thing
Beloved most dearly: this is the first shaft
Shot from the bow of exile.   Thou shalt prove
How salt the savor is of other's bread;
How hard the passage, to descend and climb
By other's stairs.   But that shall gall thee most,
Will be the worthless and vile company,
With whom thou must be thrown into these straits;
For all ungrateful, impious all, and mad,
Shall turn 'gainst thee: but in a little while,
Theirs, and not thine, shall be the crimsoned brow.
Their course shall so evince their brutishness,
To have ta'en thy stand apart shall well become thee.

   " First refuge thou must find, first place of rest,
In the great Lombard's courtesy, who bears,
Upon the ladder perched, the sacred bird.
He shall behold thee with such kind regard,

That 'twixt ye two, the contrary to that
Which 'falls 'twixt other men, the granting shall
Forerun the asking.   With him shalt thou see
That mortal, who was at his birth impressed
So strongly from this star, that of his deeds
The nations shall take note.   His unripe age
Yet holds him from observance; for these wheels
Only nine years have compassed him about.
But, ere the Gascon practise on great Harry,
Sparkles of virtue shall shoot forth in him,
In equal scorn of labors and of gold.
His bounty shall be spread abroad so widely,
As not to let the tongues, e'en of his foes,
Be idle in its praise.   Look thou to him,
And his beneficence: for he shall cause
Reversal of their lot to many people;
Rich men and beggars interchanging fortunes.
And thou shalt bear this written in thy soul,
Of him, but tell it not:" and things he told
Incredible to those who witness them;
Then added: " So interpret thou, my son,
What hath been told thee.—Lo ! the ambushment
That a few circling seasons hide for thee.
Yet envy not thy neighbors: time extends
Thy span beyond their treason's chastisement."
  Soon as the saintly spirit, by silence, marked
Completion of that web, which I had stretched
Before it, warped for weaving; I began,
As one, who in perplexity desires
Counsel of other, wise, benign, and friendly:
" My father ! well I mark how time spurs on
Toward me, ready to inflict the blow,
Which falls most heavily on him who most

Abandoneth himself.   Therefore 'tis good
I should forecast, that, driven from the place
Most dear to me, I may not lose myself
All other by my song.   Down through the world
Of infinite mourning; and along the mount,
From whose fair height my lady's eyes did lift me ;
And, after, through this heaven, from light to light ;
Have I learned that, which if I tell again,
It may with many wofully disrelish :
And, if I am a timid friend to truth,
I fear my life may perish among those,
To whom these days shall be of ancient date."

   The brightness, where enclosed the treasure smiled,
Which I had found there, first shone glisteringly,
Like to a golden mirror in the sun ;
Next answered : " Conscience, dimmed or by its own
Or other's shame, will feel thy saying sharp.
Thou, notwithstanding, all deceit removed,
See the whole vision be made manifest.
And let them wince, who have their withers wrung.
What though, when tasted first, thy voice shall prove
Unwelcome : on digestion, it will turn
To vital nourishment.   The cry thou raisest,
Shall, as the wind doth, smite the proudest summits ;
Which is of honor no light argument.
For this, there only have been shown to thee,
Throughout these orbs, the mountain, and the deep,
Spirits, whom fame hath note of.   For the mind
Of him, who hears, is loath to acquiesce
And fix its faith, unless the instance brought
Be palpable, and proof apparent urge."*

Cacciaguida points out to Dante the spirits of Joshua,

* Paradiso, xvii.

Judas Maccabæus, Charlemagne, Orlando, William I.
of Orange, Rinaldo, Godfrey of Bouillon, and Robert
Guiscard.

          Then the soul
Who spake with me, among the other lights
Did move away, and mix; and with the quire
Of heavenly songsters proved his tuneful skill.
 To Beatrice on my right I bent,
Looking for intimation, or by word
Or act, what next behooved; and did descry
Such mere effulgence in her eyes, such joy,
It passed all former wont. And, as by sense
Of new delight, the man who perseveres
In good deeds, doth perceive, from day to day,
His virtue growing; I e'en thus perceived,
Of my ascent, together with the heaven,
The circuit widened; noting the increase
Of beauty in that wonder. Like the change
In a brief moment on some maiden's cheek,
Which, from its fairness, doth discharge the weight
Of pudency, that stained it; such in her,
And to mine eyes so sudden was the change,
Through silvery whiteness of that temperate star,
Whose sixth orb now enfolded us. I saw,
Within that Jovial cresset, the clear sparks
Of love, that reigned there, fashion to my view
Our language. And as birds, from river-banks
Arisen, now in round, now lengthened troop,
Array them in their flight, greeting, as seems,
Their new-found pastures; so, within the lights,
The saintly creatures flying, sang; and made
Now D, now I, now L, figured i' the air.
First singing to their notes they moved; then, one

Becoming of these signs, a little while
Did rest them, and were mute.   O nymph divine,
Of Pegasean race! who souls, which thou
Inspirest, makest glorious and long-lived, as they
Cities and realms by thee; thou with thyself
Inform me; that I may set forth the shapes,
As fancy doth present them: be thy power
Displayed in this brief song.   The characters,
Vocal and consonant, were fivefold seven.
In order, each, as they appeared, I marked.
Diligite Justitiam, the first,
Both verb and noun all blazoned; and the extreme,
Qui judicatis terram.   In the M
Of the fifth word they held their station;
Making the star seem silver streaked with gold.
And on the summit of the M, I saw
Descending other lights, that rested there,
Singing, methinks, their bliss and primal good.
Then, as at shaking of a lighted brand,
Sparkles innumerable on all sides
Rise scattered, source of augury to the unwise;
Thus more than thousand twinkling lustres hence
Seemed reascending; and a higher pitch
Some mounting, and some less, e'en as the sun,
Which kindleth them, decreed.   And when each one
Had settled in his place, the head and neck
Then saw I of an eagle, livelily
Graved in that streaky fire.   Who painteth there,
Hath none to guide Him: of Himself he guides:
And every line and texture of the nest
Doth own from Him the virtue fashions it.
The other bright beatitude, that seemed
Erewhile, with lilied crowning, well content

33

To over-canopy the M, moved forth,
Following gently the impress of the bird.
    Sweet star, what glorious and thick-studded gems
Declared to me our justice on the earth
To be the effluence of that heaven, which thou,
Thyself a costly jewel, dost inlay.
Therefore I pray the Sovereign Mind, from whom
Thy motion and thy virtue are begun,
That He would look from whence the fog doth rise,
To vitiate thy beam; so that once more
He may put forth His hand 'gainst such as drive
Their traffic in that sanctuary, whose walls
With miracles and martyrdoms were built.
    Ye host of heaven, whose glory I survey!
O beg ye grace for those that are, on earth,
All after ill example gone astray.
War once had for his instrument the sword:
But now 'tis made, taking the bread away,
Which the good Father locks from none.—And thou,
That writest but to cancel, think, that they,
Who for the vineyard, which thou wastest, died,
Peter and Paul, live yet, and mark thy doings.
Thou hast good cause to cry, " My heart so cleaves
To him, that lived in solitude remote,
And for a dance was dragged to martyrdom,
I wist not of the fisherman nor Paul."*
Before my sight appeared, with open wings,
The beauteous image; in fruition sweet,
Gladdening the thronged spirits. Each did seem
A little ruby, whereon so intense
The sunbeam glowed, that to mine eyes it came
In clear refraction. And that, which next
Befalls me to portray, voice hath not uttered,

* Paradiso, xviii.

Nor hath ink written, nor in fantasy
Was e'er conceived.   For I beheld and heard
The beak discourse; and, what intention formed
Of many, singly as of one express,
Beginning: "For that I was just and piteous,
I am exalted to this height of glory,
The which no wish exceeds: and there on earth
Have I my memory left, e'en by the bad
Commended, while they leave its course untrod."
  Thus is one heat from many embers felt;
As in that image many were the loves,
And one the voice that issued from them all:
Whence I addressed them: "O perennial flowers
Of gladness everlasting! that exhale
In single breath your odors manifold;
Breathe now: and let the hunger be appeased,
That with great craving long hath held my soul,
Finding no food on earth.   This well I know;
That if there be in heaven a realm, that shows
In faithful mirror the celestial Justice,
Yours without veil reflects it.   Ye discern
The heed, wherewith I do prepare myself
To hearken; ye, the doubt, that urges me
With such inveterate craving."   Straight I saw,
Like to a falcon issuing from the hood,
That rears his head, and claps him with his wings,
His beauty and his eagerness bewraying;
So saw I move that stately sign, with praise
Of grace divine inwoven, and high song
Of inexpressive joy.

Here the eagle discourses on the mystery of the
Divine justice, and on the reason why man cannot
fully understand it.   He then concludes:—

"O animals of clay! O spirits gross!
The primal will, that in itself is good,
Hath from itself, the chief Good, ne'er been moved.
Justice consists in consonance with it, `
Derivable by no created good,
Whose very cause depends upon its beam."
    As on her nest the stork, that turns about
Unto her young, whom lately she hath fed,
Whiles they with upward eyes do look on her;
So lifted I my gaze; and, bending so,
The ever-blessèd image waved its wings,
Laboring with such deep counsel.   Wheeling round
It warbled, and did say: "As are my notes
To thee, who understand'st them not; such is
The eternal judgment unto mortal ken."

The eagle then inveighs against evil rulers, and exhorts oppressed nations to rise against them :*

    When, disappearing from our hemisphere,
The world's enlightener vanishes, and day
On all sides wasteth; suddenly the sky,
Erewhile irradiate only with his beam,
Is yet again unfolded, putting forth
Innumerable lights wherein one shines.
Of such vicissitude in heaven I thought;
As the great sign, that marshalleth the world
And the world's leaders, in the blessed beak
Was silent: for that all those living lights,
Waxing in splendor, burst forth into songs,
Such as from memory glide and fall away.
    Sweet Love, that dost apparel thee in smiles!
How lustrous was thy semblance in those sparkles,

* Paradiso, xix.

Which merely are from holy thoughts inspired.
    After the precious and bright beaming stones,
That did ingem the sixth light, ceased the chiming
Of their angelic bells; methought I heard
The murmuring of a river, that doth fall
From rock to rock transpicuous, making known
The richness of his spring-head: and as sound
Of cittern, at the fret-board, or of pipe,
Is, at the wind-hole, modulate and tuned;
Thus up the neck, as it were hollow, rose
That murmuring of the eagle; and forthwith
Voice there assumed; and thence along the beak
Issued in form of words, such as my heart
Did look for, on whose tables I inscribed them.
    " The part in me, that sees and bears the sun
In mortal eagles," it began, " must now
Be noted steadfastly: for, of the fires
That figure me, those, glittering in mine eye,
Are chief of all the greatest.   This, that shines
Midmost for pupil, was the same who sang
The Holy Spirit's song, and bare about
The ark from town to town: now doth he know
The merit of his soul-impassioned strains
By their well-fitted guerdon.   Of the five,
That make the circle of the vision, he,
Who to the beak is nearest, comforted
The widow for her son: now doth he know,
How dear it costeth not to follow Christ;
Both from experience of this pleasant life,
And of its opposite.   He next, who follows
In the circumference, for the over-arch,
By true repenting slacked the pace of death:
Now knoweth he, that the decrees of Heaven

33*

Alter not, when, through pious prayer below,
To-day is made to-morrow's destiny.
The other following, with the laws and me,
To yield the shepherd room, passed o'er to Greece;
From good intent, producing evil fruit:
Now knoweth he, how all the ill, derived
From his well-doing, doth not harm him aught;
Though it have brought destruction on the world.
That, which thou seest in the under bow,
Was William, whom that land bewails, which weeps
For Charles and Frederick living: now he knows,
How well is loved in heaven the righteous king;
Which he betokens by his radiant seeming.
Who, in the erring world beneath, would deem
That Trojan Ripheus, in this round, was set,
Fifth of the saintly splendors? now he knows
Enough of that, which the world cannot see;
The grace divine: albeit e'en his sight
Reach not its utmost depth." Like to the lark,
That warbling in the air expatiates long,
Then, trilling out his last sweet melody,
Drops, satiate with the sweetness; such appeared
That image, stamped by the everlasting pleasure,
Which fashions, as they are, all things that be.

As Dante cannot understand how pagans are found in heaven, the eagle, seeing his doubts visible in his face, as colors are seen through glass, explains to him how justice may open the gates of the paradise even to those who have died without baptism, and thus exclaims :—

         .... " O how far removed,
Predestination! is thy root from such

As see not the First Cause entire; and ye,
O mortal men! be wary how ye judge:
For we, who see our Maker, know not yet
The number of the chosen; and esteem
Such scantiness of knowledge our delight:
For all our good is, in that primal good,
Concentrate; and God's will and ours are one."
So, by that form divine, was given to me
Sweet medicine to clear and strengthen sight.
And, as one handling skilfully the harp,
Attendant on some skilful songster's voice,
Bids the chord vibrate; and therein the song
Acquires more pleasure: so the whilst it spake,
It doth remember me, that I beheld
The pair of blessed luminaries move,
Like the accordant twinkling of two eyes,
Their beamy circlets, dancing to the sounds.*
Again mine eyes were fixed on Beatrice;
And, with mine eyes, my soul, that in her looks
Found all contentment.   Yet no smile she wore:
And, "Did I smile," quoth she, "thou wouldst be
    straight
Like Semele when into ashes turned:
For, mounting these eternal palace-stairs,
My beauty, which the loftier it climbs,
As thou hast noted, still doth kindle more,
So shines, that, were no tempering interposed,
Thy mortal puissance would from its rays
Shrink, as the leaf doth from the thunderbolt.
Into the Seventh Splendor are we wafted,
That underneath the burning lion's breast
Beams in this hour commingled with his might."

* Paradiso, xx.

> . . . . I saw reared up,
> In color like to sun-illumined gold,
> A ladder, which my ken pursued in vain,
> So lofty was the summit; down whose steps
> I saw the splendors in such multitude
> Descending, every light in heaven, methought,
> Was shed thence.   As the rooks, at dawn of day,
> Bestirring them to dry their feathers chill,
> Some speed their way a-field; and homeward some
> Returning, cross their flight; while some abide,
> And wheel around their airy lodge : so seemed
> That glitterance, wafted on alternate wing,
> As upon certain stair it came, and clashed
> Its shining.   And one, lingering near us, waxed
> So bright, that in my thought I said, " The love,
> Which this betokens me, admits no doubt."

The spirit explains to Dante that the music in this planet is silent, because his mortal ears would not be able to bear it.   He reveals himself as St. Pier Damiano, of Ravenna, a cardinal of the eleventh century, known for his religious zeal and devotion.

> " 'Twixt either shore
> Of Italy, nor distant from thy land,
> A stony ridge ariseth; in such sort,
> The thunder doth not lift his voice so high.
> They call it Catria : at whose foot, a cell
> Is sacred to the lonely Eremite;
> For worship set apart and holy rites."
> A third time thus it spake; then added: " There
> So firmly to God's service I adhered,
> That with no costlier viands than the juice
> Of olives, easily I passed the heats

Of summer and the winter frosts: content
In heavenward musings.   Rich were the returns
And fertile, which that cloister once was used
To render to these heavens: now 'tis fallen
Into a waste so empty, that ere long
Detection must lay bare its vanity.
Pietro Damiano there was I yclept:
Pietro the sinner, when before I dwelt,
Beside the Adriatic, in the house
Of our blest Lady.   Near upon my close
Of mortal life, through much importuning
I was constrained to wear the hat, that still
From bad to worse is shifted.—Cephas came;
He came, who was the Holy Spirit's vessel;
Barefoot and lean; eating their bread, as chanced,
At the first table.   Modern Shepherds need
Those who on either hand may prop and lead them,
So burly are they grown; and from behind,
Others to hoist them.   Down the palfrey's sides
Spread their broad mantles, so as both the beasts
Are covered with one skin.   O patience! thou
That look'st on this, and dost endure so long."
    I at those accents saw the splendors down
From step to step alight, and wheel, and wax,
Each circuiting, more beautiful.   Round this
They came, and stayed them; uttered then a shout
So loud, it hath no likeness here: nor I
Wist what it spake, so deafening was the thunder.*
    Astounded, to the guardian of my steps
I turned me, like the child, who always runs
Thither for succor, where he trusteth most:
And she was like the mother, who her son

* Paradiso, xxi.

Beholding pale and breathless, with her voice
Soothes him, and he is cheered; for thus she spake,
Soothing me: "Know'st not thou, thou art in heaven?
And know'st not thou, whatever is in heaven,
Is holy; and that nothing there is done,
But is done zealously and well? Deem now,
What change in thee the song, and what my smile
Had wrought, since thus the shout had power to move
    thee."

Looking on, as he is directed by Beatrice, Dante
sees—

A hundred little spheres, that fairer grew
By interchange of splendor. I remained,
As one, who fearful of o'ermuch presuming,
Abates in him the keenness of desire,
Nor dares to question; when, amid those pearls,
One largest and most lustrous onward drew,
That it might yield contentment to my wish;
And, from within it, these the sounds I heard.
  "If thou, like me, beheld'st the charity
That burns among us; what thy mind conceives,
Were uttered. But that, ere the lofty bound
Thou reach, expectance may not weary thee;
I will make answer even to the thought,
Which thou hast such respect of. In old days,
That mountain, at whose side Cassino rests,
Was, on its height, frequented by a race
Deceived and ill-disposed: and I it was,
Who thither carried first the name of Him,
Who brought the soul-subliming truth to man.
And such a speeding grace shone over me,
That from their impious worship I reclaimed

The dwellers round about, who with the world
Were in delusion lost.   These other flames,
The spirits of men contemplative, were all
Enlivened by that warmth, whose kindly force
Gives birth to flowers and fruits of holiness.
Here is Macarius; Romoaldo here;
And here my brethren, who their steps refrained
Within the cloisters, and held firm their heart."

The poet asks the spirit of St. Benedict if he may
obtain the favor of gazing upon his image unveiled :—

" Brother !" he thus rejoined, " in the last sphere
Expect completion of thy lofty aim ;
For there on each desire completion waits,
And there on mine; where every aim is found
Perfect, entire, and for fulfilment ripe.
There all things are as they have ever been :
For space is none to bound ; nor pole divides.
Our ladder reaches even to that clime ;
And so, at giddy distance, mocks thy view.
Thither the patriarch Jacob saw it stretch
Its topmost round; when it appeared to him
With angels laden.   But to mount it now
None lifts his foot from earth : and hence my rule
Is left a profitless stain upon the leaves ;
The walls, for abbey reared, turned into dens ;
The cowls, to sacks choked up with musty meal.
Foul usury doth not more lift itself
Against God's pleasure, than that fruit, which makes
The hearts of monks so wanton : for whate'er
Is in the Church's keeping, all pertains
To such, as sue for Heaven's sweet sake ; and not
To those, who in respect of kindred claim,

Or on more vile allowance.   Mortal flesh
Is grown so dainty, good beginnings last not
From the oak's birth unto the acorn's setting.
His convent Peter founded without gold
Or silver ; I, with prayers and fasting, mine ;
And Francis, his in meek humility.
And if thou note the point, whence each proceeds,
Then look what it hath erred to ; thou shalt find
The white grown murky.   Jordan was turned back,
And a less wonder, than the refluent sea,
May, at God's pleasure, work amendment here."
    So saying, to his assembly back he drew :
And they together clustered into one ;
Then all rolled upward, like an eddying wind.
    The sweet dame beckoned me to follow them :
And, by that influence only, so prevailed
Over my nature, that no natural motion,
Ascending or descending here below,
Had, as I mounted, with my pennon vied.

Dante and his guide now reach the eighth sphere,
that of the fixed stars, and he takes his place in the
constellation of the Twins, under which he was born.

    "Thou art so near the sum of blessedness,"
Said Beatrice, "that behooves thy ken
Be vigilant and clear.   And, to this end,
Or ever thou advance thee further, hence
Look downward, and contemplate, what a world
Already stretched under our feet there lies :
So as thy heart may, in its blithest mood,
Present itself to the triumphal throng,
Which through the ethereal concave, comes rejoicing."
    I straight obeyed ; and with mine eye returned

Through all the seven spheres; and saw this globe
So pitiful of semblance, that perforce
It moved my smiles: and him in truth I hold
For wisest, who esteems it least; whose thoughts
Elsewhere are fixed, him worthiest call and best.
I saw the daughter of Latona shine
Without the shadow, whereof late I deemed
That dense and rare were cause.   Here I sustained
The visage, Hyperion, of thy son;
And marked, how near him with their circles, round
Move Maia and Dione; here discerned
Jove's tempering 'twixt his sire and son; and hence
Their changes and their various aspects,
Distinctly scanned.   Nor might I not descry
Of all the seven, how bulky each, how swift;
Nor, of their several distances, not learn.
This petty area (o'er the which we stride
So fiercely), as along the eternal Twins
I wound my way, appeared before me all,
Forth from the havens stretched unto the hills.
Then, to the beauteous eyes, mine eyes returned.*

As they ascend higher and higher, Dante beholds
Beatrice growing in beauty and splendor; but now a
greater light appears and illumines the heavenly sphere.
Beatrice is looking southward, from whence it approaches.

E'en as the bird, who midst the leafy bower
Has, in her nest, sat darkling through the night,
With her sweet brood; impatient to descry
Their wishèd looks, and to bring home their food,

* Paradiso, xxii.

34

In the fond quest unconscious of her toil :
She, of the time prevenient, on the spray,
That overhangs their couch, with wakeful gaze
Expects the sun ; nor ever, till the dawn,
Removeth from the east her eager ken :
So stood the dame erect, and bent her glance
Wistfully on that region, where the sun
Abateth most his speed ; that, seeing her
Suspense and wondering, I became as one,
In whom desire is wakened, and the hope
Of somewhat new to come fills with delight.
    Short space ensued ; I was not held, I say,
Long in expectance, when I saw the heaven
Wax more and more resplendent ; and " Behold,"
Cried Beatrice, " the triumphal hosts
Of Christ, and all the harvest gathered in,
Made ripe by these revolving spheres."   Meseemed,
That, while she spake, her image all did burn ;
And in her eyes such fulness was of joy,
As I am fain to pass unconstrued by.
    As in the calm full moon, when Trivia smiles,
In peerless beauty, mid the eternal nymphs,
That paint through all its gulfs the blue profound ;
In bright pre-eminence so saw I there
O'er million lamps a sun, from whom all drew
Their radiance, as from ours the starry train :
And, through the living light, so lustrous glowed
The substance, that my ken endured it not.
    O Beatrice ! sweet and precious guide,
Who cheered me with her comfortable words :
" Against the virtue, that o'erpowereth thee,
Avails not to resist.   Here is the Might,
And here the Wisdom, which did open lay
The path, that had been yearnèd for so long,

Betwixt the heaven and earth." Like to the fire,
That, in a cloud imprisoned, doth break out
Expansive, so that from its womb enlarged,
It falleth against nature to the ground;
Thus, in that heavenly banqueting, my soul
Outgrew herself; and, in the transport lost,
Holds now remembrance none of what she was.
  "Ope thou thine eyes, and mark me: thou hast seen
Things, that empower thee to sustain my smile."
  I was as one, when a forgotten dream
Doth come across him, and he strives in vain
To shape it in his fantasy again:
When as that gracious boon was proffered me,
Which never may be cancelled from the book
Wherein the past is written. Now were all
Those tongues to sound, that have, on sweetest milk
Of Polyhymnia and her sisters, fed
And fattened; not with all their help to boot,
Unto the thousandth parcel of the truth,
My song might shadow forth that saintly smile,
How merely, in her saintly looks, it wrought.
And, with such figuring of Paradise,
The sacred strain must leap, like one that meets
A sudden interruption to his road.
But he, who thinks how ponderous the theme,
And that 'tis laid upon a mortal shoulder,
May pardon, if it tremble with the burden.
The track, our venturous keel must furrow, brooks
No unribbed pinnace, no self-sparing pilot.

Beatrice bids Dante turn and behold the Word Divine made incarnate. Christ, with the Virgin Mary by his side, amidst an innumerable host of angels and saints, descends from the Empyrean.

> . . . . As erewhile,
> Through glance of sunlight, streamed through broken
>   cloud,
> Mine eyes a flower-besprinkled mead have seen;
> Though veiled themselves in shade: so saw I there
> Legions of splendors, on whom burning rays
> Shed lightnings from above; yet saw I not
> The fountain whence they flowed.   O gracious virtue!
> Thou, whose broad stamp is on them, higher up
> Thou didst exalt thy glory, to give room
> To my o'erlabored sight.

While the divine light retires upward, to enable the eyes of Dante to endure the vision, he beholds the triumph of the Virgin Mary, crowned by the angel Gabriel.   When at the name

> Of that fair flower, whom duly I invoke
> Both morn and eve, my soul with all her might
> Collected, on the goodliest ardor fixed.
> And, as the bright dimensions of the star
> In heaven excelling, as once here on earth,
> Were, in my eye-balls livelily portray'd;
> Lo! from within the sky a cresset fell,
> Circling in fashion of a diadem;
> And girt the star; and, hovering, round it wheeled.
>   Whatever melody sounds sweetest here,
> And draws the spirit most unto itself,
> Might seem a rent cloud, when it grates the thunder;
> Compared unto the sounding of that lyre,
> Wherewith the goodliest sapphire, that inlays
> The floor of heaven, was crowned.   " Angelic Love
> I am, who thus with hovering flight enwheel

The lofty rapture from that womb inspired,
Where our desire did dwell: and round thee so,
Lady of Heaven! will hover; long as thou
Thy Son shalt follow, and diviner joy
Shall from thy presence gild the highest sphere."
 Such close was to the circling melody:
And, as it ended, all the other lights
Took up the strain, and echoed Mary's name.
The robe that with its regal folds enwraps
The world, and with the nearer breath of God
Doth burn and quiver, held so far retired
Its inner hem and skirting over us,
That yet no glimmer of its majesty
Had streamed unto me; therefore were mine eyes
Unequal to pursue the crownèd flame
That towering rose, and sought the seed it bore.
And like to babe, that stretches forth its arms
For very eagerness toward the breast,
After the milk is taken; so outstretched
Their wavy summits all the fervent band,
Through zealous love to Mary: then, in view,
There halted; and " Regina Cœli " sang
So sweetly, the delight hath left me never.*

Beatrice thus addresses the spirits :—

 "O ye! in chosen fellowship advanced
To the great supper of the blessed Lamb,
Whereon who feeds hath every wish fulfilled;
If to this man through God's grace be vouchsafed
Foretaste of that, which from your table falls,
Or ever death his fated term prescribe;
Be ye not heedless of his urgent will:

 * Paradiso, xxiii.

34*

> But may some influence of your sacred dews
> Sprinkle him.   Of the fount ye alway drink,
> Whence flows what most he craves."   Beatrice spake;
> And the rejoicing spirits, like to spheres
> On firm-set poles revolving, trailed a blaze
> Of comet splendor: and as wheels, that wind
> Their circles in the horologe, so work
> The stated rounds, that to the observant eye
> The first seems still, and as it flew, the last;
> E'en thus their carols weaving variously,
> They, by the measure paced, or swift, or slow,
> Made me to rate the riches of their joy.

The brightest flame, the spirit of St. Peter, now issues forth from the circle, and sings a song so divine, that the fancy of the poet cannot record it. The spirit then addresses Beatrice :—

> " O saintly sister mine ! thy prayer devout
> Is with so vehement affection urged,
> Thou dost unbind me from that beauteous sphere."

Beatrice prays St. Peter to examine Dante on his religious faith, that he may be able to exalt it more. Accordingly, the Chief of the Apostles asks him to declare what is faith. The poet raises his forehead to the light which had spoken, then turns to Beatrice, and, meeting approval in her looks, he defines faith in the words of St. Paul :—

> Faith of things hoped is substance, and the proof
> Of things not seen : and herein doth consist,
> Methinks, its essence.

He explains the definition; says that his conviction perfectly corresponds to his profession, and that he derived it from the Spirit of God, which speaks through the Old and the New Testament. St. Peter asks him how he knows that the Bible is the voice of Heaven, to which he replies that he knows it from the works which were not made by Nature—that is, from miracles. The Apostle catechises him further, and asks him how he knows that the miracles were such as they pretended to be—that is, true and divine :—

> " That all the world," said I, " should have been turned
> To Christian, and no miracle been wrought,
> Would in itself be such a miracle,
> The rest were not an hundredth part so great.
> E'en thou went'st forth in poverty and hunger
> To set the goodly plant, that, from the vine
> It once was, now is grown unsightly bramble."

The poet then thus unfolds his creed :—

> "I in one God believe;
> One sole eternal Godhead, of whose love
> All Heaven is moved, himself unmoved the while.
> Nor demonstration physical alone,
> Or more intelligential and abstruse,
> Persuades me to this faith : but from that truth
> It cometh to me rather, which is shed
> Through Moses; the rapt Prophets; and the Psalms;
> The Gospel; and what ye yourselves did write,
> When ye were gifted of the Holy Ghost.
> In three eternal Persons I believe;

Essence threefold and one; mysterious league
Of union absolute, which, many a time,
The word of gospel lore upon my mind
Imprints: and from this germ, this firstling spark,
The lively flame dilates; and, like heaven's star,
Doth glitter in me."　As the master hears,
Well pleased, and then enfoldeth in his arms
The servant, who hath joyful tidings brought,
And having told the errand keeps his peace;
Thus benediction uttering with song,
Soon as my peace I held, compassed me thrice
The apostolic radiance, whose behest
Had oped my lips: so well their answer pleased.*

Conscious of the importance of this consecration, he hopes soon to return to Florence, to claim the poet's crown there.

　　　　. . . . For I there
First entered on the faith, which maketh souls
Acceptable to God: and, for its sake,
Peter had then circled my forehead thus.

Next from the same circle a light, the spirit of St. James, moves towards St. Peter :—

　　As when the ring-dove by his mate alights;
In circles, each about the other wheels,
And, murmuring, coos his fondness: thus saw I
One, of the other great and glorious prince,
With kindly greeting, hailed; extolling, both,
Their heavenly banqueting: but when an end
Was to their gratulation, silent, each,

* Paradiso, xxiv.

Before me sat they down, so burning bright,
I could not look upon them.

Beatrice addresses St. James, and urges him to exalt the praise of hope. The Apostle asks Dante what he means by hope. Beatrice says :—

" Among her sons, not one more full of hope,
Hath the Church militant: so 'tis of him
Recorded in the sun, whose liberal orb
Enlighteneth all our tribe : and ere his term
Of warfare, hence permitted he is come,
From Egypt to Jerusalem, to see.
The other points, both which thou hast inquired,
Not for more knowledge, but that he may tell
How dear thou hold'st the virtue ; these to him
Leave I : for he may answer thee with ease,
And without boasting, so God give him grace."

The poet now answers the question :—

     .... " Hope," said I,
" Is of the joy to come a sure expectance,
The effect of grace divine and merit preceding.
This light from many a star, visits my heart ;
But flowed to me, the first, from him who sang
The songs of the Supreme ; himself supreme
Among his tuneful brethren. 'Let all hope
In thee,' so spake his anthem, 'who have known
Thy name ; and, with my faith, who know not that ?
From thee, the next, distilling from his spring,
In thine epistle, fell on me the drops
So plenteously, that I on others shower
The influence of their dew." Whileas I spake,

A lamping, as of quick and volleyed lightning,
Within the bosom of that mighty sheen
Played tremulous; then forth these accents breathed:
" Love for the virtue, which attended me
E'en to the palm, and issuing from the field,
Glows vigorous yet within me; and inspires
To ask of thee, whom also it delights,
What promise thou from hope, in chief, dost win."—
" Both Scriptures, new and ancient," I replied,
" Propose the mark (which even now I view)
For souls beloved of God.   Isaias saith,
' That, in their own land, each one must be clad
In twofold vesture,' and their proper land
Is this delicious life.   In terms more full,
And clearer far, thy brother hath set forth
This revelation to us, where he tells
Of the white raiment destined to the saints."
And as the words were ending, from above,
" They hope in thee!" first heard we cried; whereto
Answered the carols all.

The spirit of St. John now appears:

　　Like as a virgin riseth up, and goes,
And enters on the mazes of the dance;
Though gay, yet innocent of worse intent,
Than to do fitting honor to the bride:
So I beheld the new effulgence come
Unto the other two, who in a ring
Wheeled, as became their rapture.   In the dance,
And in the song, it mingled.   And the dame
Held on them fixed her looks; e'en as the spouse,
Silent, and moveless.   " This is he, who lay
Upon the bosom of our pelican:

This he, into whose keeping, from the cross,
The mighty charge was given." 'Thus she spake;
Yet therefore naught the more removed her sight
From marking them: or e'er her words began,
Or when they closed. As he, who looks intent,
And strives with searching ken, how he may see
The sun in his eclipse, and, through desire
Of seeing, loseth power of sight; so I
Peered on that last resplendence, while I heard:
" Why dazzlest thou thine eyes in seeking that,
Which here abides not? Earth my body is,
In earth; and shall be, with the rest, so long,
As till our number equal the decree
Of the Most High. The two that have ascended,
In this our blessed cloister, shine alone
With the two garments. So report below."
    As when, for ease of labor, or to shun
Suspected peril, at a whistle's breath,
The oars, erewhile dashed frequent in the wave,
All rest: the flamy circle at that voice
So rested; and the mingling sound was still,
Which from the trinal band, soft-breathing, rose.
I turned, but ah! how trembled in my thought,
When, looking at my side again to see
Beatrice, I descried her not; although,
Not distant, on the happy coast she stood.*

St. John examines the poet on charity, on its nature
and its motives, arising both from the intellect and the
heart. Meantime, the spirit of Adam appears, shining
through a bright star; and the poet bows to it, like the
leaf—

* Paradiso, xxv.

> That bows its lithe top till the blast is blown;
> By its own virtue reared, then stands aloof.

In compliance with the wishes of Dante, Adam relates when he was placed in the terrestrial paradise, how long he remained there, the language which he spoke, and the real cause of his expulsion.*

> Then " Glory to the Father, to the Son,
> And to the Holy Spirit !" rang aloud
> Throughout all Paradise; that with the song
> My spirit reeled, so passing sweet the strain.
> And what I saw was equal ecstasy:
> One universal smile it seemed of all things;
> Joy past compare; gladness unutterable;
> Imperishable life of peace and love;
> Exhaustless riches, and unmeasured bliss.

The lights in which St. Peter, St. James, St. John, and Adam are embodied, shine before him; and now that of St. Peter begins to wax in brightness, and from its white appearance is transformed into a red flame. A universal silence reigns through the sphere, and forth from the flame the following words resound :—

> " Wonder not, if my hue
> Be changed; for, while I speak, these shalt thou see
> All in like manner change with me.   My place
> He who usurps on earth (my place, ay, mine,
> Which in the presence of the Son of God
> Is void), the same hath made my cemetery
> A common sewer of puddle and of blood;

* Paradiso, xxvi.

The more below his triumph, who from hence
Malignant fell." Such color, as the sun,
At eve or morning, paints an adverse cloud,
Then saw I sprinkled over all the sky.
And as the unblemished dame, who, in herself
Secure of censure, yet at bare report
Of other's failing, shrinks with maiden fear;
So Beatrice, in her semblance, changed:
And such eclipse in heaven, methinks, was seen,
When the Most Holy suffered. Then the words
Proceeded, with voice, altered from itself
So clean, the semblance did not alter more:
"Not to this end was Christ's spouse with my blood,
With that of Linus, and of Cletus, fed;
That she might serve for purchase of base gold:
But for the purchase of this happy life,
Did Sextus, Pius, and Callixtus bleed,
And Urban; they, whose doom was not without
Much weeping sealed. No purpose was of ours,
That on the right hand of our successors,
Part of the Christian people should be set,
And part upon their left; nor that the keys,
Which were vouchsafed me, should for ensign serve
Unto the banners, that do levy war
On the baptized; nor I, for sigil-mark,
Set upon sold and lying privileges:
Which makes me oft to bicker and turn red.
In shepherd's clothing, greedy wolves below
Range wide o'er all the pastures. Arm of God!
Why longer sleep'st thou? Cahorsines and Gascons
Prepare to quaff our blood. O good beginning!
To what a vile conclusion must thou stoop!
But the high providence, which did defend,

35

> Through Scipio, the world's empery for Rome,
> Will not delay its succor: and thou, son,
> Who through thy mortal weight shalt yet again
> Return below, open thy lips, nor hide
> What is by me not hidden."

The poet continues to revolve with the constellation of the Twins, from which he looks down upon the earth. He then ascends to the Primum Mobile, the sphere which imparts movement to the planets below. Beatrice explains the functions which belong to this heaven, and takes occasion to rebuke mankind for its vices, placing the responsibility, however, on bad governments; she then foretells the advent of better times.*

The poet, taking strength from the eyes of Beatrice, looks upward to the Empyrean, and beholds a point darting so sharp light, that no mortal eye can bear it. Around this central light are nine circles of fire, and each—

> As more in number distant from the first,
> Was tardier in motion: and that glowed
> With flame most pure, that to the sparkle of truth
> Was nearest; as partaking most, methinks,
> Of its reality.

These circles are the abodes of the nine orders of angels, and they revolve around the Deity with varying motions, proportioned to their love. Beatrice discourses on the Divine essence and on the angels, and explains

* Paradiso, xxvii.

some apparent opposition between the order of the Empyrean and the economy of the cosmos.*

Beatrice speaks of the creation, and of the relation of the universe to the Creator. She rebukes the vanity and ignorance of the theologians, who presume to speak of things which are beyond their understanding. She also animadverts upon those preachers who, rather than preach the morals of the Gospel, delight to dwell on the creations of their own fancy :—

> " So that men, thus at variance with the truth,
> Dream, though their eyes be open, reckless some
> Of error ; others well aware they err,
> To whom more guilt and shame are justly due.
> Each the known track of sage philosophy
> Deserts, and has a by-way of his own :
> So much the restless eagerness to shine,
> And love of singularity, prevail.
> Yet this, offensive as it is, provokes
> Heaven's anger less, than when the Book of God
> Is forced to yield to man's authority,
> Or from its straightness warped : no reckoning made
> What blood the sowing of it in the world
> Has cost ; what favor for himself he wins,
> Who meekly clings to it.   The aim of all
> Is how to shine : e'en they, whose office is
> To preach the Gospel, let the Gospel sleep,
> And pass their own inventions off instead.
> One tells, how at Christ's suffering the wan moon
> Bent back her steps, and shadowed o'er the sun
> With intervenient disk, as she withdrew :

* Paradiso, xxviii.

Another, how the light shrouded itself
Within its tabernacle, and left dark
The Spaniard, and the Indian, with the Jew.
Such fables Florence in her pulpit hears,
Bandied about more frequent, than the names
Of Bindi and of Lapi in her streets.
The sheep, meanwhile, poor witless ones, return
From pasture, fed with wind: and what avails
For their excuse, they do not see their harm?
Christ said not to His first conventicle,
'Go forth and preach impostures to the world,'
But gave them truth to build on; and the sound
Was mighty on their lips: nor needed they,
Beside the Gospel, other spear or shield,
To aid them in their warfare for the faith.
The preacher now provides himself with store
Of jests and gibes; and, so there be no lack
Of laughter, while he vents them, his big cowl
Distends, and he has won the meed he sought:
Could but the vulgar catch a glimpse the while
Of that dark bird which nestles in his hood,
They scarce would wait to hear the blessing said,
Which now the dotards hold in such esteem,
That every counterfeit, who spreads abroad
The hands of holy promise, finds a throng
Of credulous fools beneath.   St. Anthony
Fattens with this his swine, and others worse
Than swine, who diet at his lazy board,
Paying with unstamped metal for their fare."*

　Noon's fervid hour perchance six thousand miles
From hence is distant; and the shadowy cone
Almost to level on our earth declines;

* Paradiso, xxix.

When, from the midmost of this blue abyss,
By turns some star is to our vision lost.
And straightway as the handmaid of the sun
Puts forth her radiant brow, all, light by light,
Fade; and the spangled firmament shuts in,
E'en to the loveliest of the glittering throng.
Thus vanished gradually from my sight
The triumph, which plays ever round the point,
That overcame me, seeming (for it did)
Engirt by that it girdeth.   Wherefore love,
With loss of other object, forced me bend
Mine eyes on Beatrice once again.
    If all, that hitherto is told of her,
Were in one praise concluded, 'twere too weak
To furnish out this turn.   Mine eyes did look
On beauty, such, as I believe in sooth,
Not merely to exceed our human; but,
That save its Maker, none can to the full
Enjoy it.   At this point o'erpowered I fail;
Unequal to my theme; as never bard
Of buskin or of sock hath failed before.
For as the sun doth to the feeblest sight,
E'en so remembrance of that witching smile
Hath dispossessed my spirit of itself.
Not from that day, when on this earth I first
Beheld her charms, up to that view of them,
Have I with song applausive ever ceased
To follow; but now follow them no more;
My course here bounded, as each artist's is,
When it doth touch the limit of his skill.
    She (such as I bequeath her to the bruit
Of louder trump than mine, which hasteneth on,
Urging its arduous matter to the close)
    35*

Her words resumed, in gesture and in voice
Resembling one accustomed to command:
"Forth from the last corporeal are we come
Into the heaven, that is unbodied light;
Light intellectual, replete with love;
Love of true happiness, replete with joy;
Joy, that transcends all sweetness of delight.
Here shalt thou look on either mighty host
Of Paradise; and one in that array,
Which in the final judgment thou shalt see."
 As when the lightning, in a sudden spleen
Unfolded, dashes from the blinding eyes
The visive spirits, dazzled and bedimmed;
So, round about me, fulminating streams
Of living radiance played, and left me swathed
And veiled in dense impenetrable blaze.
Such weal is in the love, that stills this heaven;
For its own flame the torch thus fitting ever.
 No sooner to my listening ear had come
The brief assurance, than I understood
New virtue into me infused, and sight
Kindled afresh, with vigor to sustain
Excess of light, however pure. I looked;
And, in the likeness of a river, saw
Light flowing, from whose amber-seeming waves
Flashed up effulgence, as they glided on
'Twixt banks, on either side, painted with spring,
Incredible how fair: and, from the tide,
There ever and anon, outstarting, flew
Sparkles instinct with life; and in the flowers
Did set them, like to rubies chased in gold:
Then, as if drunk with odors, plunged again
Into the wondrous flood; from which, as one

Re-entered, still another rose.   "The thirst
Of knowledge high, whereby thou art inflamed
To search the meaning of what here thou seest,
The more it warms thee, pleases me the more.
But first behooves thee of this water drink,
Or e'er that longing be allayed."   So spake
The daystar of mine eyes: then thus subjoined:
"This stream; and these, forth issuing from its gulf,
And diving back, a living topaz each;
With all this laughter on its bloomy shores,
Are but a preface, shadowy of the truth
They emblem: not that, in themselves, the things
Are crude; but on thy part is the defect,
For that thy views not yet aspire so high."
  Never did babe that had outslept his wont,
Rush, with such eager straining, to the milk,
As I toward the water; bending me,
To make the better mirrors of mine eyes
In the refining wave: and as the eaves
Of mine eyelids did drink of it, forthwith
Seemed it unto me turned from length to round.
Then as a troop of maskers, when they put
Their visors off, look other than before;
The counterfeited semblance thrown aside:
So into greater jubilee were changed
Those flowers and sparkles; and distinct I saw,
Before me, either court of heaven displayed.
  O prime enlightener! thou who gavest me strength
On the high triumph of thy realm to gaze;
Grant virtue now to utter what I kenned.
  There is in heaven a light, whose goodly shine
Makes the Creator visible to all
Created, that in seeing Him alone

Have peace; and in a circle spreads so far,
That the circumference were too loose a zone
To girdle in the sun.   All is one beam,
Reflected from the summit of the first,
That moves, which being hence and vigor takes.
And as some cliff, that from the bottom eyes
His image mirrored in the crystal flood,
As if to admire his brave apparelling
Of verdure and of flowers; so, round about,
Eying the light, on more than million thrones,
Stood, eminent, whatever from our earth
Has to the skies returned.   How wide the leaves,
Extended to their utmost, of this rose,
Whose lowest step embosoms such a space
Of ample radiance!   Yet, nor amplitude
Nor height impeded, but my view with ease
Took in the full dimensions of that joy.
Near or remote, what there avails, where God
Immediate rules, and Nature, awed, suspends
Her sway?   Into the yellow of the rose
Perennial, which, in bright expansiveness,
Lays forth its gradual blooming, redolent
Of praises to the never-wintering sun,
As one, who fain would speak, yet holds his peace,
Beatrice led me; and, " Behold," she said,
" This fair assemblage; stoles of snowy white,
How numberless!   The city, where we dwell,
Behold how vast! and these our seats so thronged,
Few now are wanting here.   In that proud stall,
On which, the crown, already o'er its state
Suspended, holds thine eyes—or e'er thyself
Mayst at the wedding sup,—shall rest the soul
Of the great Harry, he who, by the world

Augustus hailed, to Italy must come,
Before her day be ripe.   But ye are sick,
And in your tetchy wantonness as blind,
As is the bantling, that of hunger dies,
And drives away the nurse.   Nor may it be,
That he, who in the sacred forum sways,
Openly or in secret, shall with him
Accordant walk: whom God will not endure
I' the holy office long; but thrust him down
To Simon Magus, where Alagna's priest
Will sink beneath him: such will be his meed."*

The innumerable hosts of angels hover around the
immense snow-white rose, and like a troop of bees—

Amid the vernal sweets alighting now,
Now, clustering, where their fragrant labor glows,
Flew downward to the mighty flower, or rose
From the redundant petals, streaming back
Unto the steadfast dwelling of their joy.
Faces had they of flame, and wings of gold;
The rest was whiter than the driven snow;
And, as they flitted down into the flower,
From range to range, fanning their plumy loins,
Whispered the peace and ardor which they won
From that soft winnowing.   Shadow none, the vast
Interposition of such numerous flight
Cast, from above, upon the flower, or view
Obstructed aught.   For, through the universe,
Wherever merited, celestial light
Glides freely, and no obstacle prevents.
    All there, who reign in safety and in bliss,
Ages long past or new, on one sole mark

* Paradiso, xxx.

Their love and vision fixed.   O trinal beam
Of individual star, that charm'st them thus !
Vouchsafe one glance to gild our storm below.
If the grim brood, from Arctic shores that roamed
(Where Helice forever, as she wheels,
Sparkles a mother's fondness on her son),
Stood in mute wonder mid the works of Rome,
When to their view the Lateran arose
In greatness more than earthly; I, who then
From human to divine had passed, from time
Unto eternity, and out of Florence
To justice and to truth, how might I choose
But marvel too?   'Twixt gladness and amaze,
In sooth, no will had I to utter aught,
Or hear.   And as a pilgrim, when he rests
Within the temple of his vow, looks round
In breathless awe, and hopes sometime to tell
Of all its goodly state ; e'en so mine eyes
Coursed up and down along the living light,
Now low, and now aloft, and now around,
Visiting every step.   Looks I beheld,
Where charity in soft persuasion sat :
Smiles from within and radiance from above ;
And in each gesture grace and honor high.

The poet here turns to speak to Beatrice, but she
has disappeared ; and in her place he beholds by his
side a senior, robed, as the rest, in glory, his face glowing with joy and a father's love.   Dante asks him
where Beatrice is :—

" By Beatrice summoned," he replied,
" I come to aid thy wish.   Looking aloft
To the third circle from the highest, there

Behold her on her throne, whereon her merit
Hath placed her." Answering not, mine eyes I raised,
And saw her, where aloof she sat, her brow
A wreath reflecting of eternal beams.
Not from the centre of the sea so far
Unto the region of the highest thunder,
As was my ken from hers; and yet the form
Came through that medium down, unmixed and pure.

He addresses a prayer to her, and she looks down on him and smiles. Now the senior reveals himself to be St. Bernard, who bids him look higher, on the summit of the rose, where he will see the Virgin Mary, the Queen of Heaven, the apotheosis of womanhood.

. . . . Straight mine eyes I raised; and bright
As, at the birth of morn, the eastern clime
Above the horizon, where the sun declines;
So to mine eyes, that upward, as from vale
To mountain sped, at the extreme bound, a part
Excelled in lustre all the front opposed.
And as the glow burns ruddiest o'er the wave,
That waits the ascending team, which Phaëton
Ill knew to guide, and on each part the light
Diminished fades, intensest in the midst;
So burned the peaceful oriflamb, and slacked
On every side the living flame decayed.
And in that midst their sportive pennons waved
Thousands of angels; in resplendence each
Distinct, and quaint adornment. At their glee
And carol, smiled the Lovely One of heaven,
That joy was in the eyes of all the blest.
Had I a tongue in eloquence as rich,

As is the coloring in Fancy's loom,
'Twere all too poor to utter the least part
Of that enchantment.   When he saw mine eyes
Intent on her, that charmed him ; Bernard gazed
With so exceeding fondness, as infused
Ardor into my breast, unfelt before.*

At the feet of the Holy Virgin, St. Bernard points out Eve, Rachel, Beatrice, Sarah, Judith, Rebecca, and Ruth : on one side, the saints who lived before the advent of Christ ; on the other, those who came after Him.   St. Bernard explains to Dante the causes of the different degrees of glory bestowed upon the saints, and then asks him to raise his eyes again to the Virgin Mary, the visage most resembling the ideal of humanity, Christ ; for through her splendor only, the splendor of womanly loveliness and virtue, can man gain the power to reach perfection.   Forthwith the poet saw

Such floods of gladness on her visage showered,
From holy spirits, winging that profound ;
That, whatsoever I had yet beheld,
Had not so much suspended me with wonder,
Or shown me such similitude of God.
And he, who had to her descended, once,
On earth, now hailed in heaven ; and on poised wing,
"Ave, Maria, Gratia Plena," sang :
To whose sweet anthem all the blissful court,
From all parts answering, rang : that holier joy
Brooded the deep serene.

    *   *   *   *   *

* Paradiso, xxxi.

" But (for the vision hasteneth to an end)
Here break we off, as the good workman doth,
That shapes the cloak according to the cloth ;
And to the primal love our ken shall rise ;
That thou mayst penetrate the brightness, far
As sight can bear thee.   Yet, alas ! in sooth
Beating thy pennons, thinking to advance,
Thou backward fall'st.   Grace then must first be gained ;
Her grace, whose might can help thee.   Thou in prayer
Seek her : and, with affection, while I sue,
Attend, and yield me all thy heart."   He said ;
And thus the saintly orison began.*

The Paradiso closes with the apotheosis of man in
God, the union of the human with the divine nature,
obtained through the influence of the eternal Feminine,
symbolized in the Holy Virgin, the ideal woman, at
once the mother and the daughter of the race.   Borrowing the language of the mediæval Church, the poet
thus causes St. Bernard to pray to her in his behalf :—

" O Virgin Mother, daughter of thy Son !
Created beings all in lowliness
Surpassing, as in height above them all ;
Term by the eternal counsel preordained ;
Ennobler of thy nature, so advanced
In thee, that its great Maker did not scorn,
To make Himself His own creation ;
For in thy womb rekindling shone the love
Revealed, whose genial influence makes now
This flower to germin in eternal peace :

* Paradiso, xxxii.

Here thou to us, of charity and love,
Art, as the noonday torch; and art, beneath,
To mortal men, of hope a living spring.
So mighty art thou, lady, and so great,
That he, who grace desireth, and comes not
To thee for aidance, fain would have desire
Fly without wings.　Not only him, who asks,
Thy bounty succors; but doth freely oft
Forerun the asking.　Whatsoe'er may be
Of excellence in creature, pity mild,
Relenting mercy, large munificence,
Are all combined in thee.　Here kneeleth one,
Who of all spirits hath reviewed the state,
From the world's lowest gap unto this height.
Suppliant to thee he kneels, imploring grace
For virtue yet more high, to lift his ken
Toward the bliss supreme.　And I, who ne'er
Coveted sight, more fondly, for myself,
Than now for him, my prayers to thee prefer
(And pray they be not scant), that thou wouldst drive
Each cloud of his mortality away,
Through thine own prayers, that on the sovereign joy
Unveiled he gaze.　This yet, I pray thee, Queen,
Who canst do what thou wilt; that in him thou
Wouldst, after all he hath beheld, preserve
Affection sound, and human passions quell.
Lo! where, with Beatrice, many a saint
Stretch their clasped hands, in furtherance of my suit."

The poet looks on the central light; but he is
unable to relate his transcendent vision—in which
human nature appears to him sublimated and identified with the very nature of the Deity.

.... Thenceforward, what I saw,
Was not for words to speak, nor memory's self
To stand against such outrage on her skill.

As one, who from a dream awakened, straight,
All he hath seen forgets; yet still retains .
Impression of the feeling in his dream;   .
E'en such am I: for all the vision dies,
As 'twere, away; and yet the sense of sweet,
That sprang from it, still trickles in my heart.
Thus in the sun-thaw is the snow unsealed;
Thus in the winds on flitting leaves was lost
The Sibyl's sentence.   O eternal beam!
(Whose height what reach of mortal thought may soar ?)
Yield me again some little particle
Of what thou then appearedst; give my tongue
Power, but to leave one sparkle of thy glory,
Unto the race to come, that shall not lose
Thy triumph wholly, if thou waken aught
Of memory in me, and endure to hear
The record sound in this unequal strain.

Such keenness from the living ray I met,
That, if mine eyes had turned away, methinks,
I had been lost; but, so emboldened, on
I passed, as I remember, till my view
Hovered the brink of dread infinitude.

O grace, unenvying of thy boon! that gavest
Boldness to fix so earnestly my ken
On the everlasting splendor, that I looked,
While sight was unconsumed; and, in that depth,
Saw in one volume clasped of love, whate'er
The universe unfolds; all properties
Of substance and of accident, beheld,
Compounded, yet one individual light

The whole.   And of such bond methinks I saw
The universal form; for that whene'er
I do but speak of it, my soul dilates
Beyond her proper self; and, till I speak,
One moment seems a longer lethargy,
Than five-and-twenty ages had appeared
To that emprize, that first made Neptune wonder
At Argo's shadow darkening on his flood.

   With fixèd heed, suspense and motionless,
Wondering I gazed; and admiration still
Was kindled as I gazed.   It may not be,
That one, who looks upon that light, can turn
To other object, willingly, his view.
For all the good, that will may covet, there
Is summed; and all, elsewhere defective found,
Complete.   My tongue shall utter now, no more
E'en what remembrance keeps, than could the babe's,
That yet is moistened at his mother's breast.
Not that the semblance of the living light
Was changed (that ever as at first remained),
But that my vision quickening, in that sole
Appearance, still new miracles descried,
And toiled me with the change.   In that abyss
Of radiance, clear and lofty, seemed, methought,
Three orbs of triple hue, clipped in one bound:
And, from another, one reflected seemed,
As rainbow is from rainbow: and the third
Seemed fire, breathed equally from both.   O speech!
How feeble and how faint art thou, to give
Conception birth.   Yet this to what I saw
Is less than little.   O eternal light!
Sole in thyself that dwell'st; and of thyself
Sole understood, past, present, or to come;

Thou smiledst, on that circling, which in thee
Seemed as reflected splendor, while I mused;
 For I therein, methought, in its own hue
Beheld our image painted: steadfastly
I therefore pored upon the view.   As one,
Who, versed in geometric lore, would fain
Measure the circle; and, though pondering long
And deeply, that beginning, which he needs,
Finds not: e'en such was I, intent to scan
The novel wonder, and trace out the form,
How to the circle fitted, and therein
How placed: but the flight was not for my wing;
Had not a flash darted athwart my mind,
And, in the spleen, unfolded what it sought.

   Here vigor failed the towering fantasy:
But yet the will rolled onward, like a wheel
In even motion, by the love impelled,
That moves the sun in heaven and all the stars.*

* Paradiso, xxxiii.

THE END.

www.ingramcontent.com/pod-product-compliance
Lightning Source LLC
Chambersburg PA
CBHW021335110726
47900CB00005B/1487